Paul Sussman's two great passions have always been writing and archaeology. He fulfils the former by working as a freelance journalist and the latter by spending two months of each year excavating in Egypt. He is thirty-five and lives in London with his wife. *The Lost Army of Cambyses* is his first novel.

www.**booksattransworld**.co.uk

THE
LOST ARMY
OF
CAMBYSES

PAUL SUSSMAN

BANTAM PRESS

LONDON · NEW YORK · TORONTO · SYDNEY · AUCKLAND

TRANSWORLD PUBLISHERS
61–63 Uxbridge Road, London W5 5SA
a division of The Random House Group Ltd

RANDOM HOUSE AUSTRALIA (PTY) LTD
20 Alfred Street, Milsons Point, Sydney,
New South Wales 2061, Australia

RANDOM HOUSE NEW ZEALAND LTD
18 Poland Road, Glenfield, Auckland 10, New Zealand

RANDOM HOUSE SOUTH AFRICA (PTY) LTD
Endulini, 5a Jubilee Road, Parktown 2193, South Africa

Published 2002 by Bantam Press
a division of Transworld Publishers

A catalogue record for this book is available from the British Library.
ISBN 0593048768

Typeset in 11.5/15pt Caslon by Falcon Oast Graphic Art Ltd.

Printed in Great Britain by
Mackays of Chatham, Chatham, Kent

1 3 5 7 9 10 8 6 4 2

To beautiful Alicky,
for putting up with me,
and to Mum and Dad,
for supporting but never pushing

'The force which was sent against the Ammonians started from Thebes with guides, and can be traced as far as the town of Oasis, which . . . is seven days journey across the sand from Thebes. General report has it that the army got as far as this, but of its subsequent fate there is no news whatsoever. It never reached the Ammonians and it never returned to Egypt. There is, however, a story told by the Ammonians themselves and by others who heard it from them, that when the men had left Oasis, and in their march across the desert had reached a point about midway between the town and the Ammonian border, a southerly wind of extreme violence drove the sand over them in heaps as they were taking their mid-day meal, so that they disappeared forever.'

Herodotus, *The Histories*, Book Three,
translated by Aubrey de Sélincourt

PROLOGUE

The Western Desert, 523 bc

The fly had been pestering the Greek all morning. As if the furnace-like heat of the desert wasn't enough, and the forced marches, and the stale rations, now he had this added torment. He cursed the gods and landed a heavy blow on his cheek, dislodging a shower of sweat droplets, but missing the insect by some way.

'Damned flies!' he spat.

'Ignore them,' said his companion.

'I can't ignore them. They're driving me mad! If I didn't know better I'd think our enemies had sent them.'

His companion shrugged. 'Maybe they have. They say the Ammonians have strange powers. I heard they can turn themselves into wild beasts. Jackals and lions and suchlike.'

'They can turn themselves into anything they want,' growled the Greek. 'When I get my hands on them I'll make them pay for this damned march. Four weeks we've been out here! Four weeks!'

He swung his water-skin from his shoulder and drank from it, grimacing at its hot, oily contents. What he'd give for a cup of cool, fresh water from the hill springs of Naxos; water that didn't taste as if fifty pox-ridden whores had just bathed in it!

'I'm giving up this mercenary business,' he grunted. 'This campaign's the last.'

'You say that every time.'

'This time I mean it. I'm going back to Naxos to find a wife and a nice bit of land. Olive trees – there's money in that, you know.'

'You'd never stick it.'

'I will,' said the Greek, taking another vain swat at the fly. 'I will, you know. This time it's different.'

And this time it was different. For twenty years he'd been fighting other people's wars. It was too long, and he knew it. He couldn't stand these marches any more. And the pain from the old arrow wound had been getting worse this year. Now he could barely lift his shield arm up above the level of his chest. One more expedition and that was the end of it. He was going back to grow olive trees on the island of his birth.

'So who are these Ammonians anyway?' he asked, taking another gulp of water.

'No idea,' his companion replied. 'They've got some temple Cambyses wants destroyed. There's an oracle there, apparently. That's about all I know.'

The Greek grunted, but didn't pursue the conversation. In truth he wasn't much interested in those he fought against. Libyans, Egyptians, Carians, Hebrews, even his fellow Greeks – it was all the same to him. You turned up, killed who you had to kill and then joined another expedition, as often as not against the very people who'd just paid you. Today his master was Cambyses of Persia. Yet not so long ago he'd fought against that same Cambyses in the army of Egypt. That's how it was in this business.

He took another swig of water, allowing his mind to drift back to Thebes, to his last day there before they'd set out across the desert. He and a friend, Phaedis of Macedon, had taken a skin of beer and crossed Iteru, the great river, to the valley they called the Gates of the Dead, where it was said many great kings were buried. They'd spent the afternoon drinking and exploring, discovering a narrow shaft at the foot of a steep slope of rubble into which, as a dare, they'd both crawled. Inside the walls and ceiling had been covered in painted images and the Greek, pulling out his knife, had begun carving his name into the soft plaster: ΔΥΜΜΑΧΟΣ Ο ΜΕΝΕΝΔΟΥ ΝΑΞΙΟΣ ΤΑΥΤΑ ΤΑ ΘΑΥΜΑΣΤΑ ΕΙΔΟΝ ΑΥΡΙΟΝ ΤΟΙΣ ΤΗΙ ΑΜΜΟΝΙΔΙ ΕΔΡΑΙ ΕΝΟΙΚΟΥΣΙΝ ΕΠΙΣΤΡΑΤΕΥΣΩ ΕΙΓΑΡ . . . 'I, Dymmachus, son of Menendes of Naxos, saw these wonders. Tomorrow I march against the Ammonians. May . . .'

But before he could finish, poor old Phaedis had knelt on a scorpion, letting out an almighty scream and scrabbling out of the shaft like a frightened cat. How he'd laughed!

The joke had been on him, however, for Phaedis's leg had swelled to the size of a log and he'd been unable to march with the army the next day, thus missing four weeks of torment in the desert. Poor old Phaedis? Lucky old Phaedis more like! He chuckled at the memory.

He was dragged from his reverie by the voice of his companion.

'Dymmachus! Hey, Dymmachus!'

'What?'

'Look at that, you dolt. Up ahead.'

The Greek lifted his eyes and stared forward along the line of marching troops. They were passing through a broad valley between high dunes and there ahead, its outline warped by the fierce glare of the midday sun, rose a huge, pyramid-shaped rock, its sides so uniform they seemed to have been deliberately carved into that shape. There was something faintly menacing about it, standing silent and alone in the otherwise featureless landscape, and the Greek involuntarily raised his hand to the Isis amulet at his neck, muttering a swift prayer to ward off evil spirits.

They marched on for another half-hour before a halt was called for the midday meal, by which time the Greek's company was almost alongside the rock. He staggered towards it and slumped down in the sliver of shade at its foot.

'How much further?' he groaned. 'Oh Zeus, how much further?'

Boys came round with bread and figs and the men ate and drank. Afterwards some fell to scoring their names into the surface of the rock. The Greek leaned back and closed his eyes, enjoying the sudden breeze that had come up. He felt the tickle of a fly as it landed on his cheek, the same one, he was sure, as had been tormenting him all morning. This time he made no attempt to swat it, allowing it to wander back and forth across his lips and eyelids. It took off and landed again, took off and landed, testing his resolve. Still he didn't move and the insect, lulled into a false sense of security, finally settled on his fore-head. With infinite care the Greek raised his hand, held it for a moment six inches from his face, then slammed it violently against his temple.

'Got you, you bastard!' he cried, staring down at the remains of the fly smeared across his palm. 'At last!'

His triumph was short-lived, however, for at that moment a faint murmur of alarm came drifting forward from the rear of the column.

'What is it?' he asked, wiping away the fly and standing, hand on sword. 'An attack?'

'I don't know,' said the man beside him. 'There's something going on behind us.'

The hubbub was growing. Four camels thundered past, their packs trailing in their wake, froth dripping from their mouths. Screams could be heard and muffled shouting. The breeze, too, was getting stronger, buffeting into his face, making his hair flicker and dance.

The Greek shielded his eyes and stared southwards along the valley. There seemed to be a sort of darkness coming up behind them. A cavalry charge, he thought at first. Then a sudden furious gust of wind smacked into his face and he heard clearly what had until now been just a garbled cry.

'Oh Isis,' he whispered.

'What?' said his companion.

The Greek turned to him. There was fear in his eyes. 'Sandstorm.'

Nobody moved or spoke. They'd all heard of the sandstorms of the western desert, the way they came out of nowhere and swallowed everything in their path. Whole cities had been devoured by them, it was said, entire civilizations lost.

'If you meet a sandstorm there's only one thing to do,' one of the Libyan guides had told them.

'What?' they had asked him.

'Die,' he had replied.

'Save us!' someone croaked. 'May the gods protect us!'

And then, suddenly, everyone was running and shouting.

'Save us!' they screamed. 'Have mercy on us!'

Some threw aside their packs and charged madly up the valley. Others laboured up the side of the dune, or fell to their knees, or crouched down in the shelter of the pyramid rock. One man fell face forward into the sand, weeping. Another was trampled by a horse as he struggled to mount it.

The Greek alone held his ground. He neither moved nor spoke, just stood leaden-limbed as the wall of darkness rolled inexorably towards him, seeming to gather speed as it came. More pack animals thundered past and men too, their weapons discarded, faces twisted in terror.

'Run!' they screamed. 'It's already taken half the army! Run or you'll be lost!'

The wind was raging now, whipping sheets of sand about his legs and waist. There was a roar, too, as of a surging cataract. The sun dimmed.

'Come on, Dymmachus, let's get out of here,' cried his companion. 'If we stay we'll be buried alive.'

Still the Greek didn't move. A faint smile twisted his mouth. Of all the deaths he had imagined, and there had been many, this one had never crossed his mind. And this his last campaign, too! It was so cruel it was laughable. His smile broadened and despite himself he began to chuckle.

'Dymmachus you fool! What's wrong with you?'

'Go,' said the Greek, shouting to be heard above the rising bellow of the storm. 'Run if you want! It makes no difference. For myself, I shall die where I stand.'

He drew his sword and held it in front of him, gazing at the image of a coiling serpent inscribed onto its gleaming blade, the jaws levering open around the sword's tip. He had won it over twenty years ago in his first campaign, against the Lydians, and had carried it with him ever since, his lucky mascot. He ran his thumb along the blade, testing it. His companion took to his heels.

'You're mad!' he screamed over his shoulder. 'You filthy mad fool.'

The Greek ignored him. He gripped his weapon and stared at the great darkness looming ever closer. Soon it would be upon him. He flexed his muscles.

'Come on then,' he whispered. 'Let's see what you're made of.'

He felt suddenly light-headed. It was always like this in battle: the initial fear, the leaden limbs, and then the sudden surge of battle joy. Perhaps growing olive trees wasn't for him after all. He was a *machimos*. Fighting was in his blood. Perhaps this was for the best. He began to chant, an old Egyptian charm to ward off the evil eye:

> *'Sakhmet's arrow is in you!*
> *The magic of Thoth is in your body!*
> *Isis curses you!*
> *Nephthys punishes you!*
> *The lance of Horus is in your head!'*

14

And then the storm hit, pulsing against him with the force of a thousand chariots. The wind nearly swept him off his feet and the sand blinded him, ripping at his tunic, tearing at his flesh. Shadowy forms loomed through the darkness, arms flailing, their screams drowned by the deafening roar. One of the army's standards, torn from its mounting, flew against his legs and clung there for a moment before being snatched away again and disappearing into the maelstrom.

The Greek slashed at the wind with his sword, but it was too strong for him. It pushed him backwards and to the side, and eventually forced him down onto his knees. A fist of sand punched into his mouth, choking him. Somehow he struggled onto his feet again, but was knocked down almost immediately and this time didn't get up. A wave of sand swept over him.

For a few moments he bucked and struggled, and then lay still. He felt, suddenly, very weary and very calm, as if he was floating underwater. Images drifted slowly through his mind – Naxos, where he had been born and raised; the tomb in Thebes; Phaedis and the scorpion; his first campaign all those many years ago, against the fierce Lydians, when he had won his sword. With a final supreme effort of will he lifted the weapon high in the air above him, so that even when the rest of him had been buried its thick blade still protruded above the surface of the sands, the inscribed serpent coiling around it, marking the spot where he had fallen.

1

Cairo, September 2000

The limousine pulled slowly out of the embassy gates, long and sleek and as black as a whale, pausing momentarily before easing forward into the traffic. Two police motorcycles took up position in front of it, two behind.

For a hundred metres the convoy continued straight, trees and buildings slipping past to either side, then swung right and right again, onto the Corniche el-Nil. Other drivers glanced over, trying to see who was inside the limousine, but its windows were smoked and revealed nothing but the blurred silhouettes of two human heads. A small Stars and Stripes pennant fluttered on the corner of its front left wing.

After a kilometre the convoy came to a confused intersection of roads and flyovers. The lead motorcycles slowed, sounded their sirens, and pushed forward, leading the limousine carefully through the tarmac labyrinth and up onto an elevated carriage-way where the traffic wasn't so heavy. The convoy picked up speed, following the signs to the airport. The rear motorcyclists leaned towards each other and began talking.

The blast was sudden and so understated that it wasn't

immediately clear there had been an explosion. There was a muffled thud and whoosh, and the limousine bucked up into the air, swerving across the centre of the carriageway into a concrete wall. It was only when another thud, louder this time, rocked the stricken vehicle and a spurt of flame roared from its underside that it became clear this was more than just a road accident.

The motorcycles skidded to a halt. The limousine's front door flew open and the driver staggered out, screaming, his jacket on fire. Two of the riders smothered him with their own jackets; the others tried to reach the vehicle's rear doors, against the inside of which frantic hands were drumming. A pall of black smoke umbrellaed upwards into the sky, the air grew thick with the acrid stench of burning petrol and rubber. Cars slowed and stopped, their drivers gawping. On the limousine's front wing the Stars and Stripes pennant burst into flames and swiftly crumpled to ash.

2

THE WESTERN DESERT, A WEEK LATER

'Motherfucker!'

The driver let out a scream of exhilaration as his Toyota four-wheel-drive crested the summit of the dune and took off, hanging in the air like an ungainly white bird before thudding down again on the far side. For a moment it looked as if he might lose control of the wheel, the vehicle slewing downwards at a dangerous angle, but he managed to bring it back in line and, reaching the bottom of the slope, jammed his foot on the accelerator again, powering up and over the top of the next dune.

'Motherfuckingcocksucker!' he bellowed.

He roared on for another twenty minutes, music blaring from the jeep's stereo, his blond hair whipping in the wind, before eventually skidding to a halt on a high sandy ridge and cutting the engine. He took a drag on his joint, seized a pair of binoculars and got out, his boots crunching on the sand.

The desert was eerily silent, the air thick with heat, the bleached sky seeming to press down from above. He stood for a moment gazing at the untidy collage of dunes and gravel pans stretching all around him, a strange, unearthly landscape devoid of life and movement, and then, taking another drag on the joint, lifted the binoculars and focused them to the north-west.

A crescent-shaped limestone scarp curved across his line of sight, with a swathe of green oasis spread along its bottom. Tiny white villages were scattered among the palm groves and salt lakes, while a larger smudge of white at the western end of the cultivation marked a small town.

'Siwa,' smiled the man, exhaling a curl of smoke from his nostrils. 'Thank God.'

He remained where he was for a few minutes, running the binoculars back and forth, and then returned to the jeep and started the engine, the blast of its stereo echoing once more across the sands.

He reached the edge of the oasis in an hour, bumping out of the desert onto a compacted dirt road. Three radio masts rose to his right and a concrete water tower. A pack of wild dogs came yapping around his hubcaps.

'Hey, guys, it's good to see you too!' He laughed, beeping his horn and swerving the jeep to and fro, throwing up a cloud of dust and forcing the dogs to scatter.

He passed a pair of satellite dishes and a makeshift army camp before hitting a tarmacked road that carried him into the centre of the large settlement he'd seen from the dune-top: Siwa Town.

The place was all but deserted. A couple of donkey-carts clattered along the road and in the main square a group of women were clustered around a dusty vegetable stall, their grey cotton shawls pulled right down over their faces. Everyone else had been driven indoors by the midday heat.

He pulled over at the side of the square, beneath a high mound of rock covered with ruined buildings, and, retrieving a large manilla envelope from the back seat, got out and set off across the square, not bothering to lock the doors behind him. He stopped at a general store and spoke briefly to the owner, handing him a piece of paper and a wad of money and nodding towards the Toyota, then moved on, turning down a side street and stepping into a shabby-looking building with Welcome Hotel painted down the side. As soon as he entered the man behind the desk leaped up with a cry of delight and rushed round to greet him.

'Dr John! You are back! It is so good to see you!'

He spoke in Berber and the young man responded in the same tongue.

'You too, Yakub. How are you?'

'Well. You?'

'Dirty,' said the young man, patting dust off his 'I Love Egypt' T-shirt. 'I need a shower.'

'Of course, of course. You know where they are. No hot water, I'm afraid, but have as much cold as you want. Mohammed! Mohammed!'

A boy appeared from a side room.

'Dr John has come back. Fetch him a towel and soap so he can shower.'

The boy scampered away, his flip-flops slapping loudly on the tiled floor.

'Do you want to eat?' asked Yakub.

'Damn right I want to eat. I've been living off beans and tinned pilchards for the last eight weeks. Every night I've been dreaming of Yakub's chicken curry.'

The man laughed. 'You want chips with it?'

'I want chips, I want fresh bread, I want cold Coke, I want everything you can give me.'

Yakub's laughter redoubled. 'Same old Dr John!'

The boy reappeared with a towel and a small bar of soap, which he handed over.

'I need to make a phone call first,' said the young man.

'No problem. Come. Come.'

The owner led him into a cluttered room with a rack of dog-eared postcards leaning against the wall and a phone sitting on top of a filing cabinet. Laying his envelope on a chair, the young man lifted the receiver and dialled. It rang for a few moments before a voice echoed at the other end.

'Hello,' he said, now speaking in Arabic, 'could you put me through to . . .'

Yakub waved his hand and left him to it. He returned a couple of minutes later with a bottle of Coke, but his guest was still talking so he put the Coke on top of the filing cabinet and went off to start preparing the food.

Thirty minutes later, showered and shaved, his hair brushed back from his sunburnt forehead, the young man was sitting in the hotel garden in the shade of a knotted palm tree, wolfing down his food.

'So what's been going on in the world, Yakub?' he asked, breaking off a hunk of bread and swirling it through the gravy around the edge of his plate.

Yakub sipped his Fanta.

'You heard about the American ambassador?'

'I haven't heard anything about anything. It's like I've been living on Mars for the last two months.'

'He got blown up.'

The young man let out a low whistle.

'A week ago,' said Yakub. 'In Cairo. The Sword of Vengeance.'

'Killed?'

'No, he survived. Just.'

The young man grunted. 'Shame. Wipe out all the bureaucrats and the world would be a far healthier place. This curry is superb, Yakub.'

Two girls, European, rose from their table on the far side of the garden and walked past. One of them glanced back at the young man and smiled. He nodded in greeting.

'I think she likes you,' chuckled Yakub once they'd gone.

'Maybe,' shrugged his companion. 'But then I'll tell her I'm an archaeologist and she'll run a fucking mile. The first rule of archaeology, Yakub: never tell a woman what you do. Kiss of death.'

He finished off the last of his curry and chips and sat back, flies humming in the tree above his head. The air smelt of heat and woodsmoke and roasting meat.

'So how long are you here for?' asked Yakub.

'In Siwa? About another hour.'

'And then you go back to the desert?'

'Then I go back to the desert.'

Yakub shook his head.

'A year you have been out there. You come back, you get supplies, and then you disappear again. What do you do out there in the middle of nowhere?'

'I take measurements,' smiled the young man. 'And dig holes. And draw plans. And on a really exciting day I might take some photographs too.'

'And what do you look for? A tomb?'

The young man shrugged. 'I suppose you could call it that.'

'And have you found it yet?'

'Who knows, Yakub? Maybe. Maybe not. The desert plays tricks on you. You think you've found something and it turns out to be nothing. And you think you've found nothing and suddenly you realize it's something. The Sahara, as we say back home, is one big mother-fucking prick-teaser.'

He reverted to English for this and Yakub repeated the words, struggling to get his mouth around them.

'On beeg modder-fockin peek-taser.'

The young man laughed, pulling cigarettes and a small bag of grass from his shirt pocket.

'You've got it, Yakub. On beeg modder-fockin peek-taser. And that's on a good day.'

He rolled a joint swiftly and, lighting it, drew the smoke deep into his lungs, leaning his head back against the bole of the palm tree and exhaling contentedly.

'You smoke too much of that stuff, Dr John,' admonished the Egyptian. 'It will make you mad.'

'On the contrary, my friend,' sighed the young man, closing his eyes. 'Out in the desert it's just about the only fucking thing that's keeping me sane.'

He left the hotel half an hour later, the manilla envelope still clutched in his hand. The afternoon was moving on now and the sun had slipped away towards the west, its hue thickening from a watery yellow to a citrus orange. He strolled back through the square to the jeep, now filled with boxes of provisions, and, climbing in, started the engine and idled fifty metres onto the forecourt of the town's only garage.

'Fill it,' he said to the attendant, 'and the jerrycans too. And put some water in the plastic containers. From the tap's fine.'

He threw the man the keys and walked a hundred metres up the road to the post office. Inside he opened the manilla envelope, pulled out a series of photographs, checked them, and then returned them to the envelope and licked down the flap.

'I want to send this registered mail,' he said to the man at the counter.

The man took the envelope, weighed it and, pulling a form from a drawer beneath the desk, began filling it out.

'Professor Ibrahim az-Zahir,' he said, reading out the name written on the front, enunciating it to make sure he had it right. 'Cairo University.'

The young man took a copy of the form, paid and, leaving the envelope, strolled back to the garage. The jeep, jerrycans and water containers were all filled now and, with a last look around the market square, he climbed back into the vehicle, started the engine and motored slowly out of the town.

He stopped briefly on the edge of the desert and glanced wistfully back towards the town. Then, switching on the stereo, he revved the engine and roared forward across the sands.

*

They found his body two months later. Or at least the remains of his body, fried to a crisp in the furnace of his burnt-out jeep. A group of tourists out on desert safari stumbled on the vehicle about fifty kilometres south-east of Siwa, upside down at the foot of a dune, a broken metal hulk with something inside it that passed for a human form. He had, it seemed, rolled the jeep while cresting the dune, although it wasn't a particularly steep dune and, curiously, there were other tyre tracks in the vicinity, as though he had not been alone when the accident happened. The body was so badly disfigured it could only be conclusively identified after dental records had been sent over from the United States.

3

LONDON, FOURTEEN MONTHS LATER

Dr Tara Mullray brushed a strand of coppery hair from her eyes and continued along the gantry. It was warm up there under the lamps and a sheen of sweat glowed on her smooth, pale forehead. Beneath, through the ventilation holes in the tops of their tanks, she caught brief glimpses of the snakes, but she paid them no more attention than they did her. She'd worked in the reptile house for over four years and the novelty of its inhabitants had long since worn off.

She passed the rock python, the puff adder, the carpet viper and the Gabon viper, eventually coming to a halt above the black-necked cobra. It was curled in the corner of its tank, but as soon as she arrived it raised its head, tongue flickering, its thick, olive-brown body moving from side to side like a metronome.

'Hi, Joey,' she said, putting down the bin and snake hook she was carrying and squatting on the gantry. 'How are you feeling today?'

The snake probed the underside of the tank's lid, inquisitive. She put on a pair of thick leather gloves and also protective goggles, for the cobra could, and did, spit venom.

'OK, lover boy,' she said, grasping the snake hook. 'Medication time.'

She bent forward and eased the top off the tank, leaning backwards as the snake's head rose to meet her, its hood slightly distended. In one clean, choreographed movement she grasped the handle of the bin lid, scooped the snake up with the hook and, keeping her eyes on it all the time, dropped it into the bin and slammed the lid down on top. From inside came a soft slithering sound as the cobra explored its new surroundings.

'It's for your own good, Joey,' she said. 'Don't be getting angry now.'

The black-necked cobra was the one snake in the collection she didn't like. With the others, even the taipan, she was perfectly at ease. The cobra, however, always made her feel nervous. It was crafty and aggressive, and had a bad temper. It had bitten her once, a year ago, as she removed it from its tank for cleaning. She'd hooked it too far down the body and it had managed to swing round and lunge at the back of her bare hand. Fortunately it was just a dry bite with no venom injected, but it had shaken her. In almost ten years of working with snakes she'd never before been bitten. Since then she had treated it with the utmost caution and always wore gloves when she had to handle it, something she didn't do with the other snakes. She checked the lid to make sure it was secure and, lifting the bin, set off back down the gantry, manoeuvring her way carefully down a set of steps at the end and walking along a corridor to her office. She could feel the snake moving inside the container and slowed her step, trying not to jolt it too much. No point in disturbing it more than was necessary.

Inside the office Alexandra, her assistant, was waiting. Together they removed the cobra from the bin and laid it out on a bench, Alexandra holding it flat while Tara squatted down to examine it.

'It should have healed by now,' she sighed, probing an area midway along the snake's back where the scales were swollen and sore. 'He's been rubbing it against his rock again. I think we should leave his tank bare for a while to give it time to mend.'

She removed some antiseptic from a cupboard and began gently cleaning the wound. The snake's tongue flicked in and out, its black eyes staring up at her menacingly.

'What time's your flight?' asked Alexandra.

'Six,' replied Tara, glancing up at the clock on the wall. 'I'm going to have to go as soon as I've finished here.'

'I wish my dad lived abroad. It makes the relationship seem so much more exotic.'

Tara smiled. 'There are many ways you could describe my relationship with my father, Alex, but exotic isn't one of them. Careful of his head there.'

She finished cleaning the affected area and, squeezing a blob of cream onto her finger, smeared it along the snake's flank.

'While I'm away he needs to be cleaned every couple of days, OK? And keep up with the antibiotics until Friday. I don't want the cellulitis spreading.'

'Just go and have a good time,' said Alexandra.

'I'll call at the end of the week to make sure there aren't any complications.'

'Will you stop worrying? Everything'll be fine. Believe it or not the zoo can survive without you for two weeks.'

Tara smiled. Alexandra was right. She got too intense about her work. It was a trait she'd inherited from her father. This would be the first proper holiday she'd had for two years and she knew she ought to make the most of it. She squeezed her assistant's arm.

'Sorry. Over-reacting.'

'I mean it's not like the snakes are going to miss you, is it? They don't have feelings.'

Tara assumed a mock-insulted face. 'How dare you talk about my babies like that! They'll cry for me every night I'm away.'

They both laughed. Tara took the snake hook and, working together, they returned the cobra to its bin.

'You OK to put him back?'

'Sure,' said Alexandra. 'Just go.'

Tara grabbed her coat and crash helmet and headed for the door.

'Antibiotics till Friday, remember.'

'Go, for Christ's sake!'

'And don't forget to take out his stone.'

'Jesus, Tara!'

Alexandra snatched up a cloth and threw it. Tara ducked and, laughing, ran away down the corridor.

'And make sure you wear the goggles when you put him back,' she called over her shoulder. 'You know what a bastard he is after he's had his medication!'

The afternoon traffic was heavy, but she wove skilfully through it on her moped, crossing the Thames at Vauxhall Bridge and opening the throttle for the last couple of miles down to Brixton. Every now and then she checked her watch. Her flight left in just over three hours and she hadn't even packed yet.

'Bollocks,' she muttered beneath her helmet.

She lived alone, in a cavernous basement flat backing onto Brockwell Park. She'd bought it five years ago, with money her mother left her, and her best friend Jenny had moved into the spare room as a lodger.

For a couple of years they'd lived a life of carefree bohemianism, throwing parties, drifting in and out of relationships, not taking anything too seriously. Then Jenny had met Nick and within a few months they'd moved in together, leaving Tara to manage the flat alone. The mortgage repayments were ruinous, but she didn't take in another lodger. She enjoyed having her own space. She sometimes wondered if she could ever settle down with a man in the way Jenny had. Once, years ago, there had been someone, but that was long since over. On the whole she was happy with her own company.

The flat was a mess when she came in. She poured herself a

glass of wine, stuck on a Lou Reed CD and walked through to the study, jabbing the 'Play' button on the answerphone. A metallic female voice announced, 'You have six messages.'

Two were from Nigel, an old university friend, the first inviting her to dinner on Saturday, the second cancelling the invitation because he'd remembered she was going away. One was from Jenny warning her not to go on any camel rides because all the handlers were perverts, one from a school confirming a talk she was to give on snakes and one from Harry, a stockbroker who'd been pursuing her for two months and whose calls she never returned. The final message was from her father.

'Tara, I was wondering if you could bring me some Scotch. And *The Times*. If there are any problems call me, otherwise I'll meet you at the airport. I'm, uh . . . looking forward to seeing you. Yes, um, really looking forward to it. Bye then.'

She smiled. He always sounded so awkward when he tried to say something affectionate. Like most academics Professor Michael Mullray was only really at home in the world of ideas. Emotions got in the way of clear thinking. That was why he and her mother had split up. Because he couldn't cope with her need for feeling. Even when she'd died six years ago he'd struggled to show any emotion. At her funeral he'd sat at the back, alone, expressionless, lost in his own thoughts, and left immediately afterwards to give a lecture in Oxford.

She finished her wine and went into the kitchen to refill her glass. She knew she ought to tidy the flat, but time was pressing, so she contented herself with taking out the rubbish and doing the washing up before going into the bedroom to pack.

She hadn't seen her father for almost a year, not since he was last in England. They spoke on the telephone occasionally, but the conversations were functional rather than warm. He would tell her about some new object he'd unearthed, or a class he was teaching; she'd dredge up some gossip about friends and work. The calls rarely lasted longer than a few minutes. Each year he sent her a birthday card and each year it arrived a week late.

She'd thus been surprised when last month, out of the blue, he'd called and invited her to stay. He had lived abroad for five years and this was the first time he had suggested she come out.

'The season's all but over,' he'd said. 'Why not get yourself a flight? You can stay in the dig house and I can show you some of the sights.'

Her immediate reaction had been one of concern. He was old, well into his seventies, and had a weak heart, for which he was on constant medication. Perhaps this was his way of saying his health was failing and he wanted to make his peace before the end. When she'd asked, however, he'd insisted he was perfectly well and merely thought it would be nice for father and daughter to spend a bit of time together. It was unlike him and she'd been suspicious, but in the end she'd thought what the hell and booked a flight. When she'd called to let him know when she'd be arriving he had seemed genuinely pleased.

'Splendid!' he had said. 'We'll have a fine old time.'

She sifted through the clothes on her bed, picking out the items she wanted and throwing them into a large holdall. She felt like a cigarette, but resisted the temptation. She hadn't smoked for almost a year and didn't want to start again, not least because if she could make the full twelve months she stood to win a hundred pounds from Jenny. As she always did when the urge came upon her, she fetched an ice cube from the freezer and sucked that instead.

She wondered whether she should have bought her father a present, but there wasn't time now and, anyway, even if she had got him something he almost certainly wouldn't like it. She remembered the acute disappointment of Christmases as a child when she would plan for weeks what to give him, only for him to open her carefully chosen gift, mumble a half-hearted 'Lovely, dear. Just what I wanted,' and then disappear into his paper again. She'd get him some duty-free whisky and a *Times*, and perhaps some aftershave, and that would have to do.

Throwing a few last odds and ends into the bag, she went into the bathroom and took a shower. Part of her was dreading the trip. She knew they'd end up arguing, however hard they tried to avoid it. At the same time she couldn't help feeling excited. It was a while since she'd last been abroad and if things got really bad she could always take off on her own for a few days. She wasn't a kid any more, dependent on her father. She could do whatever she wanted. She increased the heat of the shower and threw her head back so that the water slashed against her breasts and stomach. She began humming to herself.

Afterwards, having locked all the windows, she stepped outside with her holdall and slammed the door behind her. It was dark now and a light drizzle had begun to fall, making the pavements glow under the streetlights. Normally this sort of weather depressed her, but not this evening.

She checked her passport and flight tickets, and set off towards the station, smiling. In Cairo, apparently, the temperature was up in the eighties.

4

CAIRO

'It's time to close up for the night, little one,' said old Ikhbar. 'Time for you to go home, wherever that might be.'

The girl stood motionless, playing with her hair. Her face was dirty and a dribble of snot glistened beneath her nose.

'Off you go,' said Iqbar. 'You can come and help me tomorrow if you want.'

The girl said nothing, just stared at him. He took a step towards her, limping heavily, his breath coming in gasps.

'Come on now, no games. I'm an old man and I'm tired.'

The shop was getting dark. A single bare light bulb cast a weak glow, but in the corners the shadows were thickening. Heaps of bric-à-brac sunk slowly into the gloom, as though into water. From outside came the honking of a moped horn and the sound of someone hammering.

Iqbar took another step forward, belly bulging beneath his djellaba. There was something menacing about his rotten brown teeth and black eye-patch. His voice, however, was kindly and the girl showed no fear of him.

'Are you going home or not?'

The girl shook her head.

'In that case', he said, turning away and shuffling towards the front of the shop, 'I'll have to lock you in for the night. And of course it's at night that the ghosts come out.'

He stopped at the door and removed a bunch of keys from his pocket.

'Did I tell you about the ghosts? I'm sure I did. All antique shops have them. For instance, in that old lamp there' – he indicated a brass lamp sitting on a shelf – 'lives a genie called al-Ghul. He's ten thousand years old, and can turn himself into any shape that he wants.'

The girl stared at the lamp, eyes wide.

'And you see that old wooden chest there, in the corner, the one with the big lock and the iron bands across it? Well, there's a crocodile in there, a big green crocodile. By day he sleeps, but at night he comes out to look for children. Why? So he can eat them, of course. He grabs them in his mouth and swallows them whole.'

The girl bit her lip, eyes darting between the chest and the lamp.

'And that knife, up there on the wall, with the curved blade. That used to belong to a king. A very cruel man. Each night he comes back, takes his knife and cuts the throats of anyone he can lay his hands on. Oh yes, this shop is full of ghosts. So if you want to stay here for the night, my little friend, be my guest.'

Chuckling to himself he pulled open the door, a set of brass bells jangling as he did so. The girl came forward a few paces, thinking she was going to be locked in. As soon as he heard her move, Iqbar swung around and, raising his hands as though they were claws, roared. The girl screamed and laughed, scampering off into the shadows at the back of the shop, where she crouched down behind a pair of old wickerwork baskets.

'So she wants to play hide and seek, does she?' growled the old man, limping after her, a smile on his face. 'Well, she'll have a hard job hiding from Iqbar. He might only have one eye left, but it's a good eye. No-one can hide from old Iqbar.'

He could see her lurking behind the baskets, peering out through a gap between them. He didn't want to spoil her fun too quickly and so deliberately shuffled past her and instead opened the doors of an old wooden cupboard.

'Is she in here, I wonder?'

He made a show of peering into the cupboard.

'No, not in the cupboard. She's cleverer than I thought.'

He closed the cupboard and passed into a room at the back of the shop, where he made as much noise as he could opening drawers and banging on filing cabinets.

'Are you in here, little monster?' he cried, enjoying himself. 'Hiding in my secret office? Oh she's a clever one, she is!'

He clattered around for a while longer and then hobbled out again, stopping directly in front of the baskets. He could hear the girl's muffled giggles.

'Now, let me think. She wasn't in the cupboard, and she wasn't in the office, and I'm sure she wouldn't be silly enough to hide in the wooden chest with the crocodile. Which, if I'm right, only leaves one place for her to be. And that's right here, behind these baskets. Let's see if old Iqbar's right.'

He bent down. As he did so the bells on the door jangled and someone entered the shop. He straightened and turned. The girl remained where she was, hidden.

'We were just closing,' said Iqbar, shuffling forward towards the two men who were standing in the doorway. 'But if you want a look around, please take your time.'

The men ignored him. They were young, in their early twenties, bearded; each was dressed in a grubby black robe with a black 'imma wound low around his forehead. They gazed around the shop for a moment, sizing it up, and then one of them stepped outside and signalled. He came back in, followed a moment later by another man, white-skinned.

'Can I help you?' asked Iqbar. 'Are you looking for anything in particular?'

The newcomer was a giant, tall and broad, way too big for his cheap linen suit, which strained under the pressure of his massive thighs and shoulders. He held a half-smoked cigar in one hand and a briefcase in the other, the letters CD stamped into the battered brown leather. The left side of his face, from the temple down almost to the mouth, was splashed with a livid purple birthmark. Iqbar felt a shiver of fear.

'Can I help you?' he repeated.

The huge man closed the shop door gently, turning the key in the lock and nodding at his two companions, who moved towards Iqbar, faces expressionless. The shopkeeper backed away until he came up against the shop counter.

'What do you want?' he said, beginning to cough. 'Please, what do you want?'

The huge man walked up to Iqbar and stood in front of him, their bellies almost touching. He gazed at him for a moment, smiling, and then, lifting his cigar, stubbed it out on the old man's eye-patch. Iqbar screamed, flailing his hands in front of his face.

'Please, please!' He coughed. 'I have no money. I am poor!'

'You have something that belongs to us,' said the giant. 'An antiquity. It came to you yesterday. Where is it?'

Iqbar was doubled up, arms held over his head.

'I don't know what you're talking about,' he wheezed. 'I have no antiquities. It is illegal to deal in them!'

The giant signalled to his two henchmen and they grabbed the old man's elbows, forcing him upright. He stood with his head turned to one side, cheek jammed against his shoulder, as though trying to hide. One of the men's headscarves had slid upwards slightly, revealing a thick scar running up the centre of his forehead, smooth and pale as though a leech was clinging to the skin. The sight of it seemed to terrify the old man.

'Please!' he wailed. 'Please!'

'Where is it?' repeated his inquisitor.

'Please, please!'

The giant muttered something to himself and, placing his

briefcase on the floor, took out what looked like a small grouting trowel. The diamond-shaped blade was dull, save around its edges, where the metal shone as though it had been sharpened.

'Do you know what this is?' he asked.

The old man was staring at the blade, mute with terror.

'It is an archaeologist's trowel,' grinned the giant. 'We use it to scrape back soil, carefully, like this . . .' He demonstrated, passing the trowel back and forth in front of the old man's terrified face. 'It has other applications as well, though.'

With a swift movement – surprisingly swift for a man of his size – he swept the trowel upwards, slashing its edge across Iqbar's cheek. The skin flapped open like a mouth and blood streamed down over the old man's robe. Iqbar screamed and struggled pathetically.

'Now,' said the giant, 'I ask you again. Where is the piece?'

Behind the baskets the girl prayed for al-Ghul the genie to come out of his lamp and help the old man.

It was past midnight when the plane touched down.

'Welcome to Cairo,' said the air hostess as Tara stepped out of the cabin into a blast of hot air and diesel fumes. 'Enjoy your stay.'

The flight had passed off uneventfully. She had been sat in an aisle seat beside a red-faced couple, who spent the first half of the journey warning her of the stomach problems she was bound to suffer as a result of Egyptian cooking and the second half sleeping. She'd drunk a couple of vodkas, watched half the in-flight movie, bought a bottle of Scotch from the duty-free trolley and then eased her seat back and gazed up at the ceiling. She had wanted to smoke, as she always did when she flew, but had ordered a regular supply of ice cubes instead.

Her father had worked in Egypt since she was a child. He was, according to those who knew about such things, one of the most celebrated Egyptologists of his time. 'He's right up there with Petrie and Carter,' one of his colleagues had once told her. 'If there's anyone alive who's done more to advance our understanding of the Old Kingdom I've yet to meet them.'

She ought to have been proud. As it was, her father's academic achievements had always left her cold. All she knew, and all she ever had known from earliest childhood, was that he seemed more content in a world that had been dead for 4,000 years than he did with his own family. Even her name, Tara, had been chosen because it incorporated the name of the Egyptian sun god Ra.

Each year he would travel out to Egypt to excavate. To start with he'd gone only for a month or so, leaving each November and returning just before Christmas. As she had grown older, however, and her parents' marriage had slowly broken apart, he'd spent longer and longer there.

'Your father's seeing another woman,' her mother had once told her. 'Her name's Egypt.' It had been meant as a joke, although neither of them had laughed.

Then the cancer had come and her mother had begun her rapid decline. It was during this period that, for the first time, Tara had really come to hate her father. As the disease chewed away at her mother's lungs and liver and her father had kept his distance, unable to offer even a few salutary words of support, she had felt an all-consuming fury towards this man who seemed to value tombs and old potsherds more than his own flesh and blood. A few days before her mother's death she had called him in Egypt and screamed obscenities down the phone at him, surprising even herself with the violence of her rage. At the funeral they had barely acknowledged each other, and afterwards he had moved to Egypt full time, teaching eight months of the year at Cairo's American University and excavating for the other four. They didn't speak for almost two years.

And yet, for all that, there were good memories of him too. Once, for instance, as a young child, she had been crying about something and to stop her tears he had performed a magic trick whereby he had appeared to remove his thumb from the rest of his hand. She had laughed uproariously and urged him to do it again and again, staring in wonder as he had repeatedly separated his thumb from his palm, groaning in mock agony as he waved the severed digit around in the air.

On the morning of her fifteenth birthday – and this was her favourite memory – she had woken to find an envelope addressed to her sitting on her mantelpiece. Opening it, she had found the first clue in a treasure trail that had taken her all round the house and garden before eventually leading her up into the attic, where she had discovered an exquisite gold necklace concealed at the bottom of an old trunk. Each clue had taken the form of a rhyming verse and been written on parchment, with drawings and symbols to add to the air of mystery. Her father must have spent hours arranging it all. Later he had taken her mother and her out to dinner, regaling them both with wonderful tales of excavations and discoveries and eccentric academics.

'You look beautiful, Tara,' he had told her, leaning forward to adjust the new gold necklace, which she had worn specially. 'The most beautiful girl in the world. I am very, very proud of you.'

It was moments like these – few and far between as they were – that somehow balanced out her father's coldness and self-absorption, and bound her to him. It was why she had phoned him two years after her mother's funeral, asking for a reconciliation after their long silence. And it was, in a sense, why she was travelling to Egypt now. Because she knew that deep down, in his own way and despite his innumerable faults, he was a good man and he loved her, and needed her too, just as she needed him. And of course there was always the hope – just as there was every time she saw him – that maybe this time things would be different. Maybe they wouldn't bicker and shout at each other and sulk, but would be happy and relaxed in each other's company, like a normal father and daughter. Maybe this time they could make things work.

Some chance, she had thought to herself as they'd begun their descent. You'll be pleased to see him for about five minutes, and then you'll start arguing again.

'I suppose you know', said her neighbour jovially, 'that more planes crash during landing than at any other time during the flight.'

Tara had ordered more ice cubes from the stewardess.

She emerged finally into the airport arrivals hall almost an hour after they'd touched down. There had been an interminable wait at passport control, followed by a further delay at the baggage carousel, where security guards were carrying out random luggage checks.

'Sayf al-Tha'r,' a fellow passenger had said to her, shaking his head. 'What problems he causes. That one man can bring the country to a standstill!'

Before she could ask what he meant he had spotted his luggage and, signalling a porter to collect it for him, marched off into the crowd. Her own bag had come round a few minutes later and, everything else for the moment forgotten, she had hefted it onto her shoulder and set off through customs, heart thudding with anticipation.

Since her father had first said he'd come out to meet her she had imagined herself emerging into the arrivals hall to find him standing there waiting, the two of them yelping with joy and rushing towards each other, arms open. As it was, the only person who greeted her was a taxi driver touting for work. She peered along the row of faces lining the arrivals barrier, but her father's wasn't among them.

The terminal, even at that hour, was busy. Families greeted and took leave of each other noisily, children played among the plastic chairs, package tourists crowded around harassed-looking reps. Black-uniformed policemen were very much in evidence, guns held across their chests.

She waited at the barrier for a while and then began wandering around the hall. She went outside, where a tour rep mistook her for one of his party and tried to hustle her onto a coach, then came back in again, walking around for a while longer before changing some money, buying a coffee and sitting down in a seat that afforded a good view both of the entrance and the barrier.

After an hour she called her father from a payphone, but there was no reply either from his dig house or the flat he kept in central Cairo. She wondered if his taxi had been held up in traffic – she presumed he would have come in a taxi, he'd never learnt to drive – or if he had fallen ill or, and with her father it was always a possibility, simply forgotten that he was supposed to be meeting her.

But no, he wouldn't have forgotten. Not this time. Not after sounding so pleased that she was coming. He was late. That was all. Just late. She got herself another coffee, settled back in the chair and opened a book.

Damn, she thought. I didn't get his *Times*.

5

LUXOR, THE NEXT MORNING

Inspector Yusuf Ezz el-Din Khalifa rose before dawn and, having showered and dressed, went into the living room to say his morning prayers. He felt tired and irritable, as he did every morning. The ritual of worship, the standing and kneeling and bowing and reciting, cleared his head. By the time he was finished he felt fresh and calm and strong. As he did every morning.

'*Wa lillah al-shukr*',' he said to himself, moving into the kitchen to make coffee. 'Thanks be to God. His power is great.'

He put on some water to boil, lit a cigarette and looked out at a woman hanging washing on the roof opposite, which was just below the level of his kitchen window, about three metres away. He'd often wondered whether it would be possible to jump from his building to hers, across the narrow alley that divided them. When he was younger he would probably have tried it. Ali, his brother, would certainly have been up for the challenge. Ali, however, was dead and he himself now had responsibilities. It was a twenty-metre drop to the ground and with a wife and three young children he couldn't afford to take such risks. Or perhaps that was just an excuse. After all, he'd never liked heights.

He added coffee and sugar to the boiling water, allowing it to bubble up to the rim of the flask before pouring it into a glass and going through into the front hall, a large gloomy space off which all the rooms in the flat opened. For six months now he'd been building a fountain here and the floor was an assault course of cement bags and tiles and lengths of plastic tubing. It was just a small fountain and the work should have taken only a couple of weeks. Something always came up to distract him, however, so that the weeks had dragged into months and it was still only half finished. There wasn't really room for it and his wife had complained bitterly about the mess and expense, but he'd always wanted a fountain and, anyway, it would bring a bit of colour to their otherwise drab flat. He squatted and poked at a pile of sand with his finger, thinking perhaps he'd have enough time to set a few tiles before going into the office. The phone rang.

'It's for you,' said his wife sleepily as he entered the bedroom, 'Mohammed Sariya.'

She handed him the receiver and slipped out of bed, lifting the baby from its cot and disappearing into the kitchen. His son came in and leaped onto the bed beside him, bouncing up and down.

'*Bass*, Ali!' he said, pushing the boy away. 'Stop it! Hello, Mohammed. It's early. What's going on?'

The voice of his deputy echoed at the other end of the line. Khalifa held the phone with his right hand while using his left to fend off his son.

'Where?' he asked.

His deputy answered. He sounded excited.

'You're there now?'

Khalifa's son was laughing and trying to hit him with a pillow.

'I told you to stop it, Ali. Sorry, what was that? OK, stay where you are. And don't let anyone go near it. I'll be right over.'

42

He replaced the receiver and, seizing his son, turned him upside down, kissing each of his bare feet in turn. The boy roared with laughter.

'Swing me, Dad,' he cried. 'Swing me round.'

'I'll swing you round and out of the window,' said Khalifa. 'And then maybe you'll fly away and let me have a bit of peace.'

He dropped the boy on the bed and went through into the kitchen where Zenab, his wife, was making more coffee, the baby suckling at her breast. From the living room came the sound of his daughter singing.

'How is he this morning?' he asked, kissing his wife and tickling the baby's toes.

'Hungry,' she smiled. 'Like his father always is. Do you want breakfast?'

'No time,' said Khalifa. 'I've got to go over to the west bank.'

'Without breakfast?'

'Something's come up.'

'What?'

He looked at the woman hanging washing on the roof opposite. 'A body,' he said. 'I probably won't be home for lunch.'

He crossed the Nile on one of the brightly painted motor launches that plied back and forth between the two shores. Normally he would have taken the ferry, but he was in a hurry and so paid the extra and got a boat to himself. Just as they were pulling off an old man came hurrying up, a wooden box clutched under one arm. He grasped the rail of the boat and clambered aboard.

'Good morning, Inspector,' he puffed, setting the box down at Khalifa's feet. 'Shoeshine?'

Khalifa smiled. 'You never miss a trick, do you, Ibrahim?'

The old man chuckled, revealing two rows of uneven gold teeth. 'A man has to eat. And a man has to have clean shoes, too. So we help each other.'

'Go on, then. But be quick. I've got business on the other side and I don't want to hang around when we land.'

'You know me, Inspector. Fastest shoeshine in Luxor.'

He pulled out rags, a brush and polish, and slapped the top of his box, indicating that Khalifa should put his feet up. A young boy sat silently in the stern working the outboard, his face impassive.

They slid forward through the glassy water, the Theban Hills looming ahead, their colour changing from grey to brown to yellow in the growing light of day. Other launches were crossing to either side of theirs, one, away to the right, carrying a group of Japanese tourists. Probably going for a balloon ride over the Valley of the Kings, thought Khalifa, to see the sunrise. It was something he'd always wanted to do himself, although at three hundred dollars a go he couldn't afford it. Probably never would, police wages being what they were.

They came in to the western shore, sliding into a gap between two other launches and riding up onto the gravel with a crunch. The old man gave Khalifa's toecaps a last swift buff and clapped his polish-stained hands together to show he'd finished. The detective handed him two Egyptian pounds, gave the same to the boy and leaped down onto the shore.

'I'll wait for you,' said the boy.

'Don't bother,' he replied. 'See you soon, Ibrahim.'

The detective turned and climbed to the top of the bank, where a large crowd was waiting for the ferry. He wove his way through the throng, squeezing through a gap between a wall and a rusty chain-link fence and setting off along a narrow dirt track beside the river. Farmers were out working in the fields, harvesting their maize and sugar cane, and two men were up to their waists in an irrigation ditch clearing weeds. Groups of children in neat white shirts hurried past him on their way to school. The heat was rising. He lit another cigarette.

It took him twenty minutes to reach the body, by which time the buildings of western Luxor had receded to a distant blur and his newly polished shoes were white with dust. He emerged from a forest of reeds and there in front of him was Sergeant Sariya, squatting on the shore beside what looked like a bundle of wet rags. He stood as Khalifa approached.

'I've called the hospital,' he said. 'They're sending someone over.'

Khalifa nodded and descended to the water's edge. The body was lying on its front, arms splayed, face buried in the mud, its shirt ripped and bloodstained. From the waist down it was still in the water, the lapping of the waves causing it to roll back and forth like someone rocking in their sleep. A faint odour of decay wafted upwards to his nostrils.

'When was it found?'

'Just before dawn,' replied his deputy. 'Probably floated down from upriver and got caught in a boat propeller, which is why the arms are all cut up.'

'It was like this when you got here? You haven't touched anything?'

Sariya shook his head.

Khalifa squatted beside the body, examining the ground around it. He lifted the wrist, noting a tattoo on the middle of the forearm.

'A scarab,' he said, smiling faintly. 'How inappropriate.'

'Why inappropriate?'

'To the ancient Egyptians the scarab was a symbol of rebirth and renewal. Not something that's going to happen to our friend here by the looks of things.' He laid the wrist down again. 'You've no idea who reported it?'

Sariya shook his head. 'Wouldn't give his name. Called the station from a payphone and said he'd found it when he came down here to fish.'

'You're sure it was a payphone?'

'Pretty much. He cut off mid-sentence, like he'd run out of money.'

Khalifa was silent for a moment, thinking, and then, lifting his head, nodded towards a clump of trees fifty metres away, beyond which could be seen the roof of a house. The thin black line of a telephone cable was clearly visible beneath its eaves. Sariya raised his eyebrows.

'So?'

'The nearest payphone's two kilometres away, back in town. Why didn't he just call from there?'

'I guess he was in shock. It's not every day corpses wash up along these shores.'

'Precisely. You'd have thought he'd want to report it as quickly as possible. And why wouldn't he leave his name? You know what people around here are like. Never miss a chance to get in the news.'

'You think he knew something?'

Khalifa shrugged. 'It's just strange. Like he didn't want any-one to know it was him who'd found the body. Like he was scared.'

There was a loud splash as a heron took off from among the reeds, rising clumsily into the air and arcing off downstream. Khalifa watched it for a moment, then, with a shake of his head, turned his attention back to the corpse. He worked his hands into the trouser pockets and removed a penknife, a cheap lighter and a slip of soggy paper, folded. He laid the last on the corpse's back and carefully opened it out.

'Train ticket,' he said, leaning close to examine the faded writing. 'Return to Cairo. Dated four days ago.'

Sariya handed him a plastic bag and he dropped the objects into it.

'Come on, give me a hand here.'

Together they squatted beside the body and, getting their hands beneath it, rolled it over onto its back, the mud squelch-ing beneath their feet. As soon as he saw the face Sariya staggered away, retching violently.

'*Allah u akbar*,' he choked. 'God almighty!'

Khalifa bit his lip, forcing himself to look. He had seen bodies before, of course, but never one as badly mutilated as this. Even beneath its mask of mud it was clear there wasn't much of the face left. The left eye-socket was empty, the nose a mass of ribboned flesh and cartilage. He stared at it for a while, struggling to connect it with something that might once have been alive. Then, coming to his feet, he went over to Sariya and laid his hand on his shoulder.

'Are you all right?'

Sariya nodded, putting a finger against one of his nostrils and blowing hard so that a glob of mucus flew out onto the sand. 'What happened to him?'

'I don't know. Maybe a propeller, like you said, although I don't see how a propeller could have taken the eye out, or caused those sorts of wound.'

'You're saying someone did this deliberately?'

'I'm not saying anything. Just that a propeller would churn the flesh up, not slice it like that. Look how the skin has . . .' He could see his deputy was about to retch again and stopped mid-sentence, not wishing to upset him more. 'We'll wait for the autopsy,' he said after a pause.

He lit a couple of cigarettes and handed one to Sariya, who took a deep drag before throwing it aside and scrambling up the bank to be sick again. Khalifa turned away and wandered back to the river's edge, gazing over to the far shore. A procession of Nile cruisers was lined up along the bank, with beyond them, just visible, the first pylon of Karnak Temple. A felucca crossed his line of sight, its giant triangular sail cutting across the sky like a blade. He flicked his cigarette into the water and sighed. It was, he suspected, going to be a while before he got a chance to work on his fountain again.

As Inspector Khalifa stood beside the river, a group of tourists on donkeys were winding their way up into the hills behind him.

47

There were twenty of them, Americans mostly, moving in single file, with an Egyptian boy at their head to guide them and another at the rear to make sure no-one got left behind. Some clung nervously to their saddles, uncomfortable on the precipitous path, grimacing at every bump and jolt. One in particular, a large woman with sunburnt shoulders, was not enjoying the experience.

'They never said it would be this steep,' she kept shouting. 'They said it would be easy. Oh Christ!'

Others, however, seemed more relaxed, turning from side to side in their saddles to take in the spectacular views. The sun was up now and the plain beneath them throbbed and shimmered in the heat. Far off could be seen the winding silver ribbon of the Nile, with beyond it the jumbled mass of eastern Luxor and beyond that a blur of desert and mountains, no more than a rumour against the white-blue sky. Their guide stopped every now and then to point out some of the sights below: the Colossi of Memnon, small as toys from that distance; the broken ruins of the Ramesseum; the vast compound of Ramesses III's mortuary temple at Medinet Habu. Those who were not too nervous lifted their cameras and snapped a photo. Apart from the crunch and clatter of donkeys' hooves and the voice of the woman with sunburnt shoulders, they climbed in virtual silence, awed by the scenery.

'Beats the shit out of Minnesota,' muttered one man to his wife.

Eventually they came up onto the summit of the hills and the path widened and flattened out, running evenly for a while before dipping away again into a broad rocky valley.

'That is Valley of Kings in front,' shouted their guide. 'Hold tight. Path down is very steep.'

'Christ!' came a shrill voice from behind him.

They had just started across the ridge, the donkeys zigzagging their way between scattered rocks, when a man suddenly leaped up from the shadow of a boulder where he had been lying. His djellaba was filthy and ragged, and his matted hair came down well below the level of his shoulders, giving him a wild, unkempt look. In his hand he carried something wrapped in brown paper. He hurried over to them.

'Hello hello good morning good night,' he jabbered, his words all running together. 'Look here please friends. I have something good I know you like.'

The donkey guide shouted at him in Arabic, but the man ignored him and went up to one of the tourists, a young woman in a large straw sunhat. Lifting the object in his hand he pulled back the brown paper to reveal a cat carved out of dark stone.

'You see lady very very lovely carving. You buy you buy. I very poor need eat. You beautiful lady you buy!'

He thrust the carving towards her with one hand, while lifting the other to his mouth in an eating motion.

'You buy you buy. I no eat for three days. Please you buy. Hungry. Hungry.'

The woman stared fixedly ahead, taking no notice of him, and after stumbling beside her for a few metres the man gave up and turned his attention to the rider behind.

'Look look mister lovely carving. Very good quality. How much you pay give me price give me price.'

'Ignore him,' called the guide over his shoulder. 'He's mad.'

'Yes yes mad,' laughed the ragged man, twirling round a couple of times and slamming his foot on the ground in a sort of dance. 'Mad mad. Please you buy no food I hungry. Best quality give me price mister.'

The man too ignored him and the ragged figure began to scuttle up and down the line, his cries becoming increasingly hoarse and desperate.

'You no like cat I have other carvings. Many many carvings. Please please you buy. Antiquities? I have antiquities. Three thousand per cent genuine. You need guide I very good guide I know all these hills every little bit. I show you kings valley and queens valley very cheap. I show you tomb very beautiful.

49

New tomb no-one else know. I need eat. No eat for three days.'

By now he was at the back of the line and, urging his donkey forward, the boy at the rear barged him out of the way, kicking him in the ribs as he passed. The ragged man fell to the ground in a swirl of dust and the tourists moved on.

'Thank you thank you thank you!' he cried, rolling around like a wounded animal, his hair flying from side to side. 'So kind lovely tourist to help me. No want cat no want see tomb no want guide. I die! I die!'

He screwed his face into the ground, weeping, hammering his fists on the sand.

The tourists, however, did not see him, for they had already passed round an outcrop of rock and begun their descent into the Valley of the Kings. It was steep, as the guide had warned them, with a near-vertical drop away to their right. The woman with sunburnt shoulders clutched the neck of the donkey and trembled, too frightened even to complain. The wails of the madman gradually grew fainter until they disappeared altogether.

6

CAIRO

Tara waited at the airport until past ten a.m., by which point her eyes were red from lack of sleep and she was dizzy with tiredness. She had called her father every half-hour, wandered round and round the arrivals hall, even taken a taxi over to the domestic terminal in case he'd gone to the wrong place. All to no avail. He wasn't at the airport, he wasn't at his dig house, he wasn't at his flat in Cairo. Her holiday had gone wrong before it had even started. She clambered onto her seat for the umpteenth time and gazed around the concourse. So many people were now milling to and fro, however, that even if her father had been among them she wouldn't have seen him. She jumped down, went over to the payphone and called the dig house and flat one last time. Then, swinging her bag over her shoulder and slipping on her sunglasses, she went outside and hailed a taxi.

'Cairo?' asked the driver, a burly man with a thick moustache and nicotine-stained fingers.

'No,' Tara replied, sinking wearily into the back seat, 'Saqqara.'

*

Her father had been excavating at Saqqara, the necropolis of the ancient Egyptian capital Memphis, for the best part of fifty years.

He had dug at other sites around Egypt, from Tanis and Sais in the north right down to Qustul and Nauri in upper Sudan, but Saqqara had always been his first love. Each season he would take up residence in his dig house and remain there for three or four months at a stretch, painstakingly working over a small area of sand-blown ruins, uncovering a few more metres of history. Some seasons he wouldn't dig at all, but would spend his time in restoration work or recording the previous year's finds.

It was a frugal existence, monastic almost – just himself, a cook and a small group of volunteers – but it was the one place in the world, Tara believed, where he was truly happy. His infrequent letters revealed, in their minute descriptions of the progress of his work, a sense of contentment that seemed wholly absent from the other areas of his life. That's why she had been so surprised when he had asked her out to stay with him – this was his world, his special place, and it must have taken a leap of faith on his part to invite her into it.

The journey from the airport wasn't a comfortable one. Her driver seemed to have no concept of road safety, thinking nothing of overtaking on tight corners and in the face of heavy oncoming traffic. On one stretch of road, alongside a foetid green canal, he pulled out to go past a small truck only to see a lorry approaching from the opposite direction. Tara assumed he would pull in again. Far from it. He hammered his palm on the horn and pressed his foot to the floor, moving slowly past the truck which, in response, started to go faster, as though racing. The oncoming lorry grew larger by the second and Tara felt her stomach knot, convinced they were going to crash. Only at the last minute, when it looked as if a head-on collision was inevitable, did the driver yank his wheel to the right, swerving in front of the truck and missing the front of the lorry by what looked like a matter of centimetres.

'You frightened?' he laughed as they sped on.

'Yes,' Tara replied curtly. 'I am.'

Eventually, and much to her relief, they turned right off the main road and, after following a smaller, tree-lined road for a few kilometres, came to a halt at the foot of a steep sandy escarpment, above which peeped the upper courses of a step-shaped pyramid.

'You get ticket here,' said the driver, pointing to a ticket window in a building to the right.

'Do I need one?' she asked. 'My father works here. I've come to visit him.'

The driver leaned out and shouted something at the man sitting in the window. They held a brief conversation, in Arabic, and then another man, young, came out of the building and bent down to the taxi, looking at Tara.

'Your father work here?' His English was heavily accented.

'Yes,' she said. 'Professor Michael Mullray.'

'Excellent!' The man smiled broadly. 'Everybody know the Doktora. He most famous Egyptologist in world. He my good friend. He teach me English. I take you dig house myself.'

He came round to the other side of the taxi and slipped into the passenger seat, giving instructions to the driver.

'My name Hassan,' he said as they moved off. 'I work here at main *teftish*. You very welcome.' He extended a hand, which Tara shook.

'I was supposed to meet my father at the airport,' she said. 'I think we must have missed each other. Is he here, do you know?'

'I sorry, I only just come. He probably in dig house. You look like to him, you know.'

'Like him,' smiled Tara. 'I look like him. You don't need the "to".'

The man laughed. 'You look like him,' he said carefully. 'And you are good teacher like to him too.'

They followed the road up to the top of the scarp and then

turned right onto a bumpy track that ran along the edge of the desert plateau. The step pyramid was behind them now, with two other smaller pyramids nearby, both ruined and slumped, so that Tara had the impression they were all images of the same pyramid in different stages of collapse. To the right the patch-work fields of the Nile plain shimmered in the morning heat; to the left the desert rolled and bumped off towards the horizon, barren and empty and desolate.

A hundred metres along the track they passed through the middle of a small settlement and Hassan signalled the driver to stop.

'This *teftish*,' he said, indicating a large yellow building to the right. 'Saqqara main office. I stop here. *Beit Mullray*, your father dig house, more further. I tell driver how go there. If you have problem you come back here.'

He climbed out, said something to the driver and they moved off again, continuing for another two kilometres before pulling over beside a low, one-storey house standing on the very edge of the escarpment.

'*Beit Mullray*,' said the driver.

It was a long, ramshackle building, painted a dusty pink and arranged around three sides of a sandy courtyard, in the centre of which stood a huge wood and wire excavator's sieve. A rickety wooden tower with a water tank on top stood at one end of the building, a pile of wooden crates at the other, with a mangy dog dozing in the shade beside them. The windows were all closed and shuttered. There seemed to be no-one around.

The driver said he'd wait, arguing that if her father wasn't there he could take her back to Cairo, where he knew lots of good hotels. She declined the offer and, removing her bag from the boot, paid the fare and set off towards the house, the taxi reversing behind her and driving off in a cloud of dust.

She crossed the courtyard, noticing what looked like a row of painted stone blocks beneath a tarpaulin in the corner, and hammered on the front door. No response. She tried the handle. The door was locked.

'Dad!' she called. 'It's Tara!'

Nothing.

She walked around to the rear of the house. A long shady terrace ran its full length, with pots of dusty geraniums and cacti, some gnarled lemon trees and a couple of stone benches. There were fabulous views eastwards across the green Nile plain, but she was oblivious to them. Removing her sunglasses, she went up to one of the shuttered windows and peered through the peeling slats. It was dark inside and apart from the edge of a table with a book on it she could see nothing. She looked through another shutter further along, making out a bed with a pair of battered desert boots tucked beneath it, and then walked round to the front of the house and hammered on the door again. Still nothing. She walked back out onto the track, stood looking to left and right for a few moments, then returned to the terrace and sat down on one of the concrete benches.

She was worried now. Her father had let her down on numerous occasions – too many to remember – but she sensed that this time it was different. Perhaps he had been taken ill or had had some sort of accident? Scenarios flicked through her head, each more upsetting than the one before. She stood up and banged on the shutters again, more out of frustration than hope.

'Where are you, Dad?' she muttered to herself. 'Where the fuck are you?'

She waited at the house for almost two hours, wandering around, peering through the shutters, occasionally hammering on the door, beads of sweat bubbling across her forehead, eyes heavy with exhaustion. A group of children playing in the village beneath spotted her and came scrabbling up the dusty slope at the back of the building, shouting, 'School pen! School pen!' She took some pens out of her bag and handed them round, asking if any of them had seen a tall man with white hair. They didn't seem to understand and once they had their pens they disappeared down the escarpment again, leaving her alone with the flies and the heat and the silent, shuttered house.

Eventually, when the sun was at its zenith and she was so tired she could barely keep awake, she decided to go and look for Hassan, the man she'd met earlier. She knew if her father had just been delayed somewhere he would be angry at her for making a fuss, but by now she was too concerned to care. With her one remaining pen she scribbled a note explaining what she was doing and wedged it in the front door. She then set out back along the dusty track towards the distant serrated bulk of the step pyramid, the sun burning down on her, the world silent apart from the crunch of her footfall and the occasional whirr of a passing fly.

She had been walking for about five minutes, head bowed, when something caught her eye away to the right, a momentary glint. She stopped and looked in that direction, shielding her eyes. There was someone standing over there, about two hundred metres out into the desert, on top of a sandy hillock. They were too far away, and the sun too bright, to make out much about them, except that they seemed to be extremely tall and dressed in white. There was another brief glint and she realized they must be looking through binoculars, the sun reflecting off the lenses.

She turned away, assuming it was just a tourist exploring the ruins. Then the thought struck her that perhaps it was an archaeologist who might know her father. She swung back again, intending to call out, but whoever it was had disappeared. She scanned the undulating mounds of sand and rubble but there was no-one there and, after a moment, she continued on her way, uncertain whether it wasn't just something she had hallucinated in her exhaustion and worry. Her head had started to swim and her temples were throbbing. She wished she had some water with her.

It took her another twenty minutes to reach the *teftish*, by which point her shirt was damp with sweat and her limbs ached. She found Hassan and explained what was going on.

'I sure everything OK,' he said, ushering her to a chair in his office. 'Perhaps your father go out walking. Or to excavation.'

'Without leaving a note?'

'Perhaps waiting in Cairo?'

'I've called his flat and there's no reply.'

'He knew you come today?'

'Of course he knew I was coming today,' she snapped. There was a moment's silence. 'I'm sorry,' she said. 'I'm tired and worried.'

'I am understanding, Miss Mullray. Please, be very calm. We find him.'

He picked up the walkie-talkie lying on his desk, pressed a button on the side and spoke into it, carefully enunciating the words 'Doktora Mullray'. There was a crackle of static and then several other voices, one after another, responded. The official listened, spoke again and then laid the walkie-talkie down.

'He not at excavation and no-one see him. Wait here please.'

He went into another room across the hall. There was a low murmur of voices. He was back within a minute.

'He go Cairo yesterday morning, then come back Saqqara in afternoon. No-one see him since then.'

He picked up the phone. Again he held a brief conversation, emphasizing the words 'Doktora Mullray'. He was frowning when he replaced the receiver.

'That Ahmed. He driving taxi for your father. He say your father tell him come *Beit Mullray* last night, take him to airport, but when Ahmed come your father not there. Now I worried too. This not like the Doktora.'

He was silent for a moment, tapping his fingers on the desk, and then, opening a drawer, he pulled out a set of keys. 'This spare keys to dig house,' he explained. 'We go see.'

They left the office and he pointed towards a battered white Fiat parked outside. 'We take car. Quicker.'

He drove fast, the car bumping and jolting along the uneven track, skidding to a halt in front of the house. They walked down to the front door, where Tara immediately noticed that the note she had left was gone. Her heart surged and, rushing forward, she tried the door handle. It was still locked and there was no reply to her frantic knocking. Hassan selected a key from the ring, slipped it into the lock and turned it twice, throwing the door open and walking in. Tara followed.

They were in a long whitewashed room, with a rectangular dining table at the end nearest them and at the other a couple of moth-eaten sofas and a fireplace. Other rooms opened off to left and right, in one of which Tara could make out the edge of a wooden bedframe. It was dark and cool, with a faintly sweet aroma in the air, which she realized after a moment was the smell of cigar smoke.

Hassan walked across and threw open a window. Sunlight spilled across the floor. She saw the body immediately, slumped against the far wall.

'Oh God.' She was choking. 'Oh no.'

She ran across and fell to her knees, seizing his hand. It was cold and stiff. She didn't bother trying to revive him.

'Dad,' she whispered, stroking his unkempt grey hair. 'Oh my poor Dad.'

7

LUXOR

As Inspector Khalifa stared down at the corpse, he was reminded of the day they had brought his father's body home.

He'd been six at the time and hadn't really understood what was going on. They had carried the body into the living room and laid it out on the table. His mother, weeping and tearing at her black robes, had knelt at its feet, while he and his brother Ali had stood side by side at its head, holding hands, staring at the pale, dust-covered face.

'Don't worry, Mother,' Ali had said. 'I will look after you and Yusuf. I swear.'

The accident had happened only a few blocks from where they lived. A tourist bus, going too fast for the narrow streets, had spun out of control and slammed into the rickety wooden scaffolding on which his father had been working, bringing the whole structure down. Three men had been killed, his father one of them, crushed beneath a ton of bricks and wood. The tour company had refused to accept responsibility and no compensation had ever been paid. The people in the bus had escaped unharmed.

They had lived in Nazlat al-Sammam in those days, at the foot of the Giza plateau, in a cramped mud-brick shack from whose roof you could look directly out over the Sphinx and the pyramids.

Ali had been the older by six years, strong and clever and fearless. Khalifa had idolized him, following him everywhere, mimicking the way he walked and the things he said. To this day, when he was annoyed, he would mutter 'Dammit!', a word he had learnt from his brother, who in turn had picked it up from a British tourist.

After their father had died, true to his word, Ali had left school and gone to work to support them. He had found a job at the local camel stables, mucking out, repairing the saddles, taking the camels up onto the plateau to give rides to the tourists. On Sundays Khalifa had been allowed to help him. Not during the week, however. He had begged to be allowed to work with his brother full time, but Ali had insisted he concentrate on his studies instead.

'Learn, Yusuf,' he had urged him. 'Fill your mind. Do the things I can't. Make me proud of you.'

Only years later had he discovered that every day, as well as buying them food and clothes and paying their rent, Ali had put aside a little of his meagre earnings so that when the time came he, Khalifa, would be able to afford to go to university. He owed his brother so much. Everything. That was why he had named his first son after him – to show that he recognized the debt.

His son, however, had never seen his uncle, and never would. Ali was gone for ever. How he missed him! How he wished things could have turned out differently.

He shook his head and returned to the business in hand. He was in a white-tiled room in the basement of Luxor general hospital and in front of him the body they had found that morning was stretched out on a metal table, naked. A fan whirled above his head; a single strip light added to the cold, sterile atmosphere.

Dr Anwar, the local pathologist, was bent over the body, poking at it with his rubber-gloved hands.

'Very curious,' he kept muttering to himself. 'Never seen anything like it. Very curious.'

They had photographed the corpse where it had washed up beside the river and then zipped it into a body-bag and brought it back to Luxor by boat. There had been a lot of paperwork to fill out before they could get it examined and it was now late afternoon. He had sent Sariya to make enquiries about any person reported missing within a radius of thirty kilometres, thus sparing his deputy the unpleasant business of witnessing the autopsy. He himself was finding it hard not to gag. He was desperate for a cigarette and every now and then reached instinctively into his pocket for the packet of Cleopatras, although he didn't take them out. Dr Anwar was notoriously strict about smoking in his morgue.

'So what can you tell me?' asked Khalifa, leaning against the cool tile wall, fiddling with a button on his shirt.

'Well,' said Anwar, pausing for a moment to think. 'He's definitely dead.' He let out a guffaw of laughter, slapping his belly appreciatively. Anwar's bad jokes were as notorious as his dislike of smoking. 'Apologies,' he said. 'In very bad taste.'

Another chuckle escaped him and then his face straightened and he was serious again. 'So what do you want to know?'

'Age?'

'Difficult to be precise, but I'd say late twenties, possibly a bit older.'

'Time of death?'

'About eighteen hours ago. Maybe twenty. Maximum twenty-four.'

'And he's been in the water all that time?'

'I'd say so, yes.'

'How far could he have floated in twenty-four hours do you think?'

'Absolutely no idea. I'm interested in bodies, not currents.'

61

Khalifa smiled. 'OK, cause of death?'

'I would have thought that was obvious,' said Anwar, looking down at the mutilated face. It had been cleaned of mud and looked, if anything, even more grotesque than when Khalifa had first seen it, like a badly carved joint of meat. There were lacerations elsewhere on the body, too – on the arms and shoulders, across the belly, on the tops of the thighs. There was even a small puncture mark in the scrotum, which Anwar had taken great delight in pointing out. Sometimes, Khalifa thought, the man was just a little too enthusiastic about his job.

'What I meant was . . .'

'Yes, yes, I know,' said the pathologist. 'I was being facetious. You want to know what caused the injuries.'

He leaned back against the examination table and ripped off his gloves, the rubber making a snapping sound as it peeled from his hands.

'OK, first things first. He died from shock and loss of blood, both a result of the injuries you see before you. There was comparatively little water in his lungs, which means that he didn't drown and then receive the injuries afterwards. This happened to him on dry land and then the body was dumped in the river. Probably not that far away from where it was found.'

'It couldn't have been a boat propeller, then?'

'Absolutely not. You'd have a completely different type of wound. Less clean. The flesh would have been more churned up.'

'Crocodile?'

'Don't be stupid, Khalifa. This man has been deliberately mutilated. And anyway, for your information, there are no crocodiles north of Aswan. And certainly none that smoke.' He pointed at the man's arms, chest and face. 'Three burn marks. Here, here and here. Cigar probably. Too big for a cigarette.'

He fumbled in his pocket and removed a bag of cashew nuts, offering them to Khalifa. The detective refused.

'As you like,' said Anwar, tipping his head back and pouring a rush of nuts into his mouth. Khalifa watched, wondering how he could eat with that ripped face only a few metres away.

'And what about the cuts? What caused those?'

'No idea,' grunted Anwar, chewing. 'Some sort of metal object, sharp obviously. Possibly a knife, although I've seen all manner of knife injuries and none that looked quite like this.'

'How do you mean?'

'Well, the wounds aren't neat enough. It's hard to explain. More a gut feeling than proper science. It was definitely a sharpened blade of some sort, but not one with which I'm familiar. Look at this, for instance.' He pointed to a slash on the man's chest. 'If a knife had done that the wound would have been narrower and not quite so . . . what's the word . . . chunky. And look, it's slightly deeper at one end than at the other. Don't ask me to be more precise, Khalifa, because I can't. Just accept that we're dealing with an unusual weapon here.'

The inspector pulled a small pad from his pocket and scribbled a couple of notes. The room echoed to the sound of Anwar's chewing.

'Can you tell me anything else about him?'

'Well, he liked a drink. High levels of alcohol in the blood. And he would seem to have had an interest in ancient Egypt.'

'The scarab tattoo?'

'Exactly. Not the most common of designs. And look here.'

Khalifa came closer.

'You see this bruising around the upper arms? Here, and here, where the flesh is discoloured. This man has been restrained, like this.'

Anwar went behind Khalifa and grabbed his arms, his fingers digging into the flesh.

'The bruising on the left arm is more extensive and extends further round the arm, which suggests he was probably being held by two people rather than one, each gripping him in a slightly different way. You can see by the depth of the bruising that he put up quite a struggle.'

Khalifa nodded, bent over his notebook. 'At least three altogether, then,' he said. 'Two holding, one wielding the knife or whatever it was.'

Anwar nodded and, crossing to the door, put his head out into the corridor and shouted to someone at the far end. A moment later two men appeared pushing a trolley. They lifted the body onto it, covered it with a sheet and wheeled it out of the room. Anwar finished his nuts and, going to a small basin, began washing his hands. The room was silent apart from the purr of the fan.

'I'm shocked, frankly,' said the pathologist, his tone suddenly devoid of its usual jocularity. 'I've been doing this job for thirty years and I've never seen anything like it. It's' – he paused, soaping his hands slowly, his back to Khalifa – 'ungodly,' he said eventually.

'I didn't have you marked down as religious.'

'I'm not. But there's no other way to describe what happened to this man. I mean they didn't just kill him. They butchered the poor bastard.'

He turned off the taps and started to dry his hands.

'Find who did this, Khalifa. Find them quickly and lock them away.'

The earnestness of his tone surprised Khalifa. 'I'll do my best,' he said. 'If any more information comes up, be sure to let me know.'

He put his notebook away and started towards the door. He was halfway through it when Anwar called after him.

'There is one thing.'

Khalifa turned.

'Just a hunch, but I think he might have been a sculptor. Doing carvings for the tourists, that sort of thing. There was a lot of alabaster dust underneath his fingernails and his forearms were very built up, which might indicate he used a hammer and chisel a lot. I might be wrong, but that's where I'd start making enquiries. In the alabaster shops.'

Khalifa thanked him and set off down the corridor, pulling his cigarettes from his pocket. Anwar's voice echoed after him.

'And no smoking till you're out of the hospital!'

8

CAIRO

'He hated cigars,' said Tara.

The embassy official glanced across at her. 'Sorry?'

'Cigars. My father hated them. Any form of smoking, in fact. He said it was a disgusting habit. Like reading the *Guardian*.'

'Ah,' said the official, perplexed. 'I see.'

'When we first went into the dig house there was a smell. To start with I couldn't place it. Then I realized it was cigar smoke.'

The official, a junior attaché named Crispin Oates, returned his eyes to the road, honking loudly at a truck in front of them.

'Is that significant in some way?'

'As I said, my father hated smoking.'

Oates shrugged. 'Then I guess it must have been someone else.'

'But that's the point,' said Tara. 'Smoking was banned in the dig house. It was an absolute rule. I know because he wrote to me once saying he'd sacked a volunteer for breaking it.'

A motorbike overtook on the inside and swerved in front of them, forcing Oates to slam his foot on the brakes.

'Bloody idiot!'

They drove in silence for a moment.

'I'm not sure I see what you're getting at,' he said eventually.

'Neither am I,' sighed Tara. 'Just that . . . there shouldn't have been cigar smoke in the dig house. I can't get it out of my mind.'

'I'm sure it's just . . . well, you know, the shock.'

Tara sighed. 'Yes,' she said wearily, 'I suppose it must be.'

They were on a raised carriageway coming into the centre of Cairo. It was almost dark and the lights of the city spread off into the distance around and beneath them. It was still hot and Tara had the window wound down so that her hair fluttered behind her like a streamer. She felt curiously detached, as though the events of the last few hours had all been some sort of dream.

They'd waited with her father's body for an hour until a doctor had arrived. He had examined the corpse briefly before telling them what they already knew – that the old man was dead, probably from a massive coronary, although more tests would be needed. An ambulance had arrived, followed shortly afterwards by two policemen, both in suits, who had asked Tara a series of perfunctory questions about her father's age, health, nationality, profession. ('He's a sodding archaeologist,' she had replied irritably. 'What the hell else do you think he was doing here!') She had mentioned the cigar smoke, explaining, as she was later to explain to Oates, that smoking was banned in the dig house. The policemen had taken notes, but had not seemed to consider the matter especially important. She hadn't pursued it. At no point had she cried. Indeed, her immediate reaction to her father's death had been no reaction at all. She had watched as his body was carried to the ambulance and had felt nothing inside her, nothing whatsoever, as though it was someone she didn't know.

'Dad's dead,' she had mumbled, as though trying to elicit some sort of response from herself. 'He's dead. Dead.'

The words had made no impression. She had tried to recall some of the good times they had spent together – books they had both enjoyed, days out at the zoo, the treasure trail he had laid for her fifteenth birthday – but had been unable to make any emotional connection with them. The one thing she had felt – and had been ashamed of feeling – was a sense of acute disappointment that her trip had been spoilt.

I'm going to spend the next fortnight filling out forms and making funeral arrangements, she had thought. Some fucking holiday.

Oates had arrived just as the ambulance was pulling away, the embassy having been informed of her father's death as soon as it was discovered. Blond, chinless, late twenties, quintessentially English, he had offered his commiserations politely but without real conviction, in a way that suggested he'd been through all this many times before.

He had spoken to the doctor – in faltering Arabic – and had asked Tara where she was staying.

'Here,' she had told him. 'Or at least that was the plan. I suppose it's not very appropriate now.'

Oates had agreed. 'I think the best thing would be to get you back to Cairo and booked into somewhere there. Let me make a couple of calls.'

He had pulled a mobile phone from the pocket of his suit – how on earth can people wear suits in this heat, Tara had thought – and wandered outside, returning a few minutes later. 'Right,' he had said, 'we've got you into the Ramesses Hilton. I don't think there's much more to do here, so whenever you're ready . . .'

She had lingered in the dig house for a moment, gazing around at the bookcases and moth-eaten sofas, imagining her father relaxing here after a day at his excavation, and had then joined Oates in his car.

'Funny,' he had said, starting the engine. 'I've been in Cairo for three years and it's the first time I've ever been to Saqqara. Never been much interested in archaeology, to be honest.'

'Me neither,' she had said sadly.

*

It was dark by the time they reached the hotel, an ugly concrete skyscraper rearing beside the Nile, on the edge of a tangled intersection of busy roads. The interior was brightly lit and gaudy with a cavernous marble foyer, off which various bars, lounges and shops opened and through which a constant stream of red-uniformed porters bustled with armfuls of designer luggage. It was cool – cold almost – which Tara found a relief after the heat outside. Her room was on the fourteenth floor: spacious, neat, sterile, facing away from the river. She slung her bag on the bed and kicked off her shoes.

'I'll leave you to settle in then,' said Oates, hovering at the door. 'The restaurant's quite good, or else there's room service.'

'Thanks,' said Tara. 'I'm not really hungry.'

'Of course. I quite understand.' He put his hand on the door handle. 'There'll be various formalities to go through tomorrow, so if it's all right with you I'll pick you up at, say, eleven a.m. and take you over to the embassy.'

Tara nodded.

'One small thing. Probably best not to go out at night, not on your own. I don't want to alarm you, but it's a trifle risky for tourists at the moment. There's been a bit of fundamentalist activity. Attacks, you know. Better safe than sorry.'

Tara thought of the man she had met at the airport by the baggage carousel. 'Sayf al-Tamar,' she said, remembering the name he had mentioned.

'Al-Tha'r,' said Oates, correcting her. 'Al-ta-ar. Yes, it does seem to be his lot. Bloody lunatics. The more the authorities try to clamp down on them the more trouble they cause. Parts of the country are now virtual no-go areas.' He handed her his card. 'Anyway, call me if there's anything you need and have a good night's sleep.'

Rather formally he shook her hand and then opened the door and stepped out into the corridor.

Once he was gone Tara fetched a beer from the mini-bar and threw herself onto the bed. She called Jenny in England and left a message on her answerphone, telling her where she was, and asking her to call back as soon as possible. There were other calls she knew she ought to make – to her father's sister; to the American University, where he had been Visiting Professor of Near Eastern Archaeology – but she decided to leave them until tomorrow. She wandered out onto the balcony, gazing down at the street below.

A black Mercedes had just drawn up alongside the hotel, partly blocking the road, so that the cars behind were forced to pull out and around it, something they weren't too happy about to judge by the distant sounds of hooting.

Initially Tara didn't take much notice of the car. Then the passenger door opened and a figure stepped out onto the pavement and suddenly she tensed. She couldn't be certain it was the man she'd seen at Saqqara – the one who had been watching her as she walked along the escarpment – but something told her it was. He was wearing a pale suit and, even from that height, looked huge, dwarfing the pedestrians around him.

He leaned down and said something to the driver of the Mercedes, which moved off into the traffic. He watched it go and then, suddenly, turned and looked up, straight at her, or at least she imagined he was looking straight at her, although in reality he was too far away for her to see precisely where his eyes were directed. It lasted only a moment and then he dropped his head again and strode towards the hotel's side entrance, raising his hand to his mouth and puffing on what looked like a large cigar. Tara shuddered and, stepping off the balcony, closed and locked the sliding doors behind her.

THE RIVER NILE, BETWEEN LUXOR AND ASWAN

Froth churned from the bow of the SS *Horus* as she made her way slowly upriver, her lights casting an eerie glow across the water. Shadowy reed forests slipped past on either bank, with here and there a small hut or house, but it was past midnight and there were few people left on deck to see them. A young couple cuddled on the stern, faces nuzzling, and beneath an awning at the back of the cruiser a group of old ladies were playing cards. Otherwise the decks were deserted. Most of the passengers had either retired to bed or were sitting in the saloon listening to the late-night cabaret – a paunchy Egyptian man singing popular hits to a backing tape.

There were two explosions, almost simultaneous. The first came near the prow of the boat, engulfing the young couple. The second was in the main saloon, blasting tables and chairs and fragments of glass in all directions. The cabaret singer was thrown backwards into his PA, face grilled black by the heat; a group of women near the stage were lost in a hail of splintered wood and metal. There was weeping, and groaning, and the screams of a man whose legs had been ripped off below the knees. The lady card-players, unharmed, sat motionless beneath their awning. One of them started to cry.

Away from the river, beyond the reeds, squatting on a small rocky hummock, three men gazed at the boat. The glow from its flaming decks lit their bearded faces, revealing a deep vertical scar on each of their foreheads. They were smiling.

'Sayf al-Tha'r,' whispered one.

'Sayf al-Tha'r,' repeated his companions.

They nodded and, rising to their feet, disappeared into the night.

9

CAIRO

As they had agreed, Oates met Tara in the foyer of the hotel at eleven a.m. and drove her to the embassy, which was ten minutes away.

Despite her exhaustion she hadn't slept well. The image of the huge man had stayed with her, leaving her inexplicably edgy. She had eventually drifted into a light sleep, but then the phone had rung, ripping her awake again. It was Jenny.

They had talked for almost an hour, her friend offering to catch the next flight out. Tara had been tempted to let her come, but in the end had told her not to worry. Everything was being taken care of, and anyway she'd probably be home in a few days once all the formalities had been completed. They had agreed to speak the next day and rung off. She had watched TV for a while, flicking aimlessly from CNN to MTV Asia to BBC World, before eventually dozing off.

It was deep in the night when she had woken for a second time, suddenly, sensing something was amiss. The world was silent and the room thick with shadows, although the moon was gleaming through a narrow gap in the curtains, casting a ghostly sheen across the mirror on the wall opposite.

She had lain on the bed trying to work out what was troubling her and then rolled over to go back to sleep. As she did so she had caught a soft creaking coming from the direction of the doorway. She had listened for several seconds before she realized that it was the sound of her door handle turning.

'Hello!'

Her voice had sounded unnaturally shrill.

The creaking had stopped for a moment and then resumed. Heart pounding, she had crossed to the door, where she had stood gazing at the handle as it inched carefully down and up, as if in slow motion. She had thought of shouting out again, but had instead just grabbed the handle and held it. There had been a brief resistance on the other side and then a swift padding of feet. She had counted to five and opened the door, but the corridor had been empty. Or rather almost empty, because one thing at least had lingered: a smell of cigar smoke.

After that she had kept the lights on for the rest of the night, only falling asleep again just as dawn was breaking. When Oates had asked her if she'd had a good night, her reply had been terse: 'No, I bloody didn't.'

Oates swung the car through a gate in the embassy's cream-coloured outer wall, flashing his ID at the guard, and pulled up in a small car park, taking Tara into the building through a side door. They walked down a long corridor and up some stairs to a suite of offices on the first floor, where they were met by a thin, slightly dishevelled man with white hair, thick eyebrows and a pair of glasses hanging around his neck.

'Good morning, Miss Mullray.' He smiled, extending a hand. 'Charles Squires, cultural attaché.' His tone was gentle, avuncular, unlike his grip, which was vice-like. 'Crispin, why don't you see about some coffee? We'll be in my office.'

He led Tara through a set of double doors into a large, sunlit room with four armchairs arranged around a table. Another man was standing beside the window.

'This is Dr Sharif Jemal, of the Supreme Council of Antiquities,' said Squires. 'He specifically asked if he could be here this morning.'

The man was short and broad, with a heavily pockmarked face. He stepped forward.

'May I offer my condolences on the death of your father,' he said solemnly. 'He was a great scholar and a true friend of this country. He will be much missed.'

'Thank you,' said Tara.

The three of them sat down.

'The ambassador sends his apologies,' continued Squires. 'Given your father's eminence, he would have liked to have been here in person. Unfortunately, as you may have heard, there was another terrorist incident last night, up near Aswan, and two of the fatalities were British, so he is somewhat pre-occupied at present.'

He sat very still as he spoke, his thin, hairless hands clasped in his lap.

'I know I speak for him, however, and indeed the whole embassy, when I say how very sorry we were to hear of the death of your father. I had the pleasure of meeting him on several occasions. It's a great loss.'

Oates returned carrying a tray.

'Milk?' asked Squires.

'Black, no sugar,' said Tara. 'Thank you.'

Squires nodded at Oates, who poured out cups of coffee and handed them round. There was an awkward silence.

'When I was a student I was fortunate enough to spend a season with your father at Saqqara,' said Jemal eventually. 'It was 1972. The year we found the tomb of Ptah-hotep. I shall never forget the excitement when we entered the burial chamber for the first time. It was virtually intact, untouched since the day it was sealed. There was a magnificent wooden statue near the entrance, about so high' – he indicated with his hand – 'wonderfully realistic, with inlaid eyes, in perfect condition. It is currently on display in the Cairo museum. You must let me take you to see it.'

'I should love to,' said Tara, trying to sound enthusiastic.

'Your father taught me a great deal,' continued Jemal. 'I owe him much. He was a good man.'

He removed a handkerchief and blew into it loudly, apparently overwhelmed with emotion. The four of them lapsed back into silence, sipping their coffee. It was a while before Squires spoke again.

'The doctor assures me your father's death was swift and without pain. It was a coronary, apparently. Death would have been almost immediate.'

Tara nodded. 'He was taking medication for his heart,' she said.

'Please do not take this the wrong way,' said Jemal, 'but I think if your father could have chosen anywhere to die it would have been Saqqara. He was always happy there.'

'Yes,' said Tara. 'It was like his real home.'

Oates began refilling their cups.

'I'm afraid there are various formalities to go through,' said Squires apologetically, 'all of which Crispin here can help you with.' He covered his cup with his hand. 'No more for me, thank you. And at some point you are going to have to decide what you want done with your father's body, whether it is to stay in Egypt or be returned to Britain. For the moment, however, I simply want to stress that if there's anything at all you need in this difficult time you only have to ask.'

'Thank you,' said Tara. She was silent for a moment, fiddling with her cup. 'There was . . . um . . .'

She paused, uncertain how to continue. Squires raised his eyebrows.

'I don't really know how to explain it. It sounds so ridiculous. It's just . . .'

'Yes?'

'Well . . .' Again she paused. 'When I first went into the dig house yesterday I noticed a smell of cigar smoke, which was strange because my father never allowed smoking anywhere around him. I mentioned it to the police. And Crispin.'

Oates nodded. Jemal removed a set of jade worry beads from his pocket and began telling them off one by one with his thumb. Tara could feel the three of them staring at her.

'A bit earlier I'd seen this man, a big man . . .'

'Big?' said Squires, leaning forward slightly.

'Yes, sort of tall, bigger than normal. I'm sorry, it sounds so stupid when I say it . . .'

The Englishman flashed a glance at Jemal and waved her on. The worry beads began clacking faster, like someone tap-dancing.

'Well, he seemed to be watching me, through binoculars.'

'The big man?' asked Jemal.

'Yes. And then last night I saw the same man, or at least it looked like the same man, coming into the hotel and I'm sure he was smoking a cigar. And then in the middle of the night I heard someone trying to get into my room. When I opened the door there was no-one there, but there was a smell of cigar smoke in the corridor.'

She grinned weakly, aware of how paranoid the whole thing sounded. Events that in her head had seemed suspicious and threatening, now, recounted in front of other people, appeared no more than mildly coincidental.

'I told you it sounded ridiculous,' she mumbled.

'Not at all,' said Squires, leaning forward and laying his hand on her arm. 'This is a very upsetting time for you. Given the circumstances it's hardly surprising you should feel slightly . . . insecure. You're in a foreign country, after all, and someone close to you has died. It's easy to lose one's sense of perspective in such situations.'

She could tell he was simply being polite. 'I just had this feeling there was something going on,' she said. 'Something . . .'

'Sinister?'

'Yes.'

Squires smiled thinly. 'I don't think you should worry your-self, Miss Mullray. Egypt is one of those countries where it's easy to imagine that something's going on behind one's back when in fact it isn't. Wouldn't you agree, Dr Jemal?'

'Certainly,' snorted Jemal. 'Not a day goes by without me thinking someone is plotting against me. Which in the Antiquities Service they usually are!'

The three men laughed.

'I'm sure all the things you've mentioned have a perfectly harmless explanation,' said Squires. He paused and then added, 'Unless, of course, you're not telling us everything.' He said it as a joke, although there was something vaguely threatening in his tone, as though he was accusing her of holding something back.

'Have you told us everything?' he asked.

A brief silence.

'I think so,' Tara said.

For a moment Squires stared at her, then he sat back and laughed again. 'Well, there you are then. I think you can sleep safely in your bed at night, Miss Mullray. Can we get you a biscuit?'

They made polite conversation for another ten minutes before Squires rose to his feet, followed by the other two.

'I think we've taken enough of your time. Crispin will take you along to his office, where he'll help you with whatever paperwork needs to be done.'

He handed her his card and they moved towards the door.

'Feel free to call if you have anything further you'd like to discuss. It's my direct line. We'll do whatever we can to assist.'

He shook her hand, and ushered her out into the ante-room. Jemal raised his hand in farewell.

'Come on,' said Oates. 'Let's get you some lunch.'

*

For some time Squires and Jemal sat in silence, the former staring out of the window, the latter fiddling with his worry beads. Eventually Jemal spoke.

'Is she telling the truth?'

'Oh I would say so, yes,' said Squires, a glimmer of a smile playing around the corners of his thin, pale lips. 'She doesn't know anything. Or at least she doesn't think she knows anything.'

He reached into his pocket and extracted a boiled sweet, which he began slowly to unwrap.

'So what's going on?' asked Jemal.

Squires raised his eyebrows. 'Well, that's the question, isn't it. Dravic certainly appears to be on the trail, but how Mullray got mixed up in it all . . . your guess is as good as mine. It's all very mysterious.' He removed the last of the wrapper and popped the sweet into his mouth, sucking contemplatively. The room echoed to the rhythmic clack of the worry beads.

'Have you told Massey?' asked Jemal. 'The Americans ought to know.'

'Taken care of, old boy. They're not especially happy, but that was to be expected.'

'So what do we do now?'

'Not much we can do. We can't let them know that we know about the tomb. That would be fatal. We just have to sit tight and hope things work out.'

'And if they don't?'

Squires tilted his head, but said nothing.

Jemal fiddled with his beads. 'I don't like it,' he said. 'Maybe we should just drop the whole thing.'

'Come, come. This is a once-in-a-lifetime opportunity. Think of the rewards.'

'I don't know. I just don't know. It's getting out of hand.' The Egyptian stood and began pacing around the room. 'What about the girl?'

Squires drummed his fingers lightly on the arm of the couch, rolling the sweet around with his tongue.

'It seems to me', he said after a long pause, 'that she might actually be rather useful. Help us to . . . clarify the situation. So long as she doesn't go shouting her head off. That wouldn't be at all productive. I trust you can handle things at your end?'

'The police do as I tell them,' grunted Jemal. 'They won't be asking unnecessary questions.'

'Jolly good. Then I think I should be able to take care of Miss Mullray. Crispin's keeping an eye on her. And I've got other people on the job too. The most important thing is that they don't cotton on we're using her. That would be fatal.' He rose and walked to the window, staring out across the neatly clipped lawns of the embassy garden. 'We just have to play our hand carefully. So long as we do that, I firmly believe we'll achieve our goal.'

'I hope so,' said Jemal. 'For all our sakes. Because if we don't we're down the fucking creek.'

Squires chuckled. 'You have a wonderful way with words, old boy.'

There was a loud crunching sound as his teeth ground into the boiled sweet.

10

LUXOR

Khalifa had no idea there were so many alabaster workshops in Luxor. He'd known there were a lot, of course, but only when he started visiting them each in turn did he realize what a huge task it was going to be to track down the one he wanted.

He and Sariya had started late the previous afternoon immediately after the autopsy, him on the west bank, Sariya on the east, going from shop to shop with a photograph of the scarab tattoo, asking if anyone recognized it. They'd continued late into the night and resumed at six this morning. It was now midday and by Khalifa's reckoning he'd visited over fifty workshops already without any success. He was beginning to wonder if Anwar had sent them on a wild-goose chase.

He stopped in front of yet another shop: 'Queen Tiye for Alabaster, best in Luxor'. On its front were painted an aeroplane and a camel alongside the black cube of the Ka'ba – a sign the owner had performed the Hajj to Mecca. A group of workmen sat cross-legged in the shade beneath an awning chiselling lumps of alabaster, their arms and faces white with dust. Khalifa nodded at them and, lighting a cigarette, went inside. A man emerged from a back room to greet him, smiling.

'Police,' said Khalifa, showing his badge. The man's smile faded.

'We have a licence,' he said.

'I want to ask you a couple of questions. About your workers.'

'Is this about insurance?'

'It's not about insurance and it's not about licences. We're looking for a missing person.' He pulled a photograph from his pocket and held it up. 'Recognize this tattoo?'

The man took the photo and stared at it.

'Well?'

'Maybe.'

'What do you mean, maybe? You either recognize it or you don't.'

'Yes, OK, I recognize it.'

At last, thought Khalifa. 'One of your workers?'

'Until I sacked him a week ago, yes. Why, is he in trouble?'

'You could say that. He's dead.'

The man stared down at the photo.

'Murdered,' added Khalifa. 'We found his body in the river yesterday.'

There was a pause and then the man handed the photo back and turned away. 'You'd better come through.'

They passed through a bead curtain into a large room at the back of the shop. There was a low bed against one wall, a television on a stand and a table laid for lunch with bread and onions and a slab of cheese. Above the bed hung a sepia photograph of an old bearded man in a fez and djellaba – an ancestor of the shop owner, Khalifa presumed – with beside it a framed print of the first *sura* of the Koran. An open door led onto a yard where more men were working. The shop owner kicked the door shut.

'His name was Abu Nayar,' he said, turning towards Khalifa. 'He worked here for about a year. He was a good craftsman, but a drinker. Used to come in late, not concentrate on his work. Always trouble.'

'Know where he lived?'

'Old Qurna. Up by the tomb of Rekhmire.'

'Family?'

'A wife and two kids. Girls. He treated the woman like a dog. Beat her. You know.'

Khalifa pulled on his cigarette, gazing at a painted limestone bust in the corner, a copy of the famous Nefertiti head in the Berlin museum. He'd always wanted to see the original, ever since as a child he'd stared at its likeness in the windows of craft shops in Giza and Cairo. He doubted he ever would see it, though. He could no more afford a trip to Berlin than he could a balloon ride over the Valley of the Kings. He turned back to the shop owner. 'This Abu Nayar, did he have any enemies that you know of? Anyone who bore him a grudge?'

'Where do you want me to start? He owed money left, right and centre, insulted everyone, got into fights. I can think of fifty people who'd want him dead. A hundred.'

'Anyone in particular? Any blood feuds?'

'Not that I know of.'

'Was he involved in anything illegal? Drugs? Antiquities?'

'How would I know?'

'Because everyone around here knows everything about everyone else. Come on, no games.'

The man scratched his chin and sat down heavily on the edge of the bed. Outside the workers had started to sing, a folk tune, one man taking the verse, the others joining in for the chorus.

'Not drugs,' he said after a long pause. 'He wasn't involved with drugs.'

'But antiquities?'

The man shrugged.

'What about antiquities?' pressed Khalifa. 'Did he deal?'

'Odds and ends, maybe.'

'What sort of odds and ends?'

'Nothing much. A few *shabti*s, some scarabs. Everybody deals, for God's sake. It's no big thing.'

'It's illegal.'

'It's survival.'

Khalifa ground out his cigarette in an ashtray. 'Anything valuable?' he asked.

The shop owner shrugged and, leaning forward, turned on the television. 'Nothing that would be worth killing him for,' he said. A game show flickered onto the black-and-white screen. He sat staring at it. After a long pause, he sighed. 'There were rumours.'

'Rumours?'

'That he'd found something.'

'What?'

'God knows. A tomb. Something big.' The man leaned forward and adjusted the volume. 'But then there are always rumours, aren't there? Every week someone finds a new Tutankhamun. Who knows which ones are true?'

'Was this one true?'

The shopkeeper shrugged. 'Maybe, maybe not. I don't get involved. I have a good business and that's all I'm interested in.'

He fell silent, concentrating on the game show. Outside the men were still singing, the clank and thud of their tools echoing dully in the still afternoon air. When the man spoke his voice was low, almost a whisper.

'Three days ago Nayar bought his mother a television set and a new fridge. That's a lot of money for a man who has no job. Draw your own conclusions.' He burst out laughing. 'Look at him,' he cried, pointing at a contestant who had just answered a question incorrectly. 'What an idiot!'

There was something forced about his laughter. His hands, the detective noticed, were trembling.

Khalifa had always been fascinated by the history of his country. He remembered as a child standing on the roof of their house watching the sunrise over the pyramids. Other children in his village had taken the monuments for granted, but not Khalifa. For him there had always been something magical about them, great triangles looming through the morning mist, doorways to a different time and world. Growing up beside them had given him an insatiable desire to learn more about the past.

It was a desire he had shared with his brother Ali, who if anything had been even more fanatical in his passion for history, offering as it did a sanctuary from the crushing hardships of his daily life. Each night he would return home from work, exhausted and filthy, and having bathed and eaten, would sit himself down in a corner of the room and immerse himself in one of his archaeology books. He had amassed quite a collection – some borrowed from the local mosque school, most probably stolen – and the young Khalifa had loved nothing more than to sit beside him while he read aloud by the light of a flickering candle.

'Tell me about Rasses, Ali,' he would cry, nuzzling into his brother's shoulder.

'Ramesses,' Ali would laugh, correcting him. 'Well, there was once a great king called Ramesses the Second, and he was the most powerful man in the whole wide world, with a golden chariot and a crown made of diamonds . . .'

How lucky they were to be Egyptian, Khalifa had thought. What other country on earth possessed such a wealth of fabulous stories to pass down to its children? Thank you, Allah, for letting me be born in this wonderful land!

The two of them had carried out mini-excavations up on the Giza plateau, digging up stones and old bits of pottery, imagining themselves to be famous archaeologists. Once, shortly after their father's death, they had discovered a small limestone pharaoh's head close to the base of the Sphinx and Khalifa had been speechless with excitement, thinking that here for once was something truly ancient and valuable. Only years later had he discovered that Ali had buried it there himself to take his little brother's mind off the loss of their father.

They had hitched rides south to Saqqara and Dhashur and Abusir, and into the middle of Cairo, where they had cheated their way into the Museum of Antiquities by insinuating themselves into visiting school parties. To this day he could walk round the entire museum in his head, so well had he come to know it from those surreptitious childhood excursions. On one such visit they had been befriended by an elderly academic, Professor al-Habibi. Touched by their youthful enthusiasm, the professor had shown them around the collection, pointing things out, encouraging their interest. Years later, when Khalifa won a place at university to read ancient history, the same Professor al-Habibi had become his tutor.

Yes, he loved the past. There was something mystical about it, something glittering, a chain of gold stretching all the way back to the dawn of time. He loved it for its colour and its enormity, and the way it somehow made the present appear so much richer.

Mainly, however, he loved it because Ali had loved it. It was something special they had shared: a joint heart from which they had both drawn strength and life. In time their hands reached out and touched, still, even though Ali was dead and gone. The ancient world was for Khalifa, above all, an affirmation of his love for his lost sibling.

'Who were the kings of the Eighteenth Dynasty?' Ali used to ask him, testing.

'Ahmose,' Khalifa would recite slowly, 'Amenhotep one, Tuthmosis one and two, Hatshepsut, Tuthmosis three, Amenhotep two, Tuthmosis four, Amenhotep three, Akhenaten, um . . . um . . . oh I always forget this one . . . um . . . oh . . .'

'Smenkhkare,' Ali would tell him.

'Dammit! I knew that! Smenkhkare, Tutankhamun, Ay, Horemheb.'

'Learn, Yusuf! Learn and grow!'

Good days.

*

It took him a while to find Nayar's house. It was hidden away behind a cluster of other dwellings, halfway up a hill and backing onto a row of pits that had once held ancient burials, but were now full of mouldering rubbish. An emaciated goat was tethered outside, its ribs showing through its skin like the bars of a xylophone.

He knocked on the door, which after a brief pause was opened by a small woman with bright green eyes.

She was young, no older than her mid-twenties, and must have been pretty once. Like so many *fellaha* women, however, the exertions of child-bearing and the hardships of daily life had made her old before her time. Her left cheek, Khalifa noticed, showed signs of bruising.

'I'm sorry to disturb you,' he said gently, showing her his badge. 'I've . . .' He paused, searching for the right words. He'd done this sort of thing many times before but had never got used to it. He remembered how his own mother had reacted when they had brought news of his father's death, how she had collapsed and torn at her hair, wailing like a wounded animal. He hated the idea of causing that sort of pain.

'What?' said the woman. 'Drunk again, is he?'

'May I come in?'

She shrugged and turned back into the house, leading him into the main room, where two little girls were playing together on the bare concrete floor. It was cool and dark inside, like a cave, with no furniture apart from a sofa running along one wall and a television standing on a table in the corner. A new television, Khalifa noticed.

'Well?'

'I'm afraid I have some bad news,' said the detective. 'Your husband, he's . . .'

'Been arrested?'

Khalifa bit his lip.

'Dead.'

For a moment she just stared at him, then sat down heavily on the sofa, covering her face with her hands. He presumed she was weeping and took a step forward to comfort her. Only as he came close did he realize that the muffled grunts coming from between her fingers were not sobs at all, but laughter.

'Fatma, Iman,' she said, beckoning the two girls to her. 'Something wonderful has happened.'

11

CAIRO

Having finished at the embassy Tara wanted to go to her father's apartment to look through his belongings.

He had kept few possessions with him during his four-month season at Saqqara – a change of clothes, a couple of notebooks, a camera. Most of his things had stayed in the Cairo flat. Here he had his diaries, his slides, his clothes, various artefacts the Egyptian authorities had allowed him to keep. And, of course, his books, of which he had a vast collection, several thousand volumes, all individually bound in leather, the result of a lifetime of collecting. 'With books', he used to say, 'even the poorest hovel in the world is transformed into a palace. They make everything seem so much more bearable.'

Oates offered to take her in the car, but the apartment was only a few minutes' walk away and, anyway, she felt like being alone for a while. He phoned ahead to make sure the concierge had a spare set of keys, drew her a map of how to get there and escorted her to the front gates.

'Call when you get back to the hotel,' he said. 'And as I

mentioned before, try not to stay out after dark. Especially after this river-boat thing.'

He smiled and disappeared back into the embassy.

It was by now late afternoon and the sinking sun was casting dappled patterns across the uneven pavement. She gazed around her, taking in the police emplacements along the embassy wall, a beggar squatting at the roadside, a man pulling a cart piled high with watermelons and then, glancing down at the map, set off.

Oates had explained that this part of Cairo was known as Garden City and as she navigated her way through a maze of leafy avenues she realized why. It was quieter and more sedate than the rest of the metropolis, a faded remnant of the colonial era, with large dusty villas and everywhere trees and flowering shrubs – hibiscus, oleander, jasmine, purple jacaranda. The air echoed to the twitter of birds and was heavy with the scent of mown grass and orange blossom. There seemed to be few people around, just a couple of women pushing prams and the odd suited executive. Many of the villas had limousines parked in front of them and policemen stationed at their front doors.

She walked for about ten minutes before she reached Sharia Ahmed Pasha, on the corner of which stood her father's apartment block, a turn-of-the-century building with huge windows and intricate iron-work balconies. Once it must have been a cheerful shade of yellow. Now its exterior was grey with dust and grime.

She went up the front steps and pushed open the door, stepping into a cool marble foyer. To one side, sitting behind a desk, was an old man, presumably the concierge. She approached, and after a confused conversation conducted in sign language, managed to convey who she was and why she had come. Muttering, the man came to his feet, removed a set of keys from a drawer and shuffled over to a cage lift in the corner, pulling back the doors and ushering her in.

The apartment was on the third floor at the end of a silent, gloomy corridor. They stopped in front of the door and the concierge fiddled with the keys, trying three in the lock before he found the right one.

'Thank you,' said Tara as he opened the door.

He remained where he was.

'Thank you,' she repeated.

Still he showed no sign of moving. There was an embarrassed silence and then, realizing what was expected, she fished out her purse and handed him a couple of notes. He looked at them, grunted and shuffled away down the corridor, leaving the keys in the door. She waited till he had gone, and then turned and stepped into the apartment, taking the keys and closing the door behind her.

She was in a dark, wood-floored vestibule, off which opened five rooms – a bedroom, a bathroom, a kitchen and two others, both piled high with books. All the windows were closed and shuttered, giving the place a musty, abandoned feel. For the briefest moment she thought she could sense a lingering odour of cigar smoke, but it was too intangible for her to be sure and after sniffing the air a couple of times she dismissed it. Probably just polish or something, she thought.

She went through into the main room, switching on the light as she went. There were books and papers everywhere, piles of them, like drifts of leaves. The walls were hung with pictures of excavations and monuments; in the far corner sat a dusty cabinet full of cracked earthenware pots and faience *shabti*s. There were no plants.

Like somewhere that's been preserved for posterity, she thought. To show how people lived in a different time.

She wandered around, picking things up, peering into drawers, seeking out her father. She found one of his diaries from the early 1960s, when he had been excavating in the Sudan, his small, precise writing interspersed with fading pencil drawings of the objects he had been unearthing. In one of the rooms she discovered some of the books he'd written – *Life in the Necropolis: Excavations at Saqqara, 1955–85; From Snofru to Shepseskaf – Essays on the Fourth Dynasty; The Tomb of Mentu-Nefer; Kingship and Disorder in the First Intermediate Period.* She flicked through a photo album – pictures of a large sandy trench which, as the album progressed, got deeper and deeper until, on the last pages, the outlines of what looked like a stone wall began to emerge. There seemed to be nothing in the apartment but his work. Nothing that spoke of warmth or love or feeling. Nothing of the present.

Then just as she was starting to feel oppressed by the place, two surprises. Beside her father's bed – hard, narrow, like a prison cot – she found a photograph of her parents on their wedding day, her father laughing, a white rose in his buttonhole.

And in the dusty cabinet in the living room, wedged between two earthenware pots, a child's drawing of an angel, the edges of its wings marked out with silver glitter. She had made it years ago at nursery school, for Christmas. Her father must have kept it all this time. She took it out, turned it over and read on the back, in her spidery child's writing: 'For my daddy'.

She stared at it for a moment and then, suddenly, uncontrollably, began to cry, slumping down onto a chair, her body racked with sobs.

'Oh Dad,' she choked. 'I'm sorry, I'm sorry.'

Later, when the tears had slowed, she collected the photo from the bedroom and put it in her knapsack, along with the drawing. She also took a photograph of her father standing beside a large stone sarcophagus, flanked by two Egyptian workmen. (She remembered him explaining to her as a child that the word 'sarcophagus' came from the Greek for 'flesh eater', an image that had so disturbed her she had been unable to sleep that night.)

She was just debating whether to take a couple of his books as well when the phone rang. She paused, uncertain whether or not to answer it. After a moment she decided she ought to and went through into the living room, hurrying over to the desk on the far side, where the phone was sitting on top of a pile of manuscripts. Just as she reached it the answering machine clicked on and suddenly the room was full of her father's voice.

'Hello, this is Michael Mullray. I'm away until the first week in December so please don't leave a message. You can either call me on my return or, if it's university business, contact the faculty direct on 7943967. Thank you. Goodbye.'

She stopped, startled by the sound, as though a part of her father was not properly dead but remained suspended in some sort of electronic limbo, neither in this world nor fully departed from it. By the time she had regained her senses the machine had beeped and started recording.

At first she thought the caller had hung up, for there was no voice from the other end of the line. Then she caught the faintest hiss of susurration, no more than a rumour of breath, and realized the caller was still there, just not speaking. She took a step towards the phone and reached out, but then snatched her hand away again. Still he didn't hang up – she knew instinctively it was a man – just waited, breathing, listening, as if he knew she was in the apartment and wanted her to know that he knew. The silence seemed to go on for an age before eventually there was a click and the metallic whirr of the machine resetting itself. She stood frozen for a moment and then, gathering up her things, hurried out of the flat, slamming and locking the door behind her. She felt suddenly menaced by the building: the gloomy interior, the creaking lift, the silence. She moved quickly down the corridor, wanting to get out. Halfway along something caught her eye, a large beetle sitting on the clean marble floor. She slowed to look at it, only to discover it wasn't a beetle at all but a heavy nub of grey cigar ash, thick as a backgammon counter. She began to run.

The lift wasn't there and rather than wait for it she took the stairs instead, leaping down them two at a time, desperate now to get back out into the fresh air. She reached the bottom and turned the corner into the foyer, but suddenly her way was blocked. She cried out, startled. It was only the concierge.

'I'm sorry,' she said, breathing hard. 'You surprised me.'

She handed him the keys and he took them. He said something, his voice low, gruff.

'What?'

He repeated himself.

'I don't understand.' Her voice was beginning to rise. She was desperate to get out.

Again he spoke, jabbering at her, and then reached into his pocket. She had a sudden irrational fear he was reaching for a weapon and when he whipped his hand out again and up towards her face she arched back away from him, raising her arm protectively. It was only an envelope. A small white envelope.

'Professor Mullray,' he said, waving it in her face. 'Come Professor Mullray.'

She stared at it for a moment, breathing hard, and then laughed. 'Thank you,' she said, taking the letter. 'Thank you.'

The concierge turned and shuffled back towards his desk. She wondered if she was expected to give him another tip, but he didn't seem to be expecting one and so she hurried straight out of the front door, turning left and heading down the street, enjoying the space around her and the warmth of the open air. She passed a couple of schoolchildren in starched white shirts, and a man in uniform, a kaleidoscope of medal ribbons on his chest. On the other side of the road a gardener in overalls was watering a row of dusty rose bushes with a hose.

After twenty metres she looked down at the envelope in her hand. Instantly the colour drained from her face.

'Oh no,' she whispered, staring down at the familiar handwriting. 'Not after all this time, not now.'

The gardener stared after her and then, leaning his head to one side, began talking into his collar.

12

NORTHERN SUDAN, NEAR THE EGYPTIAN BORDER

The boy emerged from the tent and started running, sprays of sand kicking up beneath his feet, a herd of goats scattering in front of him. He passed a burnt-out campfire, a helicopter covered in netting, piles of crates, before eventually coming to a halt in front of another tent, this one set slightly apart from the main encampment. He pulled a piece of paper from his robes and, drawing back the flap, stepped through.

A man was standing inside, eyes closed, lips twitching as he recited silently to himself. His face was long and thin, bearded, with a hooked nose and, between his eyes, a deep vertical scar, the damaged tissue smooth and shiny as if the skin had been polished vigorously. He was smiling slightly, as though in rapture.

He went down on his knees, placing his palms on the ground and touching the carpeted floor with his nose and forehead, oblivious to the boy, who remained where he was, watching, a look of awe on his face. A minute passed, two, three, and still the hook-nosed man continued his prayers, bowing, rising, reciting, the rapt smile never leaving his face. It looked as though he would never stop, and the boy appeared to be on the point of leaving when the worshipper lowered his head to the floor one last time, muttered amen, stood and turned. The boy came forward and handed him the piece of paper.

'This came, Master. From Doktora Dravic.'

The man took the paper and read it, his green eyes glowing in the semi-darkness.

There was something threatening about him, a rumour of suppressed violence, and yet, strangely, a gentleness too in the way he laid his free hand on the boy's head, as though to re-assure him. The boy stared at his feet, afraid and adoring in equal measure.

The man finished reading and handed the paper back.

'Allah, blessed be his name, gives, and Allah, blessed be his name, withholds.'

The boy continued staring at the floor.

'Please, Master,' he whispered, 'I do not understand.'

'It is not for us to understand, Mehmet,' said the man, raising the boy's chin so that he was looking into his eyes. The boy too had a deep scar down the centre of his forehead.

'We must simply know that God has a purpose and that we are a part of that purpose. You do not question the Almighty. You merely do his bidding. Without question. Without hesitation.'

'Yes, Master,' whispered the boy, overwhelmed.

'He has set us a great task. A quest. If we succeed, the prize will be great. If we fail . . .'

'What, Master? What if we fail?' The boy seemed terrified.

The man stroked his hair, comforting him. 'We will not fail.' He smiled. 'The road may be hard, but we shall reach its end. Have I not told you? We are God's chosen.'

The boy smiled and spontaneously threw his arms around the man's waist, hugging him. The man pushed him away.

'There is work to do. Call Dr Dravic. Tell him he must find

the missing piece. Do you understand? He must find the missing piece.'

'He must find the missing piece,' repeated the boy.

'Meanwhile everything continues as planned. Nothing changes. Can you remember that?'

'Yes, Master.'

'We strike camp in one hour. Go.'

The boy stepped out of the tent and hurried away. Sayf al-Tha'r watched him as he went.

They had found him four years ago, a street orphan, scavenging for food like an animal among the rubbish tips of Cairo. Illiterate, parentless, savage, he had been bathed and fed, and in time he had become one of them, receiving the mark of faith on his forehead and pledging to wear only black, the colour of strength and loyalty.

He was a good boy – simple, innocent, devoted. There were others like him out there, hundreds of them, thousands. While the rich filled their bellies and worshipped their false idols, children like Mehmet starved. The world was sick. Benighted. Overrun by the *Kufr*. He, however, was fighting to make things right. To raise the downtrodden. To drive back the infidel. To restore the rule of the faithful.

And now, suddenly, magically, the wherewithal to complete his task had been shown to him. Shown, but no more. God gave and God withheld. It was frustrating. And yet he knew there was a purpose to it. God always has a purpose. And here? To test his servant, of course. To try his resolve. An easy life made for a shallow faith. In adversity one discovered the depth of one's belief. Allah was challenging his devotion. And he would not disappoint. The thing would be found. However many deaths it took. He, the servant, would not fail the master. And the master, he knew, would not fail him either so long as he stayed true. So long as he did not weaken. He watched the boy for a moment longer and then, turning back into the tent, fell to his knees, bowed his face to the ground and resumed his prayers.

13

CAIRO

Tara opened the envelope as soon as she got back to the hotel. She knew she shouldn't, that she should just throw it away, but she couldn't help herself. Even after six years there was still a part of her that couldn't let him go.

'Damn you,' she muttered, sliding her finger beneath the flap and tearing it open. 'Damn you for coming back. Damn you.'

Hello Michael,

I'm in town for a few weeks. Are you back from Saqqara yet? If so, let me buy you a drink. I'm at the Hotel Salah al-Din (753127), although you'll find me most nights at the tea-room on the corner of Ahmed Maher and Bursa'id. I think it's called Ahwa Wadood.

Hope the season went well, and hope to see you.

Daniel L.

P.S. Did you hear about Schenker? Thinks he's found the tomb of Imhotep! Twat.

She smiled, despite herself. Typical Daniel, to affect seriousness only to puncture it with some random expletive. For the first time in ages she felt again the tightening in her throat, the hollow emptiness in the pit of her stomach. God, he'd hurt her.

She reread the note and then scrunched it into a ball and flung it across the room. Grabbing a vodka from the mini-bar she went outside onto the balcony, but came back in almost immediately and threw herself onto the bed, staring at the ceiling. Five minutes passed, ten, twelve. She got up again, grabbed her knapsack, left the room.

'Ahwa Wadood tea-room,' she said to the first driver on the taxi rank outside the hotel. 'Corner of Ahmed Maher and . . .'

'Bursa'id,' said the man, reaching his hand behind him and swinging open the door for her. 'I know it.'

She got in and they moved off.

You idiot, Tara, she thought to herself, staring out of the window at the brightly lit shopfronts. You sad, weak idiot.

Across the street a dusty Mercedes eased away from the kerb and swung in behind them, a panther stalking its prey.

She remembered so well the first time they'd met. How long ago was it now? God, almost eight years.

She had been in her second year at University College London, reading zoology, renting a flat with three friends. Her parents were living in Oxford, their marriage fast approaching collapse, and she had gone home one evening to have dinner with them.

It was supposed to be a family affair, just the three of them, which was bad enough given that her parents barely talked those days. On arrival, however, her father told her a colleague of his would be joining them.

'Interesting chap,' he said, 'half English, half French, not much older than you. Doing a PhD in Late Period funerary practice in the Theban necropolis; just got back from three months' excavating in the Valley of the Kings. Absolute genius.

Knows more about tomb iconography and the afterlife books than anyone I've ever met.'

'Sounds fascinating,' Tara grunted.

'Yes, I think you will like him,' her father smiled, missing the sarcasm. 'He's an odd fellow. Driven. Of course, we're all driven to some extent, but he's particularly intense. You get the impression he'd cut off his own hand if he thought it might further his knowledge of the subject. Or anyone else's hand, for that matter. He's a fanatic.'

'Takes one to know one.'

'True, I suppose, although at least I have you and your mother. Daniel doesn't seem to have anyone. I worry for him, frankly. He's too obsessed. If he's not careful he's going to drive himself into an early grave.'

Tara downed her pre-dinner vodka. Late Period funerary practice in the Theban necropolis. Jesus.

He was almost an hour late and they'd just started debating whether to begin without him when the doorbell rang. Tara went to answer it, slightly drunk by this point, urging herself to be polite.

With a bit of luck he'll go straight after dinner, she thought. Please let him go straight after dinner.

She stopped for a moment to compose herself and then went forward and opened the front door.

Oh, my God, you're gorgeous!

She thought it, fortunately, and didn't say it out loud, although some sort of surprise must have registered in her face, for he was the complete opposite of everything she'd been expecting: tall, dark, with high cheekbones and eyes that were brown to the point of blackness, like pools of peat-darkened water. She stood staring at him.

'I'm so sorry I'm late,' he said, his accent English with a faint Gallic fuzz around the edge of the vowels. 'I had some work to finish.'

'Late Period funerary practice in the Theban necropolis,'

she replied, sounding embarrassingly embarrassed.

He laughed. 'Actually I was filling out a grant application. Probably a bit more interesting.' He held out his hand. 'Daniel Lacage.'

She took it. 'Tara Mullray.'

They stood like that for just a beat longer than was necessary and then went through into the house.

Dinner was wonderful. The two men spent most of it arguing about an obscure point of New Kingdom history – whether or not there had been a co-regency between Amenhotep III and his son Akhenaten. She'd heard and switched off from these sorts of discussions a hundred times before. With Daniel involved, however, the argument assumed a curious immediacy, as though it affected them there and then rather than being a dry academic debate about a time so distant even history had forgotten it.

'I am sorry.' He smiled at Tara as her mother served pudding. 'This must be excruciating for you.'

'Not at all,' she replied. 'For the first time in my life Egypt actually sounds interesting.'

'Thank you very much,' her father said gruffly.

After dinner the two of them went into the back garden for a cigarette. It was a warm night, the sky heavy with stars, and they wandered across the lawn and sat down on a rusty swing chair.

'I think you were just being polite in there,' he said, putting two cigarettes in his mouth, lighting them and handing one to her. 'There was no need.'

'I'm never polite,' she said, accepting the cigarette. 'Or at least not tonight.'

They sat in silence for a while, swinging gently to and fro, their bodies close but not quite touching. He had a smell to him, not aftershave, something richer, less manufactured.

'Dad says you've been excavating in the Valley of the Kings,' she said eventually.

'Just above it, actually. Up in the hills.'

'Looking for anything in particular?'

'Oh, some Late Period tombs. Twenty-sixth Dynasty. Nothing very interesting.'

'I thought you were fanatical about it.'

'I am,' he said. 'Just not tonight.'

They laughed, their eyes holding for a moment before they turned away and looked up at the sky. Above them the branches of an old pine tree twisted like interlocked arms. There was another long silence.

'It's a magical place, you know, the Valley of the Kings,' he said eventually, his voice low, almost a whisper, as if he was talking to himself rather than to her. 'It sends a shiver down your spine to think of the treasures that must once have been buried there. I mean, look at what they found with Tutankhamun. And he was just a minor pharaoh. A nobody. Think what must have been buried with a truly great ruler. An Amenhotep III, or a Horemheb, or a Seti I.'

He dropped his head back, smiling, lost suddenly in his own thoughts.

'I often wonder what it must be like to find something like that. Of course it will never happen again. Tutankhamun was unique, a billion-to-one chance his tomb survived. I can't help thinking about it, though. The excitement. The intensity. Nothing could ever compare with that. Nothing on earth. But then, of course . . .'

He sighed.

'What?'

'Well, it probably wouldn't last, the excitement. That's the thing about archaeology. One find is never enough. You're always trying to better yourself. Look at Carter. After he'd finished clearing the tomb of Tutankhamun he spent the last ten years of his life telling everyone he knew where Alexander the Great was buried. You'd have thought the greatest find in the history of archaeology would have been enough, but it wasn't. It's Catch-22. You spend your whole life digging up the secrets of the past and at the same time worrying that one day there won't be any secrets left to find.'

He was silent for a moment, brow furrowed, and then tamped his cigarette out on the armrest of the swing and laughed. 'Listen to me. I bet you wish you'd stayed inside and helped with the washing up.'

Their eyes met again and, as if acting independently of the rest of their bodies, their fingers crept across the seat and touched. It was an innocent gesture, barely noticeable, and yet at the same time one loaded with intent. They looked away. Their fingertips, however, remained connected, something irreversible flowing between them.

They met in London three days later and within the week had become lovers.

It had been a magical time, the finest of her life. He had a flat off Gower Street – a tiny garret with two murky skylights and no central heating – and this had been their lair. They had made love day and night, played backgammon, eaten picnics among the sheets, made love again, devoured each other.

He was a brilliant draughtsman, and she had stretched naked on the bed, bashful and blushing, while he'd drawn her, in pencil, in charcoal, in crayon, covering sheet after sheet of paper with her image, as though each drawing was somehow an official affirmation of their togetherness.

A friend of his owned a battered old Triumph motorbike and at weekends the two of them rode out into the country, Tara's hands clutched around his waist, seeking out secret corners in which to be alone together – a silent forest, a deserted riverbank, an empty stretch of shoreline.

He took her round the British Museum, pointing out objects that were particularly special to him, enthusing about them, discussing their history: a cuneiform tablet from Amarna; a blue-glazed hippopotamus; a Ramessid ostrakon with a sketch of a man taking a woman from behind.

'Calm is the desire of my skin,' he said, translating the

hieroglyphic text down one side of the stone.

'Not mine,' she laughed, grabbing his face and kissing him passionately, oblivious to the tourists eddying around them.

They visited other collections together – the Petrie, the Bodleian, the Sir John Soane Museum to see the sarcophagus of Seti I – and she in turn took him to London Zoo, where a friend of hers, who was working there, brought out a python for him to hold, which he hadn't enjoyed at all.

Her parents had finally broken apart at this time, but she had been so buried inside her life with Daniel that their separation barely affected her. She graduated from her course and enrolled to read for a PhD, still hardly aware of what was happening, as if it was going on in some parallel universe, far removed from the all-enveloping reality of her relationship. She had been so happy. So complete.

'What else is there?' she asked one night as they lay together after a particularly intense bout of love-making. 'What else could I want?'

'What else could you want?' asked Daniel.

'Nothing,' she replied, snuggling against him. 'Nothing on earth.'

'Daniel is a hugely talented person,' her father said when she told him of the relationship. 'One of the finest scholars it's ever been my privilege to teach. You make a very fine couple.'

He paused and then added, 'But be careful, Tara. Like all gifted people, he has a darkness to him. Don't let him hurt you.'

'He won't, Dad,' she said. 'I know he won't.'

Curiously, the fact that he did was something she had always, deep down, blamed on her father rather than Daniel, as though it was the warning that had fractured their relationship rather than the person being warned about.

The Ahwa Wadood tea-room was a shabby affair with sawdust on the floor and tables packed with old men sipping tea and playing dominoes. She saw him as soon as she walked in, at the far end of the room puffing on a *shisha* pipe, head bent over a backgammon board, lost in concentration. He looked much as he had done when she'd last seen him six years ago, although his hair was a little longer, his face more sunburnt. She stared for a moment, fighting back an urge to be sick, and then started forward. She was right in front of him before he looked up.

'Tara!'

His dark eyes widened. They looked at each other for a long moment, neither saying anything, and then, leaning over the table, she raised her hand and slapped him across the face.

'You cunt,' she hissed.

LUXOR, THE THEBAN HILLS

The madman squatted beside his fire, poking at the embers with a stick. Around him the cliffs loomed large and silent, the only other sign of life apart from himself being the occasional howling of a wild dog. Over his shoulder a dazzling white curve of moon hung suspended against the night.

He stared at the flickering flames, his face hollow and dusty, knots of filthy hair dangling over the shoulders of his torn djellaba. He could see gods in the fire: strange figures with human bodies and the heads of beasts. There was one with a jackal head and another like a bird, and another with a tall headdress and an elongated crocodile face. They frightened and delighted him. He began rocking on his haunches, lips quivering, mesmerized by the fiery images at his feet.

Now the flames showed him other secrets: a dark room, a coffin, jewellery, objects piled against a wall, swords, shields, knives. He gaped in wonder.

The flames went dark, but only for a moment, and when they brightened again the room was gone and in its place was something else. A desert. Mile after mile of burning sand and across it a great army marching. He heard the thud of hooves, the clink of armour, the swelling of a song. And another sound too, distant, like a lion roaring. It seemed to come from under the sand, growing louder until all other sounds were lost within it. The man's eyelids started to flicker and his breathing grew faster. He raised his thin hands and held them over his ears, for the roar was starting to hurt them. The flames leaped, a wind started to blow and then, as he looked on in horror, the sands of the desert started to bubble and foam like water. They swayed and surged, and then rose up high in front of him, swelling like a tidal wave, up and up and up, engulfing the entire army. He screamed and threw himself backwards, knowing he too would be lost beneath the sands if he didn't get away. He scrambled to his feet and ran madly into the hills, wailing.

'No!' His cries echoed into the night. 'Allah protect me! Allah have mercy on my soul! Nooooo!'

14

CAIRO

Jenny had described it as Tara's Mike Tyson week. First Daniel had left her, then, almost immediately, she had discovered her mother had inoperable cancer. Two vicious blows coming out of nowhere, one after the other, knocking her out.

'Yup,' Jenny had said, 'that's about as Mike Tyson as it gets.'

Looking back – and for the last six years she'd done nothing but look back, turning the whole thing over in her mind as if constantly replaying the same video – she could see the signs had been there from the start.

Despite their closeness, a part of Daniel had always held away from her. They would finish making love and straight away he would disappear into his reading, as though alarmed by the depth of feeling he had just displayed. They would talk and talk, and yet somehow he never revealed anything of himself. In more than a year together she had discovered almost nothing about his background, like an excavator who tries to dig downwards only to hit solid rock almost immediately beneath the surface. He had been born in Paris, lost his parents in a car crash when he was ten, come to live with an aunt in England, got a first at Oxford. That was about it. It was as if he immersed himself in the history of Egypt to make up for the lack of a past of his own.

Yes, the signs had been there. She had shut them out, however. Refused to acknowledge them. She had loved him so much.

The end had come completely without warning. She arrived at his flat one evening, eighteen months after they'd started going out, they hugged, even kissed, and then he drew away.

'I heard from the Supreme Council of Antiquities today,' he said, staring down at her, their eyes not quite meeting. 'I've been granted a concession to dig in the Valley of the Kings. To lead my own expedition.'

'Daniel, that's wonderful!' she cried, coming forward and throwing her arms around him. 'I'm so proud of you.'

She clung to his shoulders for a moment, then pulled back, sensing he wasn't responding to the embrace, that there was more to come.

'What?'

His eyes seemed even blacker than usual. 'It's going to mean me living in Egypt for a while.'

She laughed. 'Of course it's going to mean you living in Egypt. What were you expecting to do? Commute?'

He smiled, but there was something hollow about the expression. 'It's a huge responsibility, Tara. To be allowed to excavate at one of the greatest archaeological sites in the world. A huge honour. I'm going to need to . . . focus all my attention on it.'

'Of course you have to focus all your attention on it.'

'All my attention.'

Something in the way he emphasized the 'all' sent a slight tremor through her, like the warning of a more severe earthquake to come. She stepped back, chasing his eyes with her own but unable to bring them to bay.

'What are you saying, Daniel?' Silence. She came forward

107

again, taking his hands in hers. 'It's OK. I can live without you for a few months. It'll be fine.'

There was a bottle of vodka on the desk behind him and, slipping his hands out of hers, he picked it up and poured himself a glass.

'It's more than that.'

Another tremor ran through her, stronger this time. 'I don't understand what you're saying.'

He downed the vodka in one.

'It's over, Tara.'

'Over?'

'I'm sorry to be so blunt, but I can't put it any other way. I've been waiting for an opportunity like this all my life. I can't let anything get in the way. Not even you.'

She continued to stare at him for a moment and then, as if she had been punched in the stomach, staggered backwards, grasping at the doorframe for support. The room around her thickened and became indistinct.

'How would I . . . get in the way?'

'I can't explain it, Tara. I just have to concentrate on my work. I mustn't have any . . . encumbrances.'

'Encumbrances!' She fought to control her voice, to find words. 'Is that what I am to you, Daniel? An encumbrance?'

'I didn't mean it like that. I just have to . . . be free to do my work. I can't have any ties. I'm sorry. Really I am. This last year's been the best time of my life. It's just that . . .'

'You've found something better.'

There was a pause.

'Yes,' he said eventually.

She crumpled to the floor then, shamed by her tears but unable to control them.

'Oh God.' She was choking. 'Oh God, Daniel, please don't do this to me.'

When she left twenty minutes later she felt as though everything inside her had been scraped out. For two days she heard nothing and eventually, unable to hold herself away, she returned to his flat. There was no answer to her banging.

'He's moved out,' a student living on the floor below told her. 'Gone to Egypt or something. There's a new tenant coming in next week.'

He hadn't even left her a note.

She had wanted to die. Had even gone so far as to buy five bottles of aspirin and one of vodka.

That same week, however, she had received news of her mother's cancer, and that had somehow diminished the painful but lesser sorrow of Daniel's departure, one agony cancelling out another.

She had nursed her mother for the four brief months she had left to live, and in the turmoil of watching her waste away she had somehow come to terms with the ending of the relationship. When her mother eventually died Tara had organized the funeral and then gone abroad for a year, first to Australia, then South America. On her return she had bought the flat, got the job at the zoo, re-established some sort of equilibrium.

The pain, however, had never entirely left her. There had been other relationships but she had always held back, unwilling to risk even a fraction of the torment she had suffered over Daniel.

She had neither seen nor heard from him again. Until tonight.

'I guess I deserved that,' he said.

'Yes,' she replied. 'You did.'

They had left the tea-room, stares and whispers pushing against their backs, and were now walking down Ahmed Maher towards the heart of the city's Islamic quarter, past stalls selling lamps and *shisha* pipes and clothes and vegetables. The air was heavy with the bitter-sweet odour of spices and dung and rubbish; a hundred different noises assaulted their ears – hammering and music and beeping and, from one shop doorway, the slow, rhythmic grinding of a huge vermicelli-making machine.

They came to a crossroads and turned left through an ornately carved stone gateway, a pair of minarets rearing high above them. A narrow street stretched ahead, even more crowded than the one they had left. Fifty metres along they turned into a narrow alley and stopped in front of a heavy wooden door. A sign on the wall read 'Hotel Salah al-Din'. Daniel pushed the door open and they passed into a small, dusty courtyard with a dried-up fountain at its centre and a wooden gallery running above their heads.

'Home sweet home,' he said.

His room was on the upper floor, opening off the gallery, simple but clean. He flicked on a light, pushed back the window shutters, poured them both a large whisky. From below came the rattle of cart wheels and the babble of human voices. There was a long silence.

'I don't know what to say,' he said eventually.

'Sorry, maybe.'

'Would that do any good?'

'It would be a start.'

'Then I'm sorry, Tara. Genuinely so.'

There was a pack of cheroots lying on the table beside him and he pulled one out, lighting it and exhaling a cloud of dense smoke. He seemed uneasy, nervy, his eyes flicking over to her and away again. In the clear cold light of the room she could see that he'd aged more than she had at first thought. There were flecks of grey in his dark hair, and lines across his forehead. He was still handsome though. God, he was handsome.

'When did you start smoking those?' she asked.

He shrugged.

'A few years ago. Carter used to smoke them. I thought a bit of his luck might rub off on me.'

'And has it?'

'Not really.'

He refilled his glass and hers too. There was a loud beeping from below as a moped fought its way through the crowds.

110

'So how did you find me?' he asked. 'I take it you didn't just walk into the tea-room by accident.'

'I saw the note you left my father.'

'Of course. How is he?'

She told him.

'Oh Jesus. I'm sorry. I had no idea. Really I didn't.'

He laid aside his glass and came over to her, extending his arms as if to embrace her. She raised a hand, however, warding him off, and his arms dropped back to his side.

'I'm sorry, Tara. If there's anything I can do . . . ?'

'It's all been taken care of.'

'Well, if you need . . .'

'It's all been taken care of.'

He nodded and backed away. There was another long silence. She wondered what she was doing here, what she was trying to achieve. Tendrils of cheroot smoke were curling around the light bulb.

'So what have you been doing for the last six years?' she asked eventually, conscious of how superficial the question sounded.

Daniel downed his whisky. 'The usual, I suppose. Excavating. A bit of lecturing. I've written a couple of books.'

'You live out here now?'

He nodded. 'In Luxor. I'm in Cairo just for a few days. Business.'

'I didn't know you were still in touch with Dad.'

'I'm not,' he said. 'We haven't spoken since—' He broke off, poured himself another glass. 'I just thought it would be nice to see him. I don't know why. Old times' sake and all that. I doubt he would have responded. He hated me for what I did.'

'That makes two of us.'

'Yes,' he said, 'I guess it does.'

They finished the bottle of whisky, catching up on each other's news, skating across the surface of things, not going too deep. Outside the noise in the street grew, peaked and slowly died away again as the shops began to shut up for the night and the crowds to dissipate.

'You didn't even write to me,' she said, cradling her glass. It was late now and her mind was thick with drink and exhaustion. The street outside was empty and silent, wisps of paper blowing down it as if the city's flesh were flaking away.

'Would you have wanted me to?'

She thought and then shook her head. 'No.'

She was sitting on the edge of the bed. Daniel was on a dusty sofa against the far wall.

'You fucked my life up,' she said.

He looked up at her and their eyes met, briefly, before she threw back her head and finished her drink.

'Anyway, it's in the past. Finished.'

Even as she said it, though, she knew that it wasn't. That there was still something to come. Some deeper resolution.

Outside, beyond the great stone gateway through which they'd walked earlier, the dusty black Mercedes sat silently against the kerb, waiting.

15

LUXOR

'And you know nothing about a new find?' asked Khalifa wearily, stubbing out his cigarette in an empty coffee glass.

The man in front of him shook his head.

'A tomb? A cache? Anything out of the ordinary?'

Again a shake of the head.

'Come on, Omar. If there's something out there we'll find it eventually, so you might as well tell us.'

The man shrugged and blew his nose on the sleeve of his tunic.

'I know nothing,' he said. 'Nothing at all. You're wasting your time with me.'

It was eight in the morning and Khalifa had been up all night. His eyes ached, his mouth was dry and his head swimming. For over seventeen hours, with only brief breaks for prayers and food, he and Sariya had been interviewing every person in Luxor known to have connections with the antiquities trade, hoping for a lead in the Abu Nayar case. All yesterday afternoon, all through the night and all morning a steady stream of known dealers had passed through the police station on Sharia el-Karnak, all giving precisely the same answers to his questions: no, they knew nothing about any new discoveries; no, they knew nothing about any new antiquities coming onto the market; and yes, if they could think of anything else, they would get in touch. It was like being made to listen to the same tape over and over again.

Khalifa lit another cigarette. He didn't really want it, he just needed something to keep him awake.

'How is it, do you think, that someone like Abu Nayar could afford a new television set and fridge for his mother?' he asked.

'How the hell should I know?' grunted Omar, a small, wiry man with close-cropped hair and a bulbous nose. 'I barely knew him.'

'He found something, didn't he?'

'If you say so.'

'He found something, got killed because of it and you know what it was.'

'I don't know anything.'

'You're an Abd el-Farouk, Omar! Nothing happens in Luxor without your family knowing about it.'

'Well, in this case we don't. How many times do I have to tell you that? I don't know anything. Nothing. Nothing.'

Khalifa stood and walked over to the window, puffing on his cigarette. He knew he was wasting his time. Omar wasn't going to tell him anything and that was the end of it. He could ask questions till he was blue in the face and it wouldn't do any good. He sighed deeply.

'OK, Omar,' he said without turning. 'You can go. Let me know if you think of anything else.'

'Of course,' said Omar, making swiftly for the door. 'I'll call you straight away.'

He slipped out, leaving Khalifa and his deputy alone.

'How many left?' he asked.

'That's it,' replied Sariya, hunching forward and rubbing his eyes. 'We've done them all. There's no one else.'

Khalifa collapsed into a chair and lit another cigarette, not noticing that he'd left one burning in an ashtray on the windowsill.

Maybe he'd got it wrong. Perhaps Nayar's death had nothing to do with antiquities after all. From what he'd heard there were plenty of other reasons why someone might want him dead. He didn't have a shred of evidence to connect it with antiquities. Not a single shred.

And yet he felt – he couldn't properly explain why – he just sensed, deep down, that Nayar's death was tied up with the trade in ancient artefacts, in the same way some archaeologists can feel deep down that they're close to an important find. It was a sixth sense, an instinct. As soon as he had seen the man's body with its scarab tattoo he had known: this is going to be a case where the present can only be explained by the past.

And there were hints. Enough, at least, to stop his line of enquiry looking totally pointless. Nayar had definitely been involved in the antiquities trade. He had definitely come into money recently – more money, certainly, than could be explained by the odd jobs he did to support his family. His wife, when he had questioned her briefly the previous afternoon, had denied all knowledge of her husband possessing any artefacts, which wasn't surprising, except that she had done so before he himself had mentioned them, as though it was a question for which she had been preparing. And then there had been the reaction of the dealers they'd interviewed.

'Fear,' he said, blowing a smoke ring towards the ceiling and watching as it rose, expanded and then slowly dissipated.

'What?'

'They're frightened, Mohammed. The dealers. All of them. Terrified.'

'I'm not surprised. They could get five years for handling stolen antiquities.'

Khalifa blew another ring. 'It's not us they're frightened of. It's something else. Or someone.'

Sariya narrowed his eyes. 'I don't understand.'

'Someone's got to them, Mohammed. They were trying to hide it, but they were petrified. You could see it when we showed them the pictures of Nayar. They went white, as if they could see the same thing happening to themselves. Every antiquities dealer in Luxor is crapping his pants. I've never seen anything like it.'

'You think they know who killed him?'

'They suspect, certainly. But they're not going to talk. The fact is they're a damned sight more scared of the people who cut up Nayar than they are of us.'

Sariya yawned. His mouth, Khalifa noticed, seemed to have more fillings in it than teeth.

'So who do you reckon we're dealing with?' asked the sergeant. 'Local mob? Guys from Cairo? Fundamentalists?'

Khalifa shrugged. 'Could be any of those or none. One thing's for sure, though: this is big.'

'You really think he might have found a new tomb?'

'Possibly. Or maybe someone else found one and Nayar got wind of it. Or maybe it's just a few objects. But it's something valuable. Something that was worth killing him for.'

He flicked his cigarette through the window. Sariya yawned again.

'Sorry, sir,' he said. 'I haven't been getting much sleep lately, what with the new baby.'

'Of course,' smiled Khalifa. 'I'd forgotten. How many is that now?'

'Five.'

Khalifa shook his head. 'I don't know where you get the energy. Three almost killed me.'

'You should eat more chick peas,' said Sariya. 'It, you know, gives you staying power.'

The earnestness with which his deputy offered this advice amused Khalifa and he started to chuckle. For a moment Sariya looked offended. Then he too started laughing.

'Go home, Mohammed,' said Khalifa. 'Eat some chick peas, get some sleep, relax. Then you can go over to the west bank and talk to Nayar's wife and family. See what you can dig up.'

Sariya stood and removed his jacket from the back of his chair. He turned towards the door, but then turned back again. 'Sir?'

'Hmm?'

He was fiddling with the sleeve of his shirt, not looking at Khalifa.

'Do you believe in curses?'

'Curses?'

'Yes. Ancient curses. Like, you know, the curse of Tutankhamun.'

Khalifa smiled. 'What, that those who disturb the sleep of the dead will meet a terrible end?'

'Something like that.'

'You think that's what we might be dealing with here? A curse?'

His deputy shrugged non-committally.

'No, Mohammed, I don't believe in them. It's all a load of silly superstition if you ask me.' He opened his cigarette pack but, finding it empty, scrunched it up into a ball and threw it into the corner of the room. 'I do believe in evil, though. Something dark that grabs hold of a man's mind and heart and turns him into a monster. I've seen it. And it's evil that we're up against here. Pure evil.'

He leaned forward and began massaging his eyes with his thumbs.

'Allah guide us,' he muttered. 'Allah give us strength.'

Later, after eating a couple of boiled eggs and some cheese for his breakfast, Khalifa crossed the river and hopped onto a service taxi, staying with it as far as Dra Abu el-Naga, where he got off, paid the twenty-five piastre fare and began walking up the road towards the Temple of Hatshepsut at Deir el-Bahri.

The temple had always been one of his favourite monuments. A breathtaking complex of halls and terraces and colonnades, it was cut into the living rock at the base of a hundred-metre cliff face. Every time he saw it he was staggered by its audacity. It was one of the wonders of Luxor. Of the whole of Egypt. Of the world.

A tarnished wonder, though. In 1997 sixty-two people, tourists mostly, had been massacred there by fundamentalists. Khalifa had been interviewing someone in a nearby village at the time and had been among the first policemen on the scene. For months afterwards he had woken in the night, sweat-covered, hearing again the squelch of his feet on the blood-covered floors. Now, whenever he saw the temple, his appreciation was marred by a shiver of nausea.

He walked on until he came to a point where a row of dusty souvenir shops sprang up on the right-hand side of the road. Their owners stood in front of them, calling out to passing tourists, urging them to come and inspect their postcards and jewellery and sunhats and alabaster carvings, each insisting that his particular wares were by far the cheapest and best in Egypt. One bustled up to Khalifa brandishing a T-shirt with a garish hieroglyph motif on the front, but the detective waved him away and, turning off to the right, crossed a tarmacked car park and came to a halt in front of a mobile lavatory.

'Suleiman!' he called. 'Hey, Suleiman, are you there?'

A small man in a pale green djellaba emerged, limping slightly. A long scar ran diagonally across his forehead, starting beside his left eye and disappearing up beneath his hairline.

'Inspector Khalifa, is that you?'

'*Salaam Alekum.* How are you, my friend?'

'*Kwayyis, hamdu-lillah,*' smiled the man. 'Well, thanks be to Allah. Will you have tea?'

'Thank you.'

'Sit, sit!'

The man waved Khalifa to a bench in the shade of a nearby

building and set about boiling a kettle behind the trailer. When it was ready he poured out two glasses and carried them across, picking his way carefully over the uneven ground as though fearful of tripping. He handed one glass to Khalifa and sat, setting his own glass down on the bench beside him. Khalifa took the man's hand and pressed a plastic bag into it.

'Some cigarettes.'

Suleiman fumbled in the bag and removed a carton of Cleopatras.

'You shouldn't have, Inspector. It's me who owes you.'

'You don't owe me anything.'

'Apart from my life.'

Four years ago Suleiman al-Rashid had been working as a guard at the temple. When the fundamentalists came, he had been shot in the head trying to shield a group of Swiss women and children. In the aftermath of the attack everyone assumed he was dead, until Khalifa found a faint pulse and called the medics over to help him. It had been touch and go for several weeks, but eventually he had pulled through. His injuries had left him blind, however, and he had been unable to resume his job as a guard. Now he ran one of the site toilets.

'How's the head?' Khalifa asked.

Suleiman shrugged and rubbed his temples. 'So-so,' he said. 'Today it aches a bit.'

'You see the doctor regularly?'

'Doctors! Pah! Scum!'

'If it's hurting you should get it checked.'

'I'm fine as I am, thank you.'

Suleiman was a proud man and Khalifa knew better than to press the point. Instead he asked him about his wife and family, and teased him because his team, el-Ahli, had lost to his, Khalifa's, team, el-Zamalek, in the recent Cairo derby. Then they fell silent. Khalifa sat watching a group of tourists descending from their coach.

'I need your help, Suleiman,' he said eventually.

'Of course, Inspector. Anything. You know you only have to ask.'

Khalifa sipped his tea. He felt bad about involving his friend, playing on his sense of obligation. He'd been through enough already. But he needed information. And Suleiman always kept his ear to the ground.

'I think something has been found,' he said. 'A tomb, or a cache. Something important. No-one's talking, which isn't surprising, except it's not just greed that's keeping them quiet, it's fear. People are terrified.' He finished his tea. 'Have you heard anything?'

His companion said nothing, just continued rubbing his temples.

'I don't like asking you, believe me. But one man's been killed already and I don't want anyone else to be.'

Still Suleiman said nothing.

'Is there a new tomb?' asked Khalifa. 'Not much goes on around here that you don't hear about.'

Suleiman adjusted his position and, picking up his tea, began sipping it slowly.

'I've heard things,' he said, staring straight ahead of him. 'Nothing definite. Like you say, people are frightened.'

He turned his head suddenly, looking towards the hills, running his sightless eyes across the shimmering walls of yellow-brown rock.

'You think we're being watched?' asked Khalifa, following the direction of Suleiman's gaze.

'I know we're being watched, Inspector. They're everywhere. Like ants.'

'Who's everywhere? What do you know, Suleiman? What have you heard?'

Suleiman continued to sip his tea. His eyes, Khalifa noticed, had started to water.

'Rumours,' he muttered eventually. 'Hints. A word here, a word there.'

'Saying?'

Suleiman's voice dropped to a whisper. 'That they've found a tomb.'

'And?'

'And there's something extraordinary in it. Something priceless.'

Khalifa swirled the tea dregs around the bottom of his glass. 'Any idea where?'

Suleiman nodded towards the hills. 'Out there somewhere.'

'Out there is a very big area. Anything more specific?'

A shake of the head.

'Sure?'

'Sure.'

A long pause. The tarmac of the car park undulated in the heat. From somewhere behind them came the braying of a donkey. Nearby a European couple were haggling with a taxi driver over the fare down to the river.

'Why's everyone so frightened, Suleiman?' asked Khalifa gently. 'Who's got to them?'

Silence.

'Who am I dealing with here?'

Suleiman came to his feet, picking up the two empty glasses. He seemed not to have heard the question.

'Suleiman? Who are these people?'

The attendant began making his way back towards the toilet trailer. When he spoke he didn't turn his head.

'Sayf al-Tha'r,' he said. 'It is Sayf al-Tha'r they are afraid of. I'm sorry, Inspector, I have work to do. It was good of you to come.'

He clambered up the trailer steps and disappeared inside, closing the door behind him.

Khalifa lit a cigarette and leaned back against the wall. 'Sayf al-Tha'r,' he whispered. 'Why did I know it would be you?'

The young Egyptian mingled with the crowd, his baseball cap pulled low about his eyes. He looked no different from the other tourists milling around the feet of the four giant statues, except that he seemed to be muttering to himself and to take little interest in the huge seated figures rearing overhead. Rather, his attention was focused on the three white-uniformed guards sitting on a bench nearby. He glanced at his watch, swung his knapsack off his shoulder and began undoing the straps.

It was mid-morning. Two coaches of American tourists had just arrived, disgorging a stream of passengers onto the tarmac, all of them wearing yellow T-shirts. Postcard sellers and trinket hawkers swarmed around them.

The young man now had his knapsack open. He dropped to one knee and fiddled inside it. To his left a group of Japanese tourists were grouped around their guide, who was holding a fly whisk in the air so they could see where she was.

'The great temple was built by the Pharaoh Ramesses II in the thirteenth century BC,' she shouted, 'and was dedicated to the gods Re-Harakhty, Amun and Ptah . . .'

One of the three guards was looking at the muttering figure. His two companions were smoking and talking together.

'The four seated statues represent the King-God Ramesses. Each is over twenty metres high . . .'

The American tourists had started to arrive, laughing and chattering. One of them had a video camera and was issuing instructions to his wife, telling her to go forward, move to the left, look up, smile. The young Egyptian stood again, one arm still inside the rucksack. The guard continued to stare at him, then nudged his companions, who ceased their conversation and looked towards him too.

'The smaller statues between the legs of Ramesses represent the king's mother, Muttuya, his favourite wife, Nefertari, and some of his children . . .'

The young man's voice suddenly grew louder. Several people turned to look at him. He closed his eyes briefly and then, smiling broadly, withdrew his arm from the bag, a Heckler and Koch sub-machine gun clutched in his hand. In the same movement he swept his cap from his head, revealing a deep vertical scar running between his eyebrows.

'Sayf al-Tha'r!' he cried and, pointing the gun into the crowd, pulled the trigger. There was a click, but no gunfire.

The three policemen leaped to their feet, grappling with their rifles. Everyone else just stood where they were, horrified, rooted to the spot. For a moment everything was still while the gunman clawed frantically at his weapon, then he snatched at the trigger again and this time the Heckler and Koch fired. There was a furious cracking sound and bullets scythed into the crowd, tearing flesh, snapping bone, spattering the sand with blood. People began running madly, some away from the gunman, others, confused, directly towards him, screams of pain and terror filling the air. The man with the video crumpled; the three guards were thrown backwards and down. Above the roar of his gun and cries of distress the young man could be heard singing and laughing.

The barrage continued for perhaps ten seconds, enough to leave a field of bodies at the feet of the great statues. Then the Heckler and Koch jammed again and the air was curiously silent. The gunman fought with his weapon for a moment, and then, throwing it aside, fled into the desert.

He didn't get far. Five of the trinket sellers chased after him and, dragging him to the ground, began kicking him with their bare feet, his head jerking back and forth like a ball.

'Sayf al-Tha'r,' he cried, laughing, blood bursting from his nose and mouth. 'Sayf al-Tha'r!'

16

CAIRO

Tara woke with a start. She sat up groggily and looked around, realizing she was in bed in Daniel's hotel room. For a horrified moment she thought perhaps . . . Then she saw she was still fully clothed and at the same time noticed the sheets lying on the sofa opposite, where presumably he had slept. She looked at her watch. It was almost midday.

'Bollocks,' she muttered, staggering to her feet, head throbbing.

There was a bottle of mineral water beside the bed and, unscrewing the cap, she took a long swig. Noise drifted up from the street outside. There was no sign of Daniel. No note.

Something inside her felt inexplicably soiled by the previous night's encounter, as if by coming here she had somehow let herself down. She wanted to get out quickly before he came back and, finishing the water, she scribbled a note apologizing for having fallen asleep, picked up her knapsack and left. She didn't tell him where she was staying.

Back on the street she headed towards the huge stone gateway they'd passed through the night before. Then, fearful suddenly of bumping into Daniel, she swung round and set off in the opposite direction, following the narrow street deeper into the old Islamic quarter.

It was hot and dusty, and a swell of people jostled all around her – women carrying baskets of newly baked bread on their heads, merchants hawking their wares, children juddering along on the backs of donkeys. In other circumstances she might have enjoyed the scene: the alien sounds and smells, the colourful stalls with their baskets of dates and dried hibiscus petals, the cages crammed with rabbits and ducks and chickens.

As it was, she felt tired and confused. Sudden harsh noises assaulted her ears – the clanging of hammers, the blare of a moped horn, a burst of music from a radio – drilling into her head and disorientating her. The smell of refuse and spices made her faintly nauseous, while there was something claustrophobic about the way the crowd pressed in from all sides, clasping her in a stranglehold of moving bodies. She passed a group of boys unloading sheets of brass from the back of a lorry, a girl standing on top of a pile of jute sacks, two old men playing dominoes at the roadside, and all of them seemed to be staring at her. A man on a wooden scaffold shouted something, but she ignored him and pushed on through the throng, bumping into people, struggling for breath, wishing she was back in her hotel room, cool and quiet and safe.

After about ten minutes she came upon a butcher killing chickens at the side of the road. One by one he pulled the birds from a cage, nudging back their beaks with his thumb and slitting their throats before dropping them into a blue plastic barrel, their wings still flapping feebly. A semi-circle of onlookers had gathered to watch and Tara joined them, sickened by the scene but curiously compelled by it too.

She didn't notice the men at first, so mesmerized was she by the sight of the butcher's knife slicing across the soft pink-white flesh of the chickens' throats. It was only after she'd been watching for a couple of minutes that she happened to glance up

125

and see them standing across from her, two of them, bearded, with black djellabas and *'imma*s bound low about their heads. Both were gazing directly at her.

She held their look for a moment, then returned her attention to the butcher. Two more birds were slaughtered and then she glanced up again. They were still staring at her, their expressions hard, unflinching. There was something unsettling about them and, detaching herself from the group, she moved off down the street. The men waited a few seconds, then followed.

After fifty metres she stopped in front of a shop selling backgammon boards. The black-robed figures stopped as well, making no effort to disguise the fact they were watching her. She moved on again and the men moved as well, keeping about thirty metres behind, their eyes never leaving her. She quickened her step and turned right into another street. Ten paces, fifteen, twenty, and there they were behind her again. Her heart started to pound. This street was even narrower than the one before and seemed to get narrower still the further she went along it, the buildings to either side inching together like the jaws of a vice, the crowds becoming ever more compressed. She could sense her pursuers getting closer. Another street opened up ahead and to the right and, pushing her way through the crowd, she ducked down it.

This one was deserted and for a moment she felt relieved, glad to have got out of the crowd. Then she began to wonder if she had made a mistake. Here she was exposed; there was no-one she could call to for help. The emptiness seemed suddenly threatening. She spun round, intending to burrow her way back into the throng, but the men had come up more quickly than she had expected and were now just ten metres away. For a moment she stood staring at them, frozen, then turned and started to run. Five seconds and then behind her the thud of pursuing feet.

'Someone help me!' she cried, her voice sounding muffled and weak, as though she was shouting through a cloth.

Fifty metres along she swerved left into another street, then right, then left again, no longer caring where she was going, just wanting to get away. Heavy wooden doors flashed past to either side, and at one point she stopped and hammered on one, but there was no response and after a few seconds she ran on again, terrified that if she waited any longer she would be caught. The sound of her pursuers' feet seemed to echo all around, magnified and distorted by the narrow streets, so that it seemed as if they were coming from in front as well as behind. She had lost all sense of direction. Her head throbbed. She felt sick with fear. She continued running for what felt like an age, zigzagging deeper and deeper into the labyrinth of back streets before eventually emerging into a small, sun-filled square with other streets leading off it in different directions. There was a stunted palm tree at its centre, with an old man sitting in the shade beneath it. She ran over to him.

'Please,' she pleaded. 'Please. Can you help me?'

The man looked up. Both eyes were milky white. He held out his hand.

'Baksheesh,' he said. 'Baksheesh.'

'No,' she hissed, desperate, 'no baksheesh. Help me!'

'Baksheesh,' he repeated, grabbing her sleeve. 'Give baksheesh.'

She tried to pull away, but he wouldn't let go, his fingers clutching her shirt like a claw.

'Baksheesh! Baksheesh!'

There was a shout and the sound of running feet. She looked up wildly. Four streets led into the square, including the one she had entered by. She swung her eyes from one to the other, trying to work out where the sound was coming from, the whole square throbbing with the pounding of feet, as though someone was playing a drum. For a moment she remained motionless, unable to decide which direction she should take. Then, her terror giving her an unexpected strength, she ripped her arm away from the blind man and ran full tilt towards the street opposite the one she had first come down. Even as she approached it she saw two bearded figures turn a corner up ahead and charge straight towards her. She swerved and made for one of the other streets, but then, prompted by some instinct she couldn't fully explain, swerved again and ran towards the street she had entered by.

She stopped at its mouth and turned, gasping for breath. The two black-robed men were entering the square. They spotted her and slowed, glancing to their right, towards the street she'd almost gone down but had then shied away from. There was a pause and then a huge figure emerged, the same figure she had seen at Saqqara and outside her hotel. His suit was crumpled and his piebald face beaded with sweat. For a moment he stood staring at her, breathing heavily, then he reached into his pocket and pulled out what looked like a small builder's trowel.

'Where is it?' he snarled, moving towards her. 'Where is the piece?'

'I don't know what you mean,' gasped Tara. 'You've got the wrong person.'

'Where is it?' he repeated. 'The missing piece. The hiero-glyphs. Where are they?'

He was halfway across the square now, almost at the palm tree.

'Baksheesh!' wailed the blind man, grabbing at the giant's linen jacket, clasping a handful of material. 'Baksheesh.'

The giant tried to brush him off but couldn't. He cursed and, raising the handle of his trowel, smashed it down into the blind man's nose. There was a loud cracking sound, like twigs, and a deafening scream of pain. Tara didn't wait to see any more. She turned and fled. From behind came the thunder of pursuing feet.

She ran and ran, blood pounding in her ears, swinging left beneath an arch into a sort of tunnel which led into a courtyard full of women washing clothes. She rushed past them and out through a gate into a street. There were more people here. She wheeled right into another street and suddenly there were people everywhere, and shops and stalls. She slowed momentarily, heaving for air, and then pushed on. Almost immediately, however, strong hands seized her and spun her round.

'No!' she cried. 'No! Let me go.'

She fought, punching out with her fists.

'Tara!'

'Let me go!'

'Tara!'

It was Daniel. Rearing over him, its twin minarets piercing the pale afternoon sky, was the stone gateway near the hotel. She had come full circle.

'They're trying to kill me,' she gasped. 'They're trying to kill me and I think they killed Dad too.'

'Who? Who's trying to kill you?'

'Them.'

She turned and pointed. The street, however, was so jammed with people that even if her pursuers had been among them it would have been impossible to spot them. She searched for a moment and then, turning back to Daniel, buried her face in his shoulder and clung to him.

LUXOR

As Khalifa walked away from the Temple of Hatshepsut, mulling over what Suleiman had told him, he passed a couple of young boys coming up from Dra Abu el-Naga on camelback. They were laughing together, flicking at the camels with their sticks, urging the ungainly beasts forward with the traditional camel driver's cries of '*Yalla besara!*' and '*Yalla nimsheh!*' ('Hurry up! Let's go!'). He turned to watch them and suddenly the present seemed to evaporate and he was a child himself again, back at the camel stables in Giza with his brother Ali, in the old days before everything fell apart.

Khalifa had never been sure when Ali had first gone over to Sayf al-Tha'r. It hadn't been a sudden association. Rather, a gradual assimilation; a slow ripple effect that had carried his brother inexorably away from his friends and family and into the arms of violence. Khalifa had often thought that if only he had noticed earlier how Ali was changing, hardening, perhaps he could have done something. But he hadn't noticed. Or at least he'd tried to persuade himself that things weren't as bad as they seemed. And because of that Ali had died. Because of him.

Islam had always been a part of their lives and as with any other great faith there was an element of anger in it. Khalifa remembered how the imam at their local mosque, in his Friday *khutbar*, would rail against the Zionists and the Americans and the Egyptian government, warning how the *Kufr* were trying to destroy the *ummah*, the Moslem community. No doubt his words had planted seeds in Ali's mind.

If he was honest they had planted seeds in Khalifa's mind too, for much of what the imam said was true. There was evil and corruption in the world. What the Israelis were doing to the Palestinians was unforgivable. The poor and needy were ignored while the rich lined their pockets.

Khalifa, however, had never been able to make the connection between this and the use of violence. Ali, on the other hand, had slowly begun to build that bridge.

It had started innocently enough. With conversations, reading, occasional meetings. Ali had begun attending rallies, handing out leaflets, even speaking in public himself. He had spent less and less time with his history books, more and more with religious works. 'What is history without truth?' he had said to Khalifa once. 'And truth is to be found not in the deeds of men, but the word of God.'

Much of what he did had been good and it was this that had persuaded Khalifa there was no need to fear the changes that were being wrought within him. He had collected money for the poor, spent time teaching illiterate children, spoken out on behalf of those who would otherwise have had no voice.

All the while, however, there was a slow hardening of his rhetoric, a ratcheting up of the anger within him. He had become involved with fundamentalist organizations, joining first one, then another, each a little more extreme than the previous one, getting sucked deeper and deeper into the whirlpool, the line between faith and fury becoming increasingly blurred. Until eventually, inevitably, he had come to Sayf al-Tha'r.

Sayf al-Tha'r. The name was seared into Khalifa's mind like a brand on an ox's back. It was he who had corrupted Ali. He who had made him do the things he did. He, ultimately, who had sent him to his death that terrible day fourteen years ago.

And now with this case things had come full circle. Now he was no longer just investigating a death. Now he was seeking to avenge one too. Sayf al-Tha'r. He'd known it would be him. He'd known it. The past always catches up eventually, however fast you try to run.

An urgent hooting dragged him back to the present. He had strayed out onto the road and a tourist coach was bearing down on him, horn blaring. He hopped back to the side of the tarmac, looking for the two camel riders, but they had disappeared round a bend. He lit a cigarette, waited for the coach to pass, then continued on his way, the road ahead shimmering in the midday heat.

CAIRO

'I should never have left you,' said Daniel.

'This morning or six years ago?'

He looked at her.

'I was referring specifically to this morning.'

They were back in his hotel room, Tara on the couch, legs drawn up to her chin, Daniel standing beside the window. She'd had a whisky but was still trembling, the memory of her recent experiences fresh in her mind.

'I had to meet someone at the museum,' he continued. 'It took longer than I expected. I should have warned you about the back-streets around here. They can be dangerous for foreigners, especially women. There are thieves, pickpockets . . .'

'These weren't pickpockets,' said Tara, resting her forehead against her knees. 'I knew them.'

Daniel raised his eyebrows.

'One of them at least,' she said. 'I saw him at Saqqara the day I found Dad's body. And then later at the hotel. And he wasn't Egyptian.'

'You're saying someone's following you deliberately?'

'Yes.'

He was silent for a moment, and then, crossing to the sofa, sat and took her hand.

'Look, Tara, you've had a bad couple of days. First your father, now this. I think maybe you're reading too much into—'

She snatched her hand away. 'Don't patronize me, Daniel. This isn't some hysterical fantasy. This man is following me. I don't know why, but he's following me.'

She came to her feet and went over to the window, standing where Daniel had stood, looking out across the jumbled rooftops. The air was hot and she could feel trickles of perspiration running down her chest.

'He said something about a missing piece. He kept asking me where it was. He seems to think I've got something of his. God knows what, but he seems to think I've got it.' She turned. 'And he thought my father had it too. He was in the dig house. And possibly in my father's apartment. He left a smell of cigar smoke. There's something going on, Daniel. You have to believe me. Something bad.'

He said nothing, just sat on the couch staring at her intently, brown-black eyes sweeping across her face. He pulled a cheroot from his shirt pocket and lit it.

'There's something going on,' she repeated, turning away again. 'Please believe me.'

There was a brief silence and then she heard him stand and come over to her. He laid his hand on her shoulder. She shrugged it off, but he put it back and this time she let it rest. She could feel the strength of him burning through his palm.

'I do believe you, Tara,' he said gently.

He turned her and took her in his arms. For a moment she resisted, but only a moment. He felt so strong, so secure. She buried her face in his shoulder, tears welling in her eyes.

'I don't know what to do, Daniel. I don't know what's going on. Someone's trying to kill me and I don't even know why. I tried to tell them at the embassy, but they didn't believe me. They thought I was imagining things, but I'm not. I'm not.'

'OK, OK,' he said. 'Everything's going to be fine.'

He tightened his arms around her and she allowed him to do it, knowing how dangerous it was to be so close to him, yet unable to help herself. There was a loud beeping from outside as a car nudged its way through the crowd.

They stayed like that for some time before he gently eased her away, brushing his finger beneath her eyes to wipe away the tear stains.

'There were three of them, you say.'

She nodded. 'Two Egyptians and one white guy,' she said. 'The white guy was huge and had a birthmark on his face. Like I said, I've seen him before. At Saqqara and outside my hotel.'

'And what exactly did he say to you again?'

'He asked me where it was. He kept saying, "Where is it? Where is the missing piece?"'

'That was it?'

'He said something about hieroglyphs.'

Daniel's eyes narrowed. 'Hieroglyphs?'

'Yes. He said, "Where are they? Where are the hieroglyphs?"'

'He definitely used that word? Hieroglyphs? You're sure?'

'I think so, yes. Everything was a blur.'

He drew slowly on the cheroot, ribbons of blue-grey smoke spiralling from the corner of his mouth.

'Hieroglyphs?' he said, more to himself than to her. 'Hieroglyphs? What hieroglyphs?' He took another pull on the cheroot and wandered across the room. 'You haven't bought anything since you came to Egypt? No antiquities or anything?'

'I haven't had time.'

'And you say this man was at your father's dig house?'

'Yes. I'm sure of it.'

He fell silent, rubbing his temples, thinking. A wasp flew in through the window and settled on the rim of Tara's whisky glass. Silence.

'Well, they obviously think you have something that belongs to them,' he said eventually. 'And presumably they think you have it because they think your father had it before you. So we have to answer two questions: first, what is this object? And second, why did they think your father had it in the first place?'

He went over to the couch and sat down, lost in thought. She remembered him like this from their time together, how he would sit in a sort of trance thinking through a problem, mind whirring like a machine, his expression half-grimace, half-smile, as though he was pained by the process, yet enjoying it too. He was silent for a whole minute before coming to his feet again.

'Come on.'

He picked up his cheroots and moved towards the door.

'Where? The police?'

He grunted. 'Not if you want any answers. They'll just take a statement and forget about it. I know what they're like.'

'So where, then?'

He reached the door and threw it open.

'Saqqara. Your father's dig house. That's where we'll start. Coming?'

She looked into his eyes. There was so much she recognized there – the strength, the determination, the power. There was something else as well, however. Something she hadn't seen in him before. It was a moment before she was able to pin it down – guilt.

'Yes,' she said, picking up her knapsack and following him out into the corridor. 'I'm coming.'

LUXOR

On his way home from Deir el-Bahri, Khalifa stopped off to see Dr Masri al-Masri, Director of Antiquities for Western Thebes.

Al-Masri was a legend in the Antiquities Service. He had joined as a young man and, given that he was now almost seventy, should by rights have occupied a higher position than he did. He'd been offered more exalted posts, on numerous occasions, but had always turned them down. He was a native of this part of the world and felt a particular affinity with its monuments. He'd devoted his life to their preservation and protection, and although he held no formal academic qualifications, was universally referred to as the Doctor, both out of respect and, also, fear. Al-Masri's temper, it was said, was worse than that of Seth, the Egyptian god of thunder.

He was in a meeting when Khalifa arrived, so the detective sat down on a wall outside his office and lit a cigarette, gazing across the road at the scattered remains of the mortuary temple of Amenhotep III. From over his shoulder came the sound of bitter argument.

There had been a time when Khalifa himself had wanted to join the Antiquities Service. Would have joined it had Ali not been taken from them, leaving him with the sole responsibility of caring for their mother. He'd been at university at the time and for a while had tried to continue his studies, earning money on the side working as a tour guide. It hadn't been enough, however, especially after he'd married Zenab and she had become pregnant with their first child.

And so he had abandoned Egyptology and joined the police force instead. His mother and Zenab had both begged him not to, as had his tutor Professor al-Habibi, but he had seen no other way of providing a decent life for his family. The pay wasn't brilliant, but it was better than that of a junior antiquities inspector and at least the force offered some sort of security for the future.

He had been sad at the time. Was still sad in a way. It would have been nice to work among the objects and monuments he so loved. He'd never regretted the decision to put his loved ones first, though. And anyway, archaeology and detective work weren't that dissimilar. They were both about following clues, analysing evidence, solving mysteries. The only real difference was that while the archaeologist tended to unearth wonderful things, it was the detective's lot, more often than not, to find terrible ones.

He drew on his cigarette. The argument behind him was getting louder. There was a hammering sound, as of someone banging his fist on a desk, and then suddenly the door of al-Masri's office flew open and a wiry man in a dirty djellaba emerged. He turned briefly to scream, 'I hope a dog shits on your grave!' before stomping angrily out of the building, gesticulating wildly with his arms.

'And I hope two dogs shit on yours!' bellowed al-Masri after him. 'And piss on it too!'

Khalifa smiled to himself and, flicking away his cigarette, stood. The office door was open and, approaching, he put his head inside.

'*Ya Doktora?*'

The old man was sitting behind a small plywood desk piled high with papers. He was tall and thin, with a long, dark-skinned face and curly, close-cropped hair – a typical Saidee, or native of upper Egypt. He looked up.

'Khalifa,' he grunted. 'Well, come in, come in.'

The detective entered, al-Masri pointing him to one of the armchairs that lined the wall.

'Damned peasant fool,' he snapped, nodding towards the door. 'We discover what looks like an extension of Seti I's mortuary temple in one of his fields and he wants to plough it up and plant *molochia* on it.'

'A man has to eat,' smiled Khalifa.

'Not if it involves destroying our history, he doesn't. Let him starve! Ignorant barbarian.' He banged his hand on the desk, sending a sheaf of papers tumbling to the floor. He bent down to retrieve them. 'Tea?' he asked, head hidden beneath the desk.

'Thanks.'

Al-Masri shouted and a young man entered.

'Get us a couple of glasses of tea, will you, Mahmoud?' He fiddled with the papers, placing them in one pile, then moving them to another, then dividing them in half and placing each half on a different pile, before finally opening a drawer and cramming them inside. 'To hell with it. I won't read the damned things anyway.'

He sat back and looked over at Khalifa, hands clasped behind his head. 'So what can I do for you? Come to ask me for a job, have you?'

The doctor knew of Khalifa's background and liked to tease him about it, albeit in a friendly way. Although he never said as much, he admired the detective. Khalifa was one of the few people al-Masri knew whose passion for the past came anywhere near to rivalling his own.

'Not exactly,' smiled Khalifa.

He leaned forward and tamped out his cigarette in an ashtray on the desk, then filled al-Masri in on the murder of Abu Nayar. The old man listened quietly, clicking his fingers behind his head.

'I presume you haven't heard anything?' asked Khalifa when he'd finished.

Al-Masri snorted. 'Of course I haven't heard anything. If there's ever a new discovery around here we're always the last to know about it. They're better informed on the moon.'

'But it's possible something could have been found?'

'Sure, it's possible. I'd say to date we've only uncovered about twenty per cent of what's left of ancient Egypt. Perhaps less. The Theban Hills are full of undiscovered tombs. They'll be finding them for another five hundred years.'

Mahmoud came back with the tea.

'I think this might be something big,' said Khalifa, taking a glass from the proffered tray and sipping it. 'Something people are prepared to kill for. Or to keep secret.'

'There are people around here who'd kill for a couple of *shabti*s.'

'No, it's more than that. People are scared. We've interviewed every antiquities dealer in Luxor and they're all shitting themselves. This is something important.'

The old man took his own tea and sipped it. He seemed relaxed, but Khalifa could tell he was interested. He sipped again and then, laying the glass aside, came to his feet and began wandering around the room.

'Intriguing,' he muttered to himself. 'Very intriguing.'

'Any idea what it might be?' asked Khalifa. 'A royal tomb?'

'Hmmm? No, not likely. Not likely at all. Most of the great royal burials are already known, except Tuthmosis II and Ramesses VIII. And possibly Smenkhkare, if you accept that the body in KV55 was Akhenaten, which personally I don't.'

'I thought Amenhotep I's tomb was still lost,' said Khalifa.

'Rubbish. He was buried in KV39, as any sensible archaeologist knows. Anyway, the point is that if it was a major royal burial it would almost certainly be in the Valley of the Kings, and you're not going to keep a new find there hushed up, however many people you kill. The place is so full of tourists you can hardly move.'

His hands were clasped behind his back, the thumbs slowly

rotating. Every now and then his tongue slipped out and ran along his lower lip.

'What about the West Valley?' asked Khalifa, referring to a smaller, less-frequented gorge that branched off the main valley about halfway along its course.

'Sure, it's less busy, but we'd still know if anything had been found there. It's not that much of a backwater.'

'A mummy cache?'

'But there aren't any mummies left to cache. Or no great ones at least, aside from a couple of the later Ramessids, and I can't see anyone considering those worth killing for.'

'A minor royal burial, then. A prince. A princess. A secondary queen.'

'Again, they would have been buried in the Valley of the Kings or the Valley of the Queens. Somewhere close to the centre of the necropolis. These people liked to stick together.'

Khalifa leaned forward and lit a cigarette. 'An important official? A noble?'

'More likely,' admitted the old man, 'although I'd still be surprised. Almost every significant official's tomb we've ever discovered has been either in the valley or close to it. Too close to make clandestine excavation possible. And these burials rarely contain anything valuable. Historically valuable certainly, but no gold or anything like that. Or at least not enough to make it worth killing someone for. The obvious exception being Yuya and Tjuju, but that was a one-off.'

He stopped in front of the window, his rotating thumbs slowing until they were almost still.

'You've got me puzzled, Khalifa. For someone to turn up a new tomb isn't surprising in itself. As I said, the hills are full of the damned things. But for someone to turn up a tomb whose contents are worth killing for and for that same tomb to be sufficiently off the beaten track for them to be able to keep it so completely under wraps, now that is unusual.'

'You've no idea, then?'

'None at all. Of course there are tales of fabulous hoards of buried treasure up in the hills. The priests of Karnak are supposed to have hidden all the temple gold in a cave underneath the Qurn somewhere, to stop it falling into the hands of the invading Persians. Ten tons of the stuff by all accounts. But they're just old wives' tales. No, Inspector, I'm afraid I'm just as much in the dark as you are.'

The doctor returned to his desk and sat down heavily. Khalifa finished his tea and got to his feet. He hadn't slept since the night before last and felt, suddenly, exhausted.

'OK, OK,' he said, 'but if you hear anything be sure to let me know. And no amateur sleuthing. This is a police matter.'

Al-Masri waved his hand dismissively. 'Do you seriously imagine I'm going to go traipsing round these hills on my own trying to find your damned tomb?'

'That's exactly what I imagine,' said Khalifa, smiling fondly at the old man.

Al-Masri scowled at him for a moment, annoyed, and then broke into a wry chuckle. 'OK, Inspector. Have it your own way. If I hear anything you will be the first to know.'

Khalifa moved to the door. '*Ma'a salama, ya Doktora*. Peace be with you.'

'And with you, Inspector. Although if what you've told me of this case is true, peace is the last thing you're going to be getting.'

Khalifa nodded and went out.

'Oh, Inspector,' al-Masri called after him.

Khalifa put his head back round the door.

'If you ever did come and ask me for a job, I'd be more than happy to give you one. Good day.'

17

SAQQARA

They took a taxi out to Saqqara, following much the same route that Tara had taken two days before. Hassan, the man with whom she had found her father's body, wasn't in the office. One of his colleagues recognized her, however, and handed over the dig-house keys. They drove on along the escarpment and pulled up in front of the building, telling the driver to wait while they went inside.

The interior was dark and cool. Daniel opened a couple of windows and pushed back the shutters. She gazed around sadly, taking in the whitewashed walls, the threadbare sofas, the rickety bookshelves, thinking how happy her father had been here, how the building had, in a sense, become a part of her own life as well as his. She wiped her sleeve across her eyes and turned to Daniel, who was gazing at a framed print on the wall.

'So what exactly are we looking for?' she asked.

'No idea.' He shrugged. 'Something that looks ancient, I guess. With hieroglyphs on it.'

He moved away from the print and began perusing one of the bookshelves. Tara threw her bag onto a chair and drifted into one of the rooms off the main lounge. There was a narrow bed in one corner, a wardrobe against the wall and, hanging from the door, a tattered old safari jacket. She delved into one of the pockets and pulled out a wallet. She bit her lip. It was her father's.

'This is Dad's room,' she called.

He came in and together they went through her father's possessions. There wasn't much, just a few clothes, some camera equipment, a couple of notebooks and, on a chair beside the bed, a leather-bound diary. Its entries were brief and un-revealing, concerned almost exclusively with the progress of that season's work. There were several mentions of Tara – whom he styled 'T' – the last on the day before her arrival in Egypt, the penultimate day of his life:

Into Cairo morning. Meeting at American Uni. re. next year's curriculum. Lunch Antiquities Service. Afternoon shopping Khan al-Khalili for T.'s arrival. Back S. late afternoon.

And that was it. Nothing that shed any light on recent events. They laid the diary aside.

'Perhaps they've already found whatever it is,' she said.

'I doubt it. Otherwise why would they have been chasing you?'

'Then how do we know it's here, not in Cairo?'

'We don't. I'm just guessing that, whatever this thing is, your father only had it for a few days. And since this is where he's been living for the past three months it makes sense to start looking here. Try the other rooms.'

They spent an hour going through the house, looking in every drawer and cupboard, even getting on their knees to peer under the beds. Without success. Aside from her father's camera equipment there was nothing there to interest even a normal thief.

'I guess I must have been wrong,' said Daniel eventually, deflated.

Tara was in one of the bedrooms. The adrenalin had been pumping through her as they searched. Now she was overcome by a sudden weariness. The pain of her father's death, momentarily forgotten, came flooding back more intensely than ever, an overwhelming sense of loss and helplessness. She ran her hands through her hair and sat down heavily on the bed, leaning backwards against the pillow. Something crunched beneath her. She sat forward again and lifted the pillow. A piece of folded papyrus was lying on the sheet, with her name, Tara, written on it in black ink. She opened it and read.

'Daniel,' she called, 'come and look at this.'

He came into the room and she handed him the sheet. He read aloud:

> *One of eight, first link in a chain,*
> *Clue to clue, like stepping stones,*
> *At the end a prize, something hidden,*
> *But is it treasure, or just old bones?*
> *The Gods might help you if you ask politely,*
> *Imhotep, perhaps, or Isis or Seth,*
> *Although personally I'd look a little closer to home,*
> *For none knows more than old Mariette.*

'Aren't you a bit old for treasure hunts?' he asked.

'When I was fifteen Dad laid a treasure trail for my birthday,' she said, smiling sadly at the memory. 'It was one of the few times I ever felt he really cared for me. I think this is his way of trying to heal old wounds. A sort of peace offering.'

Daniel squeezed her shoulder and looked down at the papyrus again.

'I wonder . . .' he said to himself.

'You think maybe . . .'

'That your dad's prize is the thing we're looking for? No idea. But it's certainly worth finding out.'

He strode back into the main room.

'Mariette is Auguste Mariette,' he said over his shoulder. 'One of the founding fathers of Egyptology. Did a lot of work here at Saqqara. Discovered the Serapeum.'

Tara followed to find him standing in front of the print he'd been looking at before.

'Auguste Mariette,' he said. The picture showed a bearded man in a suit and traditional Egyptian headdress. He lifted the frame from the wall and turned it over. Sellotaped to the back was another folded papyrus.

'Bingo.' His eyes were shining.

'Go on then,' she said, adrenalin starting to pump again. 'Open it.'

He pulled the clue from the frame and unfolded it.

> *A queen to a pharaoh, but a pharaoh herself,*
> *Ruled between husband and husband's son,*
> *Nefertiti her name, a beautiful name,*
> *And with her the beautiful one has come.*
> *Heretic husband, damned Akhenaten,*
> *Forsaken by the Gods because the Gods he forsook,*
> *Together they lived, but where did she live?*
> *The answer, perhaps, you will find in a book.*

'What the hell does that mean?' Tara asked.

'Nefertiti was the principal wife of the Pharaoh Akhenaten,' he explained. 'Her name meant the Beautiful One Has Come. After Akhenaten died she changed her name to Smenkhkare and ruled as a pharaoh in her own right. She was succeeded by Tutankhamun, Akhenaten's son by another wife.'

'Of course,' grunted Tara.

'Later generations reviled Akhenaten because he abandoned Egypt's traditional gods in favour of the worship of just one god: the Aten. He and Nefertiti built a new capital city two hundred kilometres south of here. It was called Akhetaten, the Horizon of the Aten, although today it's known by its Arab name: Tel el-Amarna. I dug there once.'

He crossed to the bookcase.

'Looks like we need to find a book on Amarna.'

She joined him and together they ran their eyes swiftly along the rows of books. There were several with titles incorporating the name 'Amarna', but no clue inside any of them. There was another bookcase in one of the bedrooms and they went through that as well, but with no greater success. Tara shook her head in frustration.

'This is so bloody typical of Dad. I mean, if I can't even get these clues with an Egyptologist to help me, what chance would I have had on my own! He never could understand that I just wasn't bloody interested in any of it!'

Daniel wasn't listening. He was squatting on the floor, eyes narrowed. 'Where did she live?' he muttered. 'Where did Nefertiti live?'

Suddenly he sprang to his feet. '*Merde!*' he cried. 'I'm an idiot.'

He hurried back into the main room, where he knelt in front of the bookcase and ran his finger along the rows of books. He pulled one out, a slim volume.

'I was trying to be too clever. The clue was more literal than it sounded.' He held the book up, pointing to its title: *Nefertiti Lived Here*. He was smiling, pleased with himself. 'Probably the best book about excavating ever written. By Mary Chubb. I met her once. Fascinating woman. Let's see what the clue says.'

This next rhyme – about the dynasties of ancient Egypt – proved easier than the last, leading them to a poster of Tutankhamun's death mask in the kitchen. Clue five was inside an amphora in one of the bedrooms, six pinned inside the flue of the chimney and seven hidden behind the lavatory cistern. Eight, the final clue, was rolled up inside a tube of tracing paper in a cupboard in the main room. By now they were both tense with anticipation. They read the last rhyme together, tripping over the words in their hurry to discover what it said.

The last at last, eight of eight,
Hardest of all, so use your head,
Near where you are, but not inside,
A five-thousand-year-old bench for the dead
Fifteen paces south (or fifteen north),
Bang in the centre, now use your eyes,
Search for the sign of Anubis the Jackal,
For Anubis it is that guards the prize.

'Bench for the dead?' she asked.

'*Mastaba,*' replied Daniel. 'A type of rectangular tomb made of mud bricks. *Mastaba* is the Arabic for bench. Come on.'

She snatched up her knapsack and followed him outside, wincing at the heat after the cool interior of the house. The taxi driver had pulled his car into a pool of shade in front of the building and gone to sleep, seat reclined, bare feet sticking out of the window. Daniel stood for a moment looking around, shielding his eyes, then pointed to an oblong hummock rising from the sands fifty metres ahead of them and to their left.

'That must be it,' he said. 'I can't see any other *mastaba*s.'

They crossed the track and hurried over to the hummock which, when she came closer, Tara could see was made of badly weathered brown mud bricks. Daniel went to one corner and counted out fifteen paces along its side, the top of the *mastaba* coming up almost to the level of his neck.

'Somewhere around here,' he said, indicating the middle of the wall. 'We're looking for an image of a jackal.'

They squatted and ran their eyes back and forth over the uneven surface. Tara found it almost immediately.

'Got it!' she cried.

Incised into the face of one of the bricks, very faint, was the figure of a reclining jackal, paws outstretched, ears erect. The brick seemed to be loose and, getting her fingers around it, Tara began working it out of the wall. It had clearly been removed before because it came out easily, revealing a deep cavity. Daniel rolled up his sleeve, checked quickly for scorpions, then drove his hand into the hole, withdrawing it holding a flat cardboard box. He laid it on his knee and began undoing the string with which it was tied.

'What is it?' she asked.

'I'm not sure,' he said. 'It's quite heavy. I think it might be . . .'

A shadow fell across them from above and there was a metallic click. Startled, they looked up. Standing on top of the *mastaba*, gun in hand, was a bearded man in black robes, a turban wrapped low around his head. He motioned them to their feet, gabbling something in Arabic.

'What did he say?' Tara's voice was tight with terror.

'The box,' said Daniel. 'He wants the box.'

He began to reach out, handing the box up to the man. Tara grabbed his arm.

'No,' she said.

'What?'

'Not till we know what's in it.'

The man spoke again, waving the gun. Again Daniel tried to extend his arm, again Tara pulled it back.

'I said no,' she hissed. 'Not till we know why these people are doing this.'

'For fuck's sake, Tara, this isn't a game! He'll kill us. I know these people!'

The man was getting agitated. He pointed his gun at Tara's head, then Daniel's, then down at the top of the *mastaba*, firing a brief burst of bullets into the mud bricks, explosions of dust spitting up around his feet and into their faces. Daniel wrenched his arm free and threw the box onto the tomb.

'Just leave it, Tara. I want to know what's in it as much as you, but it's not worth it. Trust me, it's better to let it go.'

Keeping the gun trained on them, the man dropped to his haunches, releasing one hand and feeling for the box. It was slightly to his left and his fingers kept missing it, and, for the briefest of moments, he flicked his eyes downwards. At the same instant, hardly aware of what she was doing, Tara whipped out her arm, seized his robe and yanked. The man cried out and toppled forward over the edge of the *mastaba*, crashing head first onto the sand between them, his neck twisted at a curious angle.

For a moment neither of them moved. Then, glancing across at Tara, Daniel knelt and lifted the man's hand, feeling for a pulse.

'Is he unconscious?' She was whispering for some reason.

'He's dead.'

'Oh my God!' She put her hands to her mouth. 'Oh my God!'

Daniel stared down at the body, then reached out and pushed back the man's black woollen *'imma*, revealing a deep vertical scar running up his forehead. He gazed at it for a few seconds, then came abruptly to his feet and grabbed her arm.

'We're getting out of here.'

He started pulling her away, but after a couple of metres she broke free and leaped back to the *mastaba*, grabbing the box which was still lying there.

'For Christ's sake!' cried Daniel, coming after her and seizing her shoulder. 'Just leave it! There are things going on here . . . you don't understand . . . there'll be more of them . . .'

She shrugged him away. 'They killed my father,' she said, voice defiant. 'You do what you want, but I'm not letting them have this box! Do you understand, Daniel? They're not getting it.'

Their eyes met briefly, then she pushed past him and started back towards the dig house, slipping the box into her bag as she went. For a moment Daniel stared after her, face contorted with impotent fury, then followed, muttering to himself.

The gunfire had woken their driver, who was standing on the track looking towards them.

'What happen?' he asked as they came up.

'Nothing,' snapped Daniel. 'Take us back to Cairo.'

'I hear gun.'

'Just start the bloody . . . !'

There was a sharp crack of gunfire. Whirling, they saw two black-robed figures sprinting along the track towards them. There was another crack, from behind this time. Two more figures had emerged from the desert and were also making straight for them, black smudges against the shimmering yellow of the sand. The driver screamed and dropped to the ground.

'I told you there'd be more of them!' shouted Daniel. 'The dig house! Run!'

He seized her arm and they sprinted towards the house, one bullet whizzing past Tara's head, another kicking up a spray of dust just in front of them. They reached the side of the building and jumped down onto the rear terrace. Beyond it a steep sandy slope dropped away to the village beneath, where people were coming out of their houses and looking up, wondering what all the noise was about.

'Get down the slope,' shouted Daniel.

'What about you?'

'Just get down the slope. I'll follow.'

'I'm not leaving you!'

'Jesus!'

There was a thud of running feet. Daniel cast his eyes wildly around, spotted an old *touria* leaning against a bench and, seizing it, ran back to the side of the house, shrinking against the wall. The thud of feet grew louder. He raised the *touria*, took a couple of breaths, and then swung it as hard as he could, just as one of their pursuers scrambled into view around the corner. The metal head smashed into the man's face with a sickening crack, throwing him backwards into the undergrowth, his hand still gripping his Heckler and Koch. Daniel leaped forward and prised the gun away.

'Now!' he cried. 'While we've got the chance!'

They ran to the edge of the terrace and jumped, hitting the slope together and scrabbling downwards in a shower of dust, Tara still clutching her knapsack. There was a stretch of sand at the bottom, then a track, then the village, strung out along the edge of a dense palm grove. A car was bumping towards them and Daniel ran for it, flagging it down. The driver slowed and, seeing the gun, skidded to a halt. Shots rang out from above. Daniel turned and fired. There were screams and the villagers began to scatter. He fired again, keeping his finger on the trigger, raking the escarpment until the gun's magazine was empty. He threw the weapon aside and turned back to the car. The driver had scrambled out, leaving the keys in the ignition and the engine turning. Daniel leaped behind the wheel.

'Get in!' he yelled at Tara. 'Get in!'

She dived into the passenger side and he stamped his foot on the accelerator, the wheels churning up a spray of gravel as the car careered down the track. A bullet shattered one of the rear side windows, another punctured the bonnet. They hit a pot-hole and skidded, and for a moment it looked as if they were going to hit a wall, but he managed to bring them back under control and they sped away, the sputter of gunfire echoing behind them, the dig house lost behind a curtain of dust.

'I don't know what the fuck's in that box of yours,' Daniel panted, 'but after all this I hope it was worth it!'

18

LUXOR

By the time Khalifa got home midway through the afternoon he was so exhausted he could barely keep his eyes open.

As soon as he came through the door his son leaped on him. 'Dad! Dad! Can I have a trumpet for Abu Haggag?'

The Feast of Abu el-Haggag was due to start in a couple of days. For weeks Ali and his schoolmates had been decorating a float for the children's procession and the boy could barely contain his excitement about the forthcoming festivities.

'Can I?' he cried, tugging at Khalifa's jacket. 'Mustafa's got one. And Said.'

Khalifa picked him up and ruffled his hair. 'Of course you can.'

Ali bounced up and down in his arms, delighted.

'Mum!' he cried. 'Dad says I can have a trumpet for Abu Haggag!'

Khalifa slung the boy over his shoulder and, picking his way around the building materials in the front hall, went through into the living room. Zenab was sitting on the sofa holding the baby. Beside her were her sister Sama and Sama's husband Hosni. Khalifa groaned inwardly.

'Hello, Sama. Hello, Hosni,' he said, putting his son down.

Hosni stood and the two men embraced. Ali ran round and hid behind the sofa.

'They've just come back from Cairo,' said Zenab, a faintly accusing tone in her voice. She was always going on at Khalifa to take her up to the capital for a few days, but somehow he never got around to arranging the trip. And, anyway, they would be hard pressed to afford it.

'We flew,' said Sama, showing off. 'It's so much faster than the train.'

'Business,' added Hosni. 'Had to meet a new supplier.'

Hosni worked in edible oils and rarely talked about anything else.

'I tell you, we're struggling to keep up with demand at the moment,' he went on. 'People have to eat and to eat they have to have edible oil. It's a captive market.'

Khalifa assumed an expression that he hoped conveyed enthusiasm.

'I don't know if Zenab's told you, but we're about to launch a brand-new sesame oil. It's a bit more expensive than your normal oil, but the quality is exceptional. I could send round a couple of cans if you like.'

'Thank you,' said Khalifa. 'We'd like that very much, wouldn't we, Zenab.'

He looked towards his wife, who smirked. It always amused her when he tried to sound interested in Hosni's work.

'Come on, Sama,' she said, standing. 'Let's leave the men to talk. Would you like a glass of *karkaday*, Hosni?'

'Love one.'

'Yusuf?'

'Please.'

The sisters disappeared into the kitchen. Khalifa and Hosni sat trying to avoid each other's gaze, embarrassed. There was a long silence.

'So how's the police force?' asked Hosni eventually. 'Catch any murderers today?'

His brother-in-law was even less interested in Khalifa's work than Khalifa was in his. In truth he rather looked down on the detective. Working every hour God gave and for such a meagre wage! Zenab had definitely married beneath her. OK, she could have done worse. But she could have done a lot better as well. Someone in edible oils, for instance. That was where the future lay. A captive market. And with that new sesame oil things could really take off.

'No, not today,' Khalifa was saying.

'Sorry?'

'I didn't catch any murderers today.'

'Oh, right,' said Hosni. 'Good. Or rather bad.' He paused, confused, trying to recover the thread of the conversation. 'Hey, I hear you put in a promotion application. Think you'll get it?'

Khalifa shrugged. '*Insha-Allah*. If Allah is willing.'

'I would have thought it was more a case of if your boss is willing!'

Hosni laughed loudly at his joke, slapping the arm of the sofa.

'Sama!' he called. 'Hey, Sama! Yusuf said he'd get a promotion if Allah was willing and I said it was more a case of if his boss was willing.'

There was a loud braying from the kitchen, Sama evidently finding the comment as amusing as her husband did. Ali had come up behind the sofa and was preparing to hit Hosni on the head with a cushion. Khalifa glared at him and the boy disappeared again.

'So how's the fountain going?' asked Hosni after another long silence, struggling for something to say.

'Oh, not bad. Fancy a look?'

'Why not.'

The two men went out into the hallway and stood among the clutter of cement bags and paint pots, looking down at the rather

153

sorry-looking plastic pond from which, hoped Khalifa, a fountain of water would one day spout.

'It's a bit cramped,' observed Hosni.

'There'll be more space when all this rubbish is cleared away.'

'Where's the water coming from?'

'We'll plumb it in from the kitchen.'

Hosni scratched his chin, bemused by the whole venture. 'I don't know why you don't just . . .'

He was interrupted by Ali, who chose that moment to come running out after them, knocking over a pot of paintbrushes rinsing in white spirit. A viscous grey-white liquid spread across the concrete floor.

'Dammit, Ali,' snapped Khalifa. 'Zenab! Bring out a cloth, will you?'

His wife looked out at the mess. 'I'm not ruining one of my cloths mopping that up. Use some newspaper.'

'I haven't got any newspaper.'

'I've got an old *al-Ahram* in my bag,' said Hosni. 'You can use that.'

He fetched the paper from the other room and began laying it sheet by sheet on the pool of white spirit.

'You see,' he said, 'it's soaking it up. Wonderfully absorbent.'

He detached another sheet and went to put it down. As he did so, Khalifa grabbed his arm: 'Wait!'

The detective fell to his knees.

'What date is this paper?'

'Um . . .'

'What date!'

There was an urgency to his voice.

'Yesterday's,' said Hosni, flustered.

One of Khalifa's knees was in the puddle of spirit, but he seemed unaware of it. He was leaning forward intently, reading something in the bottom right-hand corner of the page, his finger flashing back and forth along the lines of script. Ali came and knelt beside him, running his own finger over the sodden newsprint, imitating his father.

'Yesterday,' Khalifa said to himself when he'd finished the article. 'Yesterday. Let's see: Nayar's killed on Friday, they go up the same day . . . Dammit!' he cried, leaping to his feet, a dark stain now spreading slowly across his knee.

'Dammit,' cried Ali, jumping up after him.

'What?' said Hosni. 'What is it?'

Khalifa ignored him and hurried through into the kitchen, his exhaustion suddenly forgotten. 'Zenab, I have to go out.'

'Go out? Where?'

'Cairo.'

'Cairo!'

For a moment it looked like she was going to make a fuss. Then, however, she came forward and kissed him on the forehead.

'I'll get you some clean trousers.'

In the hallway Hosni was looking down at the article Khalifa had been reading. There was a photograph of an ugly old man with an eye-patch and, above it, the caption: 'Cairo Antique Dealer Brutally Murdered'. He shook his head. That sort of thing never happened in edible oils.

155

19

CAIRO

Neither of them spoke on the way back to Cairo. Daniel concentrated on the driving, eyes flicking nervously up to the rear-view mirror to check they weren't being followed. Tara just stared down at the bag on her lap. Only when they reached the main Cairo–Giza road and turned right through a scrum of traffic towards the city centre did Daniel break the silence.

'I'm sorry, Tara, but you just don't understand how dangerous this is. Those men – they were followers of Sayf al-Tha'r. The scar on the forehead, that's their mark.'

She was fiddling distractedly with the knapsack zip. 'Who is this Sayf al-Tha'r? I keep hearing the name.'

'A fundamentalist leader,' said Daniel, swerving to avoid a cyclist wobbling along with a tray of pastries on his head. 'The name means Sword of Vengeance. Preaches a mixture of Egyptian nationalism and extremist Islam. No-one knows much about him except that he appeared on the scene back in the late Eighties and has been killing people ever since, Westerners mostly. Blew up the American ambassador a year or so ago. The government's got a million-dollar bounty on his head.'

He glanced across at her, smiling humourlessly.

'Well done, Tara. You've just made an enemy of the most dangerous man in Egypt. Jesus.'

They drove on in silence for another couple of kilometres, the city closing in all around them, before eventually crossing a fly-over and hitting gridlock. They sat for five minutes, then, cursing, Daniel swung off to the left, pushing his way through the oncoming lanes of traffic and parking up in a garbage-filled side street. They got out.

'We should try and get off the street,' he said, glancing around. 'It's too exposed. I don't think they followed us, but you never know. They've got people everywhere.'

They began walking, coming to a line of railings enclosing what Tara initially thought was a large park, but then realized was actually a zoo. There was an entrance thirty metres along and, taking her arm, Daniel steered her towards it.

'Let's go in here. We're less likely to be seen. And there's a payphone we can use.'

They paid the twenty piastre entry charge and pushed through the turnstiles. The noise of the city seemed to drop away behind them and suddenly everything was quiet. Birds were chattering in the trees, families strolling together, young lovers sitting on benches, hand in hand. From somewhere nearby came the babble of running water.

They set off down a shady walkway, eyes jerking back and forth for any sign of pursuit. They passed a rhinoceros enclosure, a monkey house, a sea-lion pool and a lake full of flamingos before eventually coming to a dusty banyan tree with a stone bench beneath it, on which they sat. There was a telephone booth five metres away and, opposite, a morose-looking elephant in a cage, its leg shackled to the bars with a heavy chain. Daniel scanned the surrounding walkways, then took her knapsack, opened it and removed the box.

'First things first. We find out what this is,' he said.

He looked around again, then pulled away the string and

lifted the lid. Inside, sitting on a bed of straw, was a flat object wrapped in newspaper. There was a small card sellotaped to it:

Tara. Thought this might be appropriate. Love, as always,
Dad.

He glanced over at her, then removed the object from the box and tore away the paper. It was a fragment of what looked like plaster, roughly square in shape, the edges jagged and uneven. The surface was painted a pale yellow, with three columns of black hieroglyphic figures running down it and, on the left, part of a figure from a fourth column. A line of snakes with their heads reared slithered along the bottom – the reason, Tara assumed, her father had chosen it for her in the first place.

Daniel turned the piece over in his hand, nodding slightly as if in recognition.

'You know what it is?' she asked.

He didn't answer immediately and she had to repeat the question.

'Gypsum plaster,' he said distractedly. 'From a tomb decoration. The hieroglyphs would have been part of a longer text – see, these ones have been cut off mid-word. It's pretty good workmanship. Very good, in fact.' He smiled to himself.

'Is it genuine?'

'Definitely. Late Period by the looks of it. Greek, maybe, or Roman. Possibly Persian occupation, not much earlier. Almost certainly from Luxor, though.'

'How can you tell that?'

He nodded at the piece of paper the object had been wrapped in. Across the top was written a legend in Arabic.

'*Al-Uqsur*,' he translated. 'Luxor. It's from the local paper.'

She took the fragment from him and stared at it, shaking her head. 'I can't understand why Dad would have bought it if it's genuine. He despised the antiquities trade. Never stopped going on about how much damage it did.'

Daniel shrugged. 'I guess he must have thought it was a fake. It's not his period, after all. Unless you're an expert in late dynastic tomb art you'd be hard pressed to tell the difference. If it was Old Kingdom I expect he'd have known immediately.'

'Poor Dad.' She sighed. 'He would have been devastated if he'd realized.' She handed the piece back. 'So what do the hieroglyphs mean?'

He laid the fragment in his lap and scanned the text.

'It reads right to left. See, the text always runs into the faces of the signs. This first column translates *abed* which is month, and then those strokes are the number three, and then *peret*, which was one of the divisions of the Egyptian year, roughly equivalent to our winter. So, *in the third month of peret*. Then we've got' – he squinted down – 'looks like some kind of name,

159

ib-wer-imenty, Great Heart of the West; *ib-wer*, great heart; *imenty*, of the west. It's not a proper name, more a sort of nickname. Certainly not part of a royal titulary. Or not one I've ever heard of.'

He thought for a moment, repeating the name to himself, then moved his finger to the second column of text.

'This top word is *mer*, which means pyramid. Then *iteru*, which is an ancient unit of measurement, and then a number, ninety. So, *the pyramid ninety iteru*. Then the next column starts with what looks like *kheper-en*, although these top two hiero-glyphs are broken off so . . .' He held the fragment up, trying to catch the light. 'No, it's definitely *kheper-en*, it happened, and then *dja wer*, a great storm. Then this cut-off figure on the left seems to be another number, although it's impossible to tell what. And that's it.'

He stared down at the fragment for a moment longer, turning it over in his hands, shaking his head, then returned it to its box and slid the box back into Tara's bag.

'If it does come from a Theban tomb of the Late Period, that certainly makes it rare,' he said. 'You don't get much painted tomb decoration post New Kingdom. Even then, though, I doubt it's worth more than a few hundred dollars. Hardly worth killing anyone over.'

'So why do these people want it?'

'God knows. Maybe they want the complete version of what-ever text it was once a part of. Why that text should be so significant, though, I've no idea.' He pulled a cheroot from his shirt pocket, lit it and stood up, exhaling a billow of smoke. 'Wait here.'

He crossed to the telephone booth and, snatching up the receiver, pushed a phone card into the slot and dialled. For a moment he looked at her, then turned away and began talking. He spoke for almost three minutes, at one point seeming to gesticulate angrily, then put the receiver down and returned to the bench. His forehead, she noticed, was beaded with sweat.

'They've been at my hotel. Three of them. Turned my room upside down, apparently. The owner was terrified, poor bastard. Christ, this is a mess.'

He hunched forward, rubbing his face with his hands. A little girl ran up, looked at them and ran away again, laughing. Somewhere nearby a monkey was howling.

'We should go to the police,' said Tara.

'After we've hijacked a car and killed two Egyptian nationals? Not fucking likely.'

'We were defending ourselves! They were terrorists!'

'That's not necessarily how the police would see it. Believe me, I know how they think.'

'We have to . . .'

'I said no, Tara! It'll only make things worse. If they could possibly get any worse.'

There was a tense silence.

'Then what?' she asked. 'We can't just sit here.'

Another silence.

'The embassy,' he said eventually. 'We'll go to the British embassy. That's the only safe place. We're out of our depth here. We need protection.'

Tara nodded.

'Do you have the number?' he asked.

She fumbled in her pocket and pulled out the card Squires had given her the previous day.

'OK. Call. Tell him what's happened. Say we need help. Urgently.'

He handed her his phone card and she crossed to the booth and dialled. It was answered after just two rings.

'Charles Squires.'

That soothing avuncular voice.

'Mr Squires? It's Tara Mullray.'

'Hello, Miss Mullray.' He didn't sound especially surprised to hear from her. 'Is everything OK?'

'No. No, it's not. I'm with a friend and we're—'

'A friend?'

'Yes. An archaeologist. Daniel Lacage. He knew my father. Look, we're in trouble. I can't explain over the phone. Something's happened.'

A pause.

'Can you be any more specific?'

'Someone's trying to kill us.'

'Kill you!'

'Yes. Kill us. We need protection.'

Another pause.

'Is this something to do with the man you told me about yesterday? The man you said was following you?'

'Yes. We've found something and they're trying to kill us because of it.'

She was aware she wasn't making much sense.

'OK,' he said soothingly, 'let's just stay calm. Where are you?'

'In Cairo. In a zoo.'

'Whereabouts in the zoo?'

'Um . . . by the elephant cage.'

'And you have this artefact with you?'

'Yes.'

He was silent for a moment. She had the impression he'd put his hand over the receiver while he spoke to someone beside him.

'OK, I'm sending Crispin over immediately. You and your friend just stay there. Do you understand me? Just stay exactly where you are. We'll be with you as quickly as we can.'

'Right.'

'Everything's going to be all right.'

'Yes. Thank you.'

'See you soon.'

He hung up.

'Well?' asked Daniel as she sat back down.

'He's sending someone over. Said we should stay here.'

He nodded and they lapsed into silence, Daniel puffing on

his cheroot, Tara staring down at her bag. She'd been hoping the mysterious object would provide some sort of answer to what was going on, but instead it seemed to make things even more obscure, as though an already complex code had had an extra line of encryption added to it. She felt confused and frightened.

'Perhaps Dr Jemal can help,' she said eventually. Daniel raised his eyebrows enquiringly. 'He's an old colleague of my father's,' she explained. 'I met him yesterday at the embassy. Maybe he'll know why the object's so important.'

Daniel shrugged. 'Never heard of him.'

'He's deputy head of the Antiquities Service.'

'Mohammed Fesal's deputy head of the Antiquities Service.'

'Oh. Well, he's something in the Antiquities Service, anyway.'

There was a pause. Daniel pulled on his cheroot. 'Jemal?'

'Yes. Dr Sharif Jemal. Like Omar Sharif.'

'I've never heard of a Dr Sharif Jemal.'

'Should you have?'

'If he's someone important in the Service, yes, of course. I deal with these guys every day.' He raised the cheroot again, but this time didn't draw in, just let it hover in front of his face. 'What else did he say, this Dr Jemal?'

'Nothing much. He said he worked with my father at Saqqara. They found a tomb together. In 1972. The year I was born.'

'What tomb?'

'I can't remember. Hotep or something.'

'Ptah-hotep?'

'Yes, that was it.'

The cheroot was still suspended in front of Daniel's mouth. He looked across at her. 'Who did you just speak to, Tara?'

'What?'

'At the embassy. Who did you just speak to?'

'Why? What's wrong?'

The bubbles of sweat on his forehead seemed to have multiplied. There was unease in his eyes.

'Your father found the tomb of Ptah-hotep in 1963. The year

I was born. And he found it at Abydos, not Saqqara.' Suddenly he threw the cheroot aside and stood up. 'Who did you just speak to?' His voice was fast now, urgent.

'Charles Squires. The cultural attaché.'

'And what did he say?'

'He just said wait here. They'd send someone over to get us.'

'That's it? You told him where we were?'

'Of course I told him where we were. How else are they going to find us?'

'And the piece. Did you mention the piece?'

'Yes. I said we'd—'

'What?'

A sudden tingle of unease rippled down her back.

'He asked if we still had the artefact with us.'

'So?'

The tingle was growing stronger.

'I didn't tell him it was an artefact. I just said we'd found something.'

For a moment he remained where he was, then hoisted her to her feet.

'We're getting out of here.'

'But this is crazy. Crazy. Why would the embassy lie to us?'

'I don't know. But this Dr Jemal clearly isn't who he says he is, and if he's not then it would seem your friend the cultural attaché isn't either.'

'But why? Why?'

'I've told you I don't know! We've got to get out of here. Come on!'

The alarm in his voice was unmistakable. He seized the knapsack and they hurried away, skirting the elephant cage and following a path up the side of a tree-covered mound. At the top they turned and looked back.

'Look!'

He pointed back down to where three men, conspicuous in suits and dark glasses, had just come up to the bench on which they'd been sitting. One crossed to the telephone booth and looked inside.

'Who are they?' whispered Tara.

'I don't know. But they're not here for an afternoon stroll, that's for sure. Let's get out of here. Before they see us.'

They turned and hurried down the far side of the knoll and out of the zoo. On the street Daniel hailed a cab and they got in.

'I get the feeling we're in trouble, Tara,' he said, peering anxiously out of the rear window. 'A lot of trouble.'

Squires picked up the phone almost before the first ring had finished.

'Yes?'

The voice at the other end spoke rapidly. He listened, holding the receiver with one hand while the other slowly worked the wrapping off a boiled sweet. He said nothing himself, and his face remained impassive. When the person had finished he said, 'Thank you. Keep looking,' and replaced the receiver.

The sweet was now out of the wrapper. Instead of putting it in his mouth he laid it carefully on the desk in front of him and made three calls, one after the other, in rapid succession. In each case, when the phone was answered, he said, 'She's gone for it,' and then rang off. Only after the third call did he sit back, reach for the sweet and slip it onto his tongue.

He remained motionless for some while, eyes half closed, the tips of his fingers touching just in front of his face as though he was at prayer. Only when the last fingernail of sweet had dissolved did he lean forward, open a drawer and remove a large hardback book. On the cover was a photograph of a wall covered in multicoloured hieroglyphs, and the title: *Late Period*

Funerary Practice in the Theban Necropolis. The author was Daniel Lacage.

He slipped his glasses onto his nose, sat back and opened the volume, crossing his thin legs and smiling to himself.

20

LUXOR

'The murders are connected,' insisted Khalifa. 'I'm sure of it.'

He was sitting in a large, meticulously tidy office on the first floor of Luxor police headquarters. In front of him, reclining behind his desk in an extravagant black leather executive chair, was Chief Inspector Abdul ibn-Hassani, his boss. Khalifa himself was on a low stool, a seating arrangement designed to emphasize Hassani's superior position in the police hierarchy. The chief rarely missed an opportunity to show his men who was in charge.

'OK, take me through it again,' sighed Hassani. 'And slowly this time.'

He was a big man with broad wrestler's shoulders and close-cropped hair, his face vaguely reminiscent of President Hosni Mubarak, whose portrait hung on the wall behind him.

He and Khalifa had never got on. Khalifa disliked his boss's obsession with doing everything by the book; Hassani mistrusted Khalifa's university education, his preparedness to be swayed by intuition rather than hard fact and his fascination with the ancient past. The chief was a pragmatist. He had no time for things that had happened thousands of years ago. He was interested in solving crimes in the here and now. And you did that by hard work, attention to detail and respect for your superiors, not daydreaming about people with unpronounceable names who'd been dead for three millennia. History was a distraction, an indulgence. And Khalifa was, in his opinion, a distracted, indulgent person. That's why he was stalling over his promotion. The man didn't have what it took. He should be working in a library, not a police station.

'According to the newspaper report,' Khalifa was saying, 'this man Iqbar was found in his shop with his face and body badly slashed.'

'What newspaper?'

'*Al-Ahram.*'

Hassani snorted and waved him on.

'The same wounds as we found on our man Nayar. Nayar dealt in antiquities. So did Iqbar. Or at least he owned an antique shop, which amounts to the same thing. Two men, both in the same business, killed in the same way, within a day of each other. It has to be more than a coincidence. Especially if you factor in Nayar's train ticket. He was in Cairo the day before Iqbar was killed. There has to be a link.'

'But do we have any hard evidence? I don't want guesses. I want facts.'

'Well, I haven't seen the Cairo medical report yet . . .'

'So it could be that the manner of death wasn't the same. You know how newspapers exaggerate. Especially rags like *al-Ahram.*'

'I haven't seen the medical report yet,' repeated Khalifa, 'but I know it'll show they were both killed in the same way. The cases are connected, I'm sure of it.'

'Go on then,' sighed Hassani wearily. 'What's your theory?'

'I think Nayar found a tomb . . .'

'I should have known tombs would come into it somewhere!'

'Or someone else found one and Nayar got wind of it. Either way, it was something big. He went to Cairo. Sold Iqbar a few objects. Got paid. Came back. Blew the money. Probably thought he was set up for life. Except that someone else knew about the tomb. And that someone else didn't like the idea of sharing the spoils.'

'This is speculation, Khalifa. Pure speculation.'

The detective ignored him and ploughed on.

'Maybe Nayar took something valuable and they wanted it back. Maybe the mere fact that he knew about the tomb was enough to sign his death warrant. Probably both. Whatever the case, these people caught up with him, tortured him to find out who else knew about the discovery, then went up to Cairo and did the same to Iqbar. And if we don't catch them, they're going to do the same to someone else. Have done the same, for all we know.'

'And who are these people? Who are these lunatics you're saying are prepared to butcher people for the sake of a few dusty old objects?'

He sounded as if he was humouring an over-imaginative child. Khalifa paused a moment before answering.

'I have reason to suspect Sayf al-Tha'r is involved.'

Hassani exploded. 'For God's sake, Khalifa! As if it's not enough to say we've got some marauding serial killer on our hands, now you've got to bring bloody Sayf al-Tha'r into it. What's the evidence?'

'I have a source.'

'What source?'

'Someone who works at Deir el-Bahri. At the temple. He used to be a guard.'

'Used to?'

'He was injured in the incident.'

'And now? What does this source do now?'

Khalifa bit his lip, knowing what Hassani's reaction would be. 'He runs the site toilets.'

'Oh marvellous!' roared the chief. 'Khalifa's great source: a bloody toilet attendant.'

'He knows more about what's going on around Luxor than anyone else I know. He's totally reliable.'

'I'm sure he is when it comes to scrubbing shit. But for police work? Do me a favour.'

Khalifa lit a cigarette and stared out of the window. The chief's office looked directly out over Luxor temple, one of the best views of the monument anywhere in Luxor. A shame it had to be wasted on a fool like Hassani, he thought. From outside came the amplified call of a muezzin summoning the faithful to mid-afternoon prayers.

'Every dealer in town is afraid,' said Khalifa eventually. 'Everybody I've spoken to about this case has been afraid. There's something going on, sir.'

'There most certainly is,' snapped Hassani. 'And it's in your head.'

'If I could just go up to Cairo for a day, have a poke around . . .'

'It's a wild-goose chase, man. This Nayder or whatever he was called was cut up by someone he owed money to . . . You did say he owed money, didn't you?'

'Yes, sir, but . . .'

'Or by someone he'd insulted . . . You did say he insulted people, didn't you?'

Khalifa shrugged.

'And Iqbar was cut up by a thief, if he was cut up at all, which knowing the reporting in *al-Ahram* he probably wasn't. They weren't cut up by the same person. You're reading too much into it.'

'I've just got this feeling . . .'

'Feelings have nothing to do with police work. Facts do. Clear thinking does. Hard evidence does. Feelings just confuse the issue.'

'Like on the al-Hamdi case?'

Hassani glared at him furiously.

The case of Ommaya al-Hamdi had shocked them all, even Hassani. Her body had been found at the bottom of a well, naked, strangled. She was only fourteen.

A boy from her village, a retard, had subsequently been arrested and, under intense questioning, confessed to the crime. For some reason, however, Khalifa had been uneasy, sensing things weren't quite as straightforward as they seemed. His doubts had incurred the wrath of Hassani and jibes from his colleagues, but he'd ignored them and pursued the investigation independently, eventually proving that the culprit was actually the girl's cousin, who had been infatuated with her. No recognition had ever been given to his role in solving the crime, but since then his hunches had been treated with a little more respect.

'OK,' said the chief inspector, 'what is it precisely you're asking for?'

'I want to go up to Cairo,' said Khalifa, sensing his boss was weakening. 'Find out about the Iqbar murder, see if that case can throw any light on the one we're dealing with here. I only need a day.'

Hassani swivelled in his chair so that he was facing the window. His fingers drummed on the desk. There was a knock on the door.

'Wait!' he shouted.

'I'll take the night train,' said Khalifa. 'Save the expense of flying.'

'Damn right you'll take the night train!' snapped Hassani. 'We're not a bloody tour company!' He swivelled back to face the detective. 'One day. That's all you get. Just one day. Go tonight. Come back tomorrow night. And I want a report on my desk first thing the next morning. Clear?'

'Yes, sir.'

Khalifa stood and made for the door.

'I hope you're right about this,' growled Hassani. 'For your sake. Because if you're not I'm going to think even less of you than I already do.'

'And if I am right, sir?'

'Get out!'

21

CAIRO

'Where you go?' asked the taxi driver.

'Anywhere,' said Daniel. 'The middle of town.'

'Midan Tahrir?'

'Yes, that's fine.'

They drove for a couple of minutes, then Daniel leaned forward. 'No, not Midan Tahrir. Zamalek. Take us to Zamalek. Sharia Abdul Azim.'

The driver nodded and Daniel sat back.

'Where are we going?' asked Tara.

'To see my fixer, Mohammed Samali. Probably the least trustworthy person in Cairo, but at the moment I can't think of anyone else who can help us.'

They sat back and stared out of the windows, the taxi slowly shunting its way through the traffic. After a couple of minutes Daniel reached out and took Tara's hand. Neither of them spoke or looked at the other.

Zamalek was a plush, leafy district of villas and high-rise apartment buildings. They pulled up in front of an exclusive-looking modern block, with well-tended gardens and a glass-fronted foyer and, having paid off the driver, climbed the steps to the main door. There was a polished metal intercom panel in the wall. Daniel pressed buzzer 43.

They waited thirty seconds and then he pressed again. There was another long wait, then a voice echoed out of the panel.

'Yes?'

'Samali? It's Daniel Lacage.'

'Daniel, what a wonderful surprise.' The voice was soft, musical, slightly lisping. 'You catch me at a rather inopportune moment. Would it be possible for you to—'

'It's urgent. I need to talk. Now.'

There was a pause.

'Wait downstairs for five minutes and then come up. Fourth floor, as you know.'

There was a click and they pushed the door open, stepping into a carpeted foyer, the air around them suddenly cool and air-conditioned. As requested, they waited for five minutes and then took the lift up to the fourth floor. Samali's flat was midway along a carpeted corridor with prints of ancient monuments hung along the walls. They knocked, waited and then heard the soft pad of approaching feet.

'Be careful what you say to him,' whispered Daniel. 'And keep the box in your bag. It's best he doesn't see it. Samali would sell his own mother if he thought it would turn in a profit. The fewer details he knows the better.'

There was the rattle of various locks being undone and the door swung open.

'My apologies for keeping you waiting. Please, do come in.'

Samali was tall and very thin, completely bald, with a faint sheen to his skin as though he was wearing moisturizer. He turned and led them down a hallway into a large living room, all very minimalist, with pale wood floors, white walls and a scattering of leather and metal furniture. Through a door to the side Tara glimpsed two young boys, one wearing a bathrobe. The door swung to almost immediately, however, and they were gone.

'I don't think we've met,' smiled Samali.

'Tara Mullray,' said Daniel. 'An old friend.'

'How enchanting.'

He stepped forward and took her hand, raising it and kissing the backs of her fingers, his nostrils dilating momentarily, as if he was smelling her skin. He lowered the hand again and waved them both towards a large leather sofa.

'A drink?'

'Whisky,' said Daniel.

'Miss Mullray?'

'The same. Thank you.'

He turned to a drinks cabinet and, removing a decanter, poured out two glasses, clinking an ice cube into each. He handed the drinks over and sat down opposite them, picking up a jade cigarette holder and screwing a cigarette into it.

'You're not having one?' asked Daniel.

'I prefer to watch,' said Samali, smiling.

He lit the cigarette and drew deeply on the mouthpiece. His eyebrows were very thin and very dark and, Tara realized suddenly, highlighted with liner.

'So,' he said, 'to what do I owe the pleasure?'

Daniel glanced up at him and then away towards the window, fingers drumming nervously on the edge of the sofa.

'We need help.'

'But of course you do,' said Samali, still smiling.

He turned towards Tara, crossing his legs and smoothing the material of his slacks with his hand.

'I am what is rather crudely termed a fixer, Miss Mullray. A much-maligned species, until someone actually needs something. Then, suddenly, we become indispensable. It is a rewarding vocation' – he waved his hand, indicating the expensive flat – 'although a dispiriting one. A man in my profession soon learns he is never the object of a purely social visit. There is always, what is the word, an agenda.'

He said it jokingly, although in his eyes there was something cold, as if he understood their politeness was just an act and wanted them to know that his was too. He leaned his head back and drew slowly on the cigarette holder, gazing up at the ceiling.

'So,' he said. 'What do you need, Daniel? Problems with your dig permit, is it? Or perhaps Steven Spielberg has expressed an interest in filming your work and you require help with the necessary permissions.'

He chuckled at his joke. Daniel downed his whisky and laid aside the glass.

'I need information,' he said tersely.

'Information!' cooed Samali. 'But how very flattering. That a scholar of your repute should come to me for advice. I really can't think what it might be that I could know and you don't, but please, ask away.'

Daniel hunched forward, the leather upholstery creaking beneath him. Again his eyes flicked up to Samali and again they swerved away towards the window, unwilling to meet the older man's gaze.

'I want to know about Sayf al-Tha'r.'

The briefest hint of a pause.

'Anything in particular?' asked Samali. 'Or just a general résumé?'

'I want to know about Sayf al-Tha'r and antiquities.'

Again, a whisper of a hesitation on Samali's part.

'Might I ask why?'

'It's best I don't go into details. For your safety as much as ours. There's a particular antiquity we believe he wants and we need to know why.'

'How very cryptic of you, Daniel.'

He lifted his left hand and began examining the nails. Tara thought she could hear whispering from the room to the side.

'This mysterious antiquity,' said Samali. 'Would I be right in thinking it is in that box in Miss Mullray's bag?'

Neither Tara nor Daniel spoke.

'I take it from your silence that it is.' He flicked his eyes at Tara. 'Might I see it, please?'

She stared at him, then across at Daniel, then down at the knapsack in her lap. There was a silence and then the throaty rasp of Samali's chuckle.

'No doubt Dr Lacage has told you not to show it to me. Another lesson one soon learns in my line of business. That one is very rarely trusted.'

He gazed at them for a moment and then waved his hand.

'It is of no consequence. Keep it to yourselves if you prefer it that way. It simply makes it more difficult for me to answer your question. Like trying to play a hand of poker when one is prevented from seeing all of one's cards.'

He resumed his examination of his nails.

'So you want to know about the Sword of Vengeance and antiquities, do you?' he mused. 'A most perilous line of enquiry. And what, I wonder . . .'

'Is in it for you?' Daniel stood, picked up his glass and crossed to the drinks cabinet, pouring himself another whisky. His hand seemed to be trembling. 'Nothing. I'm asking you to help us out of the goodness of your heart.'

Samali's eyebrows arched upwards. 'Well, well. First I am cast as the fount of all wisdom, then the great philanthropist. By the time we are finished I shall barely know who I am.'

'I can give you a few hundred dollars. Three, maybe four. If that's what it takes.'

Samali tutted. 'Please, Daniel. I might be a self-made man, but at least I've done my self-making in style. I am not a common street whore taking cash handouts in return for services rendered. You can keep your four hundred dollars.'

He took another slow puff on the cigarette holder, smiling faintly, as though he was enjoying Daniel's discomfiture.

'Although, of course, nothing in life is wholly free. Especially information about someone as dangerous as Sayf al-Tha'r. So let's just leave it that you owe me. And one day I might call the debt in. Agreed?'

They stared at each other for a moment and then Daniel downed his drink. 'Agreed.' He poured himself another large shot and returned to the sofa.

Samali's cigarette had burnt down to the butt and, leaning over, he tamped it into a metal ashtray.

'Of course, I have no links with Sayf al-Tha'r's organization. Let that be understood from the start. Anything I tell you is purely hearsay.'

'Go on.'

'Well,' he said, smoothing down his slacks again, 'it would appear that for some years now the dear man has been funding his operations through covert trading of antiquities.' He began screwing another cigarette into the holder. 'By all accounts he knows more about Egyptian artefacts than most experts, so it's an obvious source of income for him. The only source, given that his activities have alienated just about every other funda-mentalist group in Egypt. Even al-Jihad won't touch him.'

He came to his feet and wandered slowly over to the window, afternoon sunlight reflecting off his scalp so that it looked as if his head was made of polished brass.

'He runs a veritable little cottage industry, by all accounts. Artefacts are stolen from digs, looted from newly discovered tombs, removed from museum stores. They're sent south to the Sudan and then shipped out to middlemen in Europe and the Far East, who sell them on to private buyers. The proceeds are then filtered back into the region and used . . . well, I think we all know what they're used for.'

'There's a big man,' said Tara, 'with a birthmark on his face.'

Samali remained at the window, staring down at the street.

'Dravitt,' he said. 'Drakich, Dravich, something like that. German, I believe. Sayf al-Tha'r's eyes and ears here in Egypt.

I'm afraid I can't tell you much about him. Except that the rumours are not pleasant.'

He turned back to them.

'I don't know what's in that box of yours, Daniel, but if, as you say, Sayf al-Tha'r wants it, then I can assure you that sooner or later Sayf al-Tha'r will get it. Antiquities are his lifeblood. When it comes to acquiring them he is utterly ruthless.'

'But it's not even valuable,' said Daniel. 'Why should he be so desperate to get his hands on this one thing?'

Samali shrugged. 'How can I tell you if you will not show it to me? I can only repeat what I have already said: that if Sayf al-Tha'r wants it, Sayf al-Tha'r will get it.'

He padded slowly back to his chair and, retrieving his lighter, lit his cigarette.

'Perhaps I will have a drink after all,' he said. 'The afternoon appears to have grown uncommonly hot.'

He crossed to the cabinet and poured himself a glass of an opalescent yellow liqueur.

'What about the British embassy?' asked Tara.

There was a momentary pause and then a loud clank as Samali dropped an ice cube into his glass.

'The British embassy?'

His voice sounded innocent, although its register seemed to have risen ever so slightly, as if someone was squeezing his neck.

'It seems they want this thing too,' said Daniel. 'Or at least the cultural attaché does.'

Another clank. Samali laid aside the tongs and, lifting his drink, took a long sip, his back still to them.

'What on earth makes you think the British cultural attaché wants your antiquity?'

'Because he's been lying to us,' said Tara.

Samali took another sip and wandered back towards the window. For a long while he was silent.

'I shall give you a piece of advice', he said eventually, 'and I shall give it to you for free. Get rid of this antiquity, whatever it is, and leave Egypt. Do it quickly, do it today. Because if you do not you will die.'

A chill ran up Tara's spine. Involuntarily she reached out and took Daniel's hand. His palm was damp with sweat.

'What do you know, Samali?' he asked.

'Very little. And I'm happy to keep it that way.'

'But you know something?'

'Please,' said Tara.

Again a long silence. Samali finished his drink and stood with the empty glass hanging at his side, puffing on his cigarette holder. The windows appeared to be heavily glazed, for no sound came up from the street below. The whispering from the side room had stopped.

'There is . . . how shall I put it . . . a conduit,' he said eventually, slowly. 'For stolen antiquities. Via the British embassy. And the American one, too, if what I've heard is correct, which it may well not be. These are simply rumours, you understand. Rumours of rumours. Chinese whispers. Objects are removed from museums, it is said, taken out of the country under diplomatic cover, sold on abroad, profits paid into secret bank accounts, all very cloak and dagger.'

'Jesus Christ,' muttered Daniel.

'Oh that's only the half of it,' said Samali, turning. 'The embassies organize the export of the objects. It is, however, our own security service that arranges their theft in the first place. Or at least an element within the security service. This runs high and deep, Daniel. These people have contacts everywhere. They know everything. For all we know they could be watching and listening to us this very minute.'

'We have to go to the police,' said Tara. 'We have to.'

Samali laughed bitterly. 'You are not listening to what I'm saying, Miss Mullray. These people are the police. They're the establishment. I cannot overemphasize how much power they wield. They manipulate you without you even knowing you are being manipulated. Compared to them Sayf al-Tha'r is your closest ally.'

'But why?' said Daniel. 'Why for this one piece?'

Samali shrugged. 'That, as I have already told you, I can't answer. What I can see is that on the one side there are the embassies and the secret service . . .' He raised the hand with the glass in it. 'And on the other side Sayf al-Tha'r . . .' He raised his other hand. 'And in between, about to be crushed into a million pieces . . .'

'Us,' whispered Tara, stomach churning.

Samali smiled.

'What can we do?' she said. 'Where can we go?'

The Egyptian didn't reply. Daniel was sitting forward, staring at the floor. The box in Tara's lap suddenly felt as if it weighed a ton. It was actually hurting her legs. The air seemed to hum with silence.

'We need transport,' said Daniel eventually. 'A car, a motorbike, anything. Can you arrange that?'

Samali looked down at them for a moment and then, his eyes softening slightly, crossed the room, picked up a phone, dialled and spoke rapidly into the receiver. There was a faint murmur at the other end and then he hung up.

'There will be a motorbike downstairs in five minutes,' he said. 'The keys will be in the ignition.'

'How much?' asked Daniel.

'Oh, no charge.' Samali grinned. 'Even I would not be so mercenary as to take money from a condemned man.'

It was warm in the room, but Tara found that she was shivering uncontrollably.

The motorbike – a battered orange Jawa 350 – was waiting for them just as Samali had said. There was no sign of the person who had delivered it. Daniel slammed down the kickstart, revving the engine into life. Tara swung up behind him, the knapsack on her back, the box in the knapsack.

'So where to?' she asked.

'The one place where we might find out why this artefact is so important,' he said.

'Which is?'

'Where it came from. Luxor.'

He clicked the bike into gear, yanked back the accelerator and they roared away down the street, Tara's hair streaming behind her.

From his apartment window Samali watched as they disappeared round the corner and then crossed to the telephone, lifted the receiver and dialled.

'They've just left,' he said. 'And they have the piece with them.'

NORTHERN SUDAN

The helicopter flew directly over the camp and descended onto a flat patch of ground a hundred metres beyond it. The downdraught from its blades threw up sheets of sand and gravel, which whipped across the tents like hail. The boy who had come out to meet it turned his back and covered his face with his arm. Only when the helicopter was down and the rotors almost stationary did he turn again, run across to it and heave open its side door.

A man in a crumpled suit jumped out, a briefcase in one hand and a cigar in the other. He towered over the boy.

'He is waiting, *ya Doktora*.'

The two of them started towards the camp, the boy keeping his eyes firmly on the ground, away from the man's face, which frightened him, the way its left side was covered with that terrible purple stain. The man strode beside him, swinging his case, oblivious.

They skirted the side of the camp until they reached a tent set slightly apart from the others. The boy pulled back the flap and stepped in. The man threw away his cigar and followed, stooping as he entered.

'Welcome, Dr Dravic,' came a voice. 'Will you take tea?'

Sayf al-Tha'r was sitting cross-legged in the centre of the tent, his face half lost in the gloom. There was a book beside him, although it was too dark to see what it was.

'I'd prefer beer,' answered Dravic irritably.

'As you know, we do not drink alcohol here. Mehmet, bring Dr Dravic some tea.'

'Yes, Master.' The boy left.

'Please, sit.'

The giant lumbered forward and sank onto the carpeted floor. He was clearly not used to sitting on the ground for he shifted this way and that, trying to find a comfortable position. Eventually he settled in a semi-kneeling posture, one leg curled under him, the other drawn up in front of his chest.

'I don't know why you can't get some chairs,' he muttered.

'We prefer to live simply.'

'Well, I don't.'

'Then I suggest that next time you bring your own chair.'

Sayf al-Tha'r's voice was not angry, just firm. Dravic mumbled something, but didn't pursue the matter. He seemed subdued in the man's presence, unnerved by him. He pulled a handkerchief from his pocket and rubbed it over his brow, which in the two minutes since he had stepped from the helicopter had become sodden with sweat.

'So?' said Sayf al-Tha'r. 'Do we have it yet?' In contrast to Dravic he sat very still, hands resting on his knees.

'No,' mumbled the German. 'It was at Saqqara, like I said it would be, but the girl got away with it before we could stop her. Killed two of our men.'

'The girl did?'

'Her and some guy she was with. An archaeologist. Daniel Lacage.'

'Lacage?' The man's green eyes glowed in the darkness. 'How . . . interesting. His book on Late Period tomb iconography is one of my favourites.'

Dravic shrugged. 'Never read it.'

'You should. It's an excellent piece of scholarship.'

A spasm of annoyance passed across the giant's face. Not for the first time he wondered why the man bothered to employ him when his own knowledge of ancient Egypt was clearly so extensive. It was as though he was poking fun at him. Emphasizing the fact that he, an Egyptian, knew so much more about his country's past than any foreigner ever could. Black cunt. If it had been left to people like him, Egypt wouldn't have a past. It would all have been dug up long ago and sold off to the highest bidder. His fist clenched and unclenched, knuckles whitening.

Mehmet arrived with the tea, handing one glass to Dravic and placing the other on the ground beside his master.

'Thank you, Mehmet. Wait outside.'

The boy left again, keeping his eyes away from Dravic.

'Why is this Lacage helping the girl?' asked Sayf al-Tha'r.

'God knows. She stayed with him last night, they went to Saqqara this afternoon, got the piece and disappeared again.'

'And now?'

'Now I don't know.'

'Have they gone to the police?'

'No. We'd have heard if they did.'

'The embassy?'

'No. We've been watching it all day.'

'Then where?'

'To the moon, for all I know. Like I told you, they've dis-appeared. They could be anywhere.'

'Are they going after the prize themselves? Is that it?'

'Look, I don't fucking know, all right! I'm not a mind-reader.'

There was a faint tightening around Sayf al-Tha'r's mouth, the first hint of displeasure.

'It is a shame you were not more careful at Saqqara, Dr Dravic. Had you been less forceful with the old man we might have saved ourselves a lot of trouble.'

'I told you, it wasn't my fault,' said the giant. 'I didn't lay a finger on the old bastard. We waited for him in the dig house, but before we had a chance to start asking questions he had a fucking heart attack. Took one look at the trowel and dropped dead right in front of me. I didn't touch him.'

'Then it's a shame you didn't search the dig house more thoroughly.'

'The piece wasn't in the dig house. That's why we couldn't find it. He'd hidden it outside, in the wall of one of the *mastaba*s.'

The man nodded slowly and, without taking his eyes off Dravic, reached for his tea. He raised the glass to his mouth and tipped it slightly, moistening his lips with the liquid, no more. Dravic lifted his own glass and slurped loudly. Sweat poured down his face. He was finding it hard to breathe, such was the heat.

'We'll find them,' he said. 'It's just a matter of time.'

'Time is something we don't have, Dr Dravic, as you well know. We can't keep this quiet for ever. We need the piece now.'

'We're watching the stations, the bus terminals, the airport. We've got men everywhere. We'll find them.'

'I hope so.'

'We'll find them!'

Again Dravic seemed to be struggling to contain his temper. Then, as if to deflect his own fury, he broke into a low chuckle, wiping his handkerchief over his brow.

'Christ, if this thing comes off, we'll all be millionaires!'

The comment seemed to interest Sayf al-Tha'r. He leaned forward slightly.

'Does that excite you, Dr Dravic? The idea of being a millionaire?'

'Are you joking? Of course it does. Doesn't it excite you?'

'What? To have a million pounds to spend on myself? To waste on useless luxuries while in the slums children go hungry?' The man smiled. 'No, it doesn't excite me. It doesn't excite me at all. It bores me.'

He lifted his tea glass and touched it to his lips again.

'To have a million pounds to spread the word of God, on the other hand.' His smile widened. 'A million pounds to cast down the oppressors and restore the law of Sharia. To cleanse the earth and do the will of God. Yes, that does excite me, Dr Dravic. It excites me very much.'

'Fuck God!' Dravic laughed, wiping the sweat from the back of his neck. 'I'll take the money any day!'

Suddenly Sayf al-Tha'r's smile was gone. He glared at Dravic, his hand clasped so tightly around his tea glass it seemed it must shatter at any moment.

'Be careful what you say,' he hissed. 'Be very careful. There are some insults one should not utter.'

His eyes were boring into Dravic, green, unblinking, as though he had no eyelids. The giant mopped at his brow again, unable to meet the man's stare.

'OK, OK,' he muttered, 'you have your priorities, I have mine. Let's just leave it at that.'

'Yes,' nodded Sayf al-Tha'r, his voice hard. 'Let's just leave it at that.'

They sat in silence for a moment and then the man called the boy in from outside.

'Mehmet, escort Dr Dravic back to his helicopter.'

Dravic stood, slowly, wincing at the stiffness in his legs, and moved towards the entrance, relieved to be getting out.

'I'll call as soon as I have news,' he said. 'I'll be in Luxor. If they turn up anywhere it'll be there.'

'Let us hope so. Everything here is ready. We can be across the border and set up within a matter of hours. All we need is to know where.'

The giant nodded and was about to step out of the tent when Sayf al-Tha'r's voice pulled him back.

'Find the missing piece, Dr Dravic. Opportunities such as this only come once in a lifetime. We must seize it while we have the chance. Find the piece.'

Dravic grunted and left. Two minutes later there was a whine and a roar as the helicopter took off and swung away across the desert.

Alone, Sayf al-Tha'r stood and went to a large chest at the back of the tent. Removing a key from his robe he undid the padlock on the front and heaved open the lid.

It shamed him to have to associate with *Kufr* like Dravic, but he had no choice. To cross the border himself was too risky. They were watching for him. Waiting. Always waiting. Soon, perhaps, when the fragment was found, but not yet. If he could have used someone else, anyone else, he would have, but Dravic alone possessed the qualifications and, more importantly, the lack of scruples. And so he relied on him. The filth of the earth, the dregs of humanity. The ways of Allah were indeed mysterious.

He bent down and, from the inky interior of the chest, as though from a pool, removed a small necklace. He raised it into a thin shaft of light and the object glittered. Gold. He shook it and the delicate tubes of which it was made tinkled musically. He replaced it and drew out other objects. A pair of sandals. A dagger. A finely worked breastplate, the leather straps still in place. A silver amulet in the shape of a cat. Each one he held up into the light, gazing at it, rapt.

There was no doubting they were genuine. Initially, when Dravic had first brought him news of the tomb, he had refused to believe it. It was too incredible. Too much to hope for. And Dravic had made mistakes before. His judgement in these matters was not always to be trusted.

Only when he had held the objects in his own hands as he was doing now, and looked at them with his own eyes, had he known for certain that they were real. That the tomb was what Dravic had claimed it was. That Allah had indeed smiled upon them. Smiled on them with the very fullness of his favour.

He returned the artefacts to their trunk and closed the lid, slipping the padlock back into its clasp and clicking it shut. In the distance he could still hear the thudding of the helicopter's rotors.

The tomb was just the start of it. And would be the end of it, too, if they didn't find the missing piece. Everything hinged on that. That was the fulcrum upon which their destiny balanced. The missing piece.

He left the tent, eyes narrowing slightly against the sun's glare but otherwise untroubled by the roasting heat. Skirting the camp, he made his way to the top of a low dune and gazed eastwards across the rolling hills of sand, a solitary black speck in the all-enveloping void. Somewhere out there, he thought. Somewhere in that immeasurable sea of burning emptiness. Somewhere. He closed his eyes and tried to imagine what it must have been like.

22

CAIRO

The ride up from Luxor took ten hours. The train was packed and Khalifa spent the journey wedged into the corner of a draughty carriage between a woman carrying a basket full of pigeons and an elderly man with a hacking cough. Despite the cramped surroundings and the asthmatic jolting of the train, he slept soundly the whole way, his jacket rolled up behind his head as a pillow, his feet resting on a large sack of dried dates. When he woke, a particularly violent lurch banging his head against the bars of the compartment window, he felt refreshed and well rested. He whispered his morning prayers, lit a cigarette and set about devouring the bread and goat's cheese Zenab had given him for the journey, sharing it with the elderly man beside him.

They hit the outskirts of Cairo just before six a.m. He wasn't due to meet Mohammed Tauba, the detective in charge of the Iqbar case, until nine, leaving him with almost three hours to kill. Rather than stay with the train all the way to the centre of Cairo, he instead got off at Giza and, coming out of the station, took a service taxi up to Nazlat al-Sammam, his old village.

It was only the third time he'd been back since he'd left thirteen years ago. As a child he had imagined he would live in the village for ever. After Ali's death, however, and that of his mother, which had come not long afterwards, the place no longer felt the same. Every street reminded him of how badly things had gone wrong, every house, every tree. He could not be there without feeling an overwhelming sense of emptiness and loss. And so he'd accepted the Luxor posting and moved away. His only other trips back had, appropriately, been for funerals.

He left the minibus at a busy crossroads and, glancing up at the pyramid of Cheops, half hidden behind a curtain of dawn mist, set off along a main road into the village, excited and nervous.

The place had changed since his childhood days. Then it had been a proper village – a smallish cluster of shops and houses scattered along the base of the Giza plateau, beneath the silent gaze of the Sphinx.

Now, with the growth of the tourist industry and the inexorable march of the city's western outskirts, it had lost much of its identity. The streets were lined with souvenir shops, and the old mud-brick dwellings had given way to an explosion of characterless concrete tenements. He wandered around for a while, gazing at the buildings, some familiar, most new, uncertain why he had come, just knowing that somehow he needed to see the old place again. He walked past his former home, or rather the site where his former home had once stood – it had long since been demolished and replaced with a four-storey concrete hotel – and looked in at the camel yard where he and his brother had worked as children. Every now and then he passed a familiar face and greetings were exchanged. The greetings were polite rather than warm, distant, cold even in some cases. Hardly surprising, given what had happened to Ali.

He stayed for perhaps an hour, feeling increasingly melancholy, wondering if he had made a mistake in coming, and then, glancing swiftly at his watch, walked out past the edge of the village onto the sands of the plateau. The sun was rising now and the mists were dissolving, the outline of the pyramids growing sharper by the minute. He stood looking at them for a while, then angled away to the left towards a walled cemetery clustered about the foot of a steep limestone scarp opposite the Sphinx.

The lower part of the cemetery was on flat ground, its ornate graves shaded by pine and eucalyptus trees. Closer to the scarp the land sloped upwards and the graves became simpler, drabber, with no greenery to shade them from the elements, like poor suburbs on the margins of a wealthy city.

It was to this part of the cemetery that Khalifa now climbed, weaving his way through a traffic jam of flat, rectangular tombs, until eventually he stopped near the top end of the enclosure, in front of a pair of simple graves, little more than crude slabs of rendered breeze-block, unadorned save for a rock cemented onto the top of each, and a couple of lines of fading Koranic verse painted onto their front end. The graves of his parents.

He gazed down at them and then, kneeling, kissed them, first his mother's, then his father's, whispering a prayer over each. He lingered a moment, head bowed, then stood again and, slowly, as if his legs had grown suddenly heavy, trudged further up the slope to the very top corner of the cemetery, where the enclosure wall was broken and tumbled and the ground was scattered with litter and goat droppings.

There was only one grave in this corner, pushed right up against the wall as though shunned by the other tombs. It was even simpler than his parents' burials, just an unadorned rectangle of cheap cement, with no inscriptions or Koranic verses. He remembered how he had had to plead with the cemetery authorities to allow it to be sited here; how he had made it with his own hands, late at night, when no-one from the village would see; how he had wept as he had worked. God, how he had wept.

He knelt down beside the grave and, bending forward, laid his cheek against its cool surface.

191

'Oh Ali,' he whispered. 'My brother, my life. Why? Why? Please, just tell me why?'

Mohammed Abd el-Tauba, the detective in charge of the Iqbar case, looked like a mummy. His skin was dry and parchment-like, his cheeks sunken, his mouth locked in a permanent rictus that was half smile, half grimace.

He worked out of a grimy office on Sharia Bur Sa'id, where he had a desk in the corner of a smoky room shared with four other officers. Khalifa arrived shortly after nine a.m. and, having exchanged pleasantries and drunk a glass of tea, the two of them got straight down to business.

'So you're interested in old man Iqbar,' said Tauba, grinding one cigarette into an already overflowing ashtray while puffing another into life.

'I think there might be a connection with a case we've got down in Luxor,' said Khalifa.

Tauba blew twin jets of smoke out of his nostrils. 'It's a bad business. We get our share of murders around here, but nothing like this. They butchered the poor old bastard.' He reached into a drawer and pulled out a file, tossing it across the desk. 'The pathologist's report. Multiple lacerations on the face, arms and torso. Burns too.'

'Cigar burns?'

Tauba grunted an affirmative.

'And the cuts?' asked Khalifa. 'What caused the cuts?'

'Strange,' said Tauba. 'The pathologist couldn't be sure. A metal object of some sort, but too clumsy for a knife. He thinks it might have been a trowel.'

'A trowel?'

'You know, like a builder's trowel. One of those ones they use for grouting, cementing in cracks, that sort of thing. It's there in the report.'

Khalifa opened the file and worked his way through it. The pictures of the old man slumped on the floor of his shop, and subsequently of his naked corpse laid out like a fish on the mortuary slab, made him grimace. The pathologist's comments were almost verbatim those used by Anwar in his report on Abu Nayar.

'Nature of instrument used to inflict aforesaid injuries uncertain,' it concluded in the abbreviated, dehumanizing language of all such documents. 'Pathology of lacerations inconsistent with knife-inflicted injury. Shape and angle of wound suggest culprit possibly trowel of some description, as used by builders, archaeologists, etc. although no conclusive evidence either way.'

Khalifa dwelt on the word 'archaeologists' for a moment before looking up at Tauba. 'Who found the body?'

'Shopkeeper next door. Got suspicious when Iqbar didn't show up for work. Tried the door, found it was open, went in and there he was, like in the photos.'

'And this was?'

'Saturday morning. God knows how the papers got hold of it so quickly. I reckon they commit half the crimes in Cairo themselves, just so they'll have something to write about.'

Khalifa smiled. 'Did Iqbar deal in antiquities?'

'Probably. They all do in his business, don't they. We haven't got a file on him, but that doesn't mean anything. We've only got the resources to deal with the big guys. When it's just a few objects we tend to let it go, otherwise we'd be filling every prison from here to Abu Simbel.'

Khalifa flicked through the report again, coming back to the word 'archaeologist'.

'You haven't heard of anything unusual coming onto the antiquities market lately, have you?'

'Unusual?'

'You know, valuable. Worth killing for.'

Tauba shrugged. 'Not that I can think of. There was some Greek guy exporting artefacts disguised as reproductions, but that was a couple of months ago. I can't think of anything

193

more recent. Unless you count that business over at Saqqara.'

Khalifa glanced up. 'Saqqara?'

'Yesterday afternoon. An English couple got involved in a gunfight and then drove away in a stolen taxi. Apparently the girl had taken something out of one of the dig houses.'

He called across the room to one of his colleagues, an over-weight man with heavy sweat stains beneath his armpits.

'Hey, Helmi! You've got a friend in the Giza force. What was the latest with that shooting at Saqqara?'

'Not much,' grunted Helmi, biting into a large cake. 'No-one seems to know what was going on, except that the girl had nicked something. A box of some sort.'

'Any idea who she was?' asked Khalifa.

Helmi pushed more cake into his mouth, treacle oozing around his lips and chin. 'The daughter of some archaeologist, apparently. One of the inspectors at the *teftish* recognized her. Murray or something.'

Murray, thought Khalifa. Murray. 'Not Mullray? Michael Mullray?'

'That's the one. Died a couple of days ago. Heart attack. The daughter found his body.'

Khalifa pulled his notebook from his pocket and a pen.

'So let me get this clear: the girl finds her father's body two days ago, then comes back yesterday and takes this thing from the dig house . . .'

'Their taxi driver thought they'd got it from one of the tombs,' said Helmi. 'He said they went out into the desert, got this thing like a pizza carton . . .'

'Trust you to get food into it, Helmi!' shouted one of his colleagues.

'Lick my arse, Aziz . . . got this box thing, came back, some-one started shooting at them. But then the people in the village below said it was the bloke the girl was with who was doing the shooting. Like I said, no-one seems to know what the hell was going on.'

'Do we know who this man was?'

Helmi shook his head. Khalifa sat silent for a moment, thinking.

'Any chance I could talk to your friend at Giza?'

'Sure, but he won't tell you anything I haven't. And anyway, he's been moved off the case now. Al-Mukhabarat took over last night.'

'Secret service?' Khalifa sounded surprised.

'Apparently they want to keep the whole thing hush-hush. Bad publicity for Egypt and all that, what with a tourist being involved. It wasn't even on the news.'

Khalifa doodled in his notebook.

'Anyone else I could talk to?' he asked after a pause.

Helmi was brushing crumbs from his desk. 'I think there was some guy at the British embassy who knew the girl. Orts or something. Junior attaché. That's about all I know.'

Khalifa scribbled the name on his pad and put it away.

'You think there's a connection?' asked Tauba.

'No idea,' said Khalifa. 'I can't see any obvious link. It just feels . . .' He paused, and then, not bothering to finish the sentence, held up the Iqbar report. 'Can I get a copy of this?'

'Sure.'

'And I'd like to see the old man's shop. Is that possible?'

'No problem.'

Tauba rooted through his desk and produced an envelope. 'Address and keys. It's up in Khan al-Khalili. We've done all the fingerprints and forensics.'

He threw it over to Khalifa, who caught it and stood.

'I should be back in a couple of hours.'

'Take your time. I'll be here till late. I'm always bloody here till late.'

They shook hands and Khalifa started across the office. He had almost reached the door when Tauba called after him.

'Hey, I forgot to ask. Khalifa . . . your family's not from Nazlat al-Sammam, are they?'

A momentary pause.

'Port Said,' said Khalifa and disappeared into the corridor.

LUXOR

The biggest regret of Dravic's life, the only regret, in fact, was that he hadn't killed the girl. After fucking her he should have cut her throat and dumped her in a ditch somewhere. But he hadn't. He'd let her crawl away. And of course she'd crawled straight to the police and told them what he'd done and bang! That had been the end of his career.

OK, so he'd got a good lawyer and they'd persuaded the jury it was consensual. Mud sticks, however. The world of Egyptology is a small one and before long everyone knew that Casper Dravic had raped one of his dig volunteers and, worse, got away with it. The teaching posts had dried up, the concessions been refused, the publishers stopped answering his calls. Thirty years old and his career was over. Why oh why hadn't he just killed her? It wasn't a mistake he'd ever make again. That he had ever made again.

He shook his head to bring himself back to the present and waved his hand at the café owner, indicating he wanted more coffee. Beside him a young couple, blond, Scandinavian, were hunched over a guidebook marking things in it with a pen. The girl was attractive, with full lips and long, pale legs. He allowed himself to dwell for a moment on the thought of her screaming in pained ecstasy as he drove himself hard into her tight pink anus, then forced his mind back to the business of the tomb.

They'd spent most of the previous night removing the last of the artefacts – the wooden funeral stelae, the basalt Anubis, the alabaster canopic jars. All that remained now was the coffin itself, with its brightly painted panels and clumsy hieroglyphic text. They'd take that out tonight. Everything else had been crated up and sent south to the Sudan, from where it would be moved on to the markets of Europe and the Far East.

It was a good haul, one of the best he'd seen. Late Period, Twenty-seventh Dynasty, a hundred separate objects, crudish workmanship but all in good condition – should raise a few hundred thousand or more. Which on 10 per cent commission meant a nice fat pay-out for him. Compared to the main prize, however, it was small fry. Compared to the main prize every object he'd ever smuggled was small fry. This was the big one. The break he'd been waiting for. The end to all his troubles.

Only if he found that missing piece, though. That was the key. Lacage and the Mullray woman had his future in their hands. Where were they? What were they planning? How much did they know?

His initial worry had been that they would take the piece straight to the authorities. The fact that they hadn't was a source both of relief and of concern to him. Relief because it meant there was still a chance of getting it back. Concern because it suggested the two of them might be going after the haul themselves.

That was his real fear now. Time was running out, as Sayf al-Tha'r had said. They couldn't wait for ever. The longer the two of them had the piece the more chance there was of the prize slipping from his grasp. All his hopes, all his dreams . . .

'What are you doing?' he muttered to himself. 'What the fuck are you doing?'

There was a tut of disapproval from nearby. Looking up he saw the Scandinavian couple staring at him.

'Yes?' he growled. 'Something wrong?'

They paid up hurriedly and left.

His coffee arrived and he slurped at it, gazing up at the Theban Hills in front of him, brown and massive against the pale-blue cushion of the sky.

What he couldn't figure out was how, if Lacage and the girl were going for the prize themselves, they could do it with just that one fragment. Sure, Lacage was supposed to be one of the best Egyptologists around. Maybe he could put it all together from a single piece. Dravic doubted it, however. They'd need more. And to get more they'd have to come to Luxor. That was why he was waiting here rather than in Cairo. This was where they'd surface. He was sure of it. It was just a matter of time. Which was, of course, something he didn't have much of.

He finished his coffee and, reaching into his jacket, pulled out a cigar, long and fat. He rolled it between finger and thumb, enjoying the crackling sound of the dried tobacco leaf, and then put it in his mouth and puffed it into life. The warm caress of the smoke on his palette calmed him and improved his mood. He stretched out his legs and began thinking about the Mullray woman, his mind wandering over her body – the slim hips, the firm breasts, the tight backside. The things he'd like to do to her. The things he *would* do. The thought of it made him purr with pleasure. Something she certainly wouldn't be doing once he got started on her. He looked down at the ungainly bulge in his trousers and burst out laughing.

23

CAIRO

Iqbar's shop was in a narrow street off Sharia al-Muizz, the jostling thoroughfare which runs like an artery through the heart of Cairo's Islamic quarter. It took Khalifa a while to find the street and even longer to find the shop, which had a dirty steel security shutter pulled down across its front and was half hidden behind a stall selling nuts and sweetmeats. He tracked it down eventually and, throwing up the shutter, unlocked the door and stepped inside, bells jangling above his head.

The interior was cluttered and murky, with racks of bric-à-brac rising from floor to ceiling, and tangles of brass lamps, furniture and other assorted oddments piled high in the corners. Wooden masks peered down at him from the walls; a stuffed bird hung from the ceiling. The air smelled of leather, old metal and, it seemed to Khalifa, death.

He looked around for a moment, eyes adjusting to the gloom, and then moved towards the counter at the back of the shop, where an area of floor had been circled in chalk, the planks stained dark brown by Iqbar's blood. Several smaller chalk circles, orbiting the larger one like moons around a planet, highlighted traces of spongy grey cigar ash. He stooped and prodded one and then, straightening, moved round to the back of the counter.

He didn't hold out much hope of finding anything. If, as he suspected, Iqbar had bought antiquities from Nayar, the chances were they had either been sold on or removed by the people who'd murdered him. Even if there was something here he doubted he'd locate it. The antique dealers of Cairo were notoriously skilful in concealing their valuables. Still, it was worth having a poke around.

He opened a couple of drawers and rummaged through their contents. He lifted the bottom of a large mirror hanging on the wall on the off chance it might conceal a safe, which it didn't. Squeezing past a pair of old wickerwork baskets he wandered into a room at the back of the shop, flicking a switch inside the door to turn on the light.

It was a small room, cluttered like the rest of the place, with a row of battered filing cabinets against one wall and, in the corner, a life-sized wooden statue in black and gold, a cheap reproduction of the guardian statues from the tomb of Tutankhamun. Khalifa walked over to it and looked it in the eyes.

'Boo!' he said.

The filing cabinets were full to overflowing with crumpled papers and after twenty minutes he gave up trying to make any sense of them and went back out into the shop.

'Like looking for a needle in a haystack,' he muttered to him-self, gazing at the junk-laden shelves. 'And I don't even know if there *is* a needle in the haystack.'

He poked around for over an hour, opening a box here, a drawer there, before eventually giving up. If there were any clues here to the old man's murder they were lost somewhere deep among the jumbled mayhem, and short of emptying the place completely there was no way he was going to find them. He took a last look behind the counter, switched off the light in the back room and, with a resigned sigh, took the keys out of his pocket and moved towards the front door.

A face was looking at him through the glass.

It was a small face, dirty, pressed so close to the pane that the tip of the nose had become flattened. Khalifa came forward and opened the door. A ragged-looking girl, no more than five or six years old, was standing on the threshold, looking intently past him into the shop behind. He dropped to his haunches.

'Hello,' he said.

The girl seemed hardly to notice him, so focused was she on the interior of the shop. He took her hand.

'Hello,' he said again. 'My name's Yusuf. What's yours?'

The girl's brown eyes flicked onto his face for a moment before returning to the scene behind him. She withdrew her hand and pointed into the gloom.

'There's a crocodile in there,' she said, indicating an old wooden chest with an intricately carved brass lock.

'Is there?' Khalifa smiled, remembering how, as a child, he had firmly believed there was a dragon living beneath his parents' bed. 'And how do you know that?'

'It's green,' she said, ignoring the question, 'and at night it comes out and eats people.'

Her limbs were painfully thin, her belly distended. A street child, he guessed, sent out to scavenge by parents who could find no other way to support her. He brushed a tangle of hair away from her eyes, sorry for her. No wonder the funda-mentalists gained so much support, he thought. Their methods might be grotesque, but at least they tried to reach out to these people, to offer them some hope of a better future.

He came to his feet.

'Do you like candy?' he asked.

For the first time the girl gave him her full attention. 'Yes,' she said.

'Wait here a moment.'

He went outside to the sweet stall in front of the shop, where

201

he bought two large slabs of pink sugar-cake. When he came back he found that the girl had wandered further into the shop. He handed her the candy and she began to nibble it.

'Do you know what's in there?' she said, pointing at a large brass lamp.

'I don't, no.'

'A genie,' she replied, mouth full. 'He's called al-Ghul. He's ten million years old and can turn himself into things. When the men came I wanted him to help Mr Iqbar, but he didn't.' She said it so innocently that it was a moment before Khalifa realized the significance of her words. Laying his hand gently on her shoulder, he turned her towards him.

'You were here when the men came and hurt Mr Iqbar?'

The girl was concentrating on her candy slab and made no reply. Rather than push her he just stood where he was, silent, waiting for her to finish her sweet.

'What's your name again?' she asked eventually, looking up.

'Yusuf,' he replied. 'And yours?'

'Maia.'

'That's a pretty name.'

She was examining her second candy slab. 'Can I keep this till later?' she asked.

'Of course.'

She made her way round to the back of the counter, where she pulled out a piece of tissue paper and wrapped up the candy, putting it in the pocket of her dress.

'Do you want to see something?' she asked.

'OK.'

'Close your eyes, then.'

Khalifa did as he was asked. He heard the soft patter of feet as she came out from behind the counter and hurried towards the back of the shop.

'Now open them,' she said.

He did so. She had disappeared.

He waited for a moment and then moved slowly in the

direction from which her voice had come, peering to left and right into the gloom, until eventually he spotted the top of her head peeping out above the old wickerwork baskets.

'That's a good hiding place,' he said, leaning over.

She looked up at him and smiled. Slowly, however, the smile seemed to tighten and collapse in on itself, and suddenly she was weeping uncontrollably, hot tears cutting lines through the muck of her face, her tiny body trembling like a leaf. He reached over and lifted her up, holding her close against his shoulder.

'There, there,' he whispered, stroking her filthy hair. 'Everything's going to be OK, Maia. Everything will be fine.'

He began pacing up and down the shop, humming an old lullaby his mother used to sing to him, allowing her tears to run their course. Eventually the trembling began to subside and her breathing returned to normal.

'You were hiding behind the baskets when the men came, weren't you, Maia?' he said quietly.

She nodded.

'Can you tell me about them?'

A long pause, and then: 'There were three,' she whispered in his ear. Another pause, and then: 'One had a hole in his head.'

She leaned away from him a little.

'Here!' she said, touching Khalifa's forehead with her finger. 'And another one was big like a giant, and white, and he had a funny face.'

'Funny?'

'It was purple,' she said, running her hand down the side of his cheek. 'Here it was purple. And here it was white. And he had a thing like a knife that he hurt Mr Iqbar with. And the other two were holding him. And I wanted al-Ghul to come out and help, but he didn't.'

She was talking fast now, the story spilling out of her in a breathless jumble of words: how the bad men had come and started asking Iqbar questions; how she'd watched from her

203

secret hiding place; how they'd cut old Iqbar and continued to cut him even after he'd told them everything they wanted to know; how after they'd gone she'd been scared because there were ghosts in the shop, and had run away, and hadn't told anybody because if her mother had known she was with Iqbar rather than out begging she would have beaten her.

Khalifa listened quietly, stroking the girl's hair, allowing her to tell the story in her own way, slowly piecing together the narrative from her rambling commentary. When, finally, she had finished speaking, stopping suddenly in the middle of a sentence like a toy whose battery has run out, he lifted her onto the counter and, removing his handkerchief, dabbed her eyes dry. She pulled out her second piece of sugar candy and began nibbling at its corner.

'You mustn't be cross with al-Ghul, you know,' he said, wiping away the snot beneath her nose. 'I'm sure he wanted to help. But he couldn't get out of his lamp, you see.'

She looked up at him over her candy. 'Why?'

'Because a genie can only come out of his lamp if someone rubs it. You have to summon him into our world.'

Her brow furrowed as she absorbed this information, and then a small smile curled across her mouth, as though a friend whom she had thought had wronged her had somehow proved to be loyal after all.

'Shall we rub the lamp now?' she asked.

'Well, we could,' replied Khalifa, 'but you have to remember that you can only summon a genie three times. And it would be a shame to summon him for no reason, wouldn't it?'

Again the girl's brow furrowed.

'Yes,' she said eventually. And then, almost as an afterthought, 'I like you.'

'And I like you too, Maia. You're a very brave girl.'

He waited a moment and then added, 'Maia, I need to ask you some questions.'

She didn't reply immediately, just bit off another piece of

candy and started swinging her legs so that the heels banged against the front of the counter.

'You see, I want to catch the people who hurt Mr Iqbar. And I think you can help me. Will you help me?'

Her heels continued to thud metronomically against the counter-front.

'OK,' she said.

He heaved himself up beside her. She snuggled up against him.

'You said that the bad men wanted something from Mr Iqbar, Maia. Can you remember what it was?'

She thought for a moment and then shook her head.

'Are you sure?'

Again a shake of the head.

'Can you remember what Mr Iqbar told the men? What he said to them when they were hurting him?'

'He said it was sold,' she replied.

'And who did he say he'd sold it to? Can you remember?'

She looked down and screwed up her face, thinking, watching her feet as they rose and fell. When she eventually looked up at him her expression was apologetic.

'It's OK,' he said, stroking her hair. 'You're doing fine. Just fine.'

He needed to help her more. Give her some clues to jog her memory. He thought about his earlier conversation with Tauba and decided to try a long shot.

'Did Mr Iqbar say he'd sold this thing to an Englishman?'

A sudden, vigorous nod.

'Did he say he'd sold it to an Englishman who was working at a place called Saqqara?' He said the word slowly, spelling it out. There was a brief pause and then another nod. He decided to backtrack.

'Maia, can you remember a man coming into this shop a few days ago?'

He had seen Professor Mullray lecture a couple of times at the

American University, years ago, and scoured his brain now for an image of the man.

'He would have been a tall man, Maia. Old. With lots of white hair, and funny little round glasses and . . .'

She interrupted him, excited. 'He could pull his thumb off!' she cried. 'It was funny.'

He had come into the shop several days ago, she explained, and while Iqbar had gone to look for something in the room at the back, he had asked her if she wanted to see a magic trick and when she had said, 'Yes!' he had gripped his thumb and pulled it right off his hand. It had made her laugh, she said.

'And did he buy something from Mr Iqbar?' asked Khalifa.

She worked one of her fingers up into her nostril. 'A picture,' she said.

'A picture?'

She removed the finger, its tip glistening, and drew a square on the counter-top.

'It was like this. There were snakes along the bottom. And . . .' She paused, searching for the right word. '. . . shapes,' she said eventually.

Shapes, thought Khalifa. Shapes. It could be hieroglyphs. An object with hieroglyphs on it.

'I helped Mr Iqbar wrap it up,' the girl continued. 'In a box. I always helped him wrap things up.'

She bit into her candy. Khalifa slipped from the counter and began pacing up and down the shop.

These are the pieces of the jigsaw, he thought to himself: Nayar comes to Cairo and sells some artefact to Iqbar. Mullray buys it from Iqbar and takes it back to Saqqara. Nayar is killed. Iqbar is killed. Mullray dies of a heart attack, which might or might not be a coincidence. Mullray's daughter comes to Saqqara and removes the object. People unknown try to stop her.

Far from becoming clearer, the whole thing seemed more confused than ever. What was Mullray doing handling stolen antiquities? What exactly had happened yesterday at Saqqara? How was Mullray's daughter involved?

The object, he thought to himself. That's the key. What is this object everyone wants so badly? What is it? What? What?

He turned back to the girl. There was no point asking her about the picture again. Clearly she'd told him everything she could about it. The only other possibility was that she knew of other artefacts Iqbar had received from Nayar and which might, just might, still be on the premises somewhere.

'Maia,' he asked gently, 'did Mr Iqbar have a secret hiding place here in the shop? A special place where he put all his important things?'

She didn't reply, her eyes revolving away from his and coming to rest on her knees. Something about her manner – the tightness of her mouth, her clenched fists – told him his question had struck a chord.

'Please help me, Maia. Please.'

Still she didn't say anything.

'I think Mr Iqbar would want you to tell me,' he said, taking her hands. 'Because if you don't I can't catch the people who did those bad things to him.'

She was silent for a moment longer and then looked up at him.

'If I show you where it is can I have al-Ghul's lamp?'

Khalifa smiled and lifted her to the ground.

'That sounds like a fair deal to me. You show me the hiding place, you get the genie.'

The girl chuckled, pleased with the bargain, and, taking Khalifa's hand, pulled him into the room at the back of the shop.

'I'm the only person in the world who knows about it,' she said, going up to the wooden guardian statue in the corner of the room. 'Even the ghosts don't know. It's a secret.'

The statue was black, with a gold headdress, staff and sandals, and a splayed gold kilt. The girl placed her hand on the underside of the kilt, which appeared to be solid wood, and pushed hard. There was a faint click and a hidden drawer slowly descended, like a clip from the butt of a pistol. The girl took it from its slot and laid it on the floor, then turned back to the statue and carefully unscrewed one of its toes, revealing a cavity from which she removed a small metal key. This she inserted into a lock in the lid of the drawer, turning it twice and opening it.

'Good, isn't it?' she said.

'It certainly is,' said Khalifa, kneeling beside her. 'Very good.'

The drawer was divided into two compartments. In one was a thick roll of banknotes, some legal documents and a jar full of nuggets of uncut turquoise. In the other was a cloth bundle done up with string. Khalifa removed the bundle and untied the string, letting out a low whistle when he saw what was inside.

There were seven objects: an iron dagger with a rough leather strip wrapped around its handle; a silver amulet in the shape of a Djed pillar; a gold pectoral; a small terracotta ointment jar with the face of the dwarf-god Bes stamped on it; and three pale-blue faience *shabti*s. He examined them one by one, turning them over in his hand, and then turned to the girl. She was no longer there.

'Maia,' he called, standing and, when she didn't reply, walking back through into the shop. 'Maia!'

She had gone. And so too, he noticed, had al-Ghul's bronze lamp. He went to the front door and stepped outside, but she was nowhere to be seen.

'Goodbye, Maia,' he said quietly. 'May Allah smile upon you.'

LUXOR

Suleiman al-Rashid was dozing on a mat in the shade behind his mobile lavatory when he heard the creak of metal steps as someone climbed into the trailer above him.

Normally he would have gone round to see if they needed toilet paper and to make sure he was suitably positioned for any baksheesh they might offer once they emerged. The midday heat was too intense, however, and so he remained where he was, head cradled on his arm, while from above came the thump of feet on the hollow trailer floor.

He didn't immediately register anything untoward. There was, admittedly, a curious splashing sound, but he presumed the customer was simply ladling water from the bucket in the corner of the trailer into the basin of the urinal to clean it out. There was no need to, since Suleiman made a point of keeping the trailer spotless, but some people, especially the Germans, were obsessive about these things and, rolling onto his side with a grunt, he left them to get on with it.

Then, however, he smelt petrol, and at the same time heard a loud dripping as something leaked from the trailer and splashed onto the sandy ground beside him. He struggled to his feet.

'Hey!' he shouted, making his way round to the front of the trailer. 'What's—'

A heavy blow from behind pitched him forward onto the trailer steps.

'Get him in here,' hissed a voice from above.

A pair of strong arms circled Suleiman's waist and he felt himself being heaved upwards. Someone else grabbed him from above and he was half dragged, half pushed into the trailer's interior. He tried to struggle, but he was still groggy from the blow to his head and offered only token resistance. The stench of petrol made him gag.

'Cuff him,' came the voice. 'There. To the pipe.'

There was a click as something closed around his wrist. His arm was yanked violently upwards and then another click. He winced as the handcuff bit into his flesh.

'Now petrol.'

Something was poured over his face and djellaba. He tried to get out of the way, but his arm was held fast by the cuff. The liquid stung his sightless eyes and made his mouth burn. He couldn't see his attackers, but then he didn't need to. He knew who they were.

The pouring stopped. There was a clatter as an empty jerrycan was thrown aside and then the clump of feet as his assailants jumped from the trailer. For a moment everything was silent and then he heard a match being struck. Curiously, he felt no fear. Anger, yes, and sorrow for his family. How would they survive without him? But not fear.

'*Ibn sharmouta! Ya kha-in!*' hissed a voice from outside. 'Son of a whore! Traitor! This is what happens to those who inform on Sayf al-Tha'r!'

There was a brief silence and then Suleiman heard a whoosh of flame and felt a fierce heat rushing towards him across the flimsy plywood floor.

'May God have mercy on your souls!' he whispered, yanking desperately at the cuff around his wrist. 'May the Almighty for-give you!'

And then the fire swallowed him and all that could be heard were his screams.

CAIRO

An hour after leaving Iqbar's shop, Khalifa was sitting opposite Crispin Oates in his office at the British embassy. He hadn't bothered to call beforehand to ask for an appointment, had just turned up unannounced. Oates clearly hadn't been pleased about the intrusion, but had had little choice other than to invite the detective in. He was getting his own back now by being as patronizing and unhelpful as possible, albeit with impeccable English politeness.

'And you've no idea where this Tara Mullray has gone?' Khalifa asked.

Oates sighed wearily. 'None at all, Mr Khalifa. As I explained to you just a few minutes ago I last saw Ms Mullray the day before yesterday when I picked her up from her hotel and brought her to the embassy. Since then I've had no contact with her at all. Um, I'm afraid it's a no-smoking office.'

Khalifa had just removed his cigarettes from his jacket. He put them back again, hunching forward slightly, the artefacts from Iqbar's shop weighing heavy in his inside pocket.

'Was she acting strangely in any way?' he asked.

'Miss Mullray?'

'Yes. Miss Mullray.'

'How do you mean strangely?'

'I mean did she seem . . . preoccupied?'

'She had just found her father's body. I would have thought we'd all seem a little preoccupied in such circumstances, wouldn't you?'

'What I mean is . . . you must excuse my English, it is not . . .'

'On the contrary, Mr Khalifa, your English is excellent. Much better than my Arabic.'

'What I mean is, when you last saw Miss Mullray did she appear as though she was in any sort of trouble? Frightened, perhaps? Under threat?'

No, replied Oates, so far as he could recall she had appeared none of these things. 'I have told all this to the men from Giza, you know. Of course, I'm more than happy to co-operate, but it does all seem a little . . . repetitive.'

'I'm sorry,' said Khalifa. 'I'll try not to take up too much more of your time.'

He stayed for a further twenty minutes. The more questions he asked the more convinced he became that Oates knew more than he was letting on. What he knew, however, and why he should wish to keep it secret, were things he clearly had no intention of revealing, and eventually Khalifa decided he'd got as much as he was going to. Pushing back his chair, he came to his feet.

'Thank you, Mr Orts,' he said. 'I am sorry to have troubled you.'

'Not at all, Mr Khalifa. My pleasure. And it's Oates. OATES.' He spelt it out.

'Of course. Apologies. And I am *Inspector* Khalifa.'

They shook hands stiffly and Khalifa started towards the door. After a couple of paces, however, he stopped and, pulling out his notebook, scribbled swiftly on a blank page.

'One last question. Does this mean anything to you?'

He showed the page to Oates. On it was a rough square, just as the girl had drawn it for him in Iqbar's shop, with some scribbled hieroglyphs inside and, along its bottom edge, a row of serpents. Oates glanced down, his mouth tightening ever so slightly.

'No,' he said after a brief pause, 'I'm afraid not.'

Liar, thought Khalifa.

He held Oates's eyes for a moment and then folded the notebook and returned it to his pocket.

'Oh well,' he said, 'just a long shot. Again, thank you for your help.'

'I don't feel I've been very helpful at all,' said Oates.

'On the contrary. You've been extremely . . . informative.'

He smiled and walked out of the door.

In his office Charles Squires flicked off the intercom on which he had been listening to the exchange and sat back in his chair. For a while he remained very still, staring up at the ceiling, a slight grimace pinching his face, and then, sitting forward again, he lifted the telephone and dialled swiftly. There were three rings and then a click.

'Jemal,' he said, 'I think we might have a problem.'

24

LUXOR

They reached Luxor midway through the afternoon, having been travelling for almost twenty hours.

They could have done the journey in a third of the time. Daniel, however, had insisted on taking an extensive detour to avoid passing through middle Egypt.

'South of Beni Suef the whole area's crawling with funda-mentalists,' he had explained. 'You can't spit without Sayf al-Tha'r knowing about it. And, anyway, there's a police road-block at every junction. Foreigners aren't supposed to travel through the area without an escort. We'd be picked up before we'd gone ten kilometres.'

Rather than go directly south as the crow flies, therefore, following the Nile highway straight down to Luxor, they had turned east at al-Wasta across the desert.

'We'll cross to the Red Sea,' he had told her, tracing their intended route on a map, 'and then follow the coast south to al-Quseir. Then we can turn inland again and hit the Nile here, at Q'us, just north of Luxor. That way we cut out the whole of this middle stretch.'

'It seems a long way round.'

'Yes,' he agreed, 'but there are benefits. Like getting to Luxor alive.'

Amazingly, given the circumstances, Tara had enjoyed the journey. There hadn't been much traffic on the road east and Daniel had pushed the speedometer up past 140 kilometres per hour, the sun dropping swiftly behind them until suddenly it was dark and they were alone in the middle of the desert. The air was clear and icy cold, and above them a twinkling canopy of stars.

'It's beautiful,' she cried as they cut through the emptiness. 'I've never seen so many stars.'

Daniel slowed slightly. 'The Egyptians thought they were the children of Nut,' he called, 'the goddess of the sky. She gave birth to them each night and then swallowed them again in the morning. They also thought they were the souls of the dead, waiting in the darkness for the return of the sun god Ra.'

She tightened her grip around his waist, enjoying the warmth and firmness of his body. Suddenly everything that had happened over the last two days seemed to recede.

They stopped for the night in a small fishing village by the sea, finding a room above a café with two beds and a window overlooking the water.

Daniel fell asleep almost immediately. Tara lay awake late into the night, listening to the hiss of the sea and gazing at Daniel's face in the moonlight, sunburnt and strong, the brow furrowed as though his thoughts were troubled ones. He began muttering and, unable to stop herself, she leaned closer to hear. It was a name. A woman's name. Mary something. Over and over again. Mary. Her stomach tightened and, rolling away, she stared out of the window, inexplicably saddened.

She said nothing of it the next morning and, after a swift breakfast, they continued south with the dawn, down past Hurghada and Port Safaga and El-Hamarawein until eventually they came to Al-Quseir and turned west again, the wind blasting into their faces, the rocky desert rushing past to either side. Daniel kept the Jawa at full speed and Tara buried her face in his back, dreading the moment when the journey would end and they would once again have to face the reality of their situation.

They reached Q'us at two, and western Luxor half an hour later. As the cars and buildings closed in around them and the streets filled with people, Tara's head slumped forward against Daniel's back, as though a great weight had descended on it. She let out a deep sigh, her lungs aching for a cigarette.

'So what now?' she asked as they pulled onto the forecourt of a small Mobil garage at the edge of town.

'We go to Omar.'

'Omar?'

'An old friend. Omar Abd el-Farouk. He was my *rais* up in the valley. A hundred years ago his family were the most famous tomb robbers in Egypt. Now they work for the archaeological missions and run a couple of souvenir shops. There's not much goes on around here that they don't know about.'

The pump attendant came over and began filling their tank.

'And what if he can't help us?' asked Tara. 'What if we don't find anything here?'

Daniel took her hand. 'It'll be OK,' he said. 'We'll get out of this. Trust me.'

He sounded far from convinced.

Omar lived in a large mud-brick house backing directly onto the ruin-field that had once been the great palace of Malqata. He was working in the garden when they arrived, raking up palm fronds and piling them in a corner, where an aged donkey was lethargically nibbling on their sun-browned leaves. As soon as he saw them he let out a shout of pleasure and came hurrying over.

215

'*Ya Doktora!*' he cried. 'It has been too long! Welcome!'

The two men embraced, kissing twice on each cheek. Daniel introduced Tara, explaining who she was.

'I hear about your father,' said Omar. 'I am very sorry. May he be peaceful.'

'Thank you.'

He shouted something towards the house and led them to a table in the shade beneath a banana tree.

'I dig with Dr Daniel for many years,' he said as they sat. 'I work with other archaeologists too, but Dr Daniel always the best. No-one knows as much about Kings' Valley as he does.'

'Omar says that to everyone he works for,' Daniel said, smiling.

'It is true.' The Egyptian winked. 'I only mean it with Dr Daniel, though.'

A pretty girl emerged from the house carrying three bottles of Coke, which she placed on the table. She glanced at Daniel, blushed and hurried away again.

'My eldest daughter,' explained Omar proudly. 'Already she has had two offers of marriage. Local boys, good families. She only thinks of one person, though.'

He tipped his head towards Daniel and chuckled.

'Just drink your fucking Coke, Omar.'

They chatted for a while, lightly: about Omar's children, their journey down from Cairo, other missions currently working in the area. The pretty girl reappeared with a tureen of lentil soup and, when they had finished that, a platter of fried chicken, rice and slippery green *molochia*. Afterwards Omar's wife came out with a *shisha* pipe, which she placed between the two men. She accepted their thanks for the meal, collected the plates and with a curious backward look at Tara, disappeared into the house again.

'So,' said Omar, exhaling smoke from his nostrils, 'you are here for a reason, I think, Dr Daniel? Not just as a friend.'

Daniel smiled. 'You can't keep anything from the el-Farouks.'

'My family has worked with English archaeologists for over a hundred years.' Omar laughed, winking at Tara. 'My great-great-grandfather was with Petrie. My great-grandfather with Carter. My great-uncle with Pendlebury at Amarna. We see through them like glass.' He passed the pipe across to Daniel. 'So speak, my friend. If there is anything I can do for you, I will. You are a part of my family.'

There was a silence and then Daniel turned to Tara. 'Show him,' he said.

She hesitated for a moment and then, bending down, pulled the cardboard box from her knapsack and handed it to Omar. He removed the lid and lifted out the decorated fragment, turning it over in his hands.

'I think it came from round here somewhere,' said Daniel. 'A tomb, probably. Have you seen it before? Do you know anything about it?'

Omar didn't answer immediately, just continued turning the piece, examining it front and back before returning it to its box and replacing the lid.

'Where did you get this?' he asked eventually.

'My father bought it for me,' said Tara. She paused and then added, 'Sayf al-Tha'r wants it. And so do people at the British embassy.'

She felt Daniel shift uncomfortably beside her and sensed he hadn't wanted her to mention that. Omar just nodded and, taking back the pipe, puffed slowly on the brass mouthpiece. 'That is why you came such a long way round from Cairo?'

'Yes,' Daniel conceded. 'We thought it best to avoid middle Egypt. You do know something, don't you?'

The Egyptian exhaled a thick billow of smoke, taking his time.

'Yesterday morning I was brought in for questioning by the police,' he said. 'Not in itself unusual. If ever a crime is committed involving antiquities, the first thing the police

217

always do is bring in an el-Farouk. We tell them over and over again that we're not involved in that sort of thing any more, haven't been for a hundred years, but it doesn't make any difference. They still bring us in.

'This time, however, it wasn't the usual sort of silly questions. This time there'd been a murder. A local man. The detective thought maybe he'd found a new tomb. Taken some things out. Upset some powerful people. Wanted to know if I knew anything about it.'

He paused, leaning forward to fan the embers of the *shisha*.

'I told the police nothing, of course. They are dogs and I'd rather die than help them. The truth is, however, I have heard things. About a new tomb up in the hills. Where I don't know, but it's something big. Something they say Sayf al-Tha'r wants very badly.'

'And you think this piece might be a part of it?' said Daniel.

Omar shrugged. 'Maybe, maybe not. I don't know. What I can tell you is that if it is you are both in very great danger. It is not good to go against the Sword of Vengeance.'

His eyes flicked back and forward between the two of them. The donkey had stopped toying with the palm fronds and was sniffing around the mouth of a clay bread oven on the corner of the house. There was a long silence.

'I need to find out where this piece came from,' said Daniel. 'We have to know why it's so important. Help us, Omar. Please.'

The Egyptian said nothing for a long while, just continued puffing on the pipe. Then, slowly, he stood and walked back towards the house. For a moment Tara thought he was abandoning them. At the doorway, however, he turned.

'Of course I will help you, Dr Daniel. You are my friend, and when a friend asks for help an Abd el-Farouk does not let him down. I will make enquiries. In the meantime you will both stay here as my guests.'

He held out his arm, ushering them into the building.

25

CAIRO

As Khalifa stood in the front foyer of Cairo's Museum of Egyptian Antiquities, gazing up at the great glass cupola in the roof and the colossal statues at the far end of the atrium, he wished he had more time. It was two years since he'd last visited the collection and he would have liked to have at least a cursory look round, revisiting some of his favourite objects: the coffins of Yuya and Tjuju, the Tutankhamun treasures, the painted limestone statuette of the dwarf Seneb.

The afternoon was already well advanced, however, and he had a train to catch, so without further ado he turned left and hurried through the Old Kingdom gallery and up a broad staircase at the far end, glancing at exhibits as he passed but resisting the temptation to stop for a longer look.

At the top of the staircase he opened a door marked Private and climbed another staircase, wooden this time, walking down a long narrow corridor until he reached a door with 'Professor Mohammed al-Habibi' stencilled on its window. He knocked twice and a cheerful voice bade him enter.

His old teacher was standing with his back to him, bent over his desk examining something intently with a magnifying glass.

'Won't be a moment,' he said, not turning. 'Make yourself at home.'

Khalifa closed the door and leaned against it, gazing affectionately at the old man's back. He knew it was pointless trying to get his attention. When the professor was engrossed in an artefact a herd of wild elephants couldn't distract him.

He looked exactly as he always had: the same rotund figure, unravelling cardigan, jeans that stopped three inches above his ankles. The shoulders were a little more stooped and his balding head a little more wrinkled, but that was to be expected: he was, after all, approaching eighty.

Khalifa remembered the day they had first met, almost twenty-five years ago. It was here, in the museum. He and Ali had been standing in front of an alabaster libation table wondering aloud what a libation was, and the professor, who was passing, had stopped and explained.

They had liked him immediately – his muddled appearance, his cheerful manner, the way he had described the table as 'she' instead of 'it', as though it was a living person rather than an inanimate object. The professor, too, had taken to them, touched perhaps by their interest in the past and their poverty, and also, maybe – although Khalifa only found this out many years later – by the fact that his own son was Ali's age when he'd been killed in a car accident several years before.

The professor had become their unofficial guide, meeting them each Friday and taking them around the museum for an hour or two before buying each a Coca-Cola and a slice of *basbousa* from a stall on Midan Tahrir. As they had grown older the Coke and *basbousa* had given way to regular Friday lunch at the professor's home, cooked by his wife, who was even more rotund and dishevelled than he was, if it were possible. He had lent them books and given them artefacts to handle, and allowed them to watch his television, which, although neither of them would ever have admitted it, was the thing they enjoyed most about going to his flat.

He had, in a way, come to fill the gap left by the death of their father. He himself had certainly looked on the two boys with a paternal eye. The pride he had felt when Khalifa won a place at university had been more that of a father for a son than a friend for a friend. Likewise the tears he had later shed when he heard about Ali.

It was several minutes before he eventually laid aside his magnifying glass and turned.

'Yusuf,' he cried when he saw Khalifa, a huge smile breaking across his face. 'Why on earth didn't you say something, you fool!'

'I didn't want to disturb you.'

'Nonsense!'

Khalifa came forward and the two men embraced.

'How are Zenab and the children?'

'Well, thank you. They all send their love.'

'And little Ali? Is he doing well at school?'

The professor was godfather to Khalifa's son and took a keen interest in the boy's education.

'Very well.'

'I knew he would be. Unlike his father, the boy's got some brains.' He winked and, shuffling round the desk, picked up a phone. 'I'll call Arwa. Tell her you're coming for dinner.'

'I'm sorry, I can't. I'm going back to Luxor tonight.'

'You haven't got time for a quick snack?'

Khalifa laughed. At Professor al-Habibi's house there was no such thing as a quick snack. His wife's idea of fast food was five courses instead of ten.

'No time. It's just a flying visit.'

Habibi tutted and replaced the receiver.

'She'll be furious she missed you. And I'll get the blame. She'll say I should have made more effort to bring you back. Drugged you if necessary. You've no idea what sort of trouble you're getting me into!'

'I'm sorry. It was a spur-of-the-moment thing.'

The professor snorted. 'Well, you should come up here on the spur of the moment a bit more often. We don't see enough of you.'

He rummaged in a drawer and produced a bottle of sherry, pouring a hefty tot into a glass on the table.

'I take it the laws of Allah haven't relaxed since I last saw you?'

'Afraid not.'

'Then I won't embarrass you by offering you a glass.' He raised his own. 'Good to see you, Yusuf. It's been too long.'

He drained the sherry in one gulp, burped lightly and then put his arm round Khalifa and drew him in to the table.

'Take a look at this,' he said.

Lying on the ink blotter was a fragment of yellow papyrus, very frayed, with six columns of black hieroglyphic text and, in one corner, badly faded, part of a hawk's head with a solar disc on top of it. Habibi handed Khalifa the magnifying glass.

'Opinion, please.'

It was a game they always played. The professor would produce an artefact of some kind and Khalifa would attempt to work out what it was. The detective bent down now and gazed at the papyrus.

'My hieroglyphs aren't so good any more,' he said. 'There's not much call for them in police work.'

He skimmed along the lines of text.

'One of the afterlife books?' he ventured.

'Very good! But which one?'

Khalifa returned to the text. 'Amduat?' he asked uncertainly. And then, before Habibi had had time to comment, 'No, the Book of the Dead.'

'Bravo, Yusuf! I really am very impressed. But now can you date it?'

That was harder. The prayers and rituals contained in the

Book of the Dead had first appeared in the royal tombs of the Eighteenth Dynasty and had hardly changed for the next 1,500 years. The hieroglyphs themselves might have given some indication of date – stylistically the signs would have altered over the centuries – but if they did Khalifa wasn't sufficiently expert to be able to spot it. The only possible clues were the hawk's head surmounted by the solar disc and a name in the text: Amenemheb.

'New Kingdom,' he guessed eventually.

'Reason?'

'The Re-Harakhty figure.' Re-Harakhty was the state god of the New Kingdom. And Amenemheb was a typical New Kingdom name.

Habibi nodded his approval.

'Impeccable reasoning. Wrong, but impeccable reasoning nonetheless. Try again, go on.'

'I've really no idea, Professor. Third Intermediate?'

'Wrong!'

'Late Period?'

'Wrong!' The professor was enjoying himself. 'One last chance,' he chuckled.

'God knows. Graeco-Roman?'

'Afraid not.' He laughed, clapping Khalifa on the shoulder. 'Actually, it's twentieth.'

'Twentieth Dynasty? But I said the New Kingdom!'

'Not Twentieth Dynasty, Yusuf. Twentieth century.'

Khalifa's jaw dropped. 'It's a fake?'

'Indeed it is. A very good one, but definitely a fake.'

'How can you tell? It looks absolutely genuine.'

Habibi laughed. 'You'd be amazed how skilled these forgers are. Not just with the artwork but with the materials too. They have ways of ageing the ink and the papyrus to make them look thousands of years old. It's an exceptional talent. A shame they use it to hoodwink people.'

He reached for the sherry bottle and refilled his glass.

'But how did you know?' asked Khalifa again. 'What gives it away?'

As before, the sherry disappeared in one gulp.

'Well, there are various tests you can do. Carbon-14 on the papyrus strands. Microscopic analysis of the ink. In this case, however, I didn't have to call in the scientists. I could see just by examining it. Go on, take another look.'

Khalifa bent over the papyrus again and surveyed it through the magnifying glass. Look as he might, however, he could find nothing to suggest it was anything other than the real thing.

'It's got me fooled,' he said, straightening and handing the glass back to the professor. 'It's absolutely perfect.'

'Exactly! And that's how you can tell. Look at any ancient Egyptian manuscript, inscription, wall painting – they're never perfect. There's always at least one tiny blemish: a drip of ink, a misaligned hieroglyph, a figure facing the wrong way. However minute, you can find at least one mistake. But not on the forgeries. They're always faultless. And that's what gives them away. They're just too good. The ancients were never that precise. It's the attention to detail that lets the forgers down.'

He leaned across Khalifa and, picking up the papyrus, scrunched it into a ball and threw it in the bin. He then lumbered back round the desk and sat down heavily in his old leather chair, pulling a briar pipe from a shelf behind him, filling it with tobacco and lighting it. Khalifa lit a cigarette of his own and, reaching into his pocket, removed the bundle of artefacts in their cloth wrapping and laid it on the desk in front of Habibi.

'OK,' he smiled. 'Now it's your turn. What can you tell me about these?'

Habibi looked up at him through wafts of blue pipe smoke and, an intrigued grin on his face, undid the bundle. Before him lay the seven objects Khalifa had found in Iqbar's shop. The professor leaned forward and ran his wrinkled hands over them, gently, lovingly, as though trying to reassure them, win their confidence.

'Interesting,' he said. 'Very interesting. Where are they from?'

'That's for you to tell me,' said Khalifa.

Habibi chuckled and returned his attention to the objects. He switched on the lamp beside him and picked up the magnifying glass. One by one he lifted the artefacts and examined them, swivelling them back and forth in the light, bringing them right up to his face, his bloodshot eye swelling and receding in the thickness of the glass. The office echoed to the rasping of his breath.

'Well?' asked Khalifa after almost five minutes had elapsed.

Habibi laid down the *shabti* he was looking at and sat back. His pipe had gone out and he spent another minute slowly refilling and lighting it. He was relishing the moment, like someone who has been asked to identify a particularly rare wine and, after careful tasting, is quietly confident he knows what it is.

'Persian occupation,' he said eventually.

Khalifa raised his eyebrows. 'Persian occupation?'

'That's right.'

There was a brief pause.

'First or second?'

Habibi chuckled. 'A ruthless examiner! He lets me get away with nothing. First, I'd say, although I couldn't give you a precise date. Some time between 525 and 404 BC. The *shabti*s, however, would seem to be a little later.'

'Later?'

'Second Persian probably, although they might possibly be Thirtieth Dynasty. Objects like that are almost impossible to tie down to a specific date, especially very simple ones like these without any legend or inscription. There are no obvious stylistic indications. You just have to go on feel.'

'And these feel Second Persian?'

'Or Thirtieth Dynasty.'

Khalifa was silent for a moment, thinking. 'Are they genuine?'

'Oh yes,' replied Habibi. 'No doubt about that. They're all real.'

He took a deep puff on his pipe. Somewhere beneath them a tannoy system announced that the museum was closing in ten minutes.

'Anything else?' asked Khalifa.

'Depends what you want to know. The terracotta ointment jar probably belonged to a soldier. We have several of the same type. They seem to have been standard military issue of that period. The dagger too suggests a military connection. You can see here, the blade's notched and worn, so it wasn't just ceremonial or votive, it was actually used. The pectoral is interesting. It's high status. Better quality than the other stuff.'

'Which tells you what?'

'Well,' mused the professor, sucking on his pipe, 'either it came from a different source from the other items, or else the person who owned the ointment jar and dagger enjoyed a dramatic improvement in their fortunes.'

Khalifa laughed. 'You should have joined the police. With those powers of deduction you'd be a chief inspector by now.'

'Maybe.' Habibi waved his pipe dismissively. 'But then I could be talking complete rubbish. That's the thing about working with the ancient past. You can put forward any crackpot theory you like – no-one's ever going to prove you wrong. It's all interpretation.'

He reached for the sherry bottle and poured himself a third glass. This time, however, he didn't down it in one, just sipped slowly.

'So tell me, Yusuf. Where are they from?'

Khalifa sucked out the last from his cigarette and ground it into the ashtray.

'Luxor, I think. From a new tomb.'

Habibi nodded slowly. 'Something to do with a case you're working on?'

It was Khalifa's turn to nod.

'I won't ask you for the details.'

'Probably best not to.'

Habibi picked up a pen from his desk and prodded at the bowl of his pipe, tamping down the ash. Another announcement drifted up from below. They sat in silence for a while.

'It's to do with Ali, isn't it?' said Habibi eventually.

'Sorry?'

'The case, these objects – it's to do with Ali?'

'What makes you . . .'

'I can read it in your face, Yusuf. In your voice. You don't spend your life studying dead people without learning a little bit about living ones as well. I can see it, Yusuf. This is about your brother.'

Khalifa said nothing. The professor came to his feet and walked slowly around the desk. He passed behind the detective, and for a moment Khalifa thought he was going to a bookcase on the far side of the room. Then he felt the professor's hand on his shoulder. Despite the man's age, the grip was still firm.

'Arwa and I . . .' the professor started, his voice unsteady. 'When you and Ali first appeared in our lives . . .'

He stopped mid-sentence. Khalifa turned and took the old man's hand in his.

'I know,' he said quietly.

'Just be careful, Yusuf. That's all I ask. Just be careful.'

They remained like that for a moment and then Habibi broke away and moved back to his chair.

'Let's have another look at these things, shall we?' he said, trying to sound cheerful. 'See what else we can tell you. Where did I put that damned magnifying glass?'

26

LUXOR

Omar showed them to a simple room on the upper level of his house, with a rough concrete floor and no glass in the window. While his wife and eldest daughter brought in cushions and sheets, his three other children lingered in the doorway, staring at the new arrivals. The youngest of them, a boy, seemed fascinated by Tara's hair. She lifted him up and he rolled a strand of it around his knuckles, whispering something to his mother.

'What did he say?' she asked.

'That it feels like a horse's tail,' said Omar.

'So much for conditioner.' She smiled, tweaking the boy's nose and putting him down again. She found something curiously comforting about having the family around her, as though they formed an invisible barrier of warmth and innocence between her and the outside world. Once he'd made sure they were comfortable Omar ushered the others from the room.

'I will go out now and see what I can find,' he said. 'In the meantime, this is your home. You will be safe here. In Luxor, at least, the name of el-Farouk still offers some protection.'

When he had gone they showered and climbed up onto the flat roof of the house, where washing was hanging on a line and a mound of red-brown dates lay drying on a sheet. They gazed at the Theban Hills for a while, rearing above them like a great brown wave, then turned and looked eastwards towards the river. Smoke was rising from fields where farmers were burning off the stubble of their harvested maize and sugar cane; a cart piled high with straw moved slowly across their line of sight, pulled by a team of water buffalo. A pair of white egrets swooped low along the surface of a muddy canal; a group of children was playing on top of a mound of earth, throwing sticks at a dog chained below. From somewhere far off came the soft putter of an irrigation pump.

'I feel we ought to be doing something,' she said after a long silence.

'Like what?'

'I don't know. It just seems wrong to come all this way and then simply stand around taking in the view. After what's happened.'

'There's not much we can do, Tara. At least not till Omar gets back. Our next move depends on what he finds out.'

'I know, I know. But I feel powerless just waiting. Like we're at the mercy of events. My father's dead. People are trying to kill us. I want to do something. Find some answers.'

He reached out and touched her shoulder. 'I know how you feel. I'm just as frustrated. But our hands are tied.'

They stood in silence for a while watching an old man lead a camel down the road beneath them. Daniel turned towards the hills again, eyes flicking back and forth across the undulating wall of rock, lost in thought. Suddenly, as if coming to a decision, he took her hand and pulled her back towards the stairs.

'Come on. It might not solve all our problems but at least it'll give us something to do.'

'Where are we going?'

'There.' He pointed to a flat ridge running like a blade across the top of the hills. 'There's no better place in Egypt to watch the sunset.'

They started down the stairs.

'And you'd better bring the box with you,' he said.

'Why? Are you worried Omar might steal it?'

'No. I just don't want him killed because of it. It's our problem, Tara. We should keep it with us.'

It took them the best part of an hour to reach the top of the ridge, following first a set of concrete steps and then, when these petered out, a steep, dusty path that zigzagged its way upwards before eventually carrying them through a narrow gully and out onto the summit of the hills. It had been a hard climb and by the end of it they were both drenched in sweat. They stood for a moment catching their breath, then Daniel sat down on a large rock and lit a cheroot, tapping his fingers on his thigh as if waiting for someone. Tara removed her knapsack and clambered up above him, awed by the extraordinary views: the setting sun, huge and red, a vast jewel suspended against the turquoise sky; the distant silver ribbon of the Nile, shimmering in the afternoon haze; the endless rippling hills, silent and empty and mysterious.

'They call this peak el-Qurn,' said Daniel, 'the horn. From most directions it just looks like a ridge running across the top of the hills. If you view it from the north, however, from the Valley of the Kings, it's shaped like a pyramid. The ancient Egyptians called it Dehenet. The brow. It's the reason they first chose the valley as a burial ground.'

'It's so peaceful,' said Tara.

'They thought the same three and a half thousand years ago. The peak was sacred to the goddess Meret-Seger: "She who loves Silence".'

He came to his feet, glancing briefly back down the way they had come before climbing up beside her.

'Look there,' he said, pointing, 'that rectangular enclosure, there, to the right: that's Medinet Habu, the mortuary temple of Ramesses III. One of the most beautiful monuments in Egypt. And then over there, where those palm trees are, that's Omar's house. Do you see it?'

She peered downwards, following the line of his finger. 'I think so.'

'And then, if you move to the left, where that road is, the one going down to the river, those are the Colossi of Memnon. And if you keep going to the left' – he leaned into her so that their cheeks were practically touching – 'to where that complex of buildings is, that's the Ramesseum, Ramesses II's mortuary temple.'

She could feel his breath against her ear and leaned back a little, looking up at him. There was something troubled in his eyes, a reflection of some inner disturbance.

'What?' she asked.

'I . . .' He paused, unable to find the words. His eyes dropped.

'What, Daniel?'

'I wanted to . . .'

There was a sudden scrabbling noise behind them. They swung round and there, framed by the sides of the gully up which they had climbed a few minutes earlier, was a wild, unkempt-looking face with sunken cheeks and haunted, bloodshot eyes.

'For Christ's sake,' muttered Daniel.

'Hello please, hello please!' gabbled the newcomer, heaving himself a little further up the gully to reveal a djellaba so torn and tattered it was a miracle it held together at all. 'Wait, wait, wait, I show you something very good. Here, here, see.'

Coming out onto the top of the ridge he hurried over to them and extended a skeletal hand, in which he was holding a large scarab carved in black stone.

'I see you come up,' he jabbered. 'Very long way. Very long. Here, look, look, best workmanship. Very, very good how much you give me.'

'*La*,' said Daniel, shaking his head. '*Mish delwa'tee*. Not now.'

'Quality, quality! Please, how much you give.'

'*Ana mish aayiz*. I don't want it.'

'Price, price. Give price. Twenty Egyptian pounds. So cheap.'

'*La*,' repeated Daniel, his voice harsh. '*Ana mish aayiz*.'

'Fifteen. Ten.'

Daniel shook his head.

'*Antika*,' said the man, lowering his voice. 'I have *antika*. You want look. Very good. Very real.'

'*La*,' said Daniel firmly. '*Imshi*. Go away.'

The man was getting desperate. He pawed at their feet.

'Good people. Good people. Try understand. No money, no food, starve, starve, like dog.' He threw his head back and let out a sudden, ear-splitting howl. 'See,' he jabbered. 'I am dog. Not man. Dog. Animal. Dog.' Another howl.

'*Khalas!*' growled Daniel. 'Enough!'

He reached into his pocket and pulled out some notes, which he handed to the man, who took them, his sobs giving way to a wide, brown-toothed smile. He broke into a clumsy jig, hopping around the mountain top.

'Good man good man good man,' he sang. 'My friend so very good to me.' He looked up at Tara as he gambolled beneath her. 'Beautiful lady, you want see tombs? You want see Hatshepsut? Kings Valley. Queens Valley. Special tombs. Secret tombs. I be guide. Very cheap.'

'That's enough,' said Daniel. 'You've got your baksheesh. Go. *Imshi!*'

'But I show you many special things. Many secrets.'

'*Imshi!*'

The man stopped dancing and, with a shrug, moved back towards the gully, fingering his money and muttering to himself.

'Money, go, money, go, money, go.'

He dropped into the narrow defile and lowered himself downwards. When all that was left was his head, however, he turned suddenly, looking Tara straight in the eyes.

'It's not what you think it is,' he said simply, his voice

232

suddenly calm and lucid. 'The ghosts tell me to tell you. It's not what you think it is. There are many lies.'

And then he dropped out of sight and all that could be heard was the hiss of stones as he scrambled back down the mountainside.

'What did he mean?' she asked, inexplicably chilled by the man's words. 'It's not what we think it is?'

'God knows,' said Daniel. He jumped from the rock and walked to the front of the ridge, gazing down at the Valley of the Kings below. 'He's obviously mad, poor bastard. He looked like he hadn't eaten for a month.'

They stood in silence, Daniel looking down at the valley, Tara looking down at Daniel.

'You had something to tell me,' she said eventually.

'Hmm?' He looked back at her. 'Oh, it doesn't matter. Come and look. It's the best time of day to see the valley, when it's empty. Like it must have been in ancient times.'

She jumped down and came to his side, their fingers brushing lightly. Below them the wadi was silent and deserted, its tributary valleys branching off it like the fingers of a splayed hand.

'Where's Tutankhamun's tomb?' she asked.

He pointed. 'You see where the valley bottlenecks, in the middle. And then just to the left there's the outline of a doorway in the hillside. That's KV9, the tomb of Ramesses VI. Tutankhamun's just beyond that.'

'And your site?'

There was a slight beat before he answered.

'You can't see it from here. It's further up the valley, towards Tuthmosis III.'

'I remember coming here with Mum and Dad once,' said Tara, 'when I was a kid. Dad was lecturing on a Nile cruise and we got to go along as well. He was so excited taking us into all the tombs, but I just wanted to get back to the boat and go in the pool. I think that's when he realized I wasn't going to be the daughter he wanted.'

Daniel looked across at her. He moved his shoulder slightly, as though he was going to take her hand. He didn't, however, and after a moment he looked away again, finishing his cheroot and flicking it aside.

'Your father loved you very much, Tara,' he said quietly.

She shrugged. 'Whatever.'

'Believe me, Tara, he loved you. Some people just find it hard to say these things. To say what they feel.'

And then, suddenly, he *was* holding her hand. Neither of them said anything, neither of them moved, as though the contact between them was so fragile it would shatter at the least twitch. The sun was below the horizon now and the light was starting to drain away. A couple of stars were out and on the plain beneath house lights were starting to come on. Opposite, on a distant saddle of rock, they could just make out a couple of soldiers moving around outside a hut, one of the string of guard posts set up across the hills after the Deir el-Bahri massacre. The wind was gusting harder.

'Is there anyone else?' she asked quietly.

'Lovers?' He smiled. 'Not really, no. There have been. But no-one . . .' He searched for the right adjective. '. . . meaningful. You?'

'The same.'

She paused and then asked, 'Who's Mary?' She hadn't wanted to, but couldn't stop herself.

'Mary?'

'Last night, when you were asleep, you kept saying her name.'

'I don't know a Mary.'

He seemed genuinely baffled.

'You said it over and over again. Mary something. Mary. Mary.'

He thought for a moment, repeating the name to himself, and then suddenly rocked back on his heels and burst out laughing.

'Mary! Oh that's wonderful! Were you jealous, Tara? Tell me you were jealous!'

'No,' she said defensively. 'Just interested.'

'For God's sake! *Mery*. That's what I was saying. Not Mary. *Mery*. *Mery-amun*. Beloved of Amun. Nothing for you to worry about, I promise. She's a man, after all, and one who's been dead for two and a half thousand years.'

He was still laughing, and now Tara joined in as well, embarrassed by her mistake but pleased too. His hand tightened on hers, hers on his, and then, before either of them really knew what was happening, he had swung her round and kissed her.

For a second she resisted, a voice in her head warning that he was dangerous, would hurt her again. It was no more than a second, however, and then she opened her mouth, threw her arms around him and pulled him close, needing him, despite what he had done to her, or perhaps because of it. His hands caressed her neck and back, her breasts pushed urgently against his chest. She had forgotten how good he felt.

She didn't know how long they stayed like that, but when, finally, they pulled apart it was to discover that the world around them had suddenly darkened. They sat down on a rock and he wrapped her in his arms against the wind. Away to their right a chain of lights snaked up the mountainside, marking the concrete path up which they had climbed earlier. More lights were twinkling on the plain beneath, white for the most part, but with the occasional green glint marking the minaret of a mosque.

'So who is this Mary?' she asked, nestling her face into his shoulder.

He smiled. 'A son of the Pharaoh Amasis. Prince Mery-amun Sehetep-ib-re. Lived about 550 BC. I have this pet theory that he was buried in the Valley of the Kings. It's what I've been doing here for the last five years. Trying to find him. I'm convinced his tomb's still intact.'

He pulled another cheroot from his shirt pocket, leaning back behind her to shelter his lighter from the wind.

'So when do you start digging again?' she asked.

He hunched forward and dragged on the cheroot, exhaling slowly, allowing the wind to catch the smoke and pull it away from him like a tattered ribbon. There was a long pause. When he spoke again his voice had changed. Suddenly there was an edge of bitterness to it, of resentment.

'I don't start digging again.'

'How do you mean?'

'Just what I say. I don't start digging again.'

'You're excavating somewhere else?'

'Maybe. Not in Egypt, though.'

He stared down at his feet, lips taut and pale. His fist, she noticed, had clenched into a ball, as though he was about to punch someone. She wriggled from his arms and swivelled so she was sitting astride the rock, looking at the side of his face.

'I don't understand, Daniel. What do you mean you're not digging in Egypt again?'

'I mean, Tara,' he said, 'that to all intents and purposes my career as an Egyptian archaeologist is finished. It's over. Caput. Fucked.'

The bitterness in his tone was unmistakable now. He glanced up at her, eyes black as if all the light and life had been sucked out of them, then dropped his head.

'They took away my concession,' he muttered. 'The bastards took away my concession. And given the circumstances it's unlikely I'll ever get it back.'

'Oh my God!' Tara had grown up surrounded by archaeologists and knew what a crushing blow this would be for him. She took his hand and stroked it protectively. 'What happened? Tell me.'

He pulled on the cheroot again and then threw it aside, his face twisting into a grimace as though there was something distasteful in his mouth.

'Not much to tell, really. We'd found traces of what looked like an ancient retaining wall on our site and I wanted to dig along it and find out where it went. Unfortunately it ran out of our concession and into the one beside ours, which belonged to a Polish team. It's a complete no-no trespassing on someone else's concession, but they weren't due on site for another couple of weeks so I thought, fuck it, and dug on. I should have contacted them, or spoken to the Egyptians about it, but . . . well, I couldn't wait. I had to know where the wall went, you see. I couldn't stop myself.'

The fingers of his free hand had started drumming agitatedly on the surface of the rock.

'When the Poles arrived there was an almighty fucking row. The head of their mission said I was irresponsible, had no respect for the past. I've devoted my whole life to Egypt, Tara. No-one has more respect for its history than me. When he said those things I just lost control. Attacked him. Literally. They had to pull me off him. I thought I was going to kill him. Of course, he reported me. The Polish embassy made a formal complaint, took it right to the top – result: my concession was revoked. Not only that, I'm banned from working with any other mission anywhere in Egypt. "Unbalanced." That's what they called me. "A danger to himself and his colleagues." "A liability." Fucking idiots. I'd like to shoot all of them. Every bloody one.'

He was speaking fast now, his breath coming in short angry bursts, his shoulders trembling. He shook his hand free of hers and, standing, walked forward to the front of the ridge, staring down at the valley below. Despite the darkness its pale floor was still clear, winding away northwards like a river of milk. Gradually his breathing calmed and his shoulders slumped.

'I'm sorry,' he mumbled. 'I just get so . . .'

He rubbed his temples and sighed deeply. There was a long silence, broken only by the popping of the wind.

'That was eighteen months ago,' he said eventually. 'I've stayed on doing tours, selling a few watercolours, hoping maybe things would change, but they haven't. And they won't. Somewhere down there there's an intact tomb waiting to be discovered and

237

I'm not allowed to look for it. I'll never be allowed to look for it. Have you any idea how hard that is? How frustrating? Jesus.'

He hung his head.

'I don't know what to say,' she said helplessly. 'I'm so sorry. I know how much this place means to you.'

He shrugged. 'The same thing happened to Carter, you know. In 1905. He was sacked from the Antiquities Service for getting into a fight with some French tourists up at Saqqara. Ended up working as a tourist guide and painter. So in a sense my dream of being the new Carter has come true. Albeit not quite in the way I'd envisaged.'

The bitterness was gone now, and the anger, replaced by a weary despair. Tara stood and came up behind him, wrapping her arms around his waist. He allowed her to hold him.

'And do you know what the real joke is?' he whispered. 'The ancient retaining wall turned out to have been built by Belzoni in the nineteenth century. My entire world goes down the pan for a wall built less than two hundred years ago by another fucking archaeologist!' He laughed, although it was a cold, hollow sound, devoid of humour.

'I'm just so sorry,' she repeated.

'Are you?' He turned so they were facing each other. 'I would have thought you'd be glad. Poetic justice and all that.'

'Of course I'm not glad, Daniel. I've never wished you harm.'

She looked up at him, holding his eyes, then came up on tiptoe and kissed him gently on the lips.

'I want you,' she said simply. 'I want you now, here, under the stars. Above the world. While we have the chance.'

He gazed down at her and then he put his arms around her and pressed his lips to hers, kissing her passionately, his tongue circling her mouth, his hands running down across her backside. She could feel him hardening against her, the pressure sending a tingle through her stomach. He broke away and took her hand.

'I know somewhere,' he said.

He picked up her knapsack and they started along a narrow

path that ran back along the top of the ridge, leading them deeper into the hills. The plain dropped away behind them, the world was silent aside from the clink of rocks beneath their feet. After twenty minutes they reached a point where the path dropped suddenly onto a broad, flat disc of gravel on which four shapes were sitting, curved, like commas on an otherwise blank page. As they approached Tara realized they were small walls, about ten feet long, coming up to the height of her knees.

'Windbreaks,' explained Daniel. 'In ancient times the patrols who guarded these hills would shelter behind them.'

He stooped and picked up what looked like a flat stone.

'See,' he said, holding the object up in the moonlight. 'Pottery.'

They went to the largest of the walls and, without a word, knelt behind it, facing each other. A breeze played against the upper part of their bodies. From the waist down, the air was still and warm, as though they were kneeling in a pool of water. They held each other's eyes for a moment and then, reaching forward, Daniel slowly undid the buttons of her shirt, her breasts coming free and glowing pale in the moonlight, the nipples hard, straining. He leaned forward and kissed them. She threw back her head, closed her eyes and groaned with pleasure, everything else for the moment forgotten.

27

CAIRO

It was almost seven before Khalifa finally got back to Tauba's office. The detective was sitting behind his desk in a pool of lamplight, typing two-fingered on a battered-looking manual typewriter, the floor around him scattered with a thin carpet of cigarette ash, as though there had been a light snowfall in his corner of the office.

Khalifa handed back the key to Iqbar's shop and filled him in about the girl and the artefacts. Tauba whistled.

'I know it's not procedure,' Khalifa added, 'but I've left the objects with a friend of mine at the museum. He'll look at them and send them down first thing tomorrow morning. I hope you don't mind.'

Tauba waved his hand dismissively. 'No problem. I wouldn't have done anything with them before then anyway.'

'The girl gave a pretty good description of Iqbar's attackers,' Khalifa said. 'It looks like two of them were Sayf al-Tha'r's men.'

'Fucking great.'

'The third one wasn't Egyptian. European by the sound of it, maybe American. Big, with some sort of scar or birthmark down the left side . . .'

'Dravic.'

'You know him?'

'Every police force in the Near East knows Casper Dravic. I'm surprised you haven't heard of him. A real piece of shit. German.'

He shouted across the room to one of his colleagues, who began rummaging through a filing cabinet.

'That would certainly tie in with Sayf al-Tha'r,' said Tauba. 'So far as we know, Dravic has been working for him for the last few years, authenticating antiquities, smuggling them out of the country. Sayf al-Tha'r wouldn't dare set foot in Egypt himself, so he stays in the Sudan while Dravic handles everything at this end.'

Tauba's colleague deposited three bulging red folders on his desk. Tauba opened the top one.

'Dravic,' he said, taking out a large black and white photograph and passing it across.

'Handsome,' grunted Khalifa.

'He did a couple of months in Tura a while back for possession of antiquities, but we've never been able to tie him down to anything big. He's clever. Gets other people to do his dirty work. And because he's with Sayf al-Tha'r no-one's going to come forward and give evidence against him. A girl he'd raped did once and that's what happened to her.'

Tauba threw another photograph across the desk.

'God Almighty,' whispered Khalifa.

'Like I said, a real piece of shit.'

Tauba pushed back his chair and crossed his legs on the corner of the desk, lighting a cigarette. Khalifa flicked through the files.

'I went to see that guy at the British embassy,' he said after a while.

'And?'

'Nothing really. Didn't tell me anything new. I had the impression he was keeping something from me, though. Any idea why he'd do that?'

'Why the hell do you think?' Tauba snorted. 'They've never forgiven us for nationalizing Suez and telling them to fuck off back to their own country. If they can put a spanner in the works they will.'

'It was more than that. He knows something about this case. And he doesn't want me to know that he knows.'

Tauba's eyes narrowed. 'You're saying the British embassy is involved in this?'

'To be honest, I don't know what I'm saying any more.' Khalifa sighed wearily, leaning forward and rubbing his eyes. 'There's something going on here, but I just can't see what it is. I just can't bloody see what it is. Dammit!'

Charles Squires slipped his glasses onto his nose and began perusing the menu. For almost two minutes he sat in absorbed silence before eventually laying it aside with a nod of satisfaction.

'The quail, I think. Yes, the quail is always very good here. And to start, well, the seafood pancake sounds most intriguing. Jemal?'

'I'm not hungry.'

'Oh come, come. We can't have you wasting away. You must eat something.'

'I came here to talk, not to eat.'

Squires tutted disapprovingly and turned to the figure on his left, an overweight man with a balding head and an improbably large Rolex watch on his wrist.

'What about you, Massey? Surely you're not going to leave me to eat on my own?'

The American peered down at his menu, rubbing a

handkerchief over the back of his neck, which, despite the restaurant's air-conditioning, was wet with sweat.

'Have they got steak here?' he asked, his accent deep south.

Squires pointed to the menu. 'I think you'll find the *filet mignon* fits the bill.'

'Has it got a sauce on it? I don't want anything with a sauce on it. Just a plain steak.'

Squires summoned the waiter. 'The *filet mignon*,' he asked, 'does it come with a sauce?'

'Yes, sir. A pepper sauce.'

'I don't want a pepper sauce,' insisted Massey. 'Just a plain steak. No shit on it. Can you do a plain steak?'

'I'm sure we can, sir.'

'OK, give me one of those, medium rare, with french fries.'

'And to start, sir?'

'Christ, I don't know. What's that thing you're having, Squires?'

'The seafood pancake.'

'OK, give me one of those. And medium rare on the steak.'

'Jolly good,' smiled Squires. 'The seafood pancake and quail for me, and could you please bring the wine list.'

He handed his menu up to the waiter, who bowed deferentially and disappeared.

Massey tore off half a bread roll and, smearing it with butter, jammed it in his mouth. 'So what's going on?' he asked, chewing.

'Well,' said Squires, watching the American's mouth with a mixture of fascination and disgust, 'it seems our friends have finally turned up in Luxor. Isn't that right, Jemal?'

'They got in this afternoon,' confirmed the Egyptian.

'This whole charade is fucking ridiculous.' Massey grunted. 'We know where the piece is. Why don't we just go in and get it? Stop pussying around.'

'Because there's too great a danger of giving ourselves away,' explained Squires. 'We shouldn't show our hand until we absolutely have to.'

'We're not playing pinochle here.' The American sniffed. 'There's a lot riding on this.'

'I appreciate that,' said Squires. 'For the moment, however, it's better that we stay in the background. Why take unnecessary risks when Lacage and the girl can take them for us?'

'I don't like it,' said Massey, chewing. 'I don't fucking like it.'

'Everything will work out.'

'I mean, Sayf al-Tha'r . . .'

'Everything will work out', repeated Squires, a faint hint of annoyance creeping into his voice, 'so long as we keep our nerve.'

The waiter came back with the wine list and, returning his glasses to his nose, Squires began to study it. Massey got to work buttering the second half of his roll.

'There is one slight problem,' said Squires after a moment, not raising his eyes.

'Here it comes,' growled Massey. 'What?'

'A policeman. From Luxor. It appears he's found out about the missing hieroglyphs.'

'Fucking Jesus fuck! Do you have any idea what's at stake here?'

'I have every idea,' said Squires, the annoyance in his voice now unmistakable. 'I do not, however, intend to get hysterical about it.'

'Don't you patronize me, you cock-sucking limey—'

Jemal slammed his fist on the table, making their cutlery jump and glasses rattle. 'Stop it,' he hissed. 'This is not helpful.'

The three of them sank into an angry silence. Massey devoured the rest of his roll. Squires played distractedly with his fork. Jemal started telling off his worry beads.

'Jemal is right,' said the Englishman eventually. 'Arguing among ourselves is less than productive. The question is, what do we do about this fellow from Luxor?'

'I would have thought that was obvious,' snapped Massey.

'This thing's too important to let some hick paper-pusher screw everything up.'

'Holy God,' hissed Jemal. 'You're saying we should kill him? A policeman?'

'No, we buy him a dress and take him dancing for the night! What the fuck do you think I'm saying?'

The Egyptian stared at Massey with undisguised loathing, his fists clenching and unclenching on the tablecloth. Squires laid aside the wine list and, placing his hands together, rested his chin on the tips of his fingers.

'Elimination does seem rather drastic in the circumstances,' he said quietly. 'Using a sledgehammer to crack a nut and all that. I see no reason why we shouldn't be able to solve the problem without recourse to violence. Jemal?'

'I'll get him taken off the case,' he said. 'No problem.'

'I think that would be best,' agreed Squires. 'A dead policeman could lead to all sorts of unnecessary complications. Make sure you keep an eye on him, though.'

Jemal nodded.

'I still say we should take him out,' grumbled Massey. 'Keep things clean.'

'It might come to that eventually,' said Squires. 'But for the moment I would suggest restraint is the order of the day. This thing's led to too many deaths already.'

'If you want a Nobel Peace Prize you're in the wrong fucking business.'

Squires ignored the sarcasm and returned to his examination of the wine list, running his finger up and down the selection. At the far end of the restaurant a man started playing the piano.

'There is one interesting thing about this police chap,' he said. 'It seems he has a bit of a history with Sayf al-Tha'r. Isn't that right, Jemal?'

'Apparently he has a score to settle,' said the Egyptian, clicking his beads. 'Family business.'

'For fuck's sake,' snorted Massey.

'Yes, it is somewhat extraordinary, isn't it?' Squires smiled, his composure now fully restored. 'What a tiny world we live in, eh? Ah! I do believe those are our seafood pancakes approaching. A half-bottle of Chablis to wash them down, perhaps, and then onto a Burgundy for the main course.'

He flapped open his napkin and laid it carefully on his lap, waiting for his food to arrive.

Professor Mohammed al-Habibi's eyes were aching. He rubbed them slowly, working the knuckles of his clenched fists deep into the wrinkled sockets, and for a moment the pain lessened a little. As soon as he started looking at the artefacts again the ache returned, as bad as before, making his temples throb. It was a problem he often experienced these days. He was getting old and his eyes could no longer take the strain. He knew he ought to pack up and go home, give himself a rest, but he couldn't. Not yet. Not until he'd discovered everything the objects had to tell him. Yusuf was his friend, after all. He owed it to him. And, in a sense, to Ali too. Poor Ali.

He poured another slug of sherry into his glass, the last of the bottle, relit his pipe and, lifting his magnifying glass, bent down to resume his examination of the gold pectoral.

There was something puzzling about the objects his young friend had brought him. Not so much in the way they looked, but rather in the way they felt. Artefacts were, to Habibi, like living things. They sent out signals. Communicated. Provided you knew how to listen, they could tell you all sorts of interesting things. In this case, however, the more he listened, the more perplexed he became.

When he had first examined them, while Khalifa was there, he had not been struck by anything especially out of the ordinary. The artefacts were of simple manufacture and common design, easily datable, the same as dozens of similar objects on display in the museum below.

It was only after Khalifa had left that he'd started to have doubts. There was no particular reason: just a niggling sense that despite their apparent plainness, the objects were nonetheless trying to tell him something specific.

'What are you saying?' he pondered aloud, roving across the face of the pectoral with his magnifying glass. 'What do you want me to hear?'

It was completely dark in the office now, apart from the pool of light cast by his desk lamp. Occasionally he heard the footfall of a security guard passing along the corridor outside, but otherwise the museum was silent. A thick fug of bluish pipe smoke hung over his head like a raincloud.

He laid aside the pectoral and picked up the dagger, holding it by the blade and turning the handle back and forth in the light. It was a simple piece, perfectly common, twelve inches long, iron, with some crude bronze inlay at the top of the blade and a strip of browned leather wrapped tightly around the handle to improve the grip. Typical of its period. He had authenticated one almost exactly the same only a few months previously.

He finished his sherry and took a puff on his pipe, a cloud of smoke for a moment obscuring the object in front of him. When he could see it clearly again he noticed that the leather wrapping was ever so slightly loose at the lower end of the handle, close to where it joined the blade. He tweaked it gently and the strip began to unwind.

At first he thought they were just tiny scratch marks. Only when he twisted the handle so that the glare of the lamp was not falling directly on it, and held the magnifying glass right up close, did he realize that the marks were actually letter signs. Not Persian or Egyptian, as he would have expected, but Greek. A series of tiny Greek letters crudely inscribed into the metal of the handle. ΔΥΜΜΑΧΟΣ ΜΕΝΕΝΔΟΥ – Dymmachus, son of Menendes. His eyes blinked in surprise.

'Well, well, well,' he muttered. 'So that's your little secret, is it?'

He wrote the words down on the pad beside him, spelling them out letter by letter, checking and rechecking to make sure he had them right. Then he laid the dagger down, lifted the pad and sat back in his chair.

'Where have I seen that before?' he said aloud. 'Where? Where?'

For twenty minutes he sat without moving, staring into space, occasionally lifting his sherry glass and tilting it up to his mouth, even though there was no longer any sherry in it. Then, suddenly, he threw aside the pad, scrambled to his feet and made for the bookcase on the far side of the room, moving surprisingly quickly for a man his age.

'Impossible!' he said. 'It can't be!'

He ran his finger urgently along the rows of books before eventually levering one from the middle of the case: an old leather-bound volume with thick, parchment-like pages and its title inscribed in gold lettering on the spine: *Inscriptions grecques et latines de tombeaux des rois ou syringes à Thèbes. J. Baillet.* He hurried back to his desk and, swiping his arms across it to clear a space, laid the book down beneath the lamp and began leafing rapidly through the pages. Outside the security guard shouted, 'Good evening, professor,' as he passed the door, but the old man ignored the greeting, so engrossed was he in the volume before him. The silence of the room seemed to magnify the excited rasping of his breath.

'It's impossible,' he muttered. 'Impossible! But, my God, if it's not . . .'

28

LUXOR, THE THEBAN HILLS

It was too cold to lie naked for long, even behind the windbreak. After they had made love they pulled their clothes back on and, with Daniel taking the knapsack, wandered further into the hills, the wind pushing at their backs, the landscape glowing a dull silver in the moonlight. Tara clutched Daniel's arm, her body suffused with a rich, warm glow, a delicious ache between her legs. She had forgotten what a powerful lover he was.

'What are you looking for?' she asked after a while, noticing the way his head was turning this way and that, eyes scanning the shadowy slopes.

'Hmm? Oh, nothing really. It's just been a while since I was last up here.'

She tightened her grip on his arm.

'Do you wish we hadn't?'

'What, made love?' He smiled. 'No, it was wonderful. Why, do you?'

She pulled him to a halt and, standing on tiptoe, kissed him passionately on the lips.

'I'll take that as a no then,' he said, laughing.

They wandered on, arms round each other, deeper and deeper into the hills, the world about them deathly silent apart from the clunk of their feet, the whisper of the wind and, occasionally, the far-off howl of a wild dog.

So far as Tara could make out, they were crossing a broad plateau on top of the massif. To their right the land sloped upwards slightly, blocking any view in that direction. To the left it ran flat for several hundred yards before dropping away into a shadowy confusion of cliffs and wadis. Ahead loomed the distant outline of higher peaks, black against the deep grey-blue of the sky. She had no idea where they were going, nor did she really care. She was happy just to be at his side, holding him, feeling his warmth and strength and power.

Eventually, after they had been walking for over an hour, Daniel slowed and stopped. The path at this point dipped slightly, crossing a shallow, dried-up watercourse that cut directly across their way, meandering from right to left like the track of some enormous snake. Tara circled her arms around his waist.

'You're trembling,' she said.

'I'm just cold. I'd forgotten how chilly it gets up here at night.'

She dug her hands into the back pockets of his jeans and nuzzled her face against his neck. 'I suppose we ought to think about going back. We've been away for almost three hours. Omar might be worrying.'

'Yes,' he said, 'I suppose we should.'

Neither of them moved. A shooting star flashed above them.

'If it was light we could try going down a different way,' he said eventually. 'There are all sorts of paths you can follow. Best not to risk it in the dark, though. These hills are full of old tomb shafts. If you stray off the track and fall into one, chances are you won't get out again. A few years ago a Canadian woman went into one over by Deir el-Bahri. No-one heard her screaming. She eventually died of starvation. When they found her body . . .'

He stopped suddenly, body tensing.

'What?' said Tara.

'I thought I heard . . . Listen!'

She tilted her head but could hear nothing but the gusting of the breeze.

'What?' she repeated.

'There was a . . . there, again! Listen!'

Now she could hear it too. Away to their left, towards the cliffs. A faint clanking of stones, as if a hammer was being tapped lightly on an anvil. Someone was coming towards them. She strained her eyes, trying to make them out, but it was too dark.

'Probably an army patrol,' said Daniel, dropping his voice. 'We'd better make ourselves scarce.'

He pulled her across the watercourse and round behind a huge boulder on its far side, where they crouched down in the shadows.

'What's the problem?' she whispered.

'They get suspicious if anyone's up here after dark. Think they're up to no good. We're Westerners, so the chances are there wouldn't be any problems, but in our current situation I think it's best if we avoid any brushes with the authorities.'

They peered over the top of the boulder.

'What if they see us?' she asked.

'Stay where you are and make sure they know you're a tourist. These guys are just young conscripts and from what I've heard they're more than a little trigger happy.'

The sound of footsteps was unmistakable now. There were muffled voices too, and the low, dirge-like sound of someone singing. Tara bit her lip. Sod's law, she thought, after all they'd been through, to end up getting shot by accident. She could feel Daniel's hand on her arm. His grip was tense.

It took another minute for the patrol to come into sight. One moment the landscape was empty, a confused mesh of shadow and half-light, then, suddenly, figures began to emerge, moving along the bed of the dried-up water channel. Initially they all seemed to merge together, a single silhouette swaying against the background gloom. Gradually, however, their outlines grew

251

sharper until eventually Tara could see them clearly in the moonlight: nine men, walking in single file, the ones at the rear carrying what looked like a coffin. Striding at the head of the line, slightly in front of the others, was a huge figure in a pale suit. Tara's insides lurched violently.

'Oh God,' she hissed. 'It's him!'

She leaned out to get a better view, her foot dislodging a small shower of pebbly gravel down into the watercourse. The clatter seemed to fill the night. Daniel grabbed her arm and pulled her around the back of the rock out of sight, clamping his hand over her mouth.

The two of them remained completely still, hardly daring to breathe. The footsteps came nearer and nearer, clumping up the rocky channel until they were so close that Tara could make out the individual voices of the men. It seemed inevitable she and Daniel would be found and her leg muscles tightened, ready to run. At the last moment, however, when the men were practically on top of them and she could actually smell the odour of Dravic's cigar, they suddenly turned aside onto the path and moved off at right angles to the watercourse, away from the Nile valley, the sound of their feet gradually receding as they trudged deeper into the hills.

For several minutes Tara and Daniel remained where they were. Then slowly, cautiously, Daniel came to his feet and peered over the top of the rock. She came up beside him, watching as the column slowly dissolved into the shadows.

'What were they doing up here?' she whispered.

'They've been in the tomb.'

She looked at him questioningly.

'Well, what the hell else would they be doing up here? Having a quiet evening stroll? With a coffin?'

He stepped out from behind the rock and gazed after the men.

'They must know a different way down,' he said. 'One that

avoids going past the guards' huts around the Valley of the Kings. Like I said, these hills are full of paths if you know where to look.'

He stood staring into the darkness for a moment, then, drawing a deep breath, thrust his arms through the straps of the knapsack and swung it onto his back.

'I want you to go back to Omar's,' he said, taking her arm and steering her back onto the path. 'Just follow the track back to the top of the Qurn and then down the way we came. Don't stray off it. When you get to the bottom, go to Omar's house and stay there.'

'What are you going to do?'

'Don't worry about me. Just go.'

She shook herself free. 'You're going to look for the tomb, aren't you?'

'Of course I'm going to look for the bloody tomb! It's what we came here for, isn't it? Now go. I'll follow you down.'

He tried to grab her again, but she swiped his hand away.

'I'm going with you.'

'Tara, I know these hills. It's better if I go alone.'

'We go together. I want to know what's in there as much as you.'

'For Christ's sake, Tara, I haven't got time to argue! They might come back again!'

'Then we'd better get a move on.'

She stepped past him and started down the watercourse. He came after her and, seizing her shoulder, swung her roughly round.

'Please, Tara! You don't understand. These hills . . . they're dangerous. I've worked out here, I know my way around. You'll be . . .'

'What, Daniel?' she snapped, eyes flashing. 'An encumbrance? Is that what I'll be?'

'No, not an encumbrance, I just . . . I don't want you to get hurt.'

There was an edge of desperation to his voice. Despite the wind his forehead was peppered with beads of sweat. She could feel his body shaking beside her.

'I don't want you to get hurt,' he repeated. 'Can't you understand that? This isn't a game.'

For a brief moment they stood in silence, eyes burning into each other. Then she shook her arm free.

'You don't owe me anything, Daniel. You have no debts to pay. Nothing to prove. We're in this together. If you go, I go. OK?'

He opened his mouth to argue, but her eyes told him it would be useless.

'You don't know what you're getting into,' he mumbled.

'Whatever it is I'm already in it,' she replied. 'So there's not much point being careful now. I think we should get a move on.'

She came up on tiptoe and kissed his chin.

'I just don't want you to get hurt,' he said again, impotently.

'Did it ever occur to you that I don't want you to get hurt either?'

They followed the bed of the dried-up water channel, tracing the route they had seen Dravic and his men following. The night air was cold and shreds of mist had started to appear, floating just above the ground, glowing in the moonlight like will-o'-the-wisps. A wild dog began howling in the distance.

For two hundred metres the channel wound across the flat plateau. Then the land began to dip away and the watercourse sloped with it, down towards the southern edge of the massif.

'The hills on this side end in a series of cliffs,' said Daniel, peering ahead through the darkness. 'The tomb's probably cut into one of those, somewhere near the line of this watercourse. Where, though, is anyone's guess. It could be completely inaccessible without proper climbing equipment.'

They continued downwards, the water channel gradually turning into a steep, narrow gully, its sides rising like walls to the left and right of them. Its floor became choked with boulders and loose shale and they had to pick their way carefully, dislodging flurries of biscuit-like scree with every step. Daniel pulled a mini Maglite from his pocket and turned it on, playing the beam down the gully.

'If this lot starts sliding, we're dead,' he muttered. 'It'll sweep us down and over the cliff like a waterfall. If it gets much steeper, we'll have to go back. Christ knows how they got that coffin up here.'

Further and further they went, the gully dropping ever more precipitously, its floor becoming increasingly treacherous underfoot. Its walls were now so close together they could touch either side with their outstretched arms. Twice Daniel urged Tara to go back and let him continue alone, twice she insisted on staying with him.

'I've come this far,' she said. 'I'm not giving up now.'

Eventually they came to a point where the gully bottom suddenly stepped vertically downwards, dropping six metres onto a slope of shale, steep and slippery as a playground slide. The slope ran down for another twenty metres, and then, suddenly, as if a door had been thrown open, the walls of the gully disappeared and there was nothing, just a column of sky and, far beneath, the distant glimmer of a flat, silvery plain.

'That's the cliff edge,' said Daniel, pointing with the torch beam. 'Beyond that it's a hundred-metre drop straight down. We can't go any further.'

He gripped a crack in the gully wall, tested it to make sure it could take his weight, and leaned out over the edge of the step, shining his torch downwards.

'Is there anything down there?' asked Tara.

'There's some sort of opening,' he said. 'It cuts back into the rock underneath where we're standing.'

He leaned out further.

'I can't see much. It's choked with scree. It's definitely an entrance of some sort, though.' He pulled himself back and handed her the torch. 'Hold this for me. And keep it pointing downwards.'

He turned and, using the gully walls for support, swung himself over the edge of the step and down towards the shale slide below. He moved fast, as though used to this sort of terrain, and within thirty seconds was at the bottom. Tara followed more slowly, testing each foothold before she put her weight on it, fingers clasping at the rock.

At the bottom she found Daniel squatting in front of a small rectangular entrance cut back into the face of the step.

'Is this it?' she whispered.

'Well, it's definitely a tomb,' he said, taking the torch from her. 'See, the rock's been deliberately cut back to create a doorway. You can see the ancient chisel marks.'

Half of the entrance was blocked with shale and rubble, leaving a metre-wide opening at the top. Daniel put his head through and flashed the torch around in the pitch blackness. There was a sudden flurry and something shot out into the night.

'What the fuck?' gasped Tara.

'Bats.' He smiled. 'They love tombs. Nothing to worry about.'

He took another look around with the torch and then clambered through the opening. Tara came to her feet, ready to follow. As she did so she trod on a slab of loose shale which slid from beneath her foot, causing her to lose her balance. She swayed for a moment, clawing desperately at the sides of the gully, and then the entire shale bed gave way and she was on her back and sliding downwards towards the edge of the cliff, scree rushing beneath her like water down a chute.

'Tara!' cried Daniel.

Her arms flailed wildly as she grappled for a handhold. In the narrow funnel of the cleft the hiss of slipping stone was magnified tenfold so that it seemed as if she was caught up in a raging torrent. Dislodged scree vomited out of the mouth of the gully beneath her and disappeared into nothingness. Daniel stood helplessly in the tomb doorway, watching as she slid further and further down. Only when she was almost at the cliff edge, and it seemed certain that she would be dragged over it by the force of sliding rubble, did she finally manage to jam her foot against an outcrop of rock and stop her descent. There was a long silence and then the distant clatter of stones as they hit the ground far below.

'Shit,' she gasped.

She lay still for a moment, breathing heavily, and then, very carefully, stood up, keeping both feet planted firmly against the walls of the gully, where the rock was solid.

'Are you OK?' he called.

'Just about.'

'Stay there. Don't move.'

He clambered out of the tomb, shone the torch beam across the shale, then edged his way carefully down towards her, grasping her outstretched hand and half leading, half pulling her back up to the top of the slope again. Her clothes and face were grey with dust, her shirt torn at the elbow and stained with blood.

'You're hurt,' he said.

'It's fine,' she replied, shaking the dust out of her hair. 'Come on, let's see what's in the tomb.'

He smiled, despite himself. 'And I thought I was obsessed. You should have been an archaeologist, Tara.'

She grinned at him. 'Not enough excitement,' she said.

Inside the entrance they found themselves in a narrow sloping corridor. From this side, by the light of the torch, they could see that the bottom half of the doorway was blocked with a wall of mud bricks, against which the scree had become piled. For a long while Daniel stood in silence gazing around him.

'Originally the whole doorway would have been bricked up,' he said eventually. 'Over the years more and more rubble would have got piled up against it, until only the top part was left clear.

Whoever found the tomb knocked that in and left the bottom half of the blocking intact.'

He flicked the torch to the side.

'See, there are the bricks.'

Swept up against the wall of the corridor was a pile of whole and broken mud bricks. He poked among them and lifted one up. On its face was imprinted a design of nine kneeling men, their hands tied behind their backs, with a seated jackal above them.

'What's that?' she asked.

'The seal of the royal necropolis,' he said, smiling to himself. 'Nine bound captives surmounted by Anubis the jackal. If the door blocking was still in place, with the necropolis seal on it, that means the tomb was intact when it was found. Untouched since antiquity. About as rare as they get.'

He stared down at the brick for a moment longer, then laid it gently back on the floor and shone the torch down the corridor, its beam punching a narrow hole through the enveloping blackness. By its light they could see that the shaft sloped gently downwards for thirty metres before opening out into what looked like a chamber of some sort. Beyond the margins of the torchlight the darkness was thicker and more tangible than any darkness Tara had ever known. They began to move forwards, Daniel flashing the torch over the neatly chiselled walls, ceiling and floor. After a few paces, however, he stopped.

'What?' asked Tara.

'There's something moving down there.'

'Bats?'

'No, on the floor. There.'

He dropped the beam. Something was coming towards them, fast.

'Daniel,' she said, trying to sound calm, 'stand very still and don't make any sudden movements.'

The night train to Luxor was less crowded than it had been coming in the opposite direction and Khalifa had almost an entire carriage to himself. He removed his shoes, lit a cigarette and began going through the files on Dravic, which Tauba had had photocopied for him. Behind him, at the far end of the carriage, two backpackers, a boy and a girl, were playing cards. The files didn't make pleasant reading. Born in 1951, in the former East Germany, Dravic was the son of an SS officer who had subsequently joined the Communist Party and risen through the ranks to a position of some prominence.

As a boy he had excelled at school, especially in languages, and, aged only seventeen, had won a place at the University of Rostock, where he had gained a doctorate in Near Eastern Archaeology. He had published his first book at the age of twenty – an analysis of Minoan Linear A script – and had thereafter produced a stream of other works, one of which, on Late Period Greek settlements in the Nile Delta, was still regarded as a standard text on the subject.

Khalifa finished his cigarette and lit another one, remembering how he'd read the Greek settlements book for an essay he'd written at university. He stared out of the window for a moment, the landscape flat, dark and empty apart from the occasional lights of a far-off house or village, then returned his attention to the papers in front of him.

From the outset Dravic's academic achievements had been overshadowed by a tendency to violence. At the age of twelve he had put out a fellow pupil's eye during a playground fight, only narrowly escaping criminal proceedings after the intervention of the local Party supremo, a friend of his father's. Three years later he had been implicated in the murder of a vagrant who had been found burnt to death in a local park, and the year after in the gang rape of a young Jewish girl, on each occasion escaping punishment because of his father's connections. Khalifa shook his head, appalled.

The German had begun excavating in his early twenties, first in Syria, then Sudan and then Egypt, where he had worked for five consecutive seasons at Naukratis in the Delta. Despite persistent rumours of antiquities smuggling and worse, no charge against him had ever been sustained, and his career had flourished. There was a photograph of him shaking hands with President Sadat and another of him being presented with an award by Erich Honecker.

He had seemed destined for great things. Then, however, had come the incident with the dig volunteer. Although it had occurred in Egypt, the girl had been German, and that's where he'd been tried. He'd got away with it, but this time the mud had stuck. His research fellowship had been revoked, his dig concessions cancelled, he had stopped publishing.

That was two decades ago. Since then he had earned his living on the antiquities market, putting his expertise to use procuring and authenticating items for various wealthy patrons. In 1994 he had been arrested in Alexandria for possession of stolen antiquities and had served three months in Cairo's Tura prison, where the last known photo of him had been taken. Khalifa held it up – a black-and-white prison mug shot, the German standing against a wall holding a card with a number on it to his chest, scowling at the camera, huge and malevolent. Khalifa shivered.

After his release from Tura, Dravic had gone underground, entering and leaving the country illegally, organizing the smuggling of artefacts and their sale on the black markets of Europe and the Far East. Despite warrants for his arrest in seven countries, and numerous sightings, he'd always managed to keep one step ahead of the law.

Details of his recent movements were sketchy. All that was known was that he'd started working for Sayf al-Tha'r in the mid-1990s, and had been with him ever since. There were rumours of secret Swiss bank accounts, links with neo-Nazi organizations, even covert involvement with Western intelligence agencies, but most of it was hearsay. After 1994 the German had kept a low profile. One thing was certain, however – he was about as bad as they got.

Khalifa worked his way through to the end of the file, then stood to stretch his legs, wandering up to the far end of the carriage, where the two backpackers had put away their cards and were now listening to a cassette player. He nodded a greeting and asked them where they were going. They ignored him – probably worried I'm trying to sell them something, he thought, smiling to himself – and with a shrug he wandered back to his seat, lit another Cleopatra and got started on the pathologist's report on old man Iqbar. The backpackers' music seemed to blend with the rhythm of the train's wheels, as though both were part of the same tune. He could feel his eyes drooping.

Just south of Beni Suef the train juddered to a halt. It remained stationary for five minutes, emitting a soft hissing sound as though catching its breath, and then started moving again. Another minute passed and then he heard the door of the carriage open behind him. There was a pause, then a shout and a crash. The music from the cassette player stopped abruptly. He turned.

Three men in black djellabas were standing over the backpackers, whose cassette player lay smashed on the floor. One of the men grabbed the boy by the hair, yanked his head back and, in a movement so swift Khalifa barely saw it, slashed a knife across his throat. Blood jetted out over the carriage floor.

The detective leaped to his feet, reaching for his gun. Then he realized he'd left it in Luxor and so looked around wildly for something else to use as a weapon. Someone had left a pile of books on the seat opposite him. He began throwing them at the men.

'Police!' he yelled. 'Drop your weapons.'

They laughed and began moving towards him. He held his

ground for a moment, then turned and ran, crashing through the door at the end of the carriage and into the next one along. There were more people here, including a group of children clutching brass lamps.

He ran forward between the seats, but snagged his foot on a can of edible oil and fell. A hand clasped his forehead and yanked his head backwards.

'God help me!' he coughed. 'Allah protect me!'

A face loomed right up against his, huge, big as a beach ball, half white, half purple.

'Poor little Ali,' chuckled the man. 'Ali, Ali, Ali!'

He was holding a trowel, diamond-shaped, its edges sharpened. With a bellow of laughter he drew it back and drilled it into Khalifa's neck—

He woke with a start.

The pathologist's report had slipped from his knees and lay scattered on the floor. Behind him he could hear the sound of the backpackers' cassette player. He looked round. They were both asleep, leaning against each other. Khalifa shook his head, relieved, and bent to gather up the report.

29

LUXOR, THE THEBAN HILLS

The snake came straight up the corridor towards them, eyes gleaming in the beam of the torch.

'Just keep very still,' Tara repeated.

'Oh Christ,' groaned Daniel. 'What is it?'

'*Naja nigricollis*,' she said. 'Black-necked cobra.'

'Is that bad?'

'Mm-hm.'

'How bad?'

'If one of us gets bitten we won't make it back down. They're very aggressive and very, very venomous. And they spit too. So no sudden movements.'

The snake's belly made a dry slithering sound as it swirled across the floor. Daniel tried to keep the torch on it.

'Fuck,' he shivered.

The cobra came to within a few paces of them and paused, rearing slightly, its hood distended, its eyes black and menacing. It was big, over two metres, its body thick and hose-like. Beside her Tara could feel Daniel beginning to shake.

'Try to keep calm,' she whispered. 'It'll be OK.'

The cobra swung to and fro for a moment and then dropped back to the floor and slithered forward again, right up to Daniel's boot, its black, pronged tongue seeming to lap at the dusty leather. It reared and began to explore his ankle, curling slowly around his leg.

'Turn the torch off,' said Tara.

'What?'

'Turn the torch off. Now. The light's exciting it.'

The snake's tongue was flicking up his calf. His breath was coming in short gasps.

'I can't,' he stammered. 'I can't be in the dark with it.'

'Do it!' she hissed.

'Oh Jesus.'

He flicked the switch and they were plunged into impenetrable blackness, as though their eyes had been bound with a length of thick velvet. The silence pressed in upon their ears, disturbed only by the swish of the cobra's tail and Daniel's rasping breath.

'It's going up my leg,' he choked.

'Just stay as still as you can.'

'It's going to bite me!'

'Not if you stay still.'

'It's all around my leg. I can't stand this, Tara. Please do something. Please!'

He was starting to panic. The snake would be able to feel his fear and that in turn would frighten it, making it more likely to bite.

'Tell me about Mery-amun,' she said desperately.

'Fuck Mery-amun!'

'Tell me about him!' she hissed.

He was panting with terror.

'Second son of King Amasis,' he gasped. 'Lived around 550 BC. High priest of Amun at Karnak. Jesus!'

'Keep talking!'

'Carter found an ostrakon with his name on it in the

valley. Seemed to give the location of his tomb. Beside the Southern Path, twenty cubits from the Water in the Sky. We think Water in the Sky is a cliff at the top end of the valley.'

He fell silent. The air around them seemed to throb.

'What's happening?' she asked.

'I don't know. It's not on my leg any more. I can still feel it though.'

She was silent for a moment, thinking.

'Tara?'

'OK, I want you to turn the torch on again. But point it upwards. Not at the floor. Upwards. And do it very slowly. No jerky movements.'

A beat, and then a thin column of light speared up to the ceiling. By its glow she could just make out the cobra. It was between his legs, slightly in front, its head reared up almost to the level of his crotch.

'It likes you,' she said.

'I guess I'm that sort of guy,' he muttered through clenched teeth.

Slowly she dropped to her haunches. The snake's tail swished around the back of Daniel's boot.

'Lower the beam a bit. Carefully.'

The shaft of light slid across the ceiling and down onto the floor.

The cobra was swinging back and forth, its hood stretched wide, like a cupped hand. Not a good sign. It was getting agitated. Slowly she reached into her pocket and pulled out a handkerchief, holding it away from her and fluttering it to attract the snake's attention. It rocked to and fro, looking first at the handkerchief, then at her, then at the handkerchief again. It continued swaying for a moment, then reared back and, with a sound like it was sneezing, launched a jet of venom at the white material. She felt globs of it spatter on her hand and arm, making the flesh burn.

'What's happening?' hissed Daniel, trying to look down without moving his head.

'Just stay still. I'm going to try and get it off.'

'You're not going to touch it, Tara! Please tell me you're not going to touch it!'

'It'll be fine. We've got a cobra at the zoo. I handle it all the time.'

Only with a snake hook, though, she thought to herself. And wearing protective gloves and goggles. She tried to block out memories of the time she'd been bitten and, continuing to flutter the handkerchief with her left hand, began moving her right one towards the cobra, aiming for the collar of blackish scales just beneath its head, trying not to tremble too much. Blood was pounding in her ears.

'Jesus Christ!' groaned Daniel.

She ignored him and concentrated all her attention on the snake. Twice it arched its head back and spat at the handkerchief, twice she stopped her right hand dead and snapped her eyes shut, waiting for several agonizing seconds before slowly opening them again and continuing to move her fingers towards the snake's neck, expecting at any moment to feel the snap of fangs puncturing her flesh. I have to get this just right, she thought. If I take it too low I'll leave it enough room to switch round and bite me. Too high and I'll end up putting my hand right into its jaws. I have to judge it perfectly.

'What's going on?' Daniel's voice was desperate.

'Almost there,' she whispered. 'Almost . . .'

Her hand was just a few inches from the cobra's neck. Droplets of sweat were stinging her eyes. The tips of her fingers were shaking so badly it looked like she was waving.

'Please, Tara, what's . . .'

The snake lunged. It went for the handkerchief rather than her hand and, driven purely by instinct, she snatched her left hand back while at the same time whipping her right one forward and up, grasping the cobra just below the head. It writhed furiously, tail lashing against Daniel's leg.

'Christ Almighty!' he screamed, leaping backwards, dropping the torch.

'It's all right,' she said, 'I've got it. I've got it.'

The cobra coiled and flailed around her arm, struggling furiously. It was strong, but her grip was firm and it was unable to break free. Trembling, Daniel picked up the torch and shone it at them. The snake's mouth had levered open in fury, revealing dripping, needle-like fangs.

'Jesus, I can't believe you just did that!'

'Neither can I.'

She moved past him back to the doorway and clambered outside, the cobra flipping about in her hand as though she was waving a streamer. Carefully she edged her way down the gully till she was almost at its mouth and then, dropping her arm, threw the snake out into the void. It spiralled through the air, like a thin line pencilled against the sky, and fell out of sight. She made her way back up the gully and into the tomb, breathing heavily.

'Right,' she said, sounding calmer than she felt, 'let's have a look what's in here, shall we?'

The chamber at the end of the corridor was rectangular in shape, small, no more than eight metres long by four across, its walls decorated with columns of black hieroglyphic text and vivid scenes in red, green and yellow. Around the bottom of the walls ran a continuous line of rearing serpents like the ones on the plaster fragment they'd found at Saqqara. The place was completely empty.

There was a metre drop from the level of the corridor to the chamber floor. Tara jumped down immediately. Daniel remained where he was for a moment, playing the torch back and forth across the floor, then jumped down too. He circled the torch around the floor again, then lifted the beam and slowly ran it over the walls, images appearing and disappearing as the light passed over them. He seemed uneasy, his gaze flicking constantly downwards and back towards the chamber entrance. Gradually, however, as his attention focused on the painted images – the brilliant colours, the strange faces, the teetering columns of hieroglyphs – he seemed to relax. A smile spread slowly across his face and his eyes began to sparkle.

'It's good,' he muttered to himself, nodding. 'Oh, it's very good.'

He shone the torch up at one of the painted scenes: a jackal-headed figure leading a man towards a set of scales, on the far side of which stood another figure, this one with the head of an ibis, a pen and tablet in its hand.

'What is it?' asked Tara.

'From the Book of the Dead,' he replied, gazing up at the scene. 'Anubis, god of the necropolis, leads the deceased to the scales of judgement. His heart is weighed and the result is written down by the god Thoth. It's a typical Egyptian tomb scene. Like that one . . .' He ran the torch along the wall to another image: a man, red-skinned and wearing a white kilt, extending his arms with what looked like a jar clasped in each hand. In front of him stood a woman, yellow-skinned, her head surmounted by a pair of bull's horns with between them a circular disc.

'The deceased making offerings to the goddess Isis. Red for the man's skin, yellow for the woman's. Wonderfully painted. Look at the precision of the lines, the richness of the colours. I can't believe I . . . It's just incredible.'

He stared up, spellbound.

'What about these figures?' asked Tara, pointing to a scene on one of the side walls: two men with intricately braided wigs and beards facing each other, one sitting, one kneeling. 'They look different.'

Daniel shone the torch at them.

'You're right,' he said. 'Stylistically they're Persian, not

Egyptian. You can tell by the way they wear their hair and beards. Go to the ruins of Susa or Persepolis and you'll find this sort of tableau everywhere. You don't see them in Egyptian tombs, though. Same with this one.' He flicked the torch round to an image on the opposite wall: a bearded man in a white robe standing in front of a table piled high with fruit.

'Here the style's Greek,' he said. 'See, he's wearing a toga and his skin is pale, and the beard's shorter, more ragged. Again, it's extremely unusual to find this sort of figure in an Egyptian tomb. It's not entirely unheard of – the tomb of Petosiris at Tuna el-Gebel has the same sort of thing. And the tomb of Si-Amun at Siwa. It's still very rare, though. Unique if you factor in the Persian scene as well. It's almost as if three different people have been buried here. It's incredible.'

He turned round slowly, circling the torch beam over the walls, something hungry in his eyes, possessive, as if by analysing the tomb he was somehow claiming it as his own. Tara wandered over to a small recess at the back of the chamber.

'The canopic niche,' he said, coming up behind her. 'For the canopic jars. When the deceased was mummified his internal organs were removed and placed in four containers – one for the liver, one for the intestines, one for the stomach and one for the lungs. This is where they would have stood.'

He sounded as if he was giving a guided tour. She smiled to herself, remembering how he had dragged her around the British Museum when they had been lovers, giving lengthy explanations of every object they came to.

'And what about this, Professor?' she asked, indicating a painted panel just to the left of the recess. 'What's this all about?'

He ran the torch beam over the panel. It was divided into three sections, one above the other. In the upper one a line of figures was marching across a yellow landscape. In the next one down the figures appeared to be tumbling and cartwheeling, a creature with the body of a man and the head of some long-snouted animal towering over them, wielding a mace. In the last scene there was only a single figure, still against the same yellow background, with behind him, taller, a young man holding an ankh-sign in his hand, and wearing a headdress shaped like a lotus flower.

'It's telling a story,' said Daniel. 'These figures in the upper register, they're soldiers. See: spears, bows, shields. They seem to be marching across a desert. And then in the next register, that figure with the mace and the animal head, that's Seth, the god of war and chaos. And deserts too. He's striking them down. So it looks like they were defeated in battle, although there's no indication of who the enemy was. And then in the bottom register that figure with the lotiform headdress, that's Nefertum, god of regeneration and rebirth.'

'Meaning?'

Daniel shrugged. 'Maybe that the spirit of the army lives on despite its defeat. Or that some of the soldiers survived the battle. It's hard to be sure with Egyptian symbolism. They thought very differently from the way we do now.'

He stared at the images for a while longer, then turned away and shone the torch at the walls to either side of the corridor opening, which were covered in columns of neat black hiero-glyphs. At the bottom of the left-hand wall, about midway along, was a small gap in the text.

'That's where our piece comes from,' he said. 'See, the snakes fit into the line along the bottom of the wall.'

He squatted down, Tara at his side. The darkness seemed to push in around them as though they were immersed in a black liquid. She could hear her heart beating.

'Well, go on then,' she urged. 'Put it back. It's what we came here for.'

He glanced over at her, then swung the knapsack from his back, took out the box and, removing the piece of plaster, fitted it carefully back into position. Once it was in place it was almost impossible to tell it had ever been taken out.

'So what does it say?' she asked.

He looked over at her again, then stood, took a few paces back and wove the torch over the hieroglyphs.

'The text starts here,' he said, 'to the left of the door, and reads top to bottom and right to left.'

He stared at the wall a while longer, and then began to read, the torch beam rising and falling as it followed the columns of text, his translation swift and assured. In the narrow confines of the tomb his voice took on a distant, echoing quality, as though it was coming from far back in time. Tara felt the hairs on her neck stand up.

'*I, ib-wer-imenty and am laid here in year twelve of the king of upper and lower Egypt Se-tut-ra Tar-i-ush* . . . that's the Egyptian royal titulary of the Persian emperor Darius . . . *day four, first month of Akhet. Beloved of Darius, true servant of his affection, king's protector beloved of his lord, follower of the king, overseer of the army, the justified, the faithful, the true. In Greece I was at his side. In Lydia I was with him. In Persia I did not fail him. In Ashkalon I was there.*'

He paused. They had reached the bottom of the third column.

'What does all that mean?' she asked.

'Well, it dates the tomb to the First Persian Period. The Persians conquered Egypt under Cambyses in about 525 BC. Darius succeeded Cambyses in 522 BC. This guy died in year twelve of Darius's reign, so about 510 BC.'

She could almost hear his mind whirring.

'This guy must have been one of Darius's generals. That's what titles like *shemsu nesu*, follower of the king, and *mer-mesha*, overseer of the army, usually mean. You've no idea how important this is. The tomb of one of the king's generals. And from the sixth century, too. Almost no burials from that period have ever been found in Thebes. It's fabulous.'

'Go on,' she said. 'What does the rest say?'

He swung the torch up to the top of the fourth column.

'*The Nubians I destroyed at my master's bidding, grinding them to dust, winning great fame. The Greeks I made to bow low. The Libyans*

I smote to the farthest horizon, and made to taste death. My sword was mighty. My strength was great. I had no fear. The gods were with me.'

He flashed the torch downwards momentarily.

'OK. Our piece starts at the beginning of this next column.'

He raised the beam again, and continued.

'*In year three under the person of the king of upper and lower Egypt Mes-u-ti-ra Kem-bit-jet* . . . again, an Egyptian royal titulary, Cambyses this time . . . *before I found great fame, **in the third month of peret, I, ib-wer-imenty** went into the western desert, to sekhet-imit, to destroy the king's enemies.*'

He stopped again, a sudden, puzzled look on his face.

'What?' she asked.

'Sekhet-imit, that's . . .'

He paused for a moment, thinking, and then, without finishing his sentence, began translating again, his voice slower now, more deliberate, as though he was checking and rechecking every word.

'*At the place **of the pyramid, 90 iteru** to the south and east of sekhet-imit, in the midst of the valley of sand, as we took our noonday meal, **a great storm happened**. The world was black. The sun no more. 50,000 went down into the sand. I alone was spared by the mercy of the gods. Sixty iteru I walked alone through the desert, south and east to the land of the cows. Great was the heat. Great thirst I suffered. Great hunger I suffered. Many times I died. But I came to the land of the cows. The Gods were with me. I was very great in their favour . . .*'

His voice trailed off. She looked over at him. His lips were moving, but no sound was coming out. Even in the enveloping blackness she could see that his face had gone a deathly, luminous white. His hand was trembling, causing the torch beam to judder over the wall.

'My God,' he whispered, voice hoarse, as though the darkness had somehow flooded his throat.

'What?'

He didn't answer.

'What, Daniel?'

'It's the army of Cambyses.'

His eyes were wide, full of shock and triumph.

'What's the army of Cambyses?'

Again he didn't answer immediately, just stood staring up at the wall, oblivious to her questions, as though in a sort of trance. It was almost a minute before he eventually shook his head, as though to wake himself up. Taking her hand, he led her across the chamber, back to the panel they had been looking at earlier. He shone the torch up at it.

'In 525 BC Cambyses of Persia conquered Egypt and absorbed it into the Persian empire.' He could barely keep the torch beam still. 'Some time thereafter, probably around 523 BC, he sent out two armies from Thebes. He led the first one himself, marching due south against the Ethiopians. The second army was sent north-west across the desert to destroy the oracle of Amun at the oasis of Siwa, which the Egyptians knew as sekhet-imit, the Place of the Palm Trees.'

He shone the torch up at the first of the three images within the panel, a group of figures marching across a desert.

'According to the Greek historian Herodotus, who was writing about seventy-five years later, the army reached an oasis called the Island of the Blessed, which is probably modern al-Kharga. Somewhere between there and Siwa, however, out in the Great Sand Sea, it was overwhelmed by a sandstorm and the entire army was destroyed. Fifty thousand men wiped out, just like that.'

He dropped the torch to the second register, the marching figures crushed beneath the mace of Seth.

'No-one has ever known if the story was true. This text proves it was. Not only that, but that one person at least, this ib-wer-imenty, survived the disaster. God knows how, but he did.' He lowered the beam to the final register. 'Ib-wer-imenty with Nefertum, god of regeneration and rebirth. That's what this last scene means: the army was destroyed, but our man survived.'

'But why is this so important?' she asked.

Without taking his eyes from the wall, he pulled a cheroot from his pocket and lit it, the flare of the match momentarily driving back the shadows and illuminating the entire chamber.

'The mere fact that it confirms Herodotus is significant enough. But there's more here, Tara. Much more.'

He took her hand and led her back to the text.

'Look. Ib-wer-imenty doesn't just tell us he survived the sandstorm. He gives the precise location where it overwhelmed the army. See: "At the place of the pyramid, ninety *iteru* to the south and east of sekhet-imit". I don't know what "the place of the pyramid" is; presumably some sort of pyramid-shaped limestone outcrop. But we do know that an *iteru* is an ancient unit of measurement, equivalent to about two kilometres. And there's more further on: "Sixty *iteru* I walked alone through the desert, south and east to the land of the cows." The land of the cows is a translation of *ta-iht*, which was the ancient name for al-Farafra, another oasis between Kharga and Siwa. Don't you see, Tara? What we've got here is effectively a map of where the army of Cambyses was lost. Sixty *iteru* north-west of al-Farafra, ninety *iteru* south-east of Siwa, at the place of the pyramid. It's about as exact as you could ever get in an ancient text. It's fabulous.'

It was hot in the tomb and his face was glistening with sweat. He pulled excitedly on his cheroot.

'Do you have any idea what this means? People have been looking for the army of Cambyses for thousands of years. It's become a sort of holy grail for archaeologists. But the western desert's a big place. All Herodotus says is that the army was lost somewhere in the middle of it. That doesn't tell you anything. It could be anywhere.

'With these indicators, however, you can pinpoint the spot almost precisely. The measurements from Siwa and al-Farafra narrow it down to perhaps a few dozen square miles. If you surveyed that area from the air it shouldn't be too difficult to locate a pyramid-shaped rock. Anything like that would stick out from the dunes like a sore thumb. You could find it in a couple of days. Less.'

'But only if you had the measurements,' she said, starting to understand.

'Exactly. That's why our piece of text is so crucial. It's got the distance from Siwa, and part of the hieroglyph indicating the distance from al-Farafra. Without it you've got no more chance of finding the army than any of the hundreds of other explorers who've gone looking for it. No wonder Sayf al-Tha'r wanted it so badly.'

He fell silent, staring up at the wall, eyes burning in the glow of the torch. Thoughts were spinning through Tara's mind.

'How valuable would this army be?' she asked after a long silence.

'An entire ancient army? Fifty thousand men, full equipment, perfectly preserved under the desert sands? Fuck, it would be the greatest find in the history of archaeology. Nothing would come close to it. Tutankhamun's tomb would look like a cheap bric-à-brac shop by comparison. I mean a couple of years ago a breastplate from this period sold for over a hundred thousand dollars. Provided he sold it off bit by bit and didn't flood the market . . . Jesus, a find like this would make Sayf al-Tha'r one of the richest men in the Middle East. I dread to think what he could do with resources like that at his disposal.'

They stood in silence. The beam of the torch was starting to weaken, its light gradually softening from a crisp white to a flaccid yellow.

'And what about the British embassy?' asked Tara. 'Squires and Jemal?'

'They must have found out about the tomb. If what Samali said was true they'd have wanted the missing bit of text as much as the fundamentalists. The stakes are unbelievably high here. Higher than I ever thought possible.'

They stood gazing up at the wall. Despite the heat she found she was shivering. There was another long silence.

'So what does the rest of it say?' she asked eventually. 'You didn't finish.'

He shone the torch up again, to the place where he had stopped reading.

'Where were we? Ah yes: "But I came to the land of the cows. The Gods were with me. I was very great in their favour." OK, here we go.' He stared up, eyes narrowed with concentration. 'The next word seems to be a name, although it's not an Egyptian one.' He moved nearer, squinting at the wall. 'It looks like an Egyptian rendering of a Greek name. It's hard to know precisely what – the Egyptians didn't use vowels, just consonants.'

He spelled the word out slowly.

'*Demmichos*. Or *Dimmachos*. Something like that. *Dimmachos was my name, son of* . . .' He paused again.

'. . . *Menendes of Naxos. When my deeds were known, however, I was named ib-wer-imenty*. Of course!' He was laughing.

'What?'

'Ib-wer-imenty. It's a play on words. I should have seen it before. *Ib-wer*, great heart; *imenty*, of the west. But *ib-wer* can also be read as Great Thirst. Appropriate for a man who'd just walked a hundred and twenty kilometres alone through the desert. This man must originally have been a Greek. A mercenary, probably. Egypt was full of them at the time. A Greek soldier, in service to a Persian ruler with an Egyptian nickname.'

He flashed the torch at the images they'd looked at earlier: the pale-skinned man before the table piled with fruit; the man with braided hair and beard, kneeling before his king; the red-skinned figure offering to the goddess Isis.

'That's why we have three different styles of representation here. To highlight three different aspects of the same person. Greek, Persian, Egyptian. It's wonderful. Absolutely wonderful.'

He returned the beam to the wall, and ran through the last five columns of text.

'*When my deeds were known, how I had returned from the dead, Cambyses placed me at his right hand, and advanced me, and made me his beloved friend, for I had come alive from the desert, and he knew the Gods were with me.*

'*Land I was given, and titles, and riches. Under the person of Darius, living enduringly, I prospered and became great. I surpassed any peer of mine in all kinds of dignity and wealth. A wife I took. Three sons she bore. Great I became in the king's counsel. Faithful always. Strong of heart. True protector. Foremost in position in the house of his lord.*

'*In Waset I had my estates . . .* Waset was the ancient Egyptian name for Thebes, modern Luxor . . . *In Waset I was content. In Waset I lived long. I never again came to Naxos, place of my birth.*

'*Oh living ones upon the earth who may pass by this tomb and who love life and who hate death, may you say: "Osiris transfigure ib-wer-imenty . . ."*'

His voice dropped off and he lowered the torch.

'The rest is just prayers from the books of the afterlife.' He shook his head, pulling on the cheroot, its tip glowing bright orange in the darkness. 'What an incredible story, eh? A lowly Greek mercenary who marched with the army of Cambyses, came back from the dead and rose to become the friend and confidant of kings. Like something out of a Homeric myth. I could spend the rest of my life—'

There was a clatter of stones from the gully outside. Daniel looked at Tara, eyes wide, and flicked off the torch, grinding his cheroot out on the floor. Blackness smothered them. There was a muffled whispering from the top end of the passageway and then a scrabbling sound as someone climbed into the tomb. They shrank back into a corner, pressing themselves against the wall, Tara clasping Daniel's shoulder, wanting to scream but unable to summon any sound from her throat.

There was more scrabbling and then a pale beam of light lanced down the corridor and into the chamber. The whispering grew louder and there was the slow thud of approaching feet. Twenty metres, ten, five, and then they were at the chamber entrance. There was a pause and then a black-robed figure leaped from the passageway into the room.

With a cry Daniel charged at him, knocking him to the ground.

'Get out, Tara!' he cried. 'For Christ's sake . . .'

Two more figures leaped into the chamber, punching him to the floor.

'Daniel!'

She rushed forward, screaming his name. Someone grabbed her and threw her to the ground. She struggled to her feet, lashing out with her fists, but was knocked down again, harder this time, so that the breath was driven out of her. There was shouting and movement and then, suddenly, the chamber was filled with searing white light. Unaccustomed to the brightness, her eyes clamped shut.

'So,' laughed a triumphant voice, 'the rats are caught in a trap!'

She blinked. Four men were standing in front of her, two holding machine-guns, one a rifle and one a cudgel. Above, in the entrance to the corridor, a halogen lamp in his hand, was Dravic. Several other men were crowded into the shaft behind him. Tara clambered unsteadily to her feet. Daniel too was getting up, his nose streaming blood. He came to her side.

'Are you OK?' she asked.

He nodded. Dravic cast his eyes around the floor of the chamber, then handed the lamp to the man beside him and jumped down.

'I see our friend the cobra is no longer here,' he remarked. 'Obviously not as effective a guard as we thought. A shame. I should have enjoyed watching you die slowly from his venom.'

He came towards them, his huge frame seeming to fill half the chamber, blocking out the light of the lamp. Tara shrank back against the wall, her cheek burning from where she had been hit.

'How did you know we were here?' mumbled Daniel, voice thick, mouth smeared with blood.

Dravic laughed. 'Did you seriously think the only thing we'd do to protect the tomb would be to put a fucking snake down here? You stupid idiots! We had a lookout hidden at the top of the gully. When he saw you he called us and we came straight back.'

'What are you going to do with us?' asked Tara, her voice unsteady.

'Kill you, of course.' The giant's tone was matter of fact. 'It's just a question of how and when. And what I do to you first.'

He looked down at her, smiling, his lips glistening moistly, like long pink worms.

'And be assured, there are things I want to do to you first.'

He reached out a hand and ran a finger across her breast. She swiped it away, a spasm of disgust pinching her face.

'You killed my father,' she hissed.

'Oh, I wanted to,' he laughed. 'I would have enjoyed it. Unfortunately he dropped dead before I had the chance. I was as upset as you were about it.'

He noticed the pain in her eyes and his laughter redoubled.

'He went down right in front of me,' he said, goading. 'One minute he was standing, the next he was wriggling around on the floor like a stuck pig. I've never seen anyone die so pathetically.'

He turned and said something in Arabic to the men. They started laughing too. Despite her fear, a wave of fury surged through Tara. She drew her head back and spat as hard as she could in Dravic's face. The laughter stopped abruptly. She braced herself, ready for the inevitable blow.

It didn't come, however. For a moment the giant stood where he was, a wad of spittle inching down his purple cheek and then, raising a hand, he scooped it off.

'Have you ever been raped?' he asked quietly, staring down at the liquid on his fingers. 'Violated? Your body used as a plaything by others, quite against your will? Vagina, anus, mouth? No? Then, believe me, you have something to look forward to.'

'Don't, Dravic,' growled Daniel.

'Oh don't worry, Lacage. You won't be left out.'

He flicked the spittle away and, reaching into his pocket, drew out a small metal trowel, the edges gleaming sharply in the light of the lamp.

'Not all violations need be of a sexual nature, after all.'

His arm whipped out and the blade of the trowel sliced across Daniel's arm. He winced in pain as a line of blood swelled up beneath his shirt.

'Those pleasures, however, are for later.' The giant returned the trowel to his pocket. 'We have certain things to deal with first.'

He turned and looked at the wall of hieroglyphs, motioning to the man with the lamp to come closer.

'So, at last we have the final piece of the jigsaw. A shame it was ever removed in the first place. If things had been left as they were we might have saved ourselves a lot of time and trouble. And pain.'

He glanced across at Tara, grinned lasciviously, then went over to the wall and squatted in front of it, examining the text.

'Normally if a new tomb is discovered in these hills, we are the first to hear about it. The locals know it is in their interests to come straight to us. Otherwise they risk incurring the wrath of Sayf al-Tha'r. And of myself. And they know that's not a good thing to do.

'In this case, however, it was found by someone who decided to go it alone. He paid for his greed, but not before he had removed certain objects. Including, of course, this one vital piece.'

He plucked the plaster fragment from the wall and turned it over in his hands.

'Ironic that he should have hacked out this particular part of the text. He had no idea of its importance, of course. He simply wanted a bit of decoration to sell. Given time, he would have stripped every wall in the place. Unfortunately for him, he started with the one piece that pinpointed the precise location of the army, thus condemning not merely himself but several others to a most distressing end.'

Even from three metres away Tara could smell the thick, sour odour of his body. It made her want to gag.

'None of that matters now, however,' he continued. 'We have the piece. And this time tomorrow we will have the army too. And then . . .' Again that mocking, lascivious look at Tara. 'And then the fun really begins.'

He shouted something in Arabic and two men with sledge-hammers jumped into the chamber. He nodded towards the section of text Daniel had translated earlier and, coming forward, they raised the sledgehammers and flung them against the wall, shattering the plaster, knocking great holes in it, ripping it from the rock.

'Oh Jesus!' cried Daniel, leaping forward. 'No! Please God, stop!'

A gun barrel was jabbed into his stomach, pushing him back.

'You can't destroy it!' He was choking. 'For God's sake, you can't!'

'An unfortunate but necessary precaution,' said Dravic. 'The rest of the decoration can stay, but we cannot risk someone else finding the tomb and reading about the army. Not yet.'

Broad slabs of hieroglyph-covered plaster were crashing to the floor in an explosion of white dust. While one of the men continued to hammer at the wall the other began pounding the pieces on the floor, breaking them into hundreds of tiny fragments. Daniel lowered his head in despair.

When the entire section of wall had been destroyed Dravic waved the men away. The atmosphere in the chamber was heavy with dust. Tara began coughing.

'So what now?' whispered Daniel, unable to take his eyes off the heap of crushed plaster.

Dravic moved towards the chamber entrance, the piece of

text in his hand. He passed it to one of the men, and was hoisted up into the mouth of the corridor.

'Now,' he said, turning to look at them, 'something rather unpleasant is going to happen to you.'

He signalled with his hand and disappeared up the shaft. The man in front of Daniel raised his gun.

'No!' screamed Tara, thinking he was going to shoot. Instead he swung the weapon so the butt was towards Daniel, and smashed it into the side of his head. Daniel crumpled to the ground, unconscious, a trickle of blood running down his neck. Tara went down on her knees beside him, touching his face. She heard movement behind her, something coming down through the air, and then, suddenly, she was falling very fast towards what seemed like an immense ocean of still black water.

Northern Sudan

The boy sprinted through the camp with the radio message in his hand. A herd of goats, startled by his approach, sprang to their feet and scattered before him, but he ignored them and continued running until he reached his master's tent. He threw back the flap, panting with exertion, and stepped inside.

The interior was dimly lit by a single kerosene lamp. Sayf al-Tha'r was sitting cross-legged on the carpeted floor, a book held up close to his face, so still he might have been a statue. The boy came towards him.

'They've found it!' he cried, unable to contain his excitement. 'The piece. Doktora Dravic has found it!'

The man rested the book on his lap and looked up at the boy, face expressionless.

'It is written that we should be moderate in all things, Mehmet,' he said quietly, 'both in our joy and in our despair. There is no need to shout.'

'Yes, Sayf al-Tha'r.' The boy lowered his head, crestfallen.

'It is also written, however, that we should rejoice mightily in the goodness of Allah. So do not be ashamed of your joy. But control it, Mehmet. Always control it. That is the way to God. By becoming master of yourself.'

He held out his hand, and the boy passed him the message. He inclined his head and read. When he had finished he folded the message carefully and slipped it into a pocket of his robe.

'Did I not tell you we were God's chosen?' he said. 'So long as we stay true and trust in his greatness, all things will come to us. And now they have. This is a great day, Mehmet.'

A huge smile suddenly broke across his face, like water over parched land. The boy had never seen him smile like that, and his heart leaped at the sight. He wanted to fall to his knees and kiss his master's feet, tell him how much he loved him, how grateful he was for all he had done for him.

He fought the urge, however. The way to Allah is by becoming master of yourself. His master's words still rang in his ears. The lesson had been learnt. He allowed himself a smile, but no more, even though his chest was bursting with joy.

The man seemed to understand what was going on in his head, for he came to his feet and laid his hand on the boy's shoulder.

'Well done, Mehmet,' he said. 'Allah will always reward the good pupil. Just as he will always punish the bad one. Now go and tell our people to make ready. As soon as we know the place we begin flying in the equipment.'

The boy nodded and stepped back towards the entrance.

'Master,' he said, turning, 'will all bad things stop now? Will the *Kufr* be destroyed?'

The man's smile grew even broader. 'Of course they will be, Mehmet. How could they not when we have an entire army to help us?'

'*Allah u akbar.*' The boy laughed. 'God is great.'

'He is. Greater than any of us could ever understand.'

When the boy had gone Sayf al-Tha'r returned to his place beside the kerosene lamp and retrieved his book. Its leather binding was worn and tattered, and he cradled it gently in both hands. The text inside was in neither Arabic nor English, but Greek, as was the title on the cover: ΗΡΟΔΟΤΟΥ ΙΣΤΟΡΙΑΙ – *The Histories of Herodotus.*

He turned up the kerosene lamp slightly, and lifted the book to within a few inches of his face, sighing with pleasure as he lost himself within it.

30

LUXOR

Khalifa's train pulled into Luxor just before eight a.m. After his nightmare he hadn't slept again and he now felt tired and heavy-eyed. He decided to go home and freshen up before going into the office.

The town was already busy. The Feast of Abu el-Haggag was due to start that afternoon and even at that hour crowds were gathering in anticipation, jostling around the brightly coloured roadside stalls piled with sweets and cakes and party hats. Normally Khalifa would have been looking forward to the festivities. Today, however, he had other things on his mind and, lighting a cigarette, he set off down al-Mahatta Street, oblivious to the bustle around him.

His flat was fifteen minutes' walk from the centre of town, in a drab concrete block wedged like a domino in the midst of a row of other drab concrete blocks. Batah and Ali had already left for school when he got in and baby Yusuf was fast asleep in his cot. He took a shower and Zenab sat him down and brought him coffee and bread and cheese. He watched her appreciatively as she moved to and from the kitchen, her hair falling in a black cascade almost to her waist, her hips slim and provocative. Sometimes he forgot how lucky he was to have her as his wife. Her family hadn't wanted her to marry him, a penniless student from a poor family. Zenab, however, was a wilful woman. He smiled at the memory.

'What's funny?' she asked, carrying through a plate of sliced tomatoes.

'I was thinking of when we first got married. How your parents were dead against it and you told them it was me or nothing.'

She handed him the tomatoes and sat down at his feet.

'I should have listened to them. If I hadn't been so stubborn, I could have had my very own Hosni by now.'

Khalifa laughed and, leaning forward, kissed her on the head. Her hair was warm and scented and, despite his tiredness, he found it distinctly arousing. He laid aside the plate of tomatoes and wrapped his arms around her shoulders.

'How was Cairo?' she asked, kissing his arm.

'So-so. I saw the professor.'

'Is he well?'

'Seems so, yes. He sends his love.'

She shifted slightly and hooked her arm over his knee. Her dress had slipped down slightly, revealing her shoulder, and the top of her chest, just where her breasts started to swell. Khalifa lowered his elbow and nudged the plate of tomatoes further away.

'What's this case you're working on, Yusuf?' she asked gently, drawing patterns on his thigh. 'It's important, isn't it?'

'Yes,' he replied. 'I suppose it is.'

'Can you tell me?'

'It's complicated,' he said, stroking her hair.

She knew this was his way of saying he didn't want to talk about it and she didn't push him. Instead, she moved round some more and, lifting her face, kissed him softly on the lips.

'The baby's asleep,' she whispered.

Khalifa caressed her neck, breathing in the perfume of her hair.

'I should be getting down to the office,' he said.

She kissed him again and, coming to her feet, allowed her dress to slip off her. She was naked underneath.

'Should you?'

He gazed at her body – slim and dark, with high, firm breasts and a soft mound of coal-black hair between her legs. God, she was beautiful. He stood up and took her in his arms.

'I guess it won't matter if I'm a bit late.'

They kissed and, taking his hand, she led him into the bedroom. She sat on the bed and unbuttoned his shirt and trousers, pulling them down and clasping him around the waist. He pushed her back and lay down beside her, stroking her breasts and belly and thighs, kissing her shoulders, feeling her against him, breathing her . . .

The telephone rang.

'Leave it,' said Zenab, rolling on top of him and kneading his chest, draping her hair across his face.

They continued for a moment longer, but then the baby, disturbed by the ringing, started to cry and with a groan of frustration she got up and went over to the cot. Khalifa swung himself onto the side of the bed and picked up the phone. It was Professor al-Habibi.

'I hope I'm not disturbing you,' he said.

'Not at all. I was just . . . helping Zenab with something.'

She shot him an amused look and, pulling the screaming baby from his cot, went through into the other room, stooping to kiss his head as she passed. He kicked the door shut.

'Listen, Yusuf,' said the professor, 'there's something I thought you ought to know. About those objects you brought me yesterday.'

Khalifa bent and pulled his cigarettes from the pocket of his trousers. 'Go on.'

'I was looking at them last night, after you'd gone, and I found an inscription on the handle of the dagger, underneath the leather grip. Not a proper inscription. Just words scratched into the metal, very crude. The letters were Greek.'

'Greek?'

'That's right. And they spelled out a name. Presumably the dagger's owner.'

'Go on.'

'The name was Dymmachus, son of Menendes.'

'Dymmachus?' Khalifa turned the name over in his head. 'Does that mean anything to you?'

'That's the funny thing,' said Habibi, 'I was sure I'd seen it before. It took me a while to remember where, but then it came to me.' He paused for dramatic effect.

'Yes?'

'In the Valley of the Kings. The tomb of Ramesses VI. The walls are covered in ancient graffiti, Greek and Coptic, and one of them was left by a certain Dymmachus, son of Menendes of Naxos. I looked it up in my Baillet.'

'The same man?'

'Well, I can't be a hundred per cent certain, but I'd be surprised if there were two people in Thebes named Dymmachus with a father called Menendes. They're hardly common names.'

Khalifa let out a low whistle. 'Incredible,' he said.

'Indeed so. But not as incredible as what comes next.'

Again he paused for effect, and again Khalifa had to urge him on.

'This Dymmachus didn't just leave his name in the tomb. He left a short inscription as well.'

'Saying what?'

'Well, it seems to be incomplete. Either it's been written over or else he broke off in the middle of inscribing it . . .'

There was a sound of rustling paper at the other end of the line.

'It says: "I, Dymmachus, son of Menendes of Naxos, saw these wonders. Tomorrow I march against the Ammonians. May . . ." And then it stops.'

Khalifa still hadn't lit his cigarette. 'The Ammonians,' he said, thinking aloud. 'Wasn't that the name the Greeks gave to the people of Siwa?'

'Exactly. From the name of the god Amun, who had his oracle at the oasis. And so far as we are aware there was only one military expedition sent against the Ammonians during this period.'

'Which was?'

Again the dramatic pause.

'The army of Cambyses.'

Khalifa's cigarette snapped in his hand. 'The army of Cambyses! The one that was lost in the desert?'

'So the story goes.'

'But no-one survived that. How can we have a dagger belonging to one of its soldiers?'

'Well, that's the question, isn't it?'

Khalifa could hear the professor puffing his pipe into life. He pulled another cigarette from his pack and lit it. There was a long pause.

'The dagger definitely came from a Theban tomb?' asked Habibi eventually.

'I think so,' said Khalifa. 'Yes.'

'Then there would seem to be several possible explanations. Perhaps this Dymmachus didn't go with the army after all. Or perhaps the dagger had already passed to another owner by the time he did go with it. Or perhaps Herodotus simply got it wrong and the army wasn't overwhelmed by a sandstorm.'

'Or perhaps it was and this Dymmachus survived.'

The professor was silent for a moment.

'I would say that was the least likely of the possibilities. Although certainly the most intriguing.'

Khalifa pulled deeply on his cigarette. He wasn't supposed to smoke in the bedroom because the baby slept there and, leaning forward, he pushed open the window. Thoughts were rushing through his mind, too quickly for him either to keep track or make sense of them.

'I presume the tomb of a soldier from the army of Cambyses would be a significant find?' he said.

'If it was proved to be genuine,' said Habibi. 'Of course. A huge find.'

Was that it, then? Abu Nayar had discovered the tomb of a man who'd been part of the lost army of Cambyses. Like the professor said, it would be a huge find. One of the most important in Egypt for years. Yet that didn't explain why Dravic would go to so much trouble for just one small piece of hieroglyphic text. He had, after all, not bothered about the other objects in Iqbar's shop. Just that one piece. There was something missing here. Something more.

'And the army itself?' The question seemed to come from his mouth before he'd even thought of asking it.

'How do you mean?'

'The lost army of Cambyses. How significant a find would that be?'

There was a long pause.

'I think possibly we're entering the realms of fantasy here, Yusuf. The army's buried somewhere in the middle of the western desert. It'll never be found.'

'But if it was?'

Another pause.

'I don't think you need me to tell you how important that would be.'

'No. I don't.'

He threw his cigarette out of the window and waved his hand around to clear some of the smoke.

'Yusuf?'

'Yes, sorry, I was just thinking. What else do you know about the army, Professor?'

'Not a lot, I'm afraid. Not my period. The person you need to speak to is Professor Ibrahim az-Zahir. He's spent most of his life studying it.'

'And where do I find him?'

'Right there in Luxor. He spends six months of the year at Chicago House. But he's getting on a bit. Had a stroke last year. His mind's starting to go.'

There was another silence and then, thanking the professor and promising to come for dinner next time he was in Cairo, Khalifa rang off. He went through into the living room. Zenab was cradling the baby in her arms, still naked. He went over and hugged them both.

'I have to go down to the office.'

'And there's me doing everything I can to get him back to sleep!'

'I'm sorry. It's just . . .'

'I know.' She smiled, kissing him. 'Go on. And don't forget it's the children's parade this afternoon. I told Ali and Batah we'd be there to watch them. Four o'clock. Don't be late.'

'Don't worry,' he said. 'I'll be back. I promise.'

THE WESTERN DESERT

Tara woke twice during the journey – brief chinks of consciousness in an otherwise all-enveloping shroud of oblivion.

First, in a hot, cramped, vibrating space that stank of petrol, and which, despite the impenetrable blackness and the excruciating pain in her head, she knew instantly was the boot of a car. She was alone, curled in a foetal position, her hands tied to her ankles, her mouth taped. She presumed they must be driving along a tarmacked road because, although the car was juddering, the jolts were not violent and they seemed to be moving at quite a speed. She found herself thinking of all the films she had seen in which people locked in boots are able to work out where they are going by paying careful attention to the various sounds and sensations encountered during the journey. She tried to do the same now, listening for any external noises that might give a clue as to her whereabouts. Apart from the occasional beep of a car horn, however, and, once, a blare of loud music, there was nothing to tell her either where she was or where she was going, and she soon sank back into unconsciousness.

The second time she woke there was a loud thudding over-head. She listened to it for a while and then opened her eyes. She was sitting upright, strapped into a seat. Daniel was beside her, head lolling on his chest, blood caked around the side of his cheek and neck. Strangely, she didn't feel any concern for him. She merely noted he was there and then turned away and stared down at an endless expanse of yellow beneath her. For some reason the thought struck her that she was looking at a huge steaming sponge cake, and she started to laugh. Almost immediately she heard voices and some sort of sack was forced over her head. She began to sink again, but not before she had experienced a sudden, blinding instant of clarity: 'I am in a helicopter,' she said to herself, 'flying over the desert towards the lost army of Cambyses.' And then the blackness swept over her, and she remembered no more.

LUXOR

Khalifa had two surprises when he arrived at the police station. The first was that he bumped into Chief Inspector Hassani in the front foyer and, far from being shouted at for coming in late, was greeted with something approaching cordiality.

'Good to have you back, Yusuf!' said the chief, using his first name, which, so far as Khalifa was aware, he had never done before. 'Do me a favour. As soon as you've got a moment pop up to my office, will you? Nothing to worry about. On the contrary. Some rather good news.'

He slapped Khalifa on the back and strode off down a corridor.

The second surprise was that he found Omar Abd el-Farouk sitting in his office.

'He wouldn't wait downstairs,' explained Sariya. 'Didn't want anyone to see him. Claimed he had information about the Abu Nayar case.'

Omar was hunched in a corner of the office drumming his fingers on his knees, clearly uncomfortable with his surroundings.

'Well, well,' said Khalifa, walking to his desk and sitting down. 'I never thought I'd see the day when an Abd el-Farouk came in here of his own free will.'

'Believe me,' snorted Omar, 'I don't do it lightly.'

'Tea?'

Omar shook his head. 'And tell him to go.' He indicated Sariya. 'What I have to say is for you and you only.'

'Mohammed is my colleague,' said Khalifa. 'He's as much—'

'I speak to you alone or I don't speak,' snapped Omar.

Khalifa sighed and nodded at Sariya. 'Give us a few minutes, will you, Mohammed? I'll fill you in later.'

His deputy left the room, shutting the door behind him.

'Cigarette?' He leaned forward, proffering his Cleopatras. Omar waved him away.

'I came here to talk, not exchange pleasantries.'

Khalifa shrugged and, sitting back, lit a cigarette for himself. 'OK,' he said. 'So talk.'

The drumming of Omar's fingers grew faster.

'I think some friends of mine are in danger,' he said, lowering his voice. 'Yesterday they came to my house seeking help. Now they have disappeared.'

'And what does that have to do with Abu Nayar?'

Omar glanced around, as though to reassure himself no-one else was listening. 'Two days ago, when you brought me in, you asked if a new tomb had been found up in the hills.'

'And you said you knew nothing about it. Do I take it you've suddenly remembered something?' There was sarcasm in the question.

Omar glared at him. 'You must enjoy this,' he hissed. 'An el-Farouk coming to you for help.'

Khalifa said nothing, just drew slowly on his cigarette.

'OK, so Abu Nayar found a tomb. Where I don't know, so don't bother asking me. But he found a tomb. He removed a piece of wall decoration from that tomb. My friends had that piece of wall decoration. And now they have disappeared.'

Outside the window a firecracker went off. Omar jerked in his seat, startled.

'And who were these friends?'

'An archaeologist. Dr Daniel Lacage. And a woman. English.'

'Tara Mullray,' guessed Khalifa.

Omar raised his eyebrows. 'You know her?'

'It seems she and Lacage were involved in a shooting at Saqqara two days ago.'

'I know what you're thinking, Khalifa, but I have worked with Dr Lacage for six years. He is a good man.'

Khalifa nodded. 'I believe you.' He paused, then added, 'I never thought I'd see the day when I said that to an el-Farouk.'

For a moment Omar said nothing. Then a slight smile crossed his face. His shoulders relaxed a little. 'Maybe I will have that cigarette.'

Khalifa leaned forward and offered him the pack. 'So what exactly happened yesterday, Omar?'

'Like I said, they came to my house asking for help. They had this piece of decorated plaster in a box. The woman said her father had bought it for her and Sayf al-Tha'r wanted it. And the British embassy.'

'The British embassy?'

'She said people at the British embassy wanted the piece too.'

Khalifa pulled a pen from his jacket and began doodling on a piece of paper. What the hell was going on here?

'What else?' he asked.

'They wanted to know where the piece came from. I told them it was dangerous and they should leave it, but they wouldn't. Dr Lacage is my friend. If a friend asks for help, I do not refuse. I said I would make enquiries. I went out about four p.m. When I came back they had gone. I have not seen them since.'

'Do you know where they went?'

'They told my wife they were going to the top of el-Qurn. I fear for their safety, Inspector. Especially after what happened to Abu Nayar. And Suleiman al-Rashid.'

Khalifa stopped doodling. 'Suleiman al-Rashid?'

'You know, getting burnt like that.'

The colour drained from Khalifa's face. 'Dead?'

Omar nodded.

'Oh no,' groaned Khalifa. 'Oh God, not Suleiman.'

'You didn't know?'

'I've been in Cairo.'

Omar lowered his head. 'I'm sorry,' he said. 'I thought you'd have heard.' He paused, then added, 'Everyone knows what you did for Suleiman.'

Khalifa's face was buried in his hands.

'I'll tell you what I did for Suleiman. I killed him. That's what I did for him. If I hadn't gone to see him the other day . . . Dammit! How could I have been so stupid?'

His voice tailed away. Somewhere out on the street someone was banging a drum. There was a long silence.

'Perhaps I should leave you, Inspector,' said Omar quietly, standing. 'It is not right to intrude upon your grief like this.' He began moving towards the door.

'The piece,' said Khalifa.

'Sorry?'

'The piece of wall. Did you see it?'

'Yes,' said Omar. 'I saw it.'

'Snakes along the bottom? Hieroglyphs?'

Omar nodded.

'The signs. The hieroglyphic signs. Can you remember any of them?'

Omar thought for a moment and then, coming forward, took Khalifa's pen and drew on the piece of paper in front of him. The detective looked down.

'You're sure this is what you saw?'

'I think so. Do you know what it is?'

'*Mer*,' said Khalifa. 'The sign for a pyramid.'

He stared down for a moment longer and then, folding the paper, put it in his pocket.

'Thank you, Omar,' he said. 'I know how difficult it was for you to come here today.'

'Just find my friends, Inspector. That's all I ask. Just find my friends.'

For a moment it looked as if he was going to extend his hand, but in the end he just nodded curtly and left the room.

Khalifa spent twenty minutes filling Sariya in on what had happened in Cairo and getting the details of Suleiman's death. Then, as requested, he went upstairs to see the chief inspector.

Normally Hassani liked to keep him waiting for at least a few minutes before admitting him to his office. Today, however, he was ushered straight in. Not only that, but for once he was given a halfway decent chair to sit on.

'I'll have a progress report on the case typed up by noon,' he began, hoping to pre-empt the inevitable questions about where the report was. Hassani, however, waved his hand dismissively.

'Don't worry about that. I've got some good news, Yusuf.'

He sat back in his chair and jutted out his chin, adopting much the same pose as President Mubarak in the photograph above him.

'I'm pleased to inform you', he said portentously, 'that your promotion application has been approved. Congratulations.'

He smiled, although something about his expression suggested he wasn't quite as pleased as he was trying to look.

'You're joking,' said Khalifa.

The smile faded slightly.

'I never tell jokes. I'm a policeman.'

'Yes, sir. Sorry.' He didn't know what to say. It was the last thing he'd been expecting.

'I want you to take the rest of the day off, go home, tell the wife, celebrate. Then tomorrow I'm sending you up to a conference in Ismailiya.'

'Ismailiya?'

'Some hokum about urban policing in the twenty-first century. Three days of it, God help you. These are the sort of things you have to put up with if you want to get on in the force.'

Khalifa said nothing. He was delighted, of course. At the same time, however, there was something . . .

'What about the case?' he asked.

Again that dismissive wave of the hand, that not-quite-genuine smile.

'Don't worry about the case, Yusuf. It can wait for a couple of days. Go up to Ismailiya, do the conference, then when you get back you can pick it up again. It'll wait.'

'I can't just leave it, sir.'

'Relax! You've been promoted! Enjoy it!'

'I know, but . . .'

Hassani started laughing. A loud, boisterous laugh that filled the room and drowned out Khalifa's words.

'Here's a turn-up for the books, eh! Me telling one of my men to work a bit less hard! I hope you're not going to tell anyone. It could ruin my reputation!'

Khalifa smiled, but wouldn't be deflected. 'Three people have been murdered, sir. Two more have disappeared. I've got a definite link with Sayf al-Tha'r, and possibly the British embassy as well. I can't just drop this.'

Hassani continued to chuckle. In his eyes, however, Khalifa could see annoyance. Annoyance bordering on anger.

'Don't you want this promotion?' he asked.

'Sir?'

'It's just that you don't seem particularly happy about it. Or particularly *grateful*.'

He stressed the last word, as though urging Khalifa to take note of it.

'I am grateful, sir. But people's lives are in danger. I can't just disappear to Ismailiya for three days.'

Hassani nodded. 'Think we can't take care of things here without you, is that it?'

'No, sir. I just—'

'Think the force won't be able to operate in your absence?'

'Sir—'

'Think you're the only one who's interested in law and order and right and wrong?'

His voice was getting louder. A vein was pulsing up in his neck. 'Well, let me tell you, Khalifa, I've spent my entire life working for the good of this country and I'm not going to sit here and listen to a little shit like you make out you're the only one who cares.' He was breathing heavily. 'Now you've got what you wanted. You've got your fucking promotion. And tomorrow, if you know what's good for you, you're going to Ismailiya. And that's the end of it.'

He pushed himself away from the desk, got to his feet and strode to the window, where he stood looking out with his back to Khalifa, cracking his knuckles. Khalifa lit a cigarette, not bothering to ask permission.

'Who got to you, sir?' he said quietly.

Hassani didn't reply.

'That's what this promotion's about, isn't it? Somebody got to you. Somebody wants me off this case.'

Still Hassani was silent.

'It's a trade-off. I get the new job and in return I forget about the investigation. That's the deal, isn't it? That's the bribe.'

Hassani's fingers were cracking so loudly it seemed as though they were going to break.

Slowly he turned round.

'I don't like you, Khalifa,' he growled. 'I never have and I never will. You're arrogant, you're insubordinate, you're a fucking pain in the arse.' He took a step forward, jaw set, like a fighter stepping into the ring. 'You're also the best detective we've got on this force. Don't think I don't know that. And although you might not believe it, I've never wished you any harm. So listen to me, and listen closely: take this promotion, go to Ismailiya, forget about the case. Because trust me, if you don't, there's nothing I can do to protect you.'

He held Khalifa's eyes for a moment and then turned back towards the window.

'And shut the door behind you,' he said.

31

THE WESTERN DESERT

The first thing Tara noticed was the heat. It was as though she was drifting upwards from the depths of a cool lake, and with every fathom she rose the water around her grew hotter and hotter until eventually she surfaced into what felt like a raging inferno. She was sure that if she stayed up there she would be burnt alive and, flipping over, she tried to swim back down again, back into the cool, dark depths below. Her body, however, seemed to have assumed an irresistible buoyancy and, try as she might, she couldn't get herself more than a few inches below the surface. She struggled for a while, fighting to propel herself downwards, but it was no good and eventually she gave up and, rolling onto her back, floated resignedly upwards into the flames. Her eyes blinked open.

She was lying inside a tent. Beside her, gazing down, was Daniel. He reached out and stroked her hair.

'Welcome back,' he said.

Her head ached and her mouth felt dry and thick, as though it was full of paper. She lay still for a while and then struggled into a sitting position. Two metres away, in front of the tent doorway, sat a man with a gun cradled in his lap.

'Where are we?' she mumbled.

'In the middle of the western desert,' replied Daniel. 'In the Great Sand Sea. I'd guess about midway between Siwa and al-Farafra.'

She was struggling to breathe it was so hot. The air seared her mouth and throat, as though she was drinking lava. She couldn't see much through the tent door, just a lot of sand rising up in front of her. From somewhere nearby she could hear shouting and the putter of generators. She was painfully thirsty.

'What time is it?'

He glanced at his watch.

'Eleven.'

'I was in the boot of a car,' she said, trying to marshal her thoughts. 'And then a helicopter.'

'I don't remember anything about the journey.' He shrugged. 'Just the tomb.'

He reached up gingerly and touched the side of his head. The blood she had seen on his face and neck had been wiped away, if indeed she hadn't just dreamed it. She moved her hand along the matted floor and grasped his fingers.

'I'm so sorry, Daniel,' she said. 'I should never have got you involved in this.'

'I got myself involved.' He smiled. 'It's not your fault.'

'I should have just left the piece of wall at Saqqara, like you said.'

Leaning forward, he kissed her forehead. 'Maybe. But think of all the fun we'd have missed if you had. I never had this much excitement digging.' He ran his hands through his hair. 'And, anyway, this way we get to be around when they make the greatest discovery in the history of archaeology. I reckon that's worth a little bump on the head.'

She knew he was trying to cheer her up and did her best to respond. The truth was, however, that she felt sick and frightened and hopeless and, despite the jokes, knew Daniel felt exactly the same. She could see it in his eyes and the listless slump of his shoulders.

'They're going to kill us, aren't they?'

'Not necessarily. There's a good chance that once they've found the army—'

She looked him in the eyes. 'They're going to kill us, aren't they?'

He was silent for a moment and then looked down at the floor. 'Yes,' he said. 'I expect they probably are.'

They lapsed into silence. Daniel hunched forward, clasping his arms around his legs, resting his chin on his knees. Tara stood and stretched, head throbbing. The guard continued to stare at them, expressionless. He was making no effort to cover them with his gun and for a moment she had a wild notion that they could overpower him and escape. Almost immediately she dismissed the thought. Even if they did get out of the tent where would they go? They were in the middle of a desert. The guard, she realized, was just for show. Their real captors were the sand and the heat. She felt like crying, but her eyes were too dry for tears.

'I'm thirsty,' she mumbled.

Daniel lifted his head and addressed the guard. '*Ehna aatzanin. Aazin mayya.*'

The guard stared at them for a moment and then, without taking his eyes off them, shouted to someone outside. A few minutes later a man came into the tent with an earthenware jar, which he handed to Tara. She lifted it to her lips and drank. The water was warm and tasted of clay, but she gulped at it none-theless, finishing half the jar before passing it to Daniel, who drank too. A helicopter thudded overhead, causing the material of the tent to billow and ripple.

The morning dragged by. The heat, if anything, grew even more intense, drying the sweat on Tara's face and neck almost as soon as it formed. Daniel dozed for a while, head resting in her lap. More helicopters passed overhead.

After about an hour their guard was changed and they were brought food – raw vegetables, cheese, pieces of flat, unleavened bread, sour and dry and difficult to swallow. She tried to force it down, but had no appetite. Neither did Daniel and most of the food went uneaten. The new guard was as silent and impassive as his predecessor.

She must have fallen asleep because when she woke again the food had been removed and the original guard was back. She caught and held his eye, trying to make some sort of connection with him. He just stared at her, his expression cold and unyielding, and after a while she dropped her gaze.

'There's no point trying to communicate,' said Daniel. 'So far as they're concerned, we're no better than animals. Worse. We're *Kufr*. Heathens.'

She lay down again, her back to the guard, and closed her eyes. She tried to think of her flat, of the reptile house, of Jenny, of crisp December afternoons in Brockwell Park. Anything to take her away from the present. She couldn't hold the images. They would drift into her head, but then dissipate again as soon as she reached out to them. And behind them, always, would be the face of Dravic, gazing out at her with that repugnant leer. She tossed and turned and then sat up again and buried her face in her hands, despairing.

Eventually, some time in the early afternoon, when the sun was at its zenith and the air in the tent was so hot she didn't think she could stand it any more, the door flap flew back and a head poked through. Something was said to their guard, who stood and, pointing his gun at them, motioned them outside. They looked at each other and then, coming to their feet, stepped past him and out into the sunlight, their eyes narrowing to thin slits against the glare. Their tent was part of a large encampment pitched in the middle of a valley between high dunes, the one to the left sloping steeply upwards, the other, to the right, rising more gently. Everywhere were piles of oil drums, ropes, bales of straw and wooden packing crates. A

303

helicopter swept in low overhead, a net holding more crates and drums suspended beneath it, dropping down into the valley and landing on a flat area of sand, where a dozen black-robed figures swarmed around it, unloading the equipment and carrying it away.

Tara barely noticed any of this, however, for the thing that immediately caught her eye was neither the helicopter nor the encampment but rather a vast, pyramid-shaped rock rearing up ahead of her. Her line of vision was partly blocked by the tents and crates so she could see only the upper part of it, but even that was enough to give an indication of its huge size. There was something faintly threatening about it sitting there in the middle of the desert, black and solid against the surrounding sands, and a shiver rippled down her spine. The men, she noticed, were doing their best to avoid looking at it.

They set off through the camp, one guard walking in front, two behind, emerging from its northern end and climbing to the top of a steep sandy mound, where Dravic was standing beneath an umbrella, a straw sunhat perched on his head.

'I hope you both slept well,' he said, chuckling, as they were led up to him.

'Fuck you,' snarled Daniel.

From the summit of the mound they were afforded an un-interrupted view straight up the valley, which curved gently northwards into the distance, like a trough between tidal waves of sand. The huge rock was directly in front of them, its entire bulk now visible, erupting from the flank of the left-hand dune like a needle-head jutting through soft yellow material. Beneath it, dwarfed by the towering mass above them, were a crowd of men wielding spades and *tourias*, while from its base five long tubes snaked out, running up the side of the dune and disappearing over the top. The chug of generators was much louder now, filling the air with a heavy rhythmic flutter, like the beating of thousands of wings.

'I thought you might like to see,' said Dravic. 'After all, it's not as if you'll have the chance to tell anyone.'

Again that insidious throaty chuckle. Tara could feel him staring at her, eyes roving lasciviously across her body. She shivered with disgust and moved back a step, placing Daniel between them. Dravic grunted and turned away, looking back up the valley. He removed a cigar from his shirt pocket and jammed it into his mouth.

'The place was even easier to find than we thought,' he boasted. 'I had feared that the measurements in the tomb might only be rough estimates, as is so often the case with ancient texts, but our friend Dymmachus pinpointed the spot to within five kilometres. A remarkable feat, given that he had no modern technology to guide him.' He raised a lighter and ignited the cigar, puffing it slowly into life, his lips making a popping sound as they drew on its end. 'We began an aerial sweep of the area at first light', he continued, 'and had located the site within an hour. After all the complications of the last four days it was a bit of an anticlimax. I had been expecting more drama.'

Away to their right a pair of scrambler bikes powered up the flank of the dune, engines whining, their tyres cutting a deep swathe in the sand as though unzipping the slope beneath them.

'As it is, everything has gone like clockwork,' Dravic said, smiling broadly, goading them with his success. 'Better than clockwork. We've flown in enough equipment to be getting on with: fuel for the generators, packing crates, straw to protect the finds. More is on its way by camel. We've already located a cluster of inscriptions down there on the rock face, so we know the army must be nearby. All we have to do now' – he broke off, sucking deeply on his cigar – 'is to find it. Which I am expecting to do in a matter of hours.'

'It might not be as easy as you think,' said Daniel, glaring at him. 'These dunes are shifting all the time. God knows what level the desert floor was at two and a half thousand years ago.

The army could be fifty metres down. More. You could dig for weeks and still not find it.'

Dravic shrugged. 'With traditional methods, perhaps. Fortunately, we have slightly more up-to-date equipment at our disposal.'

He pointed down at the five tubes snaking away from the base of the giant outcrop. Each one, Tara now noticed, had two men standing to either side of its open end. They were gripping what looked like handles, and passing the mouth of the tube back and forth across the sand, which was being sucked up into the snaking plastic gullet behind.

'Sand-vacuums,' explained Dravic. 'Apparently they're all the rage in the Gulf. They use them to clear sand away from airport runways, oil pipelines, that sort of thing. They work on exactly the same principle as a normal vacuum cleaner. The sand is drawn in, passes through the tube and is then deposited a suitable distance away, in this case on the far side of that dune. Each one can, I am told, shift almost a hundred tons per hour. So I think we'll be finding our army rather sooner than you think.'

'You'll be seen,' said Daniel. 'You can't keep this size of operation secret for long.'

Dravic laughed, sweeping his arm around him in a wide arc. 'Who's going to see us? We're in the middle of a desert, for God's sake! The nearest settlement's a hundred and twenty kilometres away, there are no commercial flight paths overhead. You're clutching at straws, Lacage.' He blew a billow of smoke into Daniel's face and his laughter redoubled. 'What a dilemma all this must be for you! On the one hand you must be yearning for me to fail in my task. Yet at the same time, as an archaeologist, a part of you must also be desperate for me to succeed.'

'I don't give a shit about the army,' snapped Daniel.

'You lie, Lacage! You lie with every bone in your body. You're as anxious to know what's down there as I am. We are the same, you and me.'

'Don't flatter yourself.'

'Yes, Lacage, we are! We're the same. We both live by the past. We have an irresistible need to dig into it. It is not enough for us simply to know that somewhere out here in the desert there is a buried army. We must find it. We must see it. We must make it our own. For both of us it is intolerable that history should keep things from us. Oh, I understand you, Lacage. Better than you understand yourself. You care more about what's down there than you do about your own life. Than you do about the life of your friend here.'

'That's bullshit!' snapped Daniel. 'Bullshit!'

'Is it?' Dravic chuckled. 'I think not. I could cut her throat right here in front of you and a part of you would still be willing me to succeed. It's an addiction, Lacage. An impossible addiction. And we both suffer from it.'

Daniel stared at him and for a brief moment it seemed to Tara that Dravic's words had touched something deep inside him. There was a confusion in his eyes, a disgust almost, as if he had been shown a part of himself that he would prefer not to acknowledge. It disappeared almost immediately and, shaking his head, he thrust his hands defiantly into his pockets.

'Fuck you, Dravic.'

The giant smiled. 'I can assure you that if there's any fucking to be done around here, I'm the one who's going to be doing it.'

He leaned back slightly and looked at Tara, then nodded at the three guards. They raised their guns, and prodded them back down the side of the mound towards the camp.

'And don't think about trying to escape,' Dravic called after them. 'If the heat doesn't get you, the sinking sand certainly will. It's everywhere around here. In fact maybe that's how I should dispose of you both. Much more entertaining than a bullet through the head.'

He grinned and turned back towards the excavation. Below him the workmen started to sing.

32

LUXOR, THE THEBAN HILLS

There was a place Khalifa used to go when he needed to think, up in the Theban Hills, beneath the shadow of the Qurn, and he went there now.

He'd discovered it years ago when he'd first arrived in Luxor – a natural seat in the rock, cut into a low cliff halfway up the mountain, with spectacular views down into the Valley of the Kings below. He would sit there for hours, alone and peaceful, and however confused he was feeling at the time, however miserable or hopeless or wretched, his head would always clear and his spirits lift. His thinking seat, he called it. There was no place in the world he felt more in touch with himself or with Allah.

The sun was already past its zenith by the time he got up there. He sat down and rested his back against the cool lime-stone, staring out across the sun-baked hills. Far below he could see people wandering through the valley, small as ants. He lit a cigarette.

The meeting with Hassani had rattled him. Badly. His immediate reaction, of course, had been to reject the promotion and continue with the case. Two people's lives were in danger, after all – if indeed they were still alive – and he couldn't simply turn his back on them. Nor could he forget what had been done to Suleiman and Nayar and Iqbar. Nor, in a sense, his brother Ali, too.

And yet, despite that, he had doubts. He didn't want to, but he did. This wasn't a movie, after all, where everything was guaranteed to work out OK in the end. This was reality and, although he despised himself for it, he was afraid.

To go up against Sayf al-Tha'r was dangerous enough. Now it seemed there were enemies on his own side too. God knows who and God knows why, but they were powerful. Powerful enough to scare Hassani, and that took some doing.

'There's nothing I can do to protect you,' the chief had said. And he hadn't just been talking about Khalifa's career. He had meant his life. And perhaps the lives of his family too. Was it right to put at risk those he loved most in the world? He owed nothing to Nayar and Iqbar and Suleiman, after all, nor to the English couple. And Ali? Well, yes, that would always torment him, but was it worth this? Maybe he should drop the case. Take the promotion, go to Ismailiya. Sure, he'd hate himself for it. But at least he'd be alive. And his loved ones too. He flicked his cigarette away and looked up at some crude hieroglyphs scratched into the cliff face beside the seat. There were three cartouches – those of Horemheb, Ramesses I and Seti I.

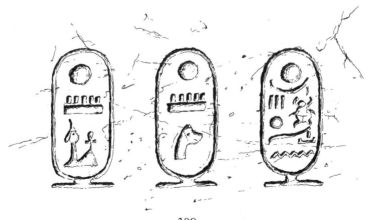

Beneath them was a brief inscription, left by someone styling himself 'The Scribe of Amun, Son of Ipu'. One of the ancient necropolis workmen, probably, who must have sat in this very same seat more than three thousand years ago, enjoying the same view as Khalifa, and listening to the same silence, and perhaps even feeling the same things. He reached out and touched the inscription.

'What should I do?' he sighed, running his fingers across the crudely incised images. 'What's the right thing? Tell me, Son of Ipu. Give me some sign. Because I sure as hell—'

He was interrupted by a clatter of stones. He turned and looked up. A gaunt, filthy man was staring down at him from a shelf a few metres above.

'Sorry sorry forgive me Allah have mercy!' gabbled the man in Arabic, slapping his head. 'Clumsy stupid fool tread in the wrong place.'

He tied his djellaba in a knot around his waist and, swinging his emaciated legs over the edge of the shelf, clambered down the cracked rock face.

'You talk to the ghosts!' he jabbered as he descended. 'I talk to the ghosts too. Hills full of ghosts! Thousands of ghosts. Millions of ghosts. Some good, some bad. Some are terrible! I have seen.'

He was on the ground now and scrabbled round to crouch at Khalifa's feet. 'I live with the ghosts. I know them. They are everywhere.' He pointed behind Khalifa's head. 'There is one. And there is another. And there, and there, and there. Hello ghosts!' He waved. 'They know me. They are hungry. Like me. We are all hungry. So hungry.' He fumbled among the folds of his robes, pulling out a crumpled paper packet. 'You want scarab?' he asked. 'Best quality.'

Khalifa shook his head. 'Not today, my friend.'

'Look, look, very best, no better in Egypt. Just look. Please.'

'Not today,' repeated Khalifa.

The man glanced around and shuffled a little closer, lowering his voice. 'You like antiquities? I have antiquities. Very good.'

'I'm a policeman,' said Khalifa. 'Be careful what you say.'

The man's smile faded. 'Fake antiquities,' he said hurriedly. 'Not real. Fake, fake. Make them myself. Make the fake. Ha, ha, ha.'

Khalifa nodded and, pulling out a cigarette, lit it. The man stared at him, like a dog waiting for a titbit. Feeling suddenly sorry for him, Khalifa threw him the pack of Cleopatras.

'Have them,' he said, 'and leave me in peace. OK? I want to be alone.'

The man took the cigarettes. 'Thank you,' he said. 'So kind. Ghosts like you. They tell me to tell you. They like you very much.' He held his hand to his ear as if listening. 'They say if you ever have problems you come up here and talk to them and they give you many good answers. Ghosts will protect you.' He stuffed the cigarettes into a pocket of his robe and stood. 'You want guide?' he asked.

'I want to be left in peace,' said Khalifa.

The man shrugged and, blowing his nose on the hem of his djellaba, set off along the path at the foot of the cliff face, oblivious to the rocks beneath his bare feet.

'You want to see Kings Valley,' he called over his shoulder, 'Hatshepsut, tombs of nobles? I know all places round here. Very cheap.'

'Some other time,' Khalifa shouted after him. 'Not today.'

'I show you places no-one else see. Very good places. Special places.'

Khalifa shook his head and, turning away, gazed out across the empty hills. The madman stumbled on, until he was almost at the point where the path curved out of sight behind a high shoulder of rock.

'I take you to secret places!' he cried.

Khalifa ignored him.

'New tomb that no-one else knows! Very good!'

He disappeared round the shoulder of rock. There was a brief hiatus and then, suddenly, as if someone had kicked him from behind, Khalifa flew to his feet.

'Wait!' he shouted, his voice magnified and echoed by the rock walls. 'Wait!'

He scrambled down to the path and ran after the man, who, on hearing his cry, had stepped back round the corner.

'A new tomb that no-one else knows,' panted Khalifa, coming up to him. 'You said a new tomb that no-one else knows.'

The man clapped his hands. 'I found it!' he cried. 'Very secret. The ghosts took me there. You want to see?'

'Yes,' said Khalifa, his heart racing. 'I do want to see. I want to see it very much. Take me.'

He clapped the man on the shoulder and they set off together up into the hills.

At first Khalifa couldn't be sure the madman's tomb was the same as the one Nayar had found. As al-Masri had pointed out, these hills were full of old shafts. It was more than possible his guide had stumbled on a completely different one, one that had no relevance at all to the case he was dealing with.

Then, after much cajoling, he persuaded the man to show him the antiquities of which he had spoken and his doubts were dispelled. There were three *shabti*s, each identical to the ones he'd found in Iqbar's shop, and a terracotta ointment jar with a Bes face stamped onto it, again identical to the one from Iqbar's cache. It was clear they all came from the same hoard. He handed the artefacts back and reached for his cigarettes, realizing only when his hand was in his pocket that he'd given them away.

'Give me a cigarette, will you?' he said.

'No!' replied the man. 'They're mine!'

It took them over an hour to reach the top of the gully and a further thirty minutes to work their way down to the tomb entrance. The last part of the descent, when they had to clamber down the six-metre rock face above the tomb, was particularly

312

painful for Khalifa, who had never liked heights. The madman swarmed down without a care in the world. Khalifa, on the other hand, took five minutes just to pluck up the courage to begin the descent, and when he finally did start climbing, he inched his way downwards so slowly and with such care that he seemed to be moving in slow motion.

'Allah protect me,' he mumbled, pressing his face against the reassuring solidity of the rock face, 'Allah have mercy on me.'

'Come, come, come!' The madman laughed, jumping up and down below him. 'Here's the tomb, why do you wait, thought you wanted to see it?'

The detective reached the bottom eventually and, scrambling through the entrance, sank against the wall of the corridor, breathing hard.

'Give me a cigarette,' he panted. 'And no arguments, or I'll arrest you for possession of stolen antiquities.'

Grudgingly the pack was proffered and Khalifa took one, lighting it, closing his eyes and inhaling deeply. After a couple of drags he started to relax. He opened his eyes again.

A thin shaft of sunlight was pushing through the tomb entrance, just enough to illuminate the corridor and, at its bottom, the dark well of the burial chamber.

'How did you find it?' Khalifa asked, looking around.

'The ghosts tell me,' said the madman. 'Seven days, ten days. Not long. They tell me to come down here. They say there is something special. So I come down and here it is, beautiful tomb, very secret, very special.'

He hopped to the entrance and pointed at the gap through which they had climbed.

'See, here, when I first come there is a wall, big wall, cover up all the door so you can't see inside. But I knock down the wall and get inside, just like the ghosts tell me. Very dark inside, very secret, goes down down down. I am scared, I shake with fear, but I go down because I want to see, like someone is pulling me.'

313

His voice was getting faster. He started to move down the corridor. Khalifa followed.

'A room,' he said, pointing downwards. 'Dark, black, like night. I light match. Many things inside. Hundreds of things. Wonderful things, and terrible things. Very magic. Home of ghosts.'

They were standing in the doorway to the burial chamber now. As Khalifa's eyes adjusted to the gloom he could make out vague colours and images on the wall opposite.

'Treasures, treasures, so many treasures,' gabbled the man. 'I stay here for a night. I sleep here with the treasures, like a king! Many dreams I have, many strange things come to me in my head, like I am flying over the world and see everything, even what people think.' He jumped down into the chamber. 'Later I tell my friend.'

'Your friend?' asked Khalifa.

'Sometimes he comes in the hills, when he has drunk, we talk, he gives me cigarettes. He has a picture. Here.'

He pointed to his left wrist. To the spot where Nayar had had his scarab tattoo. The detective was starting to understand.

'I tell my friend what the ghosts have shown me. He says, "Take me!" So I take him. He laughs very loud. He says, "You and me will be very rich! You and me will live like kings!" I must leave it to him, he says. He will take things to show special people. He will buy me a television. I mustn't come here again, he says. I mustn't say anything. And so I wait and wait and wait. But he doesn't come back. And then the others come at night. And I am alone. And there is no television. And I am hungry. And only the ghosts are my friends.'

He sniffed and wandered forlornly round the room, trailing his hand along the walls. Khalifa jumped down too, noting how the section of wall to the left of the doorway had been destroyed. He squatted beside the pile of smashed plaster on the floor, shaking his head, dismayed at such wanton vandalism.

He could see the chain of events clearly. This man had

stumbled on the tomb. He had told Nayar, Nayar had removed certain objects, including, presumably, a piece of the wall now lying in ruins at his feet. Sayf al-Tha'r had got wind of it. Nayar had been killed. The rest he already knew.

He stood and began to examine the chamber. His eyes had adjusted to the gloom now and much of the decoration was visible, although the sides of the room were still lost in impenetrable shadow, as though hung with black drapes. The man sat down on the floor, staring at Khalifa through doleful eyes, humming to himself.

'Have you been back here', asked Khalifa, 'since you found it?'

The man shook his head. 'But I have seen. I hide in the rocks, very quiet, like I am a rock too. They come at night, every night, like jackals. They take things from the tomb, one night, two night, three night, every night more things.'

'Last night?'

'Last night they come. Then they go. Then others come.'

'Others?'

'Man and woman. White. I had seen them before. They go into the tomb. They are eaten.'

'Killed?'

The madman shrugged.

'Killed?' repeated Khalifa.

'Who knows? I have not seen them with the ghosts. Maybe they live. Maybe they don't. The man I had seen . . .'

'What?'

He wouldn't say any more, however, and fell to drawing patterns in the dust with his finger.

Khalifa turned back to the walls. He worked his way slowly round the chamber, using his lighter to illuminate the decoration where it was too dark to see with natural light. He spent a long while in front of the triptych that had so interested Daniel, gazing intently at each of its three sections, and then moved on again. He peered into the canopic niche, at the image of the two Persians, the Greek man before his table of fruit, Anubis weigh-

315

ing the heart of the deceased, examining every inch of the walls, the flame of his lighter growing weaker all the time until eventually, just as he completed the circuit, it puttered out altogether, plunging him into gloom. He returned the lighter to his pocket and stepped back into the light.

'It's perfect,' he said quietly. 'Absolutely perfect.'

The man looked up at him. 'There was sand,' he mumbled. 'Sand, men, an army, all drowned.'

'I know,' said Khalifa, laying his hand on his shoulder. 'And now I need to find out where.'

Chicago House, the home of the University of Chicago Archaeological Mission, sits amid three acres of lush gardens on the Corniche el-Nil, midway between the temples of Luxor and Karnak. A sprawling hacienda-style building, all courtyards and walkways and arched colonnades, it is, for the six months of each year that it is open, home to a disparate collection of Egyptologists, artists, students and conservators, some engaged in their own private studies, most working across the river at the temple of Medinet Habu, whose reliefs and inscriptions the Chicago Mission has been painstakingly recording for the best part of three-quarters of a century.

It was afternoon when Khalifa arrived at its front gate and flashed his ID at the armed guards. A call was put through to the main house and three minutes later a young American woman came down to meet him. He explained why he had come and was ushered through into the compound.

'Professor az-Zahir is such a darling,' said the girl as they walked back through the gardens. 'He comes here every year. Likes to use the library. He's practically part of the furniture.'

'I hear he hasn't been well.'

'He gets a bit confused sometimes, but then name me an Egyptologist who doesn't. He's OK.'

They passed along a tree-lined path and up to a colonnade at the front of the building, the air heavy with the scent of hibiscus and jasmine and newly mown grass. Despite its proximity to the Corniche, the compound was quiet, the only sounds being the twittering of birds and the spitting of a garden sprinkler.

The girl led him through the colonnade, across a courtyard and out into the gardens at the back of the house.

'He's over there,' she said, pointing to a figure sitting in the shade beneath a tall acacia tree. 'He's having his afternoon nap, but don't worry about waking him. He loves visitors. I'll get some tea sent out.'

She turned and went back into the house. Khalifa walked over to the professor, who was slumped in his chair, his chin resting on his chest. He was a small man, bald and wrinkled as a prune, with liver spots on his hands and scalp, and large ears that glowed translucently in the afternoon light. Despite the heat he was wearing a thick tweed suit. Khalifa took the seat beside him and laid his hand on his arm.

'Professor az-Zahir?'

The old man mumbled something, coughed, and slowly – first one, then the other – his eyes levered open and he turned towards Khalifa. He looked, thought the detective, distinctly like a tortoise.

'Is it tea?' he asked, his voice frail.

'They're bringing some.'

'What?'

'They're bringing some,' repeated Khalifa more loudly.

Az-Zahir lifted his right arm and looked at his watch. 'It's too early for tea.'

'I've come to talk to you,' said Khalifa. 'I'm a friend of Professor Mohammed al-Habibi.'

'Habibi!' grunted the old man. 'Habibi thinks I'm senile! And he's right!' Chuckling to himself, he extended a quivering hand. 'You are?'

'Yusuf Khalifa. I used to study under Professor Habibi. I'm a policeman.'

The old man nodded, shifting slightly in his chair. His left hand, Khalifa noticed, lay heavily in his lap, like something dead. Az-Zahir noted the direction of his eyes.

'The stroke,' he explained.

'I'm sorry, I didn't mean to . . .'

He waved his good hand dismissively. 'Worse things happen in life. Like being taught by that dolt Habibi!' He chuckled again, his face crumpling into a broad, toothless grin. 'How is the old dog?'

'Well. He sends his regards.'

'I doubt it.'

A man came out with two cups of tea, which he set down on a small table between them. Az-Zahir couldn't reach his cup, so Khalifa passed it up to him. He slurped noisily at its contents. From somewhere behind them came the rhythmic smack and thud of a game of tennis.

'What's your name again?'

'Yusuf. Yusuf Khalifa. I wanted to talk to you about the army of Cambyses.'

Another loud slurp. 'The army of Cambyses, eh?'

'Professor Habibi says no-one knows more about it than you do.'

'Well, I certainly know more than him, but then that's not saying much.'

He finished his tea and motioned to Khalifa, who placed the empty cup back on the table. A wasp swung in and hovered over the tray. For a long while they sat in silence, az-Zahir's chin gradually sinking into his chest again, as though he was made of wax and was slowly melting in the afternoon heat. It looked as if he was going back to sleep, but then, suddenly, he sneezed and his head jerked upright.

'So,' he grunted, tugging a handkerchief from his jacket and blowing his nose on it, 'the army of Cambyses. What do you want to know?'

318

Khalifa pulled out the cigarettes he'd bought on the way back from the west bank and lit one. 'Anything you can tell me really. It was lost in the Great Sand Sea, right?'

Az-Zahir nodded.

'Can we be any more precise than that?'

'According to Herodotus it went down midway between a place called Oasis, or the Island of the Blessed, and the land of the Ammonians.' He sneezed again, and buried his nose in the handkerchief. 'So far as we know Oasis refers to al-Kharga,' he said, voice muffled by the handkerchief, 'although some people maintain it's actually al-Farafra. No-one really knows, to be honest. The Land of the Ammonians is Siwa. Somewhere between the two. That's what Herodotus said.'

'He's our only source?'

'Yes, unfortunately. Some people say he made the whole thing up.'

He finished blowing his nose and slid his hand down the side of his jacket, trying to get the handkerchief back in his pocket. It kept missing the opening, however, and eventually he gave up and stuffed it into the sleeve of his immobile left arm. There was a crunch of gravel behind them as the two tennis players, their game over, walked past and up into the house. 'Ridiculous game, tennis,' mumbled az-Zahir. 'Hitting a ball back and forth over a net. So pointless. The sort of thing only the English could invent.'

He shook his wrinkled head in disgust. There was another long pause.

'I wouldn't mind one of those cigarettes,' he said eventually.

'I'm sorry. I should have offered.'

Khalifa passed one over and lit it for him. The old man took a deep puff.

'Nice, that. After the stroke the doctors said I shouldn't, but I'm sure one won't do any harm.'

For a while he smoked in silence, holding the cigarette close to the bottom of the butt, leaning forward to puff on it, a look of intense concentration on his face. It was almost finished before he spoke again.

'It was probably the *khamsin* that buried them,' he said. 'The desert wind. It can be very fierce when it blows up, especially in springtime. Very fierce.' He waved away a fly. 'They've been looking for the army almost from the moment it was lost, you know. Cambyses himself sent an expedition to find it. So did Alexander the Great. And the Romans. It's attained a sort of mystical allure. Like Eldorado.'

'Have you looked for it?'

The old man grunted. 'How old do you think I am?'

Khalifa shrugged, embarrassed.

'Come on, how old?'

'Seventy?'

'You flatter me. I'm eighty-three. And I've spent forty-six of those eighty-three years out in the western desert looking for that damned army. And in those forty-six years do you know what I've found?'

Khalifa said nothing.

'Sand, that's what I've found. Thousands and thousands of tons of sand. I've found more sand than any other archaeologist in history. I've become an expert in it.'

He chuckled mirthlessly and, leaning forward, finished the cigarette, tamping it out on the arm of his chair and dropping the crumpled butt into his teacup.

'Shouldn't leave it on the ground,' he said. 'Litters the garden. It's a beautiful garden, don't you think?'

Khalifa agreed.

'It's the main reason I come to stay here. The library's wonderful, of course, but it's the garden I really love. So peaceful. I rather hope I die here.'

'I'm sure . . .'

'Spare me your platitudes, young man. I'm old and I'm sick, and when I go I hope it's right here in this chair in the shade of this wonderful acacia tree.'

He coughed. The man who had brought their tea came out and removed the tray.

'So no trace of the army has ever been found?' asked Khalifa. 'No indication of where it might be?'

Az-Zahir didn't appear to be listening. He was rubbing his hand up and down the arm of his chair, mumbling something to himself.

'Professor?'

'Eh?'

'No trace of the army has ever been found?'

'Oh, there are always people who claim to know where it is.' He grunted. 'There was an expedition thought they'd found it earlier this year. But it's all just hogwash. Crackpot theories. When you push them for hard evidence they can never provide any.' He drove his finger into his ear, screwing it back and forth. 'Although there was that American.'

'American?'

'Nice man. Young. Bit of a maverick. Knew his stuff, though.' He continued digging his finger into his ear. 'Worked out there on his own. In the desert. Had some theory about a pyramid.'

Khalifa's ears pricked up. 'A pyramid?'

'Not a pyramid pyramid. A large outcrop of rock shaped like a pyramid, that's what he said. He'd found inscriptions on it. Was convinced they were left by soldiers of the army. He called me, you know. From Siwa. Said he'd uncovered traces. Said he'd send me photographs. But they never arrived. And then a couple of months later they found his jeep. Burnt out. With him inside it. Tragedy. John. That was his name. John Cadey. Nice man. Bit of a maverick.' The old man removed his finger from his ear and stared at it.

'Can you remember where he was digging?' asked Khalifa.

Az-Zahir shrugged. 'Somewhere in the desert.' He sighed. He seemed to be getting tired. 'But then it's a big place, isn't it? I've spent enough time there myself. Near a pyramid. That's what he said. Nice young man. For a moment I really thought he might have found something. But then he had a crash. Very sad. It'll never be found, you know. The army. Never. It's fool's gold. A trick of the mind. Cadey. That was his name.'

His voice was growing fainter and fainter, until eventually it petered out altogether. Khalifa looked across. The old man's head had sunk down onto his chest, the skin rucking up around his chin and jowls so that his face seemed less like a face than a bowl full of wrinkles. His good arm had dropped over the side of the chair, and he began snoring. Khalifa watched him for a while and then, standing, left him to his slumber and walked back into the house.

The library of Chicago House, the finest Egyptological library anywhere outside Cairo, occupied two cool, whitewashed rooms on the ground floor of the building, with high ceilings, rows of metal shelving and an all-pervasive smell of polish and old paper. Khalifa showed the librarian his ID and explained why he had come.

The man – young, American, with round glasses and a thick beard – rubbed his chin thoughtfully. 'Well we've certainly got things that might be useful. Do you read German?'

Khalifa shook his head.

'Shame. Rohlfs' *Drei Monate in der Libyschen Wüste* is very good. Probably the best thing ever written about the western desert, even though it is a hundred years old. But it's never been translated, so I guess that's no use. Still, there's quite a few things in Arabic and English. And we've got some pretty good maps and aerial surveys. I'll go and see what I can find.'

He disappeared into a side room, leaving Khalifa beside a stack full of volumes from the very earliest days of Egyptology – Belzoni's *Researches in Egypt and Nubia*, Rosellini's *Monumenti dell'Egitto e della Nubia*, all twelve volumes of Lepsius' *Denkmäler aus Aegypten und Aethiopien*. Khalifa ran his fingers along them, pulling out a copy of Davies's *Ancient Egyptian Paintings*, laying it on top of the stack and gently opening it. He was still looking at it twenty minutes later when the librarian returned and gently tapped him on the shoulder.

'I've put some books in the reading room for you. On the table by the window. It's not everything on the subject, but it's enough to make a start. Give me a shout if you need anything else. Or perhaps a whisper would be better, given that we're in a library.'

He sniggered at his joke and returned to his desk. Khalifa replaced the Davies and went through into the second room, which had shelves to either side and a row of tables down the middle. On the one furthest from him, beside a window overlooking the gardens, were two teetering piles of books. He sat down and, taking the top volume from the nearest pile, started reading.

It took him three hours to find what he wanted. He eventually tracked it down in a slim volume entitled *A Journey across the Great Sea of Dunes*, written in 1902 by an English explorer, Captain John de Villiers.

De Villiers had set out to retrace, in reverse, Rohlfs' landmark expedition of 1874, starting from Siwa with local guides and a train of fifteen camels, and heading out across the desert towards the oasis of Dakhla 600 kilometres to the south-east. Twenty days later sickness and insufficient supplies had forced them to divert to al-Farafra, where the journey had been abandoned. What interested Khalifa, however, was not how the expedition had ended, but something that had happened eight days after it had first set out:

It was on the morning of this eighth day that Abu, the boy of whom I have already spoken, pointed out a most extraordinary sight far off across the dunes, somewhat to the east of our line of march.

My first impression was that the pyramid, for such it was, must be a mirage, or optical illusion . . .'

Khalifa paused, pondering the unfamiliar words, then stood and went over to the librarian, asking for an English–Arabic dictionary. The man pointed one out, and, taking it from the shelf, Khalifa returned to his desk and flicked through it.

'Ah!' he said, finding the words. '*Sirab. Tawahhum basari.* I see.'

He returned to the text, keeping the dictionary open beside him, referring to it frequently.

It certainly did not seem possible that it could be of natural provenance, both because of the extreme precision of its form, and, more telling, the absence of any other such formations anywhere within the vicinity.

As we drew closer, however, I was forced to reconsider this initial appraisal. The pyramid was, it transpired, both real and of natural creation. How it had arisen, and when, I cannot say, for my expertise does not, sadly, extend to matters geological. All I can report is that it was a most exceptional addition to the landscape, huge beyond reckoning, erupting from the dunes like the head of a javelin, or, a perhaps more appropriate simile, the prong of a trident, such as that wielded by Poseidon (we were, after all, in the midst of a Sea of Sand!).

Some sort of joke, Khalifa presumed.

It took us much of the day to reach this fantastic object, and necessitated a not inconsiderable diversion from our set course. Several of the men were against going towards it at all, believing it to be a thing of ill omen and harbinger of evil, the sort of charming superstitious bunkum to which the mind of the Egyptian Arab appears particularly susceptible (they are, in many ways, as Lord Cromer has so rightly indicated, little better than a nation of children).

Khalifa shook his head, half amused by the comment, half annoyed. Bloody arrogant English!

I gave ear to the men's concerns and did my best to quell them, conceding that large rocks could indeed be frightening, although generally in my experience only to those of a feminine or childlike disposition, and certainly not to such hardened men as they. That seemed to have the desired effect and, despite some churlish mutterings, we continued onwards, attaining our goal late in the afternoon and setting up camp at its base.

There is, I am sure you will concede, only so much that can be said about an outcrop of rock, even one as curious as this, and I believe I have exhausted most of it in the previous few paragraphs. I would, however, draw attention to one particular aspect of the feature, namely certain markings discovered close to its base, on the southward side, which, on closer examination, proved to be rudimentary hieroglyphs.

My command of the ancient Egyptian language is as limited as that of geology. I knew enough, however, to hazard a guess that the signs spelt out a name: 'Net-nebu'. An early traveller, no doubt, who had passed by this very spot several millennia before we ourselves came to stand upon it.

Later that same night, as Azab the cook served up dinner, I raised a toast – in tea, sadly, not wine – to the intrepid Net-nebu, wishing him retrospective good health, and hoping most sincerely that he had reached his destination safely. The men too raised their cups, solemnly repeating my words without, I suspect, having the least idea what they were talking about. It appeared to lift their spirits, however, and a sound night's sleep was had by all.

Khalifa read through the description twice to make sure he'd understood it properly, scribbling the odd note to himself, then turned to an appendix at the end of the book. Here there were extracts from de Villiers's expedition diary, with details of the distances covered each day, and on what compass bearing. By measuring these against a basic map of western Egypt he was able to get an idea of the general area in which the pyramid-shaped outcrop was located. He asked the librarian for more detailed maps, and set about pinpointing it precisely.

This took longer than he thought. He went right down to a 1:150,000 scale map, but couldn't find the outcrop anywhere. There was something that might have been it on an enhanced satellite map of the Dune Sea, but it was by no means clear, while a 1:50,000 Egyptian military survey, on which it would almost certainly have showed up, stopped just to the west of the area he was concerned with. He began to think he wouldn't find it.

In the end he did. On a Second World War RAF pilot's chart, of all things, kept in the library more as a historical memento than for any geographical information it might contain. Nonetheless it provided a detailed topographical picture of the area between 26 and 30 degrees of both longitude and latitude, and there, roughly halfway between Siwa and al-Farafra, sticking out from an otherwise empty landscape, was a small triangle with the legend 'Pyramidal Rock Formation'. Khalifa slammed his hand on the desk in delight, the sound echoing through the room like a gunshot.

'Sorry,' he whispered to the librarian, who had put his head round the door to see what was going on.

He noted down the rock's co-ordinates, checking and rechecking to make sure he had them exactly and then, wondering if his friend Fat Abdul still organized desert tours, stood up and stretched. Only then did he notice it had gone dark outside. He looked at his watch. Past eight o'clock. And he'd promised to be home by four for the children's parade.

'Dammit!' he hissed, snatching up his notebook and rushing out. Zenab would not be happy.

33

THE WESTERN DESERT

By nightfall there was still no trace of the army and Dravic was growing impatient.

All day long he had stood staring at the work below, waiting for the cry to go up that something had been found. Hour after hour had gone by, the sun burning down on him, the flies swarming around his face, the huge rock towering overhead, its outline trembling in the outrageous heat, and still the cry hadn't come. The vacuums had worked nonstop, lowering the ground around the base of the rock by almost ten metres, but there was nothing. Just sand. Thousands upon thousands of tons of it, as if the desert was mocking him.

A couple of times he had descended into the excavation trench himself, poking around with his trowel, cursing anyone who happened to be nearby. For the most part, however, he had remained beneath the shade of his umbrella, chomping on his cigars, wiping the sweat from his eyes, growing increasingly anxious and frustrated.

As the sun went down and the sky darkened, the air growing mercifully cooler, they set up giant arc lamps all around the excavation, flooding the valley with light. The chances of the illumination being spotted out there in the vastness of the desert were negligible and, anyway, it was a risk they had to take if they wanted to push on with the work. Every available man was issued with a shovel and sent down into the trench to dig. There was now a whole army down there, labouring furiously beneath the blazing white light. An army searching for an army. Yet still there was no sign of it.

He was beginning to worry that Lacage might be right. Perhaps the army was further down than he'd thought. His estimation was that it ought to be between four and seven metres below the desert surface. That was what he'd told Sayf al-Tha'r. Between four and seven metres. Ten at the outside. But they were down to ten now and there was nothing. Absolutely nothing.

They'd find it eventually, of course, but time was pressing. They couldn't stay out here for ever. As each day went by there was more chance of their activities attracting attention. The desert was remote, but not so remote that they could hide in it indefinitely. They had a week at most. And if the army was fifty metres down they wouldn't be able to get much of it out in that time.

'Where is it?' he muttered, sucking angrily on his cigar. 'We should have found it by now. Where the fuck is it?'

He clenched his fists and worked the knuckles into his temples. He had a furious headache – hardly surprising, given that he'd been standing up there for over twelve hours. He needed to calm down. Take his mind off things. He shouted to one of the men below, telling them he was going to his tent and that if anything happened they should call him immediately, and then turned and walked back down towards the camp. He had a bottle of vodka in his bag. A few shots of that and he'd feel a lot better. And perhaps he'd get a couple of hours' sleep as well. He could do with it.

As he walked, however, another idea gradually came into his

head, causing a smile to spread slowly across his huge face. Yes, he thought, that would really take his mind off things. He'd get a wash, have a few drinks, eat, and then . . .

He reached the camp and, weaving his way through the stacks of equipment, stopped in front of a tent and put his head through the flap. Inside Tara and Daniel were lying curled on the floor. They sat up when they heard him enter. He looked briefly at Tara and then spoke to the guard in Arabic. Daniel grimaced.

'You animal, Dravic,' he hissed. 'One day I'll kill you.'

Dravic burst out laughing. 'Then you'll have to come back from the dead to do it.' He spoke to the guard again and left.

'What was all that about?' Tara asked.

Daniel didn't say anything, just sat staring at the ends of his boots. He seemed reluctant to answer.

'What did he say?'

He muttered something.

'What?'

'He said they're to take you to his tent in two hours.'

She looked down at her watch. Eight-fifteen. She felt as if she was going to be sick.

LUXOR

As Khalifa had expected, Zenab wasn't happy with him. She was watching television with Ali and Batah when he came in, and fixed him with one of her fiercest glares.

'You didn't see me, Dad,' chided Ali. 'I was on the Tutankhamun float. I was one of his fan-bearers.'

'I'm sorry,' said Khalifa, squatting in front of his son and ruffling his hair. 'There was something I had to finish at work. I would have been there if I could. Here, I bought you something. And you, Batah.'

He reached into the plastic bag he was carrying and pulled out a shell necklace, which he gave to his daughter, and a plastic trumpet.

'Thanks, Dad!' cried Ali, seizing the instrument and blowing loudly on it. Batah rushed out to look at herself in the mirror. Ali followed.

'It's once a year, Yusuf,' said Zenab when they were alone. 'One afternoon a year. They so wanted you to be there.'

'I'm sorry,' he said again, reaching for her hand. She withdrew it and, standing, moved across the room and closed the door.

'I got a call this morning,' she said, turning. 'From Chief Hassani.'

Khalifa said nothing, just pulled out his cigarettes.

'To say how pleased he was about your promotion. How it would mean more money, a subsidized flat, a new school for the kids. I said, "It's the first I've heard about it." He said you'd be home soon to tell me. That it was a really good career move for you. Went on and on about it.'

'Bastard,' muttered Khalifa.

'What?'

'He's getting at me, Zenab. Getting at me through you. Telling you all the good things this promotion will mean and hoping you'll persuade me to take it.'

'You're not going to take it?'

'It's complicated.'

'Don't fob me off! Not this time. What's happening, Yusuf?'

Ali started banging on the door. 'Mum! I want to watch television.'

'Your father and I are talking. Go and play with Batah.'

'I don't want to play with Batah.'

'Ali, go and play with Batah! And keep the noise down or you'll wake the baby.'

There was a defiant trumpet toot and the sound of a door slamming. Khalifa lit his cigarette. 'I have to go back to Cairo,' he said. 'Tonight.'

She was still for a moment and then came over and knelt before him, her hair spilling across his thighs.

'What is this, Yusuf? I've never known you like this before. Tell me. Please. I have a right to know. Especially when it's affecting our lives like this. What is this case? Why won't you take the promotion?'

He put his arms around her and rested his forehead on her head. 'It's not that I don't want to tell you, Zenab. It's just that I'm frightened. Frightened of getting you involved. It's so dangerous.'

'Then I have even more right to know. I am your wife. What affects you affects me too. And our children. If there is danger I should know about it.'

'I don't fully understand it myself. All I know is that innocent people's lives are in danger and I'm the only one who can save them.'

They remained like that for a moment and then she pushed him away, looking up into his eyes.

'There's something else, isn't there?'

He didn't speak.

'What?'

'It's not . . .'

'What, Yusuf?'

'Sayf al-Tha'r,' he said quietly.

Her head dropped. 'Oh God, no. That's in the past. It's finished.'

'It's never been finished,' he said, staring down at his knees. 'That's what I've realized with this case: it's always here inside me. I've tried to forget about it, to move on, but I can't. I should have stopped them. I should have helped him.'

'We've been over this, Yusuf. There was nothing you could have done.'

'But I should at least have tried. And I didn't. I just let them take him away.' He could feel tears welling in his eyes and fought to keep them back. 'I can't put it into words, Zenab.

331

It's as if I'm carrying a huge weight on my back. Always I'm thinking about Ali. About what happened. About how I could have done more. And now, with this case, I have a chance to put things right. Maybe not bring Ali back, but at least redress some of the evil that's been done. And until I do that I'll always be incomplete. Half of me will always be trapped in the past.'

'I'd rather have half a husband than a dead one.'

'Please try to understand. I have to see this through. It's important.'

'More important than me and the children? We need you, Yusuf.' She seized his hands. 'I don't care about the promotion. We don't need more money, a fancy flat. We get along fine. But I care about you. My husband. My love. I don't want you to be killed. And you will be if you carry on with this. I know you will be. I can feel it.' She was crying now and buried her face in his lap. 'I want you here, with us, safe,' she said, choking. 'I want us to grow together, a family.'

From Batah's bedroom came the muffled screech of his son's trumpet. Firecrackers were popping in the street below. He stroked her hair.

'There's nothing in the world more important to me than you and the children,' he whispered. 'Nothing. Not the past, not my brother, certainly not my own life. I love you more than I could ever express. I would do anything for you. Anything.'

He lifted her head so that their eyes were joined.

'Tell me to drop the case, Zenab. Tell me and I will, without a moment's hesitation. Tell me.'

For a long while she held his stare, her eyes huge and brown and moist. Then, slowly, she came to her feet.

'What time's your train?' she said quietly.

'The last one goes at ten.'

'Then you'll just have time for dinner.'

She shook back her hair, and went out into the kitchen.

*

He left at nine-fifteen. With him he had a holdall containing a change of clothes, some food and his revolver, a Helwan 9mm, standard police issue. He also had 840 Egyptian pounds, money they'd been putting aside towards making the Hajj to Mecca. He felt terrible about taking it, but it was the only cash they had in the flat and he'd need it to get where he was going. Whatever else happened over the next few days he promised himself he'd replace it.

He turned left out of his block and set off on the fifteen-minute walk to the station, the night air echoing to the bang of firecrackers as people celebrated the feast of Abu el-Haggag. He wondered whether he should go via the office to pick up more ammunition, but decided against it. There was too big a risk of bumping into one of his colleagues. He needed to get out of Luxor without anyone knowing. He glanced at his watch. Nine-twenty.

The crowds grew heavier as he came into the centre of town. The streets around Luxor Temple were teeming. Children in party hats ran to and fro throwing firecrackers; impromptu bands – *mizmar*s and drums mainly – played at the roadside. The sweet sellers could barely keep up with demand.

In a small park beside the temple a group of *zikr* dancers were performing – two lines of men facing each other, swaying from side to side in time to the devotional chanting of a *munshid* at their head. A large crowd had gathered to watch them and Khalifa slowed too. Not to observe the dancers, but to check out the men who were following him.

He couldn't be sure how many of them there were, nor when they'd latched onto him, but they were definitely there. Three, maybe four, mingling with the revellers, clocking his every move. One he'd spotted as he stopped to buy some cigarettes, another as he stood aside to let through a procession of men on horseback. Just a momentary glimpse, a fleeting eye-contact before they'd melted back into the throng. They were good, he could tell that much. Trained. Secret service, maybe. Or military intelligence. For all he knew, they could have been with him all day.

Standing in the park now, he ran his eyes over the crowd. Ten metres away a man was leaning against some railings. His eyes kept flicking up towards Khalifa and the detective began to think maybe he was one of them. Then a woman came up and the two of them walked off together, arm in arm. Nine-thirty. Khalifa lit a cigarette and moved away.

He had to lose them before he got to the station. He wasn't sure precisely who they were or what they wanted, but he did know that if they got any inkling of where he was going they'd try to stop him. And if they stopped him once he wouldn't get another chance. He had to lose them.

Nine-thirty-one. He turned left down a narrow street, past a group of children watching television on the pavement. He quickened his step and turned right down another street. Two old men were playing *siga* in the dust, using stones as counters. He hurried past them and dodged left again, down a winding alley. Twenty metres along a motorbike was parked up against a wall and he glanced in its wing mirror. He was alone. He broke into a trot.

For ten minutes he zigzagged through the backstreets of Luxor, taking sudden unexpected turns, constantly looking behind him, before eventually emerging into Midan al-Mahatta, the square in front of the station, with its red obelisk and fountain that never seemed to work. He breathed a sigh of relief and stepped out into the road, glancing to the right to check for traffic. As he did so he noticed a suited figure standing in a shadowy doorway opposite, staring straight at him.

'Dammit!' he hissed.

The Cairo train was already waiting at the platform, passengers jostling around it, porters hefting bags up through its doors. There was no way he was going to get to it without being seen. He looked down at his watch. Nine-forty-three. Seventeen minutes.

For a moment he stood still, uncertain what to do, then, suddenly, turned left down Sharia al-Mahatta, away from the station, walking fast. It was a crazy idea, mad, but he couldn't think of anything else. He had to get home.

He took the shortest route he knew, weaving through the back streets, not bothering to look behind him, knowing they'd be there. He reached the apartment block in ten minutes, sprinting up the stairs and bursting through the front door.

'Yusuf?' Zenab came out of the living room. 'Why have you come back?'

'No time to explain,' he gasped, pulling her into the kitchen. He threw up his watch arm. Nine-fifty-three. This was going to be horribly close.

He pulled open the kitchen window and looked down into the narrow alley below. As he'd expected there were two men standing there in the shadows, covering the building's rear entrance. The twenty-metre drop made his head spin. He looked over at the roof of the block opposite, which was just below the level of his window, about three metres away, flat, with lines of washing strung across it and, at one end, a doorway leading down into the building below. He'd often wondered if it would be possible to jump from one tenement to the other. Now he was about to find out.

He took another look down, groaning inwardly, and then, leaning out, threw his holdall across the gap. It landed with a heavy thud, disturbing a flock of pigeons, which rose into the air and flapped off into the night.

'Yusuf,' hissed Zenab, fingers digging into his arm, 'what are you doing? Why did you throw your bag over there?'

He seized her face and kissed her on the mouth.

'Don't ask. Because if I start thinking about it I won't do it.'

He clambered up onto the windowsill and, clutching the metal frame, turned towards her.

'I want you to keep the doors locked tonight,' he said. 'If anybody calls, tell them I've gone to bed early because I'm going to Ismailiya tomorrow.'

'I don't—'

'Please, Zenab! There's no time. If anybody calls tell them I'm not to be disturbed. Tomorrow morning I want you to take the kids and go to Hosni and Sama's. Stay there till you hear from me. Do you understand?'

She nodded.

'I love you, Zenab.'

He leaned forward and kissed her again, and then, turning, faced across the alley to the roof opposite. It looked a very long way away.

'And shut the window after me,' he whispered.

There was no point trying to pluck up courage and so mumbling a swift prayer he counted to three and jumped, driving himself away from the sill with all his strength, fighting back an urge to scream out in terror. For a moment time seemed to stand still and he was hovering in the air directly above the alley. Then, with a jarring thud, he landed on the opposite roof and sprawled onto his face, grazing his elbow on the concrete.

He lay still for a moment, even more terrified now the jump was over than he had been before it, and then clambered to his feet and looked back. Zenab was standing at the kitchen window, a shocked look on her face. He blew her a kiss, recovered his holdall and hurried over to the roof door, which opened onto the stairwell leading down through the building. Another glance at the watch. Nine-fifty-four. He began sprinting down the stairs.

The front entrance to this block faced in the opposite direction to his block and his theory was that with both sides of his own tenement covered there was no reason for them to be watching this one too. He could get out and away without being seen. He would have liked a few minutes to check the street was clear, but there wasn't time, and on reaching the bottom of the stairs he ran straight out into the road and back towards the centre of town. He had about a mile to cover and five minutes to do it in. Adrenalin was burning through his veins like magma.

After two minutes he had an excruciating pain in his left side, after three he couldn't breathe. He kept going, however, powering forward, forcing every last ounce of energy into his legs, until eventually he burst from a narrow grid of streets and staggered up to a level crossing, clutching his side. Two hundred metres to his right the Cairo train was slowly pulling out of the station, its wheels creaking and clanking.

Dammit! he thought. The first time a train had ever left Luxor on time and it had to be tonight.

He stayed where he was, gasping for air, until the train was almost level with him, then ducked beneath the crossing barrier and began running beside it, a high concrete wall to his left, the train's huge iron wheels to his right, coming up almost to the level of his chest. He clutched at the handrail beside a door, but couldn't hold on and had to let it go. The gap between train and wall was getting narrower. Another fifty metres and there'd be no more space left to run. He grasped another rail, desperate, and this time managed to keep hold, swinging himself up onto the footplate and, with his last ounce of strength, heaving open the door and slipping through, slamming it shut again just as the concrete wall came flush with the side of the train. He collapsed onto a seat, gasping.

'Are you OK?' asked a man sitting opposite.

'Fine.' Khalifa's lungs were raging. 'Just need . . . need . . .'

'Some water?'

'A cigarette.'

Outside the buildings of Luxor slowly slipped back into the night as the train built up speed and flew north towards Cairo.

34

The Western Desert

'I'm not going to let him rape me, Daniel.'

The two hours were almost up. They'd been the worst two hours of her life – a slow water torture as the minutes ticked relentlessly down towards her meeting with Dravic. She felt as if she was in a river being swept towards a cataract, with nothing she could do to save herself. She understood how a prisoner on death row must feel as the hour of execution approaches.

'I'm not going to let him rape me,' she repeated, standing, too nervous to sit. 'I'd rather die.'

Daniel said nothing, just stared up at her in the glow of the kerosene lamp, wanting to speak but unable to find the words. The guard gazed at them both through empty eyes. She began pacing around the tent, a heavy weight in her stomach, sickened by her powerlessness, looking down at her watch constantly. It was cold now, and she was shivering.

'We don't know that's what's going to happen,' he said, trying to offer some words of comfort.

'Sure,' she spat. 'Maybe he just wants to talk about archaeology.'

Her voice was angry, full of bitterness and sarcasm. Daniel dropped his head.

'I'm sorry,' she said after a moment. 'I'm just so scared.'

He stood and took her in his arms, holding her tight. She clung to him like a child, desperate, tears stinging her eyes.

'It's OK,' he whispered. 'Everything will be all right.'

'It won't, Daniel. It won't be all right ever again if he does that to me. I couldn't stand it. I'd feel dirty for the rest of my life.'

He was about to say it wouldn't make much difference since they were going to be killed anyway, but stopped himself. Instead he just stroked her hair and held her close against him. She was shaking uncontrollably.

They stayed like that until they heard the crunch of approaching feet. The tent flap was pulled back and someone spoke to the guard. He stood, and motioned Tara outside.

Daniel swung her behind him, shielding her. The guard motioned again and then stepped forward, reaching out his hand. Daniel slapped it away, raising his fists, ready to fight. The guard called and two other men came in. Daniel lashed out at one, but the man dodged the blow and, raising the butt of his gun, knocked Daniel to the floor, standing over him and jamming the muzzle against his chest. His companion grabbed Tara's arm and pulled her towards the entrance.

'I'm sorry,' groaned Daniel. 'I'm so sorry.'

'I love you.' Her voice was shaking. 'I've always loved you. Always.'

And then she was outside and being dragged through the camp, one guard clutching her arm, the other walking behind and jabbing at her with his gun. She struggled violently, kicking and biting, but it was no good, the man's grip was firm. Ahead the pyramid rock loomed vast and silent against the night, glowing in the light of the arc lamps below.

They came to another tent, larger than the one she and Daniel had been kept in. One of the guards said something and she was pushed through the entrance, the flap dropping down behind her. It made only a slight sound as it closed, a soft rustling of canvas against canvas, but there was something horribly final about it, as though a cell door had been slammed shut.

'Good evening.' Dravic chuckled. 'I'm so glad you could come.'

He was sitting on a canvas chair beside a wooden trestle table. In one hand he held a half-smoked cigar, in the other a glass. A three-quarters empty bottle of vodka sat on the table beside him. The pale side of his face had turned a bright pinky-red, as though his birthmark was leaking beneath the bridge of his nose and slowly colouring his other cheek. The tent stank of cigar smoke and sweat. Tara shivered with disgust.

The German shouted something and there was a sound of receding feet as the guards left her to him.

'Drink?'

She shook her head, so scared she felt as though her chest was going to split open. Dravic drained his glass and poured himself another. He downed that too and took a puff on his cigar.

'Poor little Tara.' He smiled. 'I bet you wish you'd never got mixed up in all of this, don't you? And if you don't now, you certainly will in a few minutes.' He laughed raucously.

'Why have you brought me here?' Her voice was hoarse.

He sensed her terror and his laughter grew louder. 'Surely I don't need to spell it out!'

Again he filled his glass and knocked it back in one gulp, his throat swelling as the liquid passed through it. She looked wildly around for something to use as a weapon. She could see Dravic's jacket with the trowel handle sticking out of the pocket and edged slightly towards it. There was another bellow of laughter.

'Go on,' he said, 'try and get it. I want you to. I expect you to. What's the point if there's no struggle?'

She lunged for the jacket and pulled out the trowel, backing away, holding the point towards him.

'I'll kill you,' she hissed. 'If you come near me, I'll kill you.'

He laid the glass aside and stood, wobbling slightly. She could see the bulge in his groin, and her throat tightened as though she was being strangled. He came towards her, puffing on his cigar, coils of smoke winding around his huge head.

'I'll kill you,' she repeated, stabbing at him with the trowel.

He was in front of her now. Her head barely came up to the level of his chest, his arms were as big as her thighs. She backed away against the wall of the tent, slashing at him, frantic.

'Get away from me!'

'I'm going to hurt you,' he whispered. 'I'm going to hurt you so badly.'

She slashed at him again, but he caught her arm easily and twisted so that she dropped the trowel. She cowered against the tent wall, desperate, wanting to bring her knee up into his groin but somehow unable to make her leg move. He leaned down over her, a towering monstrosity, and then his hand whipped out and clawed down the front of her shirt, ripping the material, exposing her breasts. She squirmed sideways, wrapping her arms around her.

'You fucking animal,' she screamed. 'You fucking filthy ugly animal.'

The punch hit her on the side of her head, heavy as a sledge-hammer, sending her reeling across the tent onto the floor. Half dazed, she heard him coming over and then felt the crushing weight of his body as he straddled her. She couldn't breathe.

He took the cigar from his mouth and, reaching forward, touched its glowing tip to her neck. She screamed in agony, writhing, trying to get him off, but he was too heavy, as if she had a mountain on top of her. The cigar came down again on her forearm and the top of her breast. Each time she screamed and each time he laughed in delight. He threw the cigar aside and began pawing at her breasts, squeezing them, pulping the pale flesh. Then he bent his head and, grunting like a pig, started to bite her neck and shoulders, his teeth leaving deep purple welts on her white skin. Somehow she managed to get a hand free and with all the strength she could muster, drove her thumb up into his eye. He arced backwards, roaring.

'You filthy bitch!' he screamed. 'I'll fucking teach you!'

He slapped her three times about the face, shockingly hard, knocking the breath out of her. She felt herself being flipped over onto her front, and heard the sound of a belt being un-buckled, although the noise was strangely muffled. She felt as if she had stepped out of her body and was standing to one side gazing down, a witness to the violation rather than its victim. She watched as Dravic pulled open his trousers and, reaching beneath her belly, started to undo her jeans.

I'm going to be raped, she thought to herself in a detached sort of way. Dravic is going to rape me and there's nothing I can do about it.

She could see the trowel lying on the floor ten feet away and reached towards it, even though she knew she could never reach it.

I wonder how much it'll hurt, she thought.

He grabbed her hair and yanked her head back while at the same time tugging down her jeans and knickers. She closed her eyes and clenched her teeth, waiting for the assault.

It didn't come. She could feel the weight of Dravic on top of her, his fist on her buttocks, but he seemed to have stopped still, as though frozen.

'Come on,' she said impatiently. 'Just get it over with.'

Still he didn't move. She opened her eyes again and twisted round. He was looking towards the door, head cocked, listening. She listened too. Initially it was all just a confused buzz. Then, gradually, like a radio being tuned in, the sound grew clearer. Shouting. Dozens of voices shouting. Dravic remained where he was for a moment and then, muttering, came to his feet and rebuckled his trousers. The shouting was growing louder and more urgent, although she couldn't make out what was being said. Dravic retrieved his trowel, looked back at her and then, throwing aside the tent flap, stepped out into the night. She was alone.

For some moments she lay where she was, her face thick and heavy, the burns on her skin aching viciously. Then, rolling onto her back, she pulled up her jeans and struggled to her feet.

Several minutes passed and then a guard stepped into the tent. He looked at her and there was a momentary flicker of apology in his eyes, as if he disapproved of what Dravic had done and wanted her to know that. Then, with a twist of his head, he motioned her outside.

Dravic was nowhere to be seen. The whole camp, indeed, was empty, like a ghost town. The guard pointed with his gun, up towards the mound they'd stood on earlier in the day. As she came to the top she saw that Daniel was already there, flanked by two guards. He turned.

'Oh Jesus,' he said, choking at the sight of her ripped shirt and bruised skin. 'Oh Jesus, what's the bastard done to you?' He pushed past his guards and ran to her, wrapping his arms around her. 'I'll kill him. I'll kill the animal!'

'I'm OK,' she said. 'I'm fine.'

'Did he . . . ?'

She shook her head.

'I heard you screaming. I wanted to do something, but they had a gun on me. I'm so sorry, Tara.'

'It's not your fault, Daniel.'

'I'll kill him! I'll kill all of them!'

The intensity of his embrace was hurting her and she pushed him away.

'I'm fine,' she said. 'Honestly. What's going on? There was shouting.'

He was staring at the burn marks on her skin, eyes filled with disgust and guilt.

'I think they've found something,' he mumbled. 'Dravic is down in the excavation trench.'

She grasped his hand and together they went forward to the front of the mound.

Since they'd been there that afternoon a vast round crater had been sucked out of the valley floor, exposing the base of the pyramid rock like the root of an enormous tooth. Dravic was at the bottom, side on to them, kneeling, poking at the ground with his trowel. The rest of the men were above, gazing down, expectant. The cold white light of the arc lamps lent the scene an unearthly, dreamlike quality.

'What have they found?' she asked.

'I don't know,' said Daniel. 'We're too far away.'

Dravic shouted and one of the men threw a brush down to him. He took it and began flicking at the area in front of his knees, stopping every now and then and leaning forward, staring intently at the ground. After a minute he laid the brush aside and resumed scraping with his trowel, alternating between the two as he slowly cleared back the gravelly sand before him, revealing something, although Tara couldn't make out what it was.

Several minutes passed. More of the object was exposed now and she could see that it was semi-circular in shape, like the upper part of a wheel. Dravic continued clearing around it before eventually laying aside his tools, gripping the thing with both hands and pulling. His shoulders bunched with the effort, but the object wouldn't come and he was forced to take up the brush and trowel again and clear away more sand. Despite what he'd just done to her, Tara nonetheless found herself absorbed in his actions. Daniel was leaning forward, hand tight in hers, his anger suddenly forgotten.

Again Dravic laid aside his tools, and again grasped and pulled at the object. Still it wouldn't come. He shuffled backwards slightly to give himself more leverage, adjusted his grip and, throwing back his head, heaved with all his might, veins bulging in his neck. For a moment the world seemed to stop dead, as if the scene in front of Tara was a photograph rather than an event happening in real time. Then, slowly, inch by inch, the object started to rise. Daniel took a step forward. Up it came, resisting all the way, the desert reluctant to release its treasure, up and up, until suddenly the ground's jaws broke and, in a spray of sand and small pebbles, the object came free. A shield, huge, round, heavy, its convex face gleaming in the glare of the lamps. Dravic held it aloft and the men began cheering wildly, yelling, clapping, stamping their feet.

'I've found you, you bastard!' bellowed Dravic. 'The army of Cambyses. I've found you!'

For a moment he stood with the shield held triumphantly above his head and then began screaming orders. Men swarmed down into the trench. The shield was carried away and the vacuums taken up again, their mouths swinging furiously across the sand.

'Clear it!' roared Dravic. 'Clear all of it. Work!'

Initially there was nothing, just sand and more sand, a bottomless well of yellow, so that it began to look as if the shield might have been a one-off, something thrown up by the desert to taunt and tantalize them.

Then, slowly, other shapes started to appear. Formless at first, just vague hummocks and ridges, unsightly distortions in the smooth continuum of the desert. As more sand was gasped away, however, they gradually took on recognizable forms. Bodies, dozens of bodies, hundreds of them, their flesh dried and hardened by two and a half millennia of submersion, giving them the look not of corpses, but rather of old men. An army of old men. Ancient beyond reckoning, but alive nonetheless, rising wearily from the sands, blinking in the angry light, disorientated, their weapons still clutched firmly in their skeletal hands. There was hair on their heads, and armour clamped around their torsos, and, most extraordinary, expressions on their faces – terror and pain and horror and fury. One man appeared to be screaming, another weeping, another laughing insanely, his mouth levered wide open to the sky, his throat filled with sand.

'Jesus Christ,' whispered Tara. 'It's . . .'

'. . . fabulous,' said Daniel, breath heavy with excitement. 'Horrible.'

Most of the figures were lying flat, steam-rollered by the monstrous weight of the storm that had buried them. A few, however, were on their knees, and some were still standing upright, arms raised protectively in front of their faces, overwhelmed so swiftly they hadn't even had time to fall.

As each body emerged, a host of black-robed workers descended upon it like vultures, pulling away its armour and equipment and passing them up to the top of the trench, where packing crates were being laid out ready to receive them. Occasionally an arm or leg would snap off as the body to which it belonged was roughly manhandled.

'Strip them!' yelled Dravic. 'Strip them clean! I want everything. Everything!'

An hour passed and the excavation spread out in all directions, revealing more and more of the army. Dravic strode back and forth barking orders, examining objects, directing the sand-vacuums, before eventually clambering out of the hole and looking up at Tara and Daniel.

'I told you I'd find it, Lacage,' he shouted gleefully. 'I told you!'

Daniel said nothing. His eyes burned with hatred. And also, it seemed to Tara, a hint of envy.

'I couldn't kill you without at least giving you the chance to see it. I'm not that cruel!'

The German laughed and indicated to the guards that they should take them back to their tent.

'And Ms Mullray,' he called after them, 'our little soirée hasn't been cancelled, merely postponed. I'll be sending for you again. After all this work I'll be needing to slip into something warm and tight.'

The boy found him standing on a dune top, alone, gazing eastwards into the night. He climbed up to him.

'They've found it, Master,' he said. 'The army. Dr Dravic has just radioed in.'

The man continued staring out into the wilderness, the dunes glowing silver in the moonlight, like a sea of mercury. When he eventually spoke his voice was subdued.

'This is the end and the beginning, Mehmet. From today so much will be different. Sometimes it frightens me.'

'Frightens, Master?'

'Yes, Mehmet. Even I, God's warrior, can be scared. Scared of the responsibility I have been given. There is so much to do. At times I think I would just like to sleep. It's been so long since I slept, Mehmet. Years. Not since I was a child.'

He clasped his hands behind his back. A soft wind started to blow. The boy was growing cold.

'We cross the border tomorrow. Mid-morning. Inform Dr Dravic.'

'Yes, Master.'

The boy turned and started to descend. Halfway down he stopped and looked back.

'Sayf al-Tha'r,' he called. 'You are like a father to me.'

The man continued gazing out across the desert.

'And you are like a son to me,' he said.

His voice was quiet, no more than a whisper, and the words dissolved into the night so that the boy did not hear them.

35

CAIRO

Cairo was the only practical starting point for the journey Khalifa intended to make. The alternative would have been to drive from Luxor to 'Ezba el Gaga and then follow the huge loop of the desert highway through the oases of al-Kharga and Dakhla before cutting cross-country from al-Farafra – a vast journey over badly maintained, heavily policed roads that were frequently made impassable by the drifting sands. No, it had to be Cairo. And anyway, that was where Fat Abdul was.

His train drew into Ramesses Central just after eight a.m. He jumped off before it had come to a stop and, hurrying through the cavernous marble concourse, hopped a service taxi down to Midan Tahrir. He'd had ten hours to think about what he was doing and more than once the doubts had begun to creep in again. He'd pushed them from his mind, however, and instead focused on the journey ahead. He just hoped Abdul still organized those desert tours.

He crossed the square, dodging the barrage of morning traffic, and turned down Sharia Talaat Harb, coming to a halt in front of a glass-fronted shop with 'Abdul Wassami Tours – Better Than

None in Egypt' stencilled above the window. Below was a list of the various tours on offer, including, to Khalifa's relief, a 'Thriller Five-Day Desert Adventure including camp out under beautiful stars, four-wheel drive and very exotic belly dance extravaganza'. Abdul had clearly lost none of his talent for selling a product.

He opened the door and stepped inside.

Abdul Wassami – Fat Abdul as he was generally known – was a friend from Khalifa's Giza days. They'd grown up next door to each other and gone to the same school, where, from an early age, Abdul had displayed a determinedly entrepreneurial streak, selling 'miracle power tonics' made from Coca-Cola and cough medicine, and charging ten piastres a head for surreptitious guided tours of his elder sister's bedroom (unlike her sibling, Fatima Wassami had been tall, slim and extremely good-looking).

Adulthood had tempered his exploits slightly, although not his ingenuity, and after a brief spell exporting Libyan dates to the former Soviet Union he'd settled down to run his own travel company. Khalifa saw him only occasionally these days, but the old warmth was still there, and as he entered the shop now there was a cry of delight from the far end.

'Yusuf! What a marvellous surprise! Girls, say hello to Yusuf Khalifa, one of my oldest and thinnest friends.'

Three girls, all young, all pretty, looked up from behind their computers and smiled. Abdul waddled over and enveloped the detective in a suffocating hug.

'Look at Rania,' he whispered in his ear. 'The one on the left, with the big you-know-whats. Thick as a slice of *basbousa*, but the body on her! Oh God, the body! Watch!' He released Khalifa and turned to the girls. 'Rania dear, could you fetch us some tea?'

Smiling, Rania stood and walked towards the back of the shop, hips swaying provocatively. Abdul stared after her, mesmerized, until she disappeared into a small kitchen.

'The Gates of Paradise,' he sighed. 'God, what a bum.' He ushered Khalifa over to a row of armchairs and squeezed down beside him. 'Zenab OK?' he asked.

'Fine, thanks. Jamilla?'

'As far as I know.' Abdul shrugged. 'She seems to spend most of her time round at her mother's these days. Eating. God, she eats. Makes me look like I'm on a starvation diet. Hey, you know what? I'm about to open a New York office.'

For as long as Khalifa could remember Abdul had been about to open a New York office. He smiled and lit a cigarette. Rania returned with the tea, setting the glasses down in front of them and going back to her desk, Abdul's eyes glued to her receding backside.

'Listen, I need a favour,' said Khalifa.

'Sure,' said his friend distractedly. 'Anything.'

'I need to borrow a four-by-four.'

'Borrow?'

Suddenly Abdul was all attention.

'Yes, borrow.'

'What, as in hire?'

'As in you lend me.'

'For free?'

'Exactly. I need it for four, maybe five days. Something that's equipped for rough terrain. Desert terrain.'

Abdul's brow had furrowed. Lending things for free clearly wasn't a concept with which he felt comfortable.

'And when do you need this four-by-four?'

'Now.'

'Now!' Abdul burst out laughing. 'I'd love to help you, Yusuf, but that's impossible. All the four-wheel drives are down in Bahariya. It would take at least a day to bring one back to Cairo, more if they're out on a tour, which, now I think about it, they all are. If we had one here of course you could have it. We're friends, after all. But as it is ... I'm sorry, there's no way.'

He leaned forward and slurped his tea. There was a brief silence.

'There is that one in the garage,' said Rania from behind her computer.

The slurping stopped.

'The new one that was delivered on Monday. It's all filled up and ready to go.'

'Yes, but that's no good,' said Abdul. 'It's booked out.'

'No it's not,' said Rania.

'I'm sure it is,' insisted Abdul, glaring at her. 'Booked out to that group of Italians.'

He spoke slowly and deliberately, emphasizing the words, as if prompting an actor who'd forgotten her lines.

'I don't think it is, Mr Wassami. Hang on, I'll look on the computer.'

'There's really no . . .'

Her fingers were already clattering over the keyboard.

'There!' she said triumphantly. 'I knew it wasn't. No-one's using it for another five days. Which is just how long your friend needs it for. Isn't that lucky?'

She smiled broadly, as did Abdul, although he clearly had to work at the expression.

'Yes, dear, marvellous.' He sighed, and buried his face in his hands. 'Thick as a slice of bloody *basbousa*.'

The four-by-four, a Toyota, was in a garage in the next street but one. White, cuboid, solid, with bull-bars across the front, two spare wheels bolted to the rear and a row of eight jerrycans slotted into the heavy steel roof-rack, it was exactly what Khalifa wanted. Abdul drove it out and parked it by the kerb.

'You will be careful with it, won't you?' he pleaded, clutching the steering wheel protectively. 'It's brand-new. I've only had it two days. Please tell me you'll be careful with it.'

'Of course I will.'

'It cost forty thousand dollars. And that was with a discount.

351

Forty thousand. I must be mad letting you have it. Stark raving mad.'

He clambered out and walked Khalifa round the vehicle, pointing out the various features, stressing and re-stressing how anxious he was to get it back in one piece.

'It's four-wheel drive, obviously. Manual gearing, water-cooled engine, electric fuel pump. About as top of the range as you can get.' He sounded like a car salesman. 'It's fully equipped with fuel cans, water containers, toolbox, traction mats, first-aid kit, compass. Everything you'd expect, basically. There are also blankets, maps, emergency rations, flares, binoculars and . . .' Reaching into the glove compartment he removed what looked like a large mobile phone with a stubby aerial and a liquid crystal display on the front. '. . . a portable GPS unit.'

'GPS?'

'Global Positioning by Satellite. It tells you your precise position at any given moment and, if you punch in the co-ordinates of a point you're trying to reach, it'll tell you how far away it is and on what bearing. There's an instruction manual in the compartment. They're perfectly simple. Even I can use one.'

He replaced the unit and, reluctantly, handed the keys over.

'And I'm not paying for the petrol.'

'I didn't expect you to, Abdul,' said Khalifa, climbing in.

'So long as that's understood. The petrol's down to you. And take this.'

He pulled a mobile phone from his pocket and handed it over.

'If there are any problems, anything at all, any strange noises or anything, I want you to stop, pull over, turn off the engine and call me immediately. OK?'

'Will it work in the desert?'

'As far as I can tell it works everywhere except in Cairo. Now just tell me one more time: you will be careful.'

'I will be careful,' said Khalifa, starting the engine.

'And you'll be back in five days.'

'Less, I hope. Thanks again, Abdul. You're a good man.'

'I'm a madman. Forty thousand dollars!'

The car started to move off. Abdul waddled along beside it.

'I didn't even ask which desert you're going to.'

'The western desert.'

'The oases?'

'Beyond the oases. The Great Sand Sea.'

Abdul clutched at the window. 'Hang on, you didn't say any-thing about the Sand Sea! God Almighty, the place is a car graveyard. You can't take my—'

'Thanks again, Abdul! You're a true friend!'

Khalifa gunned the engine and roared off down the street. Abdul ran after him, but his obesity was against it and after only a few paces he wobbled to a halt. In the rear-view mirror Khalifa saw him standing in the middle of the road gesticulating wildly. He beeped twice and swung round the corner out of sight.

36

THE WESTERN DESERT

The helicopter roared across the camp and landed on a flat patch of sand fifty metres beyond it. As soon as it was down its side door slid open and two people jumped out, a man and a boy. The man stood for a moment looking around him and then fell to his knees and kissed the sand.

'Egypt!' he cried, his voice drowned out by the roar of the engines. 'My land, my home! I have returned!'

He remained prostrated for several seconds, embracing the desert, and then stood and set off towards the camp, the boy at his side.

Ahead all was frantic activity. A stream of crates was being carried away up the valley, while other containers, heavier, were being lugged back into the camp and piled up along its perimeter. Black-robed figures swarmed everywhere.

So intent were the workers on their labour that the new arrivals were almost at the tents before anyone noticed them. Three men rolling an oil drum looked up, saw them and immediately stopped what they were doing and raised their arms into the air.

'Sayf al-Tha'r!' they cried. 'He is here! Sayf al-Tha'r!'

The cry spread rapidly and soon men everywhere were laying aside their burdens and running to greet their master.

'Sayf al-Tha'r!' they screamed. 'He has returned! Sayf al-Tha'r!'

The object of their attention continued through the camp, expressionless, the crowd surging behind and to either side of him like the tail of a comet. Word of his arrival flew forward to those working at the excavations, and they too dropped their tools and streamed back towards the camp, shouting and waving their arms. The guards on the dune-tops fired their guns into the air, ecstatic.

Reaching the mound on the far side of the camp Sayf al-Tha'r climbed to its summit, the boy Mehmet still at his side, and gazed down at the scene below. Work had continued throughout the night and a vast crater now cut into the valley like a deep wound. Swathes of plastic sheeting had been laid along its upper edge and were piled with heaps of artefacts – shields, swords, spears, helmets, armour. Beneath, in the trench itself, as though the earth had split open and spewed forth its entrails, lay a seething confusion of emaciated bodies, human and animal, their skin brown and crinkled, like wrapping paper. There was something apocalyptic about the scene, as though it was the end of the world and the dead had come forth to face their final judgement. Appropriate, thought Sayf al-Tha'r, for the hour was indeed at hand when men would be judged. He gazed down for a long moment and then raised his arms triumphantly.

'*Allah u akbar,*' he roared, his voice echoing across the desert. 'God is great!'

'*Allah u akbar!*' responded the crowd beneath him. 'Praise be to God.'

The cry was repeated several times, accompanied by gunfire from the dune-tops above, and then, with a wave of his arms, Sayf al-Tha'r signalled that the men should return to work. They scattered immediately. He watched as they resumed their labours, stripping, loading, carrying and stacking, and then, sending Mehmet back down to the camp, he descended to the excavations and moved towards Dravic, who was standing beneath an umbrella supervising the packing of the artefacts.

'Sorry I didn't have time to come and applaud you,' said the German. 'I've been busy down here.'

If he noticed the sarcasm, Sayf al-Tha'r did not acknowledge it. He stood quietly just beyond the shade of the umbrella, in the full glare of the sun, gazing out over the mass of twisted corpses. Now that he was close he could see that many had been mangled in the hurry to strip them of their possessions. Limbs had been ripped from torsos, hands snapped away, heads knocked loose, dried flesh torn.

'Was it necessary to destroy them like this?' he asked.

'No,' sniffed Dravic. 'We could have done it by the book and spent a week uncovering each one. In which case we'd be leaving here with a couple of spears and that's about it.'

Again, Sayf al-Tha'r did not rise to the sarcasm. Instead he leaned forward and picked up a sword, turning it over in his hand, admiring its graceful lines and intricately moulded pommel. He'd only ever seen its like in museums, locked away in glass cases, beyond reach. Now there were hundreds laid out before him. Thousands. And those only a fraction of what was still hidden beneath the sands. The enormity of the find was almost too much to take in. It was more than he could have imagined in his wildest dreams. The answer to his prayers.

'Do we know how far it extends yet?'

Dravic puffed on his cigar. 'I've got men out digging test trenches. We've found the front end, almost a kilometre up the valley. We're still looking for the rear. It's fucking huge.' He wiped his arm across his forehead. 'When does the camel train arrive?' he asked.

'The day after tomorrow. Perhaps sooner.'

'I still say we should start flying some of this stuff out now.'

Sayf al-Tha'r shook his head. 'We can't risk a stream of

helicopters going back and forth across the border. It would attract attention.'

'We flew in the men and equipment OK,' said the German.

'We were lucky. We needed to start work immediately and Allah granted us his favour. He may not do so again. We will wait for the camel train and take everything out on that. It is safer. We're patrolling the area?'

'We've got dune bikes doing sweeps out to fifty kilometres.'

'And?'

'What do you think? We're in the middle of a fucking desert. It's not like someone's just going to wander past accidentally.'

They fell silent. Sayf al-Tha'r laid aside the sword and picked up a small jasper amulet. It was no bigger than a thumbnail but beautifully carved, in the shape of Osiris, god of the underworld. He rubbed it gently between his fingers.

'We have five, maybe six days,' he said. 'How much of the army can we get out in that time?'

Dravic sucked on his cigar. 'A fraction of it. Less than a fraction. We're working round the clock and we've still only uncovered this small section. It's getting easier as we move northwards because the bodies seem to be nearer the surface, but we're still only going to be able to clear a tiny part of it. But then that's all we need, isn't it? The stuff we've already got will raise millions. We'll be dominating the antiquities market for the next hundred years.'

'And the rest of it? Preparations are being made?'

'We're working backwards from the front. Don't worry, it's all under control. And now, if you don't mind, I've got work to do.'

He jammed his cigar into his mouth and strode off towards the sand-vacuums. Sayf al-Tha'r gazed after him, a fog of distaste clouding his eyes, and then, still clasping the amulet, made his way around the edge of the excavation until he came to the great pyramid-shaped outcrop, squatting down in the shade at its foot.

It saddened him to think of what they were going to do to the army. If there had been another option he would have taken it, but there wasn't. The risk of someone else finding it was too great. They had to cover themselves. It went against his natural inclinations, but there was no choice. It had to be. Like killing. It had to be.

He sat back against the stone, rubbing the amulet between finger and thumb, surveying the lake of bodies. One, he noticed, buried up to the waist so that its torso was upright, seemed to be staring straight at him. He looked away and back again, but still the corpse's sightless eyes were turned in his direction, its dried lips pulled back from its teeth so that it appeared to be snarling. There was hatred in that face, fury, and for some reason he sensed that it was directed at him. He held its gaze for a moment and then, uncomfortable, stood and moved away. As he did so he glanced down at the amulet, only to discover that somehow it had snapped in half in his hand. He gazed at it for a moment, and then, with a grunt, cast it away into the trench.

37

CAIRO

Through the smoked glass of the limousine window Squires gazed over at two lanes of stationary traffic. Beside him was a small Peugeot with nine people squeezed inside it, a family by the looks of it, and beyond that a truck piled high with cauliflowers. Occasionally one of the three lanes would creep forward and he would find himself momentarily staring out at a new neighbour. Almost immediately the other lanes would advance too and the familiar configuration of limousine, Peugeot, truck would be restored, as though they were drums in an enormous fruit machine which, whenever it was activated, would rotate slowly only to return always to the same position.

'And what time was this?' he said into the mobile phone.

A crackly voice echoed down the line.

'You've no idea how? Or when?'

Again, a crackly echo. A boy selling bottles of perfume came up and knocked on the window. The chauffeur leaned out, shouted and the boy moved on.

'And his family?'

The response came through in a cough of static.

There was a long pause.

'Oh well, no use crying over spilt milk. We shall just have to adapt. Do what you can to find him and keep me informed.'

Squires switched off the mobile and returned it to his jacket pocket. Although he seemed calm there was something in the narrow set of his eyes that suggested disquiet.

'It seems our friend the detective has disappeared,' he said.

'Jesus fuck!' Massey slammed a fleshy hand onto the seat between them. 'I thought Jemal was having him watched.'

'It seems he managed to give them the slip.'

'I said we should have got rid of him. Didn't I say it?'

'You most certainly did, old boy.'

'Fuck, fuck, fuck!'

The American was slamming his hand harder and harder against the seat, leaving deep indentations in the leather. He continued to hit it for several seconds more before slumping backwards, breathing heavily.

'When?'

'They're not sure.' Squires sighed. 'Apparently his wife and children went out at seven this morning. By ten he still hadn't appeared so they kicked the door in and he wasn't there.'

'Amateurs!' spat Massey. 'Amateurs!'

From behind came a loud blaring as a bus driver hammered furiously, pointlessly, on his hooter.

'It seems he was at a library yesterday,' said Squires. 'Looking through maps of the western desert.'

'Jesus! So he knows about the army.'

'It looks that way.'

'Has he told anyone? Press? Antiquities Service?'

Squires shrugged. 'I'd say on balance he hasn't or we'd have heard something by now.'

'So what's he doing?'

'I really couldn't say. Going out there on his own, by the looks of things. I fear we might have to make our move rather earlier than we'd planned.'

For once Massey didn't argue.

'We have all the equipment ready?' asked Squires.

'You don't have to worry about my end. As far as Jemal goes, I've no idea. The man's a fucking clown.'

'Jemal will do what's expected of him, just as we all will.'

The American pulled out a handkerchief and blew his nose loudly. 'This isn't going to be easy,' he said, sniffing. 'Sayf al-Tha'r's going to have a lot of men protecting that army.'

'Nonetheless I feel confident that we will succeed. You'll inform your people in the States?'

Massey nodded, a series of chins sinking into one another like an elaborately layered cream cake.

'Good,' said Squires. 'Then it looks like we're on our way.'

The limousine jolted forward another few feet.

'Or we will be if we ever get out of this blessed traffic jam.' He leaned forward towards the driver. 'What on earth's going on up there?'

'There's a lorry jackknifed across the road,' came the reply.

With a sigh Squires removed a sweet from his pocket and began picking at the wrapper, gazing absent-mindedly at the Peugeot in the next lane.

The obvious route for Khalifa to have taken, and the most direct, would have been to go south-west to Bahariya Oasis and then west across the desert from there.

He decided against it. Whoever had been tailing him the previous night would know by now that he'd given them the slip, and also probably that he'd been on the ten p.m. train to Cairo. It wouldn't take a genius to work out he was heading into the desert, in which case there was a good chance they'd try to intercept him en route. And the route they'd be expecting him to take was the quickest one available.

Rather than heading south-west, therefore, he decided

instead to go in almost the opposite direction, north-west to Alexandria, picking up the coastal highway to Marsa Matruh and then turning south to the oasis at Siwa. Although longer, this route had clear advantages. The roads were in better condition; he would have less open desert to cross from Siwa than from Bahariya; and, most important, it was the last route his pursuers would think of him taking. Having filled up with petrol, therefore, he headed out of Cairo and onto Highway 11, up towards the Mediterranean coast.

He drove fast, chain-smoking, the landscape around him switching from desert to cultivation and back again. There was a cassette player built into the dashboard, but he could find only one tape – Kazim al-Saher's *My Love and the Rain* – and after playing it through four times he ejected it again and drove on in silence.

He reached Alexandria in two hours and Marsa in five, stopping only twice en route, once to fill up with petrol and once, just beyond Alexandria, to look at the sea – the first time in his life he had ever seen it.

From Marsa, having again filled up with petrol, he continued west for a further twenty kilometres before turning south onto the Siwa road, an empty ribbon of tarmac stretching away across the desert. The sun was dropping now and he pushed his foot right to the floor. The odd ruined building flashed past and a line of rusting signs marked the course of a buried pipeline. Otherwise there was nothing, just a forlorn expanse of flat orange gravel broken here and there by distant ridges and escarpments. He passed no other traffic and no other signs of life, save an occasional herd of dromedaries nibbling at the desert scrub, their coats brown and shaggy.

Halfway to Siwa he came across a roadside café – a makeshift shack optimistically styling itself the Alexander Restaurant – and stopped briefly for some tea before moving on again. Night fell and the desert melted into darkness. Every now and then he glimpsed lights way out across the flats, a settlement, perhaps, or an army camp and, once, a flickering tongue of flame from a gas well. Otherwise he was alone in the void. He put Kazim al-Saher back on.

Finally, around seven p.m., he sensed the flatness around him starting to break up. Vague hills loomed, and peaks and scarps. The road started to descend, snaking through a mess of crags and ridges before the land suddenly opened up and there, below and in front of him, was a carpet of twinkling lights, like tiny boats on a still sea. Siwa Oasis. He slowed momentarily, admiring the sight, and then continued down.

He'd been driving for nine hours and was just finishing his second packet of cigarettes.

38

THE WESTERN DESERT

The man seemed to materialize out of nowhere, as if he had formed from the darkness itself. One moment Tara and Daniel were sitting in each other's arms gazing at the flickering flame of the kerosene lamp, the next they looked up and there he was, standing just inside the tent entrance, his head and face swathed in shadows. He motioned to the guard, no more than a flick of his finger, and immediately the man came to his feet and left.

'Sayf al-Tha'r, I presume,' said Daniel.

The man said nothing, just stared at them. There was a long silence.

'Why have you come here?' asked Daniel eventually. 'To look at us before you kill us? To gloat?' He nodded towards Tara's bruised face and ripped shirt. 'Well, gloat away. I'm sure Allah's very proud of you.'

'Do not speak the name of Allah,' said the man, taking a step forward, his voice quiet but steely, his English good. 'You are not worthy.'

He stared down at Tara, taking in her swollen cheek and the

burn marks on her neck, chest and arm. A barely perceptible grimace pulled at his lips. 'Dravic did this?'

She nodded.

'It will not happen again. It was . . . unfortunate.'

'No,' said Daniel quietly. 'It was expected. It's what people like you and Dravic do.'

Again, the man grimaced almost imperceptibly. 'Do not place me and Dravic in the same bracket, Dr Lacage. He is a tool, no more. I serve a higher master.'

Daniel shook his head wearily. 'You people make me laugh. You butcher women and children and somehow convince yourselves it's all for the good of Allah.'

'I told you not to speak his name.' The man's voice was sharp now. 'Your mouth pollutes it.'

'No,' said Daniel, looking up at him, meeting his eyes. 'You pollute it. You pollute it every time you use it to justify the things you do. Do you really think Allah expects—'

The assault was so sudden, and so swift, that the man had his hand around Daniel's throat before either of them was even aware he'd moved. He lifted him to his feet, fingers tight around his windpipe. Daniel struggled, but could not break the grip.

'Stop it!' cried Tara. 'Please, stop it!'

Sayf al-Tha'r ignored her. 'You are all the same, you Westerners,' he growled. 'Your hypocrisy is extraordinary. Every day a hundred children die in Iraq because of the sanctions your governments have imposed and yet you have the audacity to lecture us on what is right and what is wrong.'

Daniel's face was turning red.

'You see this?' Sayf al-Tha'r raised his free hand to the scar on his forehead. 'This was done to me in a police cell. The interrogators kicked me so hard I was blinded for three days. My crime? I'd spoken out on behalf of the millions in this country who live in squalor and hopelessness. Do you complain about that? Do you complain that half the world lives in poverty so that a privileged few can fritter away their lives in pointless luxury? No. Like all your kind you are selective in your outrage, condemning only what it is convenient for you to condemn. To the rest you turn a blind eye.'

He squeezed for a moment longer and then released his grip. Daniel collapsed. 'You're mad,' he said, choking. 'You're a mad fanatic.'

The man's breathing seemed hardly to have changed.

'Very possibly,' he replied calmly. 'The question, however, is why. You dismiss me and my followers as extremists and fanatics, but never once do you look behind those words. Try to understand the forces that have created us.'

He stood over Daniel, his black robes seeming to merge with the darkness so that all that was visible was his face, floating disembodied above them.

'I have known horrors, Dr Lacage,' he said, his voice sunk almost to a whisper. 'Men beaten and crippled in the torture cells of the state. People so hungry they are reduced to eating scraps out of garbage cans. Children gang-raped because they have the misfortune to be a distant relative of someone whose views do not coincide with the ideas of those in power. These are the things that make men mad. These are the things you should be condemning.'

'And you think the answer's to go around shooting tourists?' coughed Daniel.

Sayf al-Tha'r smiled faintly, eyes glowing. 'The answer? No, I don't think it's the answer. We merely make a point.'

'What possible point does it make killing innocent people!'

The man raised his hands, the fingers long and thin, skeletal almost. 'That we are no longer prepared to have you meddling in our affairs. Propping up a godless regime because it happens to be in your best political interests. Using our country as a playground while we, the people of that country, remain hungry and oppressed and abused.' He stared at Daniel, the scar tissue on his forehead gleaming red in the flickering light of the kerosene lamp.

'I often wonder how you in the West would react if the tables were turned. If it was your children who were begging in the streets while we Egyptians rode around flaunting our wealth and insulting your customs. If half your national treasures had been stripped out and carried off to Egyptian museums. If a crime such as Danishaway had been committed on your soil, against your people, by Egyptian overlords. It would be an interesting experiment. It might help you to understand a little of the anger we feel.'

Still his voice was low and calm, although flecks of froth had started to bubble at the corners of his mouth.

'Do you know', he went on, 'that when Carter discovered the tomb of Tutankhamun he signed a contract with *The Times* of London stating that they and only they could report what was in that tomb? In order to find out about a discovery in our own land, which belonged to us, one of our kings, we Egyptians had to turn to an English newspaper.'

'That was eighty years ago,' coughed Daniel, shaking his head. 'It's different now.'

'No, it is not different! The attitudes are the same. The assumption that as Egyptians and Moslems we are somehow less civilized, less able to order our own affairs. That you can treat us how you want. These things persist. And those of us who try to question them are dismissed as madmen.'

Daniel stared up at him but said nothing.

'You see,' said Sayf al-Tha'r, 'you have no response to that. And, indeed, there is no response. Other than to beg forgiveness for the way this country and its people have been treated. You have pillaged our heritage, sucked out our blood, taken but not given in return. And now the time has come to redress the balance. As it says in the Holy Koran, "You have received but the recompense of what you have earned."'

His shadow bulged on the canvas behind him, black and shapeless and menacing. From outside came the sounds of excavating, but in the tent the air was silent and still, as though they were part of a different world. There was a pause. Then, slowly, Tara came to her feet.

'I don't know much about Egypt,' she said, standing in front of the man, looking into his eyes, 'but I do know that my father, whose death is on your hands, loved this country and its people and its heritage. Loved them so much more than you do. Look at what you're doing here. Destroying. My father would never have done that. He wanted to protect the past. You just want to sell it to the highest bidder. It's you who's the hypocrite.'

The man's mouth tightened and for a moment she thought he was going to hit her. His hands, however, remained at his sides.

'I derive no pleasure from plundering the army like this, Miss Mullray. Sometimes it is necessary to do unpleasant things to achieve a higher purpose. If part of our heritage must be sacrificed to free us from oppression, then so be it. My conscience is clear.'

For a moment he held her eyes and then slowly dropped to his haunches in front of the lamp. 'I do the will of God. And God knows that. God is with me.'

He reached out and placed his hand on the scalding metal. He neither blinked nor grimaced. A faint smell of burning flesh drifted upwards to Tara's nostrils. She thought she was going to gag.

'Do not underestimate the strength of our belief, Miss Mullray. That is why each of my followers takes the mark of faith on his forehead. To show the depth of his conviction. Our adherence is unwavering. We suffer no doubts.'

He remained like that for what seemed an age, staring up at Tara, hand burning, face expressionless, and then stood again, his palm scalded a livid reddish-white.

'You asked why I came here, Dr Lacage. It was not, as you suggested, to look at you, my prisoners. Rather it was to let you, my prisoners, look at me. To look, and to understand.' He stared at them for a moment and then moved towards the entrance.

Daniel called after him, 'It'll never work, you know. Digging up the army like this and selling it off. You'll only be able to uncover a fraction of what's down there. And then someone else will come along and find the rest and the value of what you've got will drop through the floor. It's pointless unless you've got the whole thing.'

Sayf al-Tha'r turned. He was smiling. 'We have our plans, Dr Lacage. God has given us the army and God will ensure that we alone reap its benefits.'

He nodded at them and melted into the night.

SIWA OASIS

Just as Khalifa was pulling onto the forecourt of Siwa's only garage, a power cut suddenly plunged the entire settlement into darkness.

'If you want petrol you'll have to wait,' said the garage attendant. 'The pumps won't work till the electricity comes back on.'

'How long?'

The man shrugged. 'Maybe five minutes. Maybe five hours. It'll come back when it does. Once we had to wait two days.'

'I hope it's sooner than that.'

'*Insha-Allah,*' said the man.

Khalifa parked at the edge of the forecourt and got out. The air was chilly and, reaching back into the car, he removed his jacket and put it on. A donkey-cart rattled past with three women in the back, their shawls pulled low around their heads to hide their faces, giving them a lumpen, shapeless look, like melted waxworks. There was a roar as a generator coughed into life.

He walked back and forth for a while, stretching the stiffness from his legs, and then, lighting a cigarette, crossed to a refreshment stall on the edge of the main square and bought a glass of tea. There was a wooden bench nearby and he went and sat on it, pulling Abdul's mobile phone from his jacket and keying in Hosni's number. His brother-in-law answered on the fourth ring.

'Hosni, it's Yusuf.'

There was a sharp intake of breath.

'What the hell's going on, Yusuf? We've had the security service round looking for you. Where are you?'

'Bahariya,' lied Khalifa.

'Bahariya! What are you doing there?'

'Police business. I can't give any details.'

'They came to my office, Yusuf! Do you understand? The security service came to my office. Have you any idea what that could do to business? Edible oils is a small world. Rumours get around.'

'I'm sorry, Hosni.'

'If they come back, I'm going to have to tell them where you are. We're at a very delicate stage with this new sesame oil project. I can't let something like this put a spanner in the works.'

'I understand, Hosni. If you have to tell them, you have to tell them. Is Zenab there?'

'Yes, she is. Just turned up on our doorstep this morning. We need to talk, Yusuf. When you get back. Man to man. There are things that need to be said.'

'OK, OK. When I get back. Just put Zenab on, will you?'

There was muttering, then a clunk and the sound of receding feet. A moment later Zenab came on the line.

'And shut the door, please, Hosni,' he heard her say. More muttering, and the sound of a door slamming. 'That man is such a busybody!'

Khalifa smiled. 'Are you OK?'

'Fine,' she said. 'You?'

'Fine.'

'I won't ask where you are.'

'Best not to. The kids?'

'Missing you. Ali says he won't blow his trumpet till you get back. So feel free to stay away as long as you like.'

They laughed, although there was something forced about it.

'They're out with Sama,' she went on. 'At the festival. I'll tell them you rang.'

'Give them my love.'

'Of course.'

He'd been thinking about her for most of the day. Now, for some reason, he couldn't think of anything to say. He wished he could just sit there for an hour listening to her breathing.

'Anyway, it was just a quick call,' he said eventually. 'To make sure Hosni isn't making life too difficult for you.'

'He wouldn't dare.' Another silence. 'These men, Yusuf . . .'

'Don't ask, Zenab. Please. The less you know the better. So long as you're OK, that's all that matters.'

'We're OK,' she said.

'Good.'

He scoured his mind for something to add, some parting line of reassurance. All he could think of was to tell her that he'd seen the sea.

'Maybe we'll go there one day. I'd love to see you in a swimsuit.'

'You'll have to wait a long time before you get me in one of those!' She laughed indignantly, the sound dying away to silence. 'I love you, Yusuf.'

'I love you too. More than anything in the world. Kiss the kids for me.'

'Of course. And be careful.'

There was a final silence and then they both hung up.

He finished his tea and stood. The electricity still hadn't come back on and the main square was full of shadows. Ahead of him a large mosque loomed, its whitish stone seeming to glow in the moonlight as if it was made of ice. He had intended to get a bite to eat but instead wandered over to the mosque's entrance, slipping off his shoes and bathing his hands and face at a tap in the wall.

The interior was dark and silent, the few candles that had been lit doing little to dispel the enveloping gloom. Initially he thought he was the only person there, but then he noticed another man towards the back of the hall, kneeling, his forehead pressed to the ground.

He stood for a while, taking in the stillness, and then moved forward, his feet making no noise on the carpeted floor, stopping midway across the hall beneath a large chandelier, thousands of lozenges of glass dripping from the shadows as if the ceiling was weeping. He gazed up at it for a moment and then, turning towards the *mihrab*, lowered his head and began to recite.

> *Praise belongs to Allah, the Lord of all being;*
> *the All-compassionate, the All-merciful,*
> *the Master of the Day of Judgement;*
> *Thee only we serve, and to Thee alone we pray for succour;*
> *Guide us in the straight path;*
> *the path of those whom Thou hast blessed,*
> *not of those against whom Thou art wrathful,*
> *nor of those who are astray.*

As he prayed thus, asking God to watch over him, and his family too, he felt his cares and concerns gradually falling away, as they always did when he spoke directly to Allah. The world outside seemed to recede; or rather the interior of the mosque to expand so that its stillness and tranquillity filled the entire universe. Sayf al-Tha'r, Dravic, Chief Hassani, the army of Cambyses – all dwindled until they were no more than motes of dust floating in the eternity of God's embrace. He felt an overwhelming sense of calm.

He continued for twenty minutes, performing ten *rek'ah*s, or prayer cycles, before eventually coming to his feet and whispering amen. As he did so the chandelier above him suddenly burst into light, filling the interior of the mosque with a radiant whiteness. He smiled, sensing that in some way it was a sign his prayers had been acknowledged.

Back outside, the town square was once more ablaze with light and the petrol pumps working again. The attendant filled his tank and the eight jerrycans, while he himself filled the three water containers from a tap in the wall. By the time he'd paid for the fuel and bought himself another three packs of Cleopatras he had almost no money left. He got back into the car, drove on through the town and out onto the low dunes that washed up against its southern edge.

He didn't go far into the desert, just a couple of kilometres, and then pulled up beside a flattish hummock of sand, its sides covered with a thin mat of scrub grass. Behind him the lights of Siwa twinkled brightly. In the other direction, out across the desert, there was nothing, just an endless vista of moonlit emptiness. Somewhere far off a dog was howling. He ate some of the food Zenab had given him – the first time he had eaten that day – and, fetching a couple of blankets from the back of the Toyota, reclined his seat and curled up, gazing out of the window at the stars above. The thought suddenly struck him that having come all the way out here he had no real idea what he was going to do once he reached the army. He tried to focus his mind on what lay ahead, but he was too tired. The more he tried to concentrate, the more the army and Sayf al-Tha'r and Dravic dissolved before him, until eventually, somehow, they had transformed into a vast fountain of water spurting out of the desert, turning the sand around them into greenery. Beside him his gun lay cocked on the passenger seat. He'd locked the doors.

THE WESTERN DESERT

Tara jolted awake. Her head was in Daniel's lap and he was staring down at her.

'You were digging my heart out,' she mumbled. 'You had a trowel and you were digging my heart out.'

'It was just a dream,' he said gently, stroking her hair. 'Everything's OK.'

'You were going to bury me. There was a coffin.'

He bent down and kissed her forehead.

'Go back to sleep,' he whispered. 'Everything will be all right.'

She gazed up at him for a while, and then slowly her eyes drifted shut and she was asleep again, her face pale, her body limp. Daniel gazed down at her, and then, easing himself away, laid her head softly on the floor and stood. He began pacing up and down the tent, eyes flicking constantly towards the doorway, his features seeming to twist and warp in the flicker of the kerosene lamp, as if he was wearing a mask and it was slowly slipping.

'Come on,' he muttered. 'Where are you? Come on.'

Their guard stared up at him, face impassive, finger curled around the trigger of his gun.

The Western Desert, near Siwa Oasis

Khalifa woke with Zenab nuzzling his face. Or at least he thought it was Zenab. Then he opened his eyes, and realized that what he had taken to be the warmth of her breath was in fact the first rays of the sun pushing through the car window. He threw off the blankets, opened the door and got out, shivering, for the world had not yet had time to warm up. He said his morning prayers, lit a cigarette and climbed to the top of the low mound beside which he'd parked. To the north the ragged green crescent of the oasis stretched off to left and right, its salt lakes glowing a delicate pink in the light of the rising sun, columns of smoke drifting up from among the palm and olive groves. Everywhere else was desert, a jagged, broken landscape of sand and gravel flats and twisted rocky outcrops. He stared at it for a while, daunted by its emptiness, and then, flicking aside his cigarette, went back down to the four-by-four and pulled the GPS unit out of the glove compartment.

It was, as Abdul had said, all fairly self-explanatory. He keyed in the co-ordinates of the pyramid-shaped rock and pressed the GoTo key. According to the display it was 179 kilometres away, on a bearing of 133 degrees. He keyed in his current position as well, and that of al-Farafra oasis, and dropped the unit into his holdall along with Abdul's mobile phone and his gun. He then let a little air out of each of the tyres to improve traction, got back into the car and, starting the engine, moved slowly off into the desert, the wheels leaving a deep wake in the sand behind him.

He had never driven on this sort of terrain before and took things carefully, keeping his speed low and even. The desert floor seemed solid, but there were unexpected dips and bumps, while occasionally he would come to the top of what seemed like a gently sloping dune only to find that the ground suddenly disappeared in front of him, plunging down twenty metres in a near-vertical wall of sand. At one point he almost rolled the car, only just managing to keep it under control as it slid sideways down a slope, cutting a deep groove in the desert's flank. After that he reduced his speed still further.

For the first few kilometres there were other tyre tracks in the sand, presumably from the vehicles that took tourists from Siwa out on desert safaris. Gradually these dwindled and then disappeared altogether. Every now and then he passed a swathe of struggling dune grass, and, twice, skeletons, half buried in the sand and bleached an unnatural white by the sun. Jackals, he thought, although he couldn't be sure. Otherwise there were no signs of life. Just sand, rock, gravel and, above, the immense powdery blue sky. The green fuzz of the oasis slowly receded until it was lost beneath the horizon.

It soon became clear that although the GPS unit had

calculated the distance he had to cover as 179 kilometres, he was going to have to travel a lot further than that to reach his destination. The unit had given him a straight-line measurement. On the ground it was impossible to hold such a course, for impassable slopes of sand, high limestone ridges and sudden explosions of jagged rock meant that he was continually having to divert to left or right to find a route that was navigable by car. Sometimes the diversions were short, only a few hundred metres, sometimes three or four kilometres. All the while he was being shunted off line, as though pulled by a strong current. After two hours of steady driving, by which point he had, by his reckoning, covered seventy kilometres, he checked the unit's display to find the pyramid rock was only forty kilometres nearer. He began to wonder if he'd ever get there.

Slowly the morning passed. At one point he stopped to relieve himself, shutting off the engine and walking a few yards from the four-by-four. The silence was extraordinary, more intense than any silence he had ever known. He realized how intrusive the vehicle's engine must sound in this all-enveloping stillness. If Sayf al-'Tha'r had patrols out, which he almost certainly had, they'd be able to hear him from miles off.

'I might as well radio in and say I'm on my way,' he muttered, walking back to the vehicle and starting it up again. He felt suddenly very exposed.

The landscape continued pretty much the same for another couple of hours. Then, around midday, he noticed what looked like a ridge of hills looming across the horizon ahead. It was impossible to make it out clearly at that distance, for the heat distorted its shape, making it swell and recede and shimmer, as if it was made of water. As it came nearer it gradually stabilized and he realized it wasn't hills at all, but rather a vast dune – a towering wall of sand stretching right across his line of sight in a single, unbroken curve, with other, higher dunes ranged behind it, like waves freeze-framed in the act of crashing down onto a beach. The outlying ranges of the Great Sand Sea.

'*Allah u akbar!*' was all he could think of saying. 'God almighty.'

He drove on until he came to the foot of the dune, which seemed to be holding the ones behind it in check, like a vast dyke. He got out and trudged to its summit. The sand was soft underfoot so that by the time he reached the top he was panting and his forehead was damp with sweat.

Before him an endless vista of dunes stretched off to the horizon, line after line of them rippling away into the far distance, silent and smooth and neat, completely different from the disordered landscape through which he had so far been travelling. He remembered a story his father had told him once about how the desert was actually a lion that had fallen asleep at the dawn of time and would one day wake again and devour the entire world. Looking out over the dune sea now he could almost believe it, for the orange-yellow sand had a velvety, fur-like quality to it, while the receding ridges looked like wrinkles on the back of some impossibly aged beast. He felt an irrational pang of guilt about stubbing his cigarette out on the ground, as if he was burning the flesh of a living creature.

He stood taking in the scene for some while and then scrambled back down to the car, his feet sinking into the sand almost to the level of his knees. He'd heard there were stretches of quicksand out here, especially at the bottom of dune slopes, and shuddered at the thought of being sucked down into one. However else this adventure ended, he told himself, it wasn't going to be like that.

Back at the car he let a little more air out of the tyres and, heaving three of the jerrycans down from the roof-rack, filled the tank, which was by now over half empty. He started the engine, selected first gear and powered slowly upwards into the dune ranges. According to the GPS unit he still had almost a hundred kilometres to go.

He drove through the afternoon, the tiny white blob of the Toyota dwarfed by the towering walls of sand, like a boat bobbing on an immense ocean. He kept the speed low, mounting each dune as it came, slowing at the top to check there wasn't a slip-face on the far side, then descending. In some places the dunes were close together. In others they were set further apart, with broad flat valleys between them hundreds of metres across. Behind him his tyre tracks stretched back into the distance like a line of stitches.

Initially he was able to steer a reasonably straight course. Gradually, however, the dunes grew higher, and their slopes steeper, so that at times he would come to the top of one and find himself gazing down at a near-vertical cliff of sand dropping away beneath him. He would then have to creep along the ridge until he found an easier place to descend, or else reverse back down and try to find a way around it, which could take him a dozen kilometres out of his path. Even with the windows closed and the air-conditioning full on he could still sense the merciless heat outside.

The further he progressed, the more it seemed to him that the landscape around him was possessed of some sort of rudimentary consciousness. The hues of the sand seemed to change as if the dunes had moods, and these were reflected in the shifting oranges and yellows of the desert surface. At one point he stopped to drink some water and a gentle breeze came up, causing the sand to hiss and sigh, as if the dunes were breathing. He felt an urge to shout out, to tell the desert he meant it no harm, that he was only a temporary intruder into its secret heart and as soon as his business was finished he would leave immediately and not come back. He had never in his life felt so small, nor so alone. He tried playing the Kazim al-Saher cassette, but it seemed inappropriate. So awed was he by his surroundings he even forgot to smoke.

At about five o'clock, the sun by now well down in the western sky, he came to the summit of a really massive dune and slowed to check the slope on the far side. As he did so, hunching forward over the wheel and peering through the windscreen, something caught his eye, ahead and to the left. He cut the engine and got out.

It was difficult to see it clearly, for the air was still unsteady with the afternoon heat. It looked like a hazy triangle floating above the dunes just this side of the horizon. He leaned back into the car and got the binoculars, putting them to his eyes and revolving the drums to bring the object into focus. For a while everything was blurred. Then, suddenly, it leaped into view: a dark, pyramid-shaped outcrop rising high above the sands like a huge black iceberg. About twenty-five kilometres away, he guessed. Twenty-eight according to the GPS unit. He swung the binoculars across the dune-tops around the rock, but could see nothing to indicate any human activity in the area, except a couple of vague black blobs that might or might not have been lookouts. He lowered the glasses and closed his eyes, listening. He didn't really expect to hear anything. To his surprise, however, he caught the vague whine of a motor, distant but unmistakable. The sound seemed to come and go, disappearing for a while and then returning again, each time stronger than before. The desert seemed to warp and stretch it so that it was hard to tell where it was coming from. Only when he'd been listening for almost a minute did he realize with a shock that it wasn't from the direction of the pyramid rock, but from behind him, back the way he had come. He swung round and focused the binoculars along the line of his tyre tracks. As he did so, a pair of motorbikes flew over the summit of the fourth dune back from where he was standing, no more than two kilometres away, following his trail.

Cursing, he looked swiftly over the edge of the dune. It dropped almost vertically down, far too steep to negotiate in the four-by-four. Leaping back into the driver's seat he started the engine and tugged the gearstick into reverse, flying back down the dune's leeward slope, the wheels skewing and swerving beneath him. At the bottom he spun the steering wheel and drove the gearstick into first, slamming his foot down on the accelerator. The car's rear end skidded round and he flew forward. After just a few metres it jerked to a halt, an angry hissing sound coming from beneath as the tyres struggled for grip on the desert floor, digging themselves deeper and deeper into the sand.

'Dammit!' he shouted, desperate.

He shunted the car into reverse, staring up at the summit of the dune opposite, expecting the two bikes to fly over it at any instant. The vehicle rolled back and up and for a moment it looked as if he had freed himself. Then the wheels spun again, embedding themselves even deeper than they had before, almost to the level of the axle.

He leaped out and looked. The tyres had all but disappeared. There was no way he was going to dig them out in time. Scrambling back into the car he threw the GPS unit into his bag, hefted one of the water containers off the back seat and began running back up the slope he'd just descended, feet sinking deep into the sand.

About halfway up the dune started to slip beneath him and he stopped making any headway. He drove himself forward, but couldn't seem to get any closer to the summit, as though he was on a giant treadmill. The water container wasn't helping, and eventually, reluctantly, he threw it aside, using his free hand to steady himself while his feet dug into the sliding sand, fighting for leverage. He could hear the bikes powering up the far side of the dune behind. If they got to the top and saw him he was dead.

'Come on!' he hissed. 'Come on!'

For a moment he still didn't get anywhere. Then, just when it seemed certain he would be seen, he managed to get a foothold and was moving upwards again, eyes popping with exertion. He came to the top and dived over just as behind him the bikes crested their dune and raced down towards his abandoned car.

He lay still for a moment trying to get his breath back and then, pulling out his gun, rolled onto his front and eased himself back up to the dune's summit, peering cautiously down at the valley beneath.

The bikes had by now almost reached the four-by-four. Skidding to a halt, the riders dismounted, swinging machine-guns from their shoulders. One of them opened the door and peered inside, removing Khalifa's jacket, which he'd left behind in his hurry to get away. The other started up the side of the dune, following the twin trails of Khalifa's footprints and the tyre tracks. The man stopped for a moment beside the discarded water container, pointing his gun down at it and blowing a hole in the plastic, then continued upwards. The sound of the gunshot echoed away across the desolate landscape.

Khalifa rolled away from the summit. There was no point trying to run. The man would see him and pick him off like a rabbit. He could shoot him as he came up from the other side, but that would still leave the one down below.

He looked around swiftly. The upper part of the dune was, at this point, slightly undercut, leaving a long hollow running just below its summit with a heavy lip of sand curling over it, like the crest of a wave turning back in on itself. Someone crouching beneath this overhang would be invisible to a person standing on the dune-top above, even though they were almost directly beneath their feet. It wasn't much of a hiding place, but it was the best the desert had to offer and, grabbing his holdall, the detective slipped down and rolled into it, lying on his back with his gun held ready on his chest, gazing up at the canopy of sand above.

For a moment nothing happened. Then he heard the crunch of feet. He could picture the man coming out onto the top of the dune, looking around, walking forward a few paces, stopping above him. A trickle of dislodged sand wept down over the edge of the overhang, confirming that the man was indeed almost directly overhead. Curling a finger around the trigger of his Helwan, Khalifa tried not to breathe.

There was an agonizing silence. He could almost feel the man thinking, trying to work out where he had gone. The trickle of sand grew heavier, turning into a small landslide, and it looked for a moment as if the man was coming down. Khalifa shrank back into his hollow. Seconds passed and nothing happened. Gradually the sandfall slackened off. The man was staying where he was. There was another long silence and then a shout: 'It looks like he's been up here, but then he went back down again. We must have missed him further back.'

There was a pause and then the crunch of receding feet. Khalifa breathed a sigh of relief, shoulders relaxing.

'Thank you, Allah,' he mumbled.

Abdul's mobile phone started ringing.

The sound was so unexpected it took Khalifa a couple of seconds to realize what it was. When he did he drove his hand desperately into the holdall in an attempt to turn the phone off. Too late. He could hear the man above him shouting and the slap of running feet. He squirmed frantically out from beneath the overhang and, raising his gun, fired off three shots in quick succession. The first was too high, the second wide. The third hit the man square in the forehead, throwing him backwards and out of sight down the far side of the dune.

Immediately Khalifa was on his feet, scrambling up to the dune's summit. As he reached it a burst of gunfire ripped up the sand in front of him, forcing him back and onto his stomach. There was a pause and then another burst of gunfire, although it wasn't aimed at the top of the dune. Khalifa eased himself upwards. The man below had shot out the tyres of the second dune bike. Raising his pistol Khalifa fired, but missed. The man swung and sprayed the dune-top with bullets again, forcing the detective back. There was another brief pause and then the sound of a motorbike starting.

Khalifa counted to three and lifted his head again. The bike was already pulling away. He came up onto his knees and, aiming, emptied the clip at the rider's back. The man jerked, but didn't come off and, with no bullets left, Khalifa could only watch helplessly as the bike roared away down the valley. After a hundred metres it came to a stop and, turning in his seat, the rider fired a volley of bullets back at the stricken Toyota. He continued firing for five seconds and then suddenly, with a deafening roar that echoed far out across the desert, the car erupted in a ball of flame, a mushroom of heavy black smoke rising into the air above it. The bike sped away.

For a long moment Khalifa stared down at the furnace below, his breath coming in short, sharp gasps, his hands trembling. Then, taking a couple of deep gulps of air, he slowly came to his feet and trudged back down to his bag, where the mobile phone was still ringing. He took it out, pressed the 'Yes' key and held it to his ear.

'Yusuf, you old rogue!' boomed Abdul's voice. 'What took you so long? Just calling to make sure my car's OK.'

Khalifa looked round at the column of velvety black smoke spiralling upwards into the air and his heart dropped.

'Yes, Abdul,' he lied. 'It's absolutely fine.'

39

The Western Desert

Sayf al-Tha'r had been on the dune-top since dawn, watching as beneath him more and more of the army had slowly been uncovered. The sun had risen, levelled and dropped again, and all the while the excavation crater had spread inexorably outwards like a vast mouth levering open. By noon so many bodies had been dug up, and so much equipment stripped from them, that they'd run out of packing crates. More would be arriving with the camel train later that night, but they still wouldn't be enough to deal with the thousands of artefacts piled up below. The valley floor looked like an enormous scrapheap, ancient weapons, armour and bodies piled up everywhere.

Now, however, Sayf al-Tha'r had turned his back on the army and was instead gazing out at the plume of smoke rising in the distance. An hour ago one of the patrols had radioed in to say they'd found a set of tracks leading across the desert. The smoke presumably indicated they'd caught up with whatever vehicle had made them. He should have felt relieved. Instead he had a curious sense of foreboding.

The boy Mehmet scrambled up beside him.

'What is it?' the man asked. 'What has happened?'

'They found a car, Master. Destroyed it.'

'The driver?'

'He got away. Killed one of our men. The other's on his way back.'

Sayf al-Tha'r was silent. The column of smoke was rising higher and higher into the air, as though some noxious black gas was hissing from a rip in the desert surface. A breeze tugged at its upper part, stretching and twisting it.

'Let me know when the patrol comes in,' he said eventually. 'And send the helicopter over. The driver can't have gone far.'

'Yes, Master.'

The boy turned and ran back down the side of the dune. Sayf al-Tha'r began pacing, hands locked behind his back, a cloth wrapped around his scorched palm.

Who was this intruder, he wondered. What was he doing out here in the middle of the desert? Was he alone or were there others?

The more he thought about it, the more uneasy he became. Not because he feared they'd been discovered. It was more elemental than that. He could feel something. It was as if a hand was stretching towards him out of the past. He stared at the plume of smoke and it seemed to him that it had assumed an almost human form, towering above the desert like a genie. He could make out a head, and shoulders, and an arm, and even two eyes where the breeze had punched holes through the fumes. They seemed to be looking directly at him, glaring angrily. He turned away, annoyed at himself for imagining such things, but he could still feel the black shape looming malevolently at his back. He closed his eyes and started to pray.

'You're breaking up, Abdul . . . I can't . . . you're . . . it's . . .'

Khalifa pressed his mouth to the receiver and made a noise

that he hoped sounded like static, then switched the mobile off. For a brief moment he wondered whether he should call for help, but immediately dismissed the idea. Who would he call, after all? Chief Hassani? Mohammed Sariya? Hosni? Even if they believed him, what could they do? No, he was on his own. He threw the phone into the holdall and hurried back to the top of the dune, the air heavy with the smell of petrol and burning rubber.

Flames were still leaping from the four-by-four's shattered windows. Directly beneath him, at the bottom of the slope, lay the body of the man he'd killed, sprawled face up on the sand, one arm twisted at an unnatural angle beneath his head. He started down towards it, stopping briefly to check the ruptured water container. Most of its contents had drained away, although there was still a small reservoir of liquid in one corner. Carefully raising the receptacle to his lips he swallowed what was left and continued down to the valley floor.

The dead man's face was a gruesome mask of blood and sand, his forehead gaping open to reveal a mash of bone and brain within. Trying not to look, Khalifa prised free the machine-gun that was still clasped in the man's hand and began to strip the body of its clothes. He didn't like doing it, but if he was to get into Sayf al-Tha'r's camp unnoticed he would need them. He rolled the robe and headscarf into a bundle, grabbed the gun and started back up the dune. After ten metres, however, his conscience got the better of him and, turning, he hurried back down and scooped a shallow grave out of the loose sand. It wasn't a proper burial, but he couldn't just leave the body to be picked at by vultures or jackals or whatever other creatures lived out here in this god-forsaken wilderness. Enemy or no enemy, the man deserved at least that small show of respect.

The gesture almost cost him dear because as he came back up to the top of the dune he heard, distant but unmistakable, the thud of helicopter rotors. Another twenty seconds and he would have been spotted. As it was, he just had time to snatch up his holdall and scramble down beneath the overhang before the helicopter swept overhead, its downdraught sweeping a spray of sand from the dune's ridge. For a minute it hovered overhead taking in the scene and then rose and swung away north-westwards.

His initial plan had been to get away from the spot as quickly as possible, but with the helicopter around it wasn't safe out in the open, so he decided to stay where he was until dark. He loaded the one remaining clip into his pistol, jammed the black robes into his holdall and lay back in his sand cave, lighting a cigarette and gazing out across the dune sea as it slowly faded in the dying light of the day. An hour, he reckoned, perhaps less. He hoped the moon wasn't going to be too bright.

The sun had dropped beneath the horizon and the first faint stars were twinkling in the sky when the bike leaped over the dune and bucked down towards the camp, skidding to a halt in front of a pile of crates. The rider dismounted, clutching his shoulder, and collapsed. A crowd gathered around him, includ-ing the boy Mehmet, who knelt at his side, took something from him and then pushed his way out through the mass of men and sprinted up the dune towards his master.

'Well?' said Sayf al-Tha'r.

'He found these', panted the boy, 'in the car.' He handed over Khalifa's wallet and police ID.

'And the helicopter?'

'It's been searching, but there's no sign of him. He's disappeared.'

The man shook his head. 'He's out there somewhere. I can feel him. Keep the helicopter searching until nightfall. And double the guards around the army. He'll have to come here. There's nowhere else. Tell every man to be alert.'

'Yes, Master.'

'And send Dr Dravic up. Immediately.'

'Yes, Master.'

The boy spun and ran back down the slope. For a moment Sayf al-Tha'r remained where he was, gazing out at the column of smoke, still just visible in the thickening twilight, and then opened the ID card and looked down at the name and photo inside. His face registered no emotion, although his eyes widened fractionally, and his Adam's apple quivered as if something was crawling beneath the skin of his throat.

He stared at the card for almost a minute, then slipped it into his pocket and began going through the contents of the wallet. He removed a picture of Khalifa's wife, another of his three children, and another of his parents, standing arm in arm in front of the pyramids. There was a Menatel phone card, twelve Egyptian pounds and a miniature book of Koranic verses. Nothing else.

Or at least he thought there was nothing else. Then, in a hidden pocket inside one of the other pockets, he discovered one more photo. It was creased and faded, the corners dog-eared, but still recognizable: a young man, handsome, similar to the one in the ID photo but sterner, more severe, with piercing eyes and a mop of black hair falling down over a high, intelligent forehead. He was staring straight into the camera, one arm hanging at his side, the other lying on the head of a small stone sphinx. On the back was written, 'Ali, outside the Cairo museum'.

Sayf al-Tha'r's hand started to tremble.

He was still staring at the photo when Dravic staggered up onto the top of the dune.

'What's going on?' puffed the German.

'We start flying the artefacts out tomorrow,' said Sayf al-Tha'r.

'What?'

'I want the helicopters here at first light.'

'I thought you said we weren't going to use helicopters.'

'The plan has changed. We take as much as we can by

helicopter, the rest goes with the camel train. I want us off this site within twenty-four hours.'

'For Christ's sake, we can't just—'

'Do it!'

Dravic glared angrily at him and, snatching a handkerchief from his pocket, began mopping at his sodden brow.

'There's no way we can get everything in place by tomorrow. No fucking way. We only found the rear of the army this morning. It's almost three kilometres away. It'll take us at least two more days to get the whole thing rigged.'

'Then we put more men on it. We put all the men on it. As of now we stop digging and concentrate on preparing the army for our departure.'

'What's the problem, for Christ's sake?'

Sayf al-Tha'r gazed down at the photo in his hand. 'Someone knows. A policeman. He's out here. In the desert. Near.'

For a moment Dravic stared at him incredulously, then burst out laughing.

'This is what you're shitting your pants over? One fucking policeman out here on his own? Jesus! We send out a patrol, we shoot him, end of story. It's not like there's anywhere he can hide.'

'We go tomorrow.'

'There's not time, I tell you! We need at least two more days to get everything ready. If we don't do this properly the stuff we've got won't be worth shit. Do you understand that? It won't be worth shit!'

Sayf al-Tha'r looked up, eyes steely. 'We go tomorrow. There is no more to be said.'

Dravic opened his mouth to argue, but realized it was futile. Instead he hawked up a glob of tobaccoey mucus, spat it a centimetre from Sayf al-Tha'r's foot and, turning, set off back down the dune.

A generator chugged into life and the arc lamps flared on, flooding the excavations with a wash of icy light. Sayf al-Tha'r took no notice, just stared back down at the photo in his hand.

'Ali,' he whispered to himself, grimacing slightly, as though the words tasted bitter on his tongue. 'Ali Khalifa.'

He was still for a moment and then suddenly, violently, he tore the picture apart and threw the pieces into the wind. They scattered across the top of the dune, fragments of face lying confusedly at his feet like the shards of a broken mirror.

It was dark when Khalifa finally crawled out from beneath the overhang. Or at least as dark as it gets in the desert, which never sees an absolute blackness, merely a ghostly half-light as if a soft gauze has been draped across the landscape. He stood for a moment gazing out across the dunes, the moon, as he had hoped, not too bright, and then brought his attention back to his immediate surroundings. He had a long walk ahead of him and no time to waste. Beneath him a precipitous, thirty-metre slide of hard-packed sand dropped sharply downwards. He looked to left and right along the ridge, casting around for a gentler place to descend, but the gradient was just as acute in both directions and so, mumbling a swift prayer, he threw his holdall down, sat at the top of the slope and, machine-gun cradled in his lap, lay back and slid.

He picked up speed immediately. He tried to brake himself with his feet, but it didn't have any effect other than to fill his shoes with sand. Faster and faster he went, the wind hissing in his ears, the bottom of his shirt rucking up so that the sand scraped viciously against the bare flesh of his lower back. Halfway down he hit a heavy ripple and went into a roll, bouncing downwards in a flurry of dislodged sand and whirling limbs, the machine-gun slamming painfully against his chest and chin. He hit the bottom shoulder-first and was slammed round onto his face, tasting sand on his lips and tongue.

'*Ibn sharmoota*,' he mumbled. 'Son of a bitch.'

He lay still for a moment and then, spitting, came shakily to his feet and looked back up the slope. It appeared even steeper from the bottom than it had from the top, a near-vertical wall of sand, with a deep, swerving groove marking the line of his descent. He whispered another brief prayer, this one of thanks for still being alive, and, brushing sand out of his hair, retrieved his bag and set out across the desert.

He walked throughout the night, the world around him silent aside from the soft crunch of his footfall and the rasp of his breath. He knew he was leaving a trail that would be easy to follow, even in the dark, but there was nothing he could do about it and so he just ploughed forward as best he could. He kept the GPS unit in his hand and referred to it occasionally to check how far he still had to go. For his bearings, however, he had no need of it, for the pyramid rock was clearly visible, glowing mysteriously in the darkness. He guessed they must have lights rigged around its base.

Gradually his feet settled into a rhythm. Slowly up each dune, faster down the far side, and then an even stride across the flattish desert floor to the bottom of the next slope. Up, down, across; up, down, across; up, down, across.

He had twenty-eight kilometres to cover and for the first half of the journey he managed to stay focused on his surroundings, keeping his ears and eyes sharp for any sign he was being pursued. As the hours passed, however, and the kilometres slipped away, so his mind began to wander.

He found himself thinking of Zenab, of the first time they'd met shortly after he'd started at university. A group of them had gone to the zoo for the afternoon and Zenab had been one of them, a friend of a friend of a friend. They'd wandered around gazing at the animals, Khalifa far too shy to talk to her, until eventually they'd stopped in front of a cage with a polar bear inside, swimming sadly round in its pool of milky water.

'Poor thing,' Khalifa had said with a sigh. 'He wants to go home to the Antarctic.'

'The Arctic, I think.' She had been beside him. 'Polar bears come from the Arctic. You don't get them in the Antarctic. Penguins, yes, but not polar bears.'

He had blushed a deep shade of magenta, overwhelmed by her long hair and huge eyes.

'Oh,' was all he had managed to say. 'I see.'

And that had been it. He hadn't spoken to her for the rest of the afternoon, too tongue-tied with shyness. He smiled at the memory. Who would have thought that from such unpromising beginnings . . .

To the west a shooting star flared brilliantly for a moment and disappeared. Up, down, across. Up, down, across.

Now he was thinking of his children. Batah, Ali, baby Yusuf. He remembered each of their births as if it had happened only yesterday. Batah, their first, had taken almost nineteen hours to arrive.

'Never again,' Zenab had muttered afterwards. 'I'm never going through that again.'

But she had gone through it again, and a few years later Ali had arrived, and then baby Yusuf, and who knows, maybe there would be more. He hoped so. He imagined a whole crowd of children playing around the fountain he was building in his hall, floating their toys in its water, their laughter echoing around the flat.

A slight breeze came up, making the dunes around him whisper, as if they were talking about him. Up, down, across. Up, down, across. He lit a cigarette.

Now his children too were drifting away and he was thinking of his father and mother. How his father used to pick him up and swing him round by his feet, how his mother would sit cross-legged on the roof of their house shelling termous beans. He stayed with them for a while and then moved on again, thinking of Professor al-Habibi and Fat Abdul, of the Cairo Museum and the camel yard, cases he'd dealt with, cases he'd solved. Image after image drifted through his mind, as if he was sitting in a cinema watching the narrative of his own life slowly unfolding in front of him.

And of course inevitably, inexorably, his thoughts came round to his brother.

Good things at first: the games they had played, the adventures they had had, an old derelict river cruiser from whose upper deck they used to dive into the Nile. Then how Ali had started to change, growing harder, more distant, getting in trouble, doing bad things. Finally, unavoidably, the day his brother had died. The day Khalifa's own life had fallen apart. It had all happened so quickly, so unexpectedly. The fundamentalists had come to their village one afternoon looking for foreigners, bent on killing. There had been shooting, seven people had died, including three terrorists. Khalifa had been at university at the time and had only heard about it on the radio. He had rushed home immediately, knowing instinctively that Ali had been caught up in it. His mother had been sitting alone in a chair staring at the wall.

'Your brother is dead,' she had said simply, face blank. 'My Ali is dead. Oh God, my poor heart is broken.'

Later Khalifa had gone out and wandered the streets. The bodies of the fundamentalists had not yet been removed and had been lying in a row on the pavement, blankets thrown over their faces, policemen standing by, chatting and smoking. He had gazed down at them, trying to connect them with the brother he had loved, and then turned away. He had walked up onto the Giza plateau, up to the pyramids, and then further up, climbing block over block to the very summit of the great Pyramid of Cheops, to the place where he and Ali had sat as children, the world spread out below like a map. And there, at what felt like the apex of the world, he had slumped down and wept, overwhelmed with shame and horror, unable to believe what had happened, unable to understand it, the late afternoon sun hovering above his head like a vast thought bubble, full of fire and pain and confusion.

Ali, his brother. The brother who had become a father. Who had made him what he was, who had inspired him in all things. So much strength. So much goodness. Dead for fourteen years now, but still it weighed him down. And always would, until he stood face to face with the man responsible for that loss. Until he stood face to face with Sayf al-Tha'r. That was why he had come out here. To look Sayf al-Tha'r in the eyes. Even if he had to die to do it. To confront the man who had destroyed his family.

Khalifa stumbled up to the top of a dune and realized with a shock that he had almost reached his destination. Ahead, less than two kilometres away, the great pyramidal rock loomed vast and menacing, a patina of brilliant light pulsing all around it. Vague black smudges spaced regularly along the surrounding dune-tops were presumably lookouts, and he dropped down immediately, fearful of being seen. He glanced at his watch. Half an hour till dawn.

He slipped back from the summit of the dune and, laying aside the machine-gun, pulled his pistol from his holdall and tucked it into his belt. He took out the black robes and dragged them over his head, wrapping the dead man's scarf around his forehead and his face, the dried blood giving the material an unpleasant, crusty feel. He then stuffed the mobile phone and GPS unit into his pockets, cast the bag aside and, picking up the machine-gun again, climbed back up to the top of the dune and started down the far side, making straight towards his enemies.

'For Ali,' he whispered.

Tara weaved her way through the camp, the guard walking slightly behind her, his gun slung across his arm. It was cold and she hugged her arms around herself, her body still stiff and painful from Dravic's assault. There was shouting and hammering and, from somewhere away to the right, a raucous braying sound, like a symphony of discordant trumpets. She gulped in the air, glad to be out of the cloying interior of the tent where she and Daniel were being held.

How many days had they been captive now? She tried to focus her mind. Two? Three? She searched for landmarks, events against which she could measure the passing of time. Sayf al-Tha'r had come the previous night. Dravic had attacked her the one before that. And that had been, what? Their second night in the desert? No, only their first. They had arrived that morning. So, three days in total. It seemed longer than that. Much longer.

They continued through the tents, skirting a wall of crates and emerging from the southern end of the encampment. To the right a herd of camels was standing, the source of the braying. A crowd of men jostled around them, loading and unloading crates.

Fifty metres further on they stopped and, pulling down her jeans, Tara squatted and began to urinate. A few days ago she wouldn't have contemplated doing such a thing in front of a complete stranger. Now she no longer cared.

The guard watched for a moment and then averted his eyes. He was young, no more than a boy. She hadn't seen him before tonight.

'You like Manchester United?' he asked suddenly.

His voice was a shock. It was the first time one of their captors had spoken to her.

'Football team,' he added.

She looked up at him, urine pattering between her feet, and despite herself started to laugh. Could the situation possibly be more absurd, pissing in the middle of a desert beside a gun-toting religious fanatic who wanted to discuss football? It was crazy. Her laughter redoubled, ratcheting towards hysteria.

'What?' said the guard, turning, confused. 'What is funny?'

'This,' said Tara, waving her arm around her, 'all of this. It's fucking hilarious.'

'You no like Manchester United?'

She came to her feet, pulling up her jeans and stepping forward so that her face was just a few centimetres from his.

'I don't care about fucking Manchester United,' she hissed. 'Do you understand? I don't give a shit. I've been kidnapped, beaten and soon I'm going to be killed. Fuck Manchester United. Fuck you.'

The guard's eyes dropped. Although it was he who was holding the gun, he seemed scared of her.

'Manchester United good,' he muttered.

His face was young, frighteningly young. She wondered how old he was. Fourteen, fifteen? She felt a sudden, inexplicable twinge of pity for him.

'What's your name?' she asked, her voice more gentle.

He mumbled inaudibly.

'What?'

'Mehmet.'

'And why are you here, Mehmet?'

The boy seemed confused by the question.

'Sayf al-Tha'r say,' he replied.

'And if Sayf al-Tha'r said kill me, would you?'

The boy's feet shifted uncomfortably. His head was still bowed.

'Look at me,' she said. 'Look at me.'

Reluctantly he lifted his eyes.

'If Sayf al-Tha'r said kill me, would you?'

'Sayf al-Tha'r good man,' he mumbled. 'He care me.'

'But would you kill me? If Sayf al-Tha'r said, would you?'

The boy's eyes flicked nervously from side to side, blinking.

'We go back now,' he said.

'Not till you answer me.'

'We go back,' he repeated.

'Answer me!'

'Yes!' he cried, lifting the gun and shaking it in her face. 'Yes, I kill you. I kill you! For Allah, I kill you! OK? OK? You want me kill you now?'

His breath was fast and uneven, his hands trembling. She knew better than to push him further.

'OK,' she said quietly, 'OK. We go back now.'

She turned and began walking towards the camp. After a few seconds she heard the boy coming up behind her. They walked in silence until they had reached the edge of the tents.

'I sorry,' whispered the boy. 'I very sorry.'

She slowed and turned. What could she say? He was a child. In a way they were all children, simple, innocent, despite the acts they committed. Children who had realized they were more powerful than the adults.

'Chelsea,' she said. 'I support Chelsea.'

The boy's face broke into a broad smile.

'Chelsea no good!' He chuckled. 'No as good as Manchester. Manchester United very good.'

They continued on into the camp.

Khalifa lay gazing at the black-robed figures ahead of him and below. There was now only one ridge between him and the army, and the air echoed to the chug of generators and the distant thud of hammering.

He could go no further without being seen. A string of guards was lined across the summit opposite and in the valley beneath, positioned at regular intervals, so there was no way he'd be able to slip through unnoticed. He could try to outflank them, but that would take time and a tinge of grey was already weeping into the western sky. Whatever else happened he had to be inside the ring by sunrise, or he'd almost certainly be picked up by the helicopter patrols that were bound to start again at dawn.

He slipped down from the dune-top and rolled onto his back, lighting a cigarette and wondering what to do.

It was Ali who decided his course of action. Or rather a piece of advice Ali had once given him, the first time they'd visited the Cairo museum together. As they approached the front gates, his brother had stopped to brief him on how they would get in without paying.

'We're going to pretend we're with a school party,' he had explained. 'Go in right through the front door.'

Khalifa had asked whether it wouldn't be better to try and slip in through a side entrance, but Ali had shaken his head.

'If they see you sneaking around the side they're bound to stop you,' he had said. 'Always go through the front. Always look confident, like you belong there. It never fails.'

And it never had. Whether it would work now was a different matter, but he couldn't think of anything else. Finishing his cigarette and pulling the scarf tightly around his forehead and face, he stood, climbed back to the top of the dune and started down the other side, waving at the guards below.

'*Salaam*,' he called to them. 'Everything OK?'

There was confused shouting and three guards hurried forward, guns raised, intercepting him at the bottom of the slope.

Always look confident, Khalifa told himself. Always look confident.

'Hey!' he laughed, holding up his hands. 'It's OK, guys! I'm on your side!'

The men continued to point their guns.

'What's going on?' said one of them. 'Where have you come from?'

'Where the hell do you think I've come from? I've been out on patrol.'

'Patrol?'

'Complete waste of time. I've been walking all night and haven't seen a thing. Any of you guys got a cigarette?'

There was a pause and then one of the men fumbled in the

pocket of his robe and pulled out a packet of Cleopatras. His companion, the one who had spoken before, motioned him back.

'There aren't any patrols out tonight. Guards around the perimeter, that was the order. Nothing about patrols.'

'Well, I wish someone had told me that,' said Khalifa, trying to keep his voice steady. 'I must have walked thirty kilometres.'

The man stared at him, eyes narrowed, and then, lifting his gun, indicated he should remove the scarf from the lower half of his face.

Brazen it out if they start asking questions, Ali had told him that day at the museum. Get angry if necessary. Never show doubt.

'For God's sake,' snapped Khalifa, 'I've been out all night. I'm cold!'

'Do it,' said the man.

With an annoyed grunt Khalifa slowly pulled the scarf down over his chin, making sure it remained wrapped closely around his forehead. The man leaned forward and stared at him.

'I don't recognize you,' he said.

'And I don't recognize you! I don't recognize half the people here, but I don't go around pointing my gun at them. This is crazy! Crazy!'

He paused and then took a risk.

'If you don't believe me why don't you go and ask Dravic? He knows me. I was with him when he cut up that old guy in Cairo. Ripped half his face off with that bloody trowel of his. Fucking animal.'

There was another brief pause and then, nodding at each other, the men lowered their guns. The one with the cigarettes stepped forward and offered Khalifa the pack. He pulled one out and put it in his mouth, hoping they didn't notice how much his hand was shaking.

'You going back to the camp?' asked the one who had been questioning him.

Khalifa nodded.

'Well, tell them to send someone down here to relieve us.'

'Sure,' said the detective. 'And do me a favour, will you? What I just said about Dravic, keep it to yourselves, eh?'

The men laughed. 'Don't worry. We feel the same about him.'

Khalifa smiled and, raising his hand in farewell, began walking away. After a few paces, however, a voice called after him.

'Hey, haven't you forgotten something!'

The detective froze. What had he forgotten? A password? A secret sign? He should have known there'd be something else. Turning, he found the three men staring at him, clutching their machine-guns.

'Well?' said the one who had given him the cigarette.

Khalifa's mind was a blank, his heart racing. He grinned inanely, his finger curling instinctively round the trigger of his gun, eyes flicking from one man to the next, sizing up his chances. There was a brief painful silence, the calm before the storm, and then, suddenly, raucous laughter.

'The cigarette, you idiot! Don't you want a light?'

It took a second for Khalifa to register what they meant, and then the air whooshed from his lungs in a deep sigh of relief. He lifted a hand and touched the cigarette in his mouth.

'That's what a night in the desert does to you,' he said, laughing with the others. 'Turns your mind.'

The man flicked a lighter and held out the flame. Khalifa leaned forward and puffed the cigarette into life.

'The sooner we get out of this god-forsaken place the better,' he said.

Murmurs of agreement.

He took a couple more puffs, nodded a farewell and started away again. This time no-one called him back. He was through.

The eastern horizon was definitely greying now. Khalifa crossed the valley and climbed to the top of the next dune, the huge rock rearing monstrously to his left, silent and immutable, a pivot on whose point the entire sky seemed to balance. At the summit he passed between two lookouts, neither of whom paid him any attention, and gazed down at the chaotic scene below – the crater, the tents, the camels, the piles of boxes and artefacts. Droves of black-robed figures were moving to and fro, most of them packing and loading crates, although a small group was working within the crater itself, wading among the tangled corpses, doing something with lengths of cable. There was a large man in a white shirt standing above them, supervising their work. Dravic, he guessed.

He gazed down at them for a few moments and then turned his attention back towards the camp, just in time to see a fair-haired woman disappearing into a tent right in the centre. He noted its position, between a row of fuel drums and a pyramid of straw bales, and then started down the slope. As he did so an amplified voice drifted up from beneath: '*Allah u akbar! Allah u akbar!*'

The call to dawn prayers. He quickened his descent, pulling the scarf back up across his face.

A tide of men streamed through the camp and out onto a flat area of sand to the south of it, where they lined up in rows, facing east. Sayf al-Tha'r moved with them, but turned aside on the edge of the camp and stepped into a tent with an antenna jutting above it. A man rose as he entered, but Sayf al-Tha'r waved him back to his seat in front of heavy radio apparatus.

'The helicopters?'

The man handed him a piece of paper. 'Just taken off.'

'No problems?'

'None. They'll be here in under an hour.'

'And the guards? Nothing?'

The man shook his head.

'Keep me informed,' said Sayf al-Tha'r and stepped out of the tent again.

The tide of men was thinning now as the last stragglers hurried towards the prayer area, leaving the camp deserted. The lookouts had remained in position, but they too were facing east, heads bowed. He gazed up at them, black hummocks strung out along the dune-tops like a line of vultures, and then turned and made his way back through the camp. The sound of prayer wafted through the air like a breeze.

He reached his own tent and threw back the flap. As he bent to step inside he stopped suddenly, shoulders tense. Slowly he stood and turned, eyes darting to left and right. He came forward half a step, eyes probing the shadowy labyrinth of canvas and equipment, but there was nothing and after a moment he shook his head, turned and disappeared inside, the canvas flap dropping down behind him.

NEAR THE LIBYAN BORDER

The helicopters flew low, hugging the desert, twenty of them, like a flock of carrion birds sweeping over the sands. One was slightly ahead of the others and those behind followed its every movement, rising and falling as it rose and fell, swinging to left and right, a perfectly choreographed dance of flight. They were large machines, heavy, their lumpen bodies somehow at odds with the grace of their movement. In their cockpits human forms could just be made out. They rushed on ahead of the dawn, slicing through the silence as the sky slowly turned to red.

40

THE WESTERN DESERT

Khalifa remained hidden among a jumble of oil drums until the camp had emptied completely. He then made his way swiftly through the twisting avenues of equipment and tents, searching for the one into which the girl had disappeared. He reckoned he had fifteen minutes, twenty at the outside.

From above the layout of the camp had seemed perfectly clear. Now, at ground level, it wasn't so easy to orientate himself. Everything looked the same and the landmarks he had noted a few moments before – the row of fuel drums, the stack of straw bales – were nowhere to be seen. He put his head through a couple of doorways, thinking they might be the ones, but there was nothing inside and he was just beginning to get desperate when he emerged from behind a teetering wall of crates and saw ahead of him, beside a heap of bales, the tent he was looking for. He grunted with relief and, hurrying forward, drew back its flap and leaned in, machine-gun held ready in front of him.

It wasn't necessary, for the guard he'd been expecting wasn't there. Neither, however, was the girl. Instead, kneeling with his back to the door, was a solitary figure, his forehead pressed to the floor. Khalifa made to step back, realizing he'd again got the wrong tent, but something stopped him. He couldn't see the man's face, nor even much of his shape beneath his costume of black robes. Somehow, however, he knew. It was Sayf al-Tha'r. He raised his gun, finger ready to squeeze the trigger.

If the kneeling figure noticed the policeman, he gave no indication, but continued with his prayers, oblivious to the presence behind him. Khalifa's finger tightened on the trigger, squeezing the metal tongue back until it was just a twitch away from firing. From this distance there was no way he could miss. The tent's interior seemed to echo with the beating of his heart.

The man straightened, stood, recited, knelt again. One twitch of the finger, thought Khalifa, that's all it would take. One twitch and the figure in front of him would be dead. He thought of Ali and raised the muzzle slightly, aiming it at the base of the man's head. He drew a deep breath, bit his lip, then lowered the weapon again, eased his finger off the trigger and stepped backwards and out of the tent.

For a moment he stared at the worn canvas flap, a strangely hollow feeling in the pit of his stomach. He could only have been looking at the man for a few seconds, but in that time the sky suddenly seemed to have become much lighter, dawn sweeping swiftly in from the east like a wave. They'd be finishing prayers soon. He turned and hurried off through the camp.

'I wonder how Joey is,' mumbled Tara.

She was sitting on the tent floor, hugging her knees, rocking back and forth. Daniel lay beside her, drumming his fingers on the ground, occasionally lifting his arm to look at his watch.

'Who's Joey?' he asked.

'Our black-necked cobra. At the zoo. He's not been well.'

'I would have thought you'd have had enough of cobras to last you a lifetime.'

She shrugged. 'I never particularly liked him, but then . . . you know . . . when you think you'll never see him again . . . I hope Alexandra's kept up with his antibiotics. And taken his rock out. He had a skin disease, you see. Was rubbing himself up against it. Damaging the scales.'

She was rambling, talking for the sake of talking, as if by making conversation she could somehow put off the moment when they would be taken outside and . . . what? Shot? Beheaded? Stabbed? She looked at their guard. Not the boy Mehmet any more, an older man. She pictured him holding a gun to her head and firing; the sound, the feel, the explosion of blood, her blood. She began wringing her hands.

'What the hell was it with you and snakes anyway?' muttered Daniel, struggling into a sitting position. 'I never understood the attraction.'

Tara smiled ruefully. 'In a funny way it was Dad who got me interested in them. He hated them, you see. It was the one chink in his armour. Made me feel like I had some sort of power over him. I remember some students once hid a rubber one in his bag and when he opened it . . .'

Her voice trailed off, as if she realized there was no point finishing the story because neither of them was going to laugh. There was a long, heavy silence.

'What about you?' she asked eventually, desperate to keep the conversation going. 'You've never told me why you became an archaeologist.'

'God knows. I've never really thought about it.' Daniel was fiddling with the lace of his boot. 'I've just always loved digging, I guess. I remember before my parents died, when we lived in Paris, we had a garden and I used to dig these holes at the bottom of it, looking for buried treasure. Huge holes, deep, like craters. Dad said if I wasn't careful I'd end up in Australia. That's where it started, I suppose. And then I was given a book with pictures of the Tutankhamun treasures, and somehow the digging and Egypt . . .'

The tent flap was drawn back and a guard stepped in, his scarf wrapped close around his face against the dawn chill. The guard on the floor started getting to his feet. As he did so, the new arrival brought the metal butt of his machine-gun down hard on the side of the man's head. He slumped backwards, unconscious. Daniel leaped to his feet, Tara beside him. Khalifa pulled the scarf down to reveal his face.

'There is very little time,' he said, bending to pick up the guard's gun. 'I am a policeman, I am here to get you out.' He handed the gun to Daniel. 'Can you use this?'

'I think so.'

'How did you get here?' asked Tara. 'How many of you are there?'

'Just me,' said Khalifa. 'There's no time to explain. In a few minutes they'll have finished prayers and the camp will be swarming with people again. You must go now, while you have the chance.'

He put his head out through the flap, looked around, turned back to them.

'Go north up the valley, past the excavations. Stay close to the bottom of the westward dune. That way you'll be out of the line of sight of the lookouts above. Go as fast as you can.'

'What about you?' asked Tara.

Khalifa ignored the question, reaching into his robe and pulling out the phone and GPS unit.

'Take these. Once you're clear of the guards call for help. Your co-ordinates will show up on the unit here. You just press—'

'I know how it works,' said Daniel, taking the unit and handing the phone to Tara.

'What about you?' she repeated, louder this time.

Khalifa turned to her. 'I have business here,' he said. 'It is not your concern.'

'We can't leave you.'

'Go,' he said, pushing them towards the entrance. 'Go now. North, and close to the left-hand dune.'

'I don't know who you are,' said Daniel, 'but thank you. I hope we'll meet again one day.'

'*Insha-Allah*. Now go.'

They ducked through the flap. On the other side Tara turned and, leaning forward, kissed Khalifa swiftly on each cheek.

'Thank you,' she whispered.

He nodded and pushed her away. 'I am sorry about your father, Miss Mullray. I saw him lecture once. He was magnificent. Now go, please.'

Their eyes locked for a second and then Tara and Daniel ran off through the tents. Khalifa watched until they had disappeared and then turned and moved swiftly in the opposite direction.

He made his way towards the south end of the camp, stopping every now and then to listen to the murmur of prayers ahead of him, gauging how much time he had. A couple of minutes. Not much more. A translucent band of pink light had appeared over the ridge of the eastern dune, widening all the time, its glow mingling with and slowly superseding that of the arc lamps.

He kept going until he reached the point where the tents began to run out, giving way to a confusion of equipment. Beyond, fifty metres away, lines of men were kneeling on the sand, their lips trembling with prayer. He slipped behind a stack of crates and cast around for a way of creating a diversion.

There were several bales of straw nearby and, beside them, a solitary fuel drum. He looked at the wooden boxes behind him, each with a skull-and-crossbones stencilled on the side, and then, crossing to the drum, unscrewed its cap. A wisp of vapour drifted out. Diesel, as he'd thought. He grasped the rim and tipped the drum up, sloshing its contents out over the nearest bale. He continued pouring until the straw was sodden, then dragged the bale back to the crates, pushing it right up against them. He repeated the process twice more, petrol splashing over his shoes and robe as he worked.

He was just pushing the third bale into place when a sudden swell of noise told him the prayers were ending. At the same time there was a shout from the dune-top above. He spun, lifting his gun, thinking he'd been spotted. Then there was a clatter of gun-fire from the other end of the camp and he realized it wasn't him who had been seen, but Tara and Daniel.

'*Fa'r!*' he hissed. 'Shit!'

He turned back towards the mass of damp straw and, fumbling in his pocket, pulled out his lighter. The gunfire intensified. There was a commotion in front of him now too as the crowd of worshippers broke ranks and began running back towards the camp. He squatted and held the lighter to the base of one of the bales.

'I wouldn't if I were you.'

The voice came from behind him.

'Just drop the lighter and stand up. And no sudden moves.'

For a moment Khalifa remained motionless, the world seem-ing to condense around him, then he closed his eyes, drew a breath and flicked his thumb down on the barrel of the lighter. There was a click and a spark, but no flame. A spurt of bullets chewed up the sand around him.

'I said drop the lighter. I won't repeat myself.'

Defeated, Khalifa opened his hand and allowed the lighter to fall. More gunfire from the far side of the camp.

'Now stand and turn around,' said the voice. 'Nice and slow. And get your arms in the air.'

The detective did as he was told. Ten metres away, a machine-gun in his hands, stood Dravic.

'You stupid little cunt,' snarled the German.

Suddenly there were men everywhere. Dravic shouted and three of them grabbed Khalifa and forced him down onto his knees.

'So this is our brave policeman, is it?' said the giant, coming forward. 'Our very own little Omar Sharif.'

He stopped in front of Khalifa and, raising his hand, smashed it across his mouth, splitting the lip.

'What did you think you were going to do? Arrest us all single-handed? You lot are even more stupid than I thought you were.'

Khalifa said nothing, just stared up at him, blood streaming across his chin. The sound of gunfire was growing more intense. A man ran into the clearing and said something to Dravic, who glared down at Khalifa.

'You'll pay for this,' he growled. 'Believe me, you'll pay.'

He signalled to one of the men, who picked up Khalifa's lighter and handed it over. The giant took it and leaned forward, nostrils flaring, sniffing the air.

'Now what's this I smell?' he said. 'This strange odour all over your lovely black robes. Could it be petrol?'

He grinned sadistically. The men around him laughed.

'We have been careless, haven't we!'

He drew back a little and, holding the lighter just in front of Khalifa's chest, struck the flint. A yellowy-blue flame leaped up.

'It's a knack, you see. All in the thumb.'

He wafted the flame back and forth, moving it closer and closer to the petrol-stained material. Khalifa struggled, but the men on either side held him firm. The flame was almost on the hem of the robe.

'Stop this! Stop it now!'

The voice came from beyond the crowd, sharp and authori-tative. Dravic's eyes rolled upwards and, muttering, he withdrew the lighter and stepped back. The circle of men opened to reveal Sayf al-Tha'r. He remained where he was for a long moment, staring at Khalifa, and then came forward, stop-ping in front of the detective and looking down at him. 'Hello, Yusuf.'

'You know him?' asked Dravic, surprised.

'Indeed,' said Sayf al-Tha'r. 'He is my little brother.'

They hurried through the camp, flitting from tent to tent and angling towards the foot of the left-hand dune, as Khalifa had told them. Daniel led, Tara followed, adrenalin pumping through her, the aching of her body forgotten for the moment.

At the camp's northern edge they stopped. Ahead the mayhem of the excavations stretched off into the distance, still and silent in the growing light of day, heaps of artefacts strewn across the ground like the wreckage of some enormous plane crash. They could see guards strung along the dune-top to their right, but they were facing away from them, eastwards, towards the rising sun. Those above were lost behind the angle of the ridge.

'OK?' said Daniel.

'OK.'

They started forward again, hugging the bottom of the slope, the pyramid rock looming huge ahead of them. With every step away from the camp, every step they weren't spotted, Tara felt they were stretching their luck just that little bit further. It had been years since she'd last prayed, not since she was a child. Now, without even being aware of it, she began mumbling to herself, pleading with whatever power would listen to protect them, to let them get away.

'Please don't let us be seen,' she whispered. 'Please don't let us be seen. Please don't let us be seen.'

It worked for fifty metres. Then, however, as they came level with the beginning of the excavation trench, there was a shout from above and an angry crack of gunfire.

'Shit,' hissed Daniel.

The shout was taken up by other voices and there was more gunfire. Forty pairs of eyes swivelled towards them. Daniel swung and fired.

'Back,' he shouted. 'We have to go back.'

'No!'

'There's no cover here!'

He grabbed her arm and pulled her back the way they had come. Men were leaping down the dunes to either side of them now, shooting wildly. Bullets cracked past Tara's head, thudded into the sand, smashed into crates and ancient armour. Daniel unleashed another volley of gunfire, and then they were back among the tents, their pursuers lost momentarily behind a mesh of canvas.

'What now?' panted Tara.

'I don't know. I don't know.'

His voice was desperate.

They ran forward, scrambling through the tents and equipment, hunted. The shouts were growing louder behind them. And in front too. They were caught in the jaws of a closing vice. There was nowhere for them to go. Fear pounded in Tara's ears. Everything had become a blur.

They skidded round the side of a tent and there, standing alone in a clearing, was a single dune bike. They ran over to it. The keys were in the ignition. Without a word Daniel thrust the gun into her arms, leaped astride the saddle and slammed the kickstart. The engine sputtered, but didn't catch. He slammed it again. Nothing.

'Come on!' he cried. 'Start, you bastard.'

The shouts were just a couple of tents away now, all around, a tightening noose of sound.

Frantic, Tara held the gun in front of her and fired, the weapon leaping violently in her hands, a hail of bullets puncturing canvas and wood. She loosed her finger, swung, fired again, in the opposite direction this time, emptying the clip. There was another clip taped to it, upside down, and, yanking the finished magazine from its slot, she flipped it over and jammed the new one in its place. The bike roared into life.

'Get on!' screamed Daniel.

She leaped up behind him, his hand twisting back on the throttle before her backside had even hit the saddle. A spray of sand lashed out from under the rear wheel and they flew forward. A figure leaped out in front of them, but Daniel raised his foot and kicked him out of the way. Other figures loomed, ahead and to either side and, clutching Daniel's waist with one hand, eyes half closed as if that would somehow protect her, Tara unleashed spasms of bullets all around, uncertain whether she was actually hitting anything. Somewhere nearby there was an explosion and a man staggered across the periphery of her sight, robes flaming.

They roared on, zigzagging madly through the tents, swerving this way and that, skidding, sliding, until eventually they burst from the northern edge of the camp and flew towards the mound on whose summit they'd stood the night the army was discovered. Black-robed figures were pouring towards them from either side of it. Daniel slowed, looked around, then heaved back the throttle.

'Hold on!'

They sped straight towards the mound. The men ahead held for an instant, then scattered. When she saw what he was about to do Tara threw the gun aside and clasped both arms tightly around his waist.

'No fucking way!' she screamed.

They hit the bottom of the slope, powered upwards and took off, arcing up, over and, after what seemed like an impossible length of time, down again on the far side, putting the mound between them and their pursuers. Their rear tyre slewed badly as it hit the ground and for a moment it looked as if they were coming off. Somehow they remained upright, however, and sped away along the valley. There were sporadic bursts of gun-fire from behind, but none from above, most of the lookouts having left their posts and run back towards the camp as soon as the shooting started. They were out.

'Jesus, look at all this stuff,' cried Daniel as they flew past the excavations.

Tara tightened her grip around his waist.

'Don't look,' she yelled. 'Drive!'

41

THE WESTERN DESERT

'You're not my brother,' said Khalifa, staring up at the man in front of him. 'My brother's dead. He died the day he and his thugs came to our village and murdered four innocent people. The day he took the name Sayf al-Tha'r.'

Now that they were beside each other the similarity was obvious: the same high cheekbones, narrow mouths, hooked noses. Only their eyes spoke of some fundamental difference. Khalifa's were clear blue; Sayf al-Tha'r's brilliant green.

Their gazes remained locked for some time, their bodies motionless, the air between them seeming to crackle and burn, and then Sayf al-Tha'r held out his hand towards Dravic.

'Your gun.'

The giant stepped forward and handed him the weapon. Sayf al-Tha'r took it and aimed the muzzle at Khalifa's head.

'Take the men and get back to work,' he ordered. 'Bring the lookouts down too. The helicopters will be here in thirty minutes and there is much still to do.'

'What about the prisoners?'

'Let them run. We don't need them.'

'And him?'

'I will deal with it.'

'We can't—'

'I will deal with it.'

Muttering, Dravic turned and walked away. The men followed, leaving the two of them alone. Sayf al-Tha'r motioned Khalifa to his feet and they stood facing each other, Sayf al-Tha'r slightly the taller of the two.

'You should have killed me when you had the chance, Yusuf. When you came into my tent just now. It was you, wasn't it? I could feel you behind me. Why didn't you pull the trigger? I know you wanted to.'

'I tried to think what my brother Ali would have done in that situation,' said Khalifa. 'And I knew he would never have shot a man in the back. Especially not when he was at prayer.'

Sayf al-Tha'r grunted. 'You talk as if I'm not your brother.'

'You're not. Ali was a good man. You are a butcher.'

The generators stopped suddenly and the arc lamps flicked off, immersing the camp in the softer, more subtle hues of dawn. Northwards a column of heavy black smoke rose into the air.

'Why did you come here, Yusuf?'

Khalifa was silent for a moment.

'Not to kill you,' he said. 'No, not that. Although you're right: I wanted to. For fourteen years I've wanted to. To wipe Sayf al-Tha'r from the face of the earth.'

He fumbled among the folds of his robe and pulled out his cigarettes. He removed one, but then realized Dravic had taken his lighter and so just stood with it in his hand, unlit.

'I came because I wanted to understand. To look you in the face and try to understand what happened all those years ago. Why you changed. Why Ali had to die and give way to this . . . wickedness.'

Sayf al-Tha'r's eyes flashed momentarily, his hand tightening around the gun. Then his grip eased and he broke into a half-smile.

'I opened my eyes, Yusuf, that is all. I looked around and saw the world for what it is. Evil and corrupt. The *sharia* forgotten. The land overrun by *Kufr*. I saw and vowed to do something about it. Your brother didn't die. He simply grew.'

'Into a monster.'

'Into God's true servant.' The man stared at Khalifa, eyes boring into him. 'It was easy for you, Yusuf. You were not the elder son. You did not have to bear the things I bore. Shoulder the same responsibilities. Eighteen, twenty hours a day I worked to feed you and Mother. I felt my life slowly draining from me. And all around the rich Westerners in their fine hotels, spending more on a single meal than I earned in a month. Such things change a man. They show him the world as it really is.'

'I would have helped,' said Khalifa. 'I begged you to let me help. You didn't have to take the whole burden.'

'I was the elder son. It was my duty.'

'Just as it is now your duty to kill people?'

'As it says in the Holy Koran: "Fight against the unbelievers until there be no opposition." '

'It also says: "Let not hatred of a people incite you to act unjustly." '

'And also: "Those who err from the way of God shall suffer a severe punishment." And also: "Against them make ready your strength to the utmost of your power to terrorize the enemies of Allah." Shall we stand here and bandy holy verses, Yusuf? I think I would outdo you.'

Khalifa stared down at the cigarette in his hand.

'Yes,' he whispered, 'I think you probably would. I'm sure you could quote from dawn to dusk and beyond. But it still wouldn't make your actions right.'

He looked up again, into Sayf al-Tha'r's face, his eyes running back and forth across it.

'I just don't recognize you. The nose, the eyes, the mouth, yes, they're Ali's. But I just don't recognize you. Not here.' He raised his hand to his heart. 'Here you are a stranger. Less than a stranger. A void.'

'I am still your brother, Yusuf. Whatever you say. Our blood is the same.'

'No, it's not. Ali is dead. I even made him a grave, built it with my own hands, although there was no body to put in it.'

He raised his sleeve and wiped away the blood on his mouth.

'When I think of Ali, I feel pride. I feel admiration. I feel love. That's why my elder son carries the same name. Because it will always fill me with joy and warmth. But you . . . with you I feel only shame. Fourteen years of it. Fourteen years of dreading to open a newspaper for fear of reading of some new atrocity. Fourteen years of hiding from my past. Of pretending I'm not who I am because who I am is the brother of a monster.'

Again Sayf al-Tha'r's eyes flashed and his hands tensed around the gun, knuckles whitening. 'You always were weak, Yusuf.'

'You confuse weakness with humanity.'

'No, you confuse humanity with subservience. To be free one sometimes has to make unpleasant decisions. But then why should you understand that? Understanding, after all, is born of suffering and I always tried to protect you from such things. Perhaps it was a mistake to have done so. You talk of shame, Yusuf, but has it occurred to you the shame I feel? My brother, whom I loved and cared for, whom I worked my fingers to the bone to feed and clothe and send to university, now a policeman. A servant of those who did this to his own flesh and blood.'

He snapped his fingers in front of his scarred forehead.

'Is this what I broke my back for? Drained away my life? Believe me, you are not the only one who feels disappointment. Nor the only one who believes he has lost a brother. Not a day goes by, not a minute of a day, when you are not in my thoughts. And not a day goes by when those thoughts are not darkened with regret and anger and bitterness.'

His voice had dropped to a low hiss.

'When I realized it was you out here, I thought perhaps . . . just for a moment . . . after all this time . . .'

His eyes glowed for an instant, then dimmed.

'But no. Of course not. You do not have the strength. You have betrayed me. And you have betrayed God. And for that you will be punished.'

He raised the gun and pointed it at Khalifa's head, finger tightening around the trigger.

Khalifa stared up at him. 'God is great', he said simply, 'and God is good. And He does not need to kill people to prove that. This is the truth. This my brother Ali taught me.'

Their eyes held, five seconds, ten, and then, with a growl, Sayf al-Tha'r squeezed the trigger. As he did so, he flipped the muzzle upwards so that the gun fired harmlessly into the sky. There was a pause and then the boy Mehmet came running into the clearing.

'Take him and guard him,' said Sayf al-Tha'r. 'Watch him closely. Do not speak to him.' He turned and began walking away.

'You're going to destroy it, aren't you?' Khalifa called after him, indicating the stack of boxes behind him. 'That's what these are. Explosives.'

Sayf al-Tha'r stopped and turned. 'What we've got is useless if the rest of the army survives. It's unfortunate, but there's no other way.'

Khalifa said nothing, just stared at him.

'Poor Ali,' he whispered.

They drove hard for ten minutes, Tara glancing constantly over her shoulder for signs of pursuit. When it became clear they weren't being followed Daniel slowed and swung off to the right, up the side of a dune, skidding to a halt at its summit. Behind them the camp had faded to a distant blur, a vague pall of smoke rising above it into the dawn sky. The pyramid rock shimmered orangey-purple in the growing light of day. They gazed at it in silence.

'We can't just leave him,' said Tara eventually.

Daniel shrugged, but said nothing.

'We could call for help.' She pulled the mobile phone from her pocket. 'The police, the army, something like that.'

'Waste of time. They'd take hours to get out here. If they believed us.'

He paused, fiddling with the ignition key. 'I'll go back,' he said.

'We'll both go back.'

He smiled. 'I get the feeling we've had this argument before.'

'Then best not to repeat it. We'll go back together.'

'And then?'

She shrugged. 'Let's worry about that when we get there.'

'Clever plan, Tara. Subtle.'

He squeezed her knee and, with a sigh, clicked the bike into gear, setting off down the far side of the dune.

'At least we've got a nice day for it,' he said over his shoulder.

'For what?'

'Suicide.'

Initially he took them due east, about a kilometre, putting two huge dunes between them and the valley where the army was buried. Only then did they turn south again, opening the throttle and flying back towards the huge rock, now lost somewhere ahead and to their right.

'We'll run parallel to the valley till we're level with the camp,' he explained. 'At least that way we've got a chance of getting close to it. If we'd gone back the way we'd come they'd have spotted us a mile off. Nothing wrong with staying alive as long as we can.'

They kept their eyes open for any sign of movement on the dunes to either side and, once, Daniel stopped and cut the

418

engine, closing his eyes and listening for anything that might indicate they'd been seen. There was nothing. Just sand and silence and stillness.

'It's like the whole thing was just a dream,' said Tara.

'If only.'

They roared on for another five minutes until Daniel judged they were about level with the camp, whereupon he angled the bike up towards the summit of the right-hand dune. The slope was steep, and they only just made it to the top, the engine whining in protest. The pyramid-shaped outcrop reared in front of them and slightly to their left, two dunes away, with below it, hidden, the camp and excavations. There was no sign of any guards.

'Where are they?' asked Tara.

'No idea. They must have all gone down into the camp.'

He eased back the throttle and took them down, across and up the side of the next dune. There was now only one dune between them and the army. They could hear vague sounds, shouts and hammering. The landscape, however, remained resolutely empty.

'It's eerie,' she said. 'Like the desert's full of invisible people.'

Daniel cut the engine and again surveyed the land in front of them. Then, slowly, he eased his hand off the brake and free-wheeled silently down the side of the dune, their velocity carrying them fifty metres across the flat before they finally came to a halt. They dismounted and he laid the bike on the sand.

'We'll go on foot from here. I don't want to risk starting the engine. Too much noise. If anyone sees us . . . Well, there's not much we can do. Run for it, I guess.'

They walked to the foot of the dune and started upwards, eyes fixed on the summit above, dreading the moment when someone would appear and spot them. No-one did, however, and, hearts thudding with exertion, they reached the top and threw themselves onto their bellies, crawling slowly forward over the cool sand until they could gaze down into the valley below.

They were directly above the excavation crater, the vast rock in front of them, the camp away to their left. Droves of men were scurrying frantically to and fro, packing away artefacts – swords, shields, spears, armour – and loading crates onto camels.

'Looks like they're getting ready to leave,' said Daniel, grimacing at the way the objects were being treated. 'Look, they're not even bothering to use straw to pack them. They're just dumping them in the boxes.'

They lay still, surveying the scene. A huge figure was striding among the workmen, shouting and gesticulating. Dravic. Tara felt a spasm of disgust and turned her eyes away.

'What's that?'

She indicated a man down by the edge of the crater, close to the base of the pyramid rock, fiddling with what looked like a small grey box, a confusion of cables tangled around his feet. Daniel's eyes narrowed.

'Oh God!' he gasped.

'What?'

'Detonator.'

A brief pause.

'You mean . . .'

'They're going to blow it up,' he said, his face pale with horror. 'That's what Sayf al-Tha'r meant the other night. It's the only way they can guarantee the value of what they've got. The greatest find in the history of archaeology and they're going to destroy it. Oh Jesus.' He grimaced as though in physical pain.

'So what do we do?' she said.

'I don't know, Tara.' He shook his head. 'I just don't know. If we try to go down here they'll see us immediately.'

He tore his eyes away from the detonator and, raising himself, looked away to his left.

'We might be able to get down further along, beside the

camp, but it's dangerous. Someone just has to look up and that's it.'

'We've come this far. If there's a chance of getting down we should try it.'

'But what then? The detective guy could be anywhere. There are a hundred tents down there.'

'Let's just get down, eh?'

He smiled, despite himself. 'That's what I love about you, Tara. Never answer a question today that you can put off till tomorrow.'

He glanced down at the camp again and then, easing himself back from the summit, came to his feet and started along the flank of the dune. Tara followed. They had gone only a few metres when they heard something behind them: a distant thud as of drums being beaten. They stopped, turned, listened. The noise grew louder.

'What is it?' she asked.

'I don't know. It sounds like . . .'

He cocked his head, concentrating.

'Shit!'

He dragged her down onto the sand.

'Helicopters!'

They lay still, faces pressed into the dune as the sound grew steadily louder. Soon it was all around them, filling their ears. Sand started to blow off the top of the dune, sheets of it, swirling over them, the wind punching down from above. The first helicopter roared past, no more than ten metres overhead. Another went over, and another, and another, more and more of them, like a swarm of giant locusts, turning the sky dark, on and on, until eventually they had all passed and the downdraught subsided again.

For a moment the two of them lay still, then crawled back up to the ridge and took in the scene below.

Three helicopters were hovering over the valley. The others were coming in to land, half to the south of the camp, the

421

others to the north. As soon as their wheels touched the ground, workers pressed in all around, ready to start loading crates. There was a brief pause and then, as one, the cargo doors slid open. The black-robed men bent to lift their loads. As they did so, suddenly, shockingly, a vicious pulse of smoke and flame erupted from the sides of the helicopters and there was a furious crackle of gunfire.

'What the . . .'

Sayf al-Tha'r's men flew backwards, the crates and their contents shredding under the hail of bullets. The gunfire intensified, now coming from the airborne helicopters too. Black-robed figures were scattering in all directions, bullets sweeping after and over them, cutting them down as they ran. Some tried to return fire, but were picked off almost immediately by the helicopters hovering overhead. Camels thundered madly to and fro, trampling anyone who got in their way.

'It's a massacre,' Tara whispered. 'God almighty, it's a massacre.'

There were shouts and screams, and the whoosh and boom of exploding oil drums. Figures began to leap out of the helicopters, a surge of khaki, crouching low, fanning out, shooting. Black-robed bodies lay strewn across the ground like spatters of ink.

Daniel came to his feet. 'I'm going down!'

She began to stand too, but he clamped his hand to her shoulder.

'Stay here! I'll try to find the detective and get him out. Watch for us!'

Before she could say anything he was gone, sprinting along the ridge and then down towards the camp. At the bottom one of Sayf al-Tha'r's men came running from between the tents. He saw Daniel and raised his gun, but was thumped to the ground by a storm of bullets from above, the sand around him staining red with blood. Barely breaking his stride Daniel stooped, seized the man's gun and ran on into the camp, disappearing behind a veil of smoke. Tara leaned forward, trying to see where he'd gone. Suddenly her head was yanked back and she was looking up at the sky.

'I believe we have some unfinished business, Miss Mullray. I do hope you don't enjoy it.'

'You love him, don't you?' said Khalifa gently. 'Sayf al-Tha'r.'

He was sitting cross-legged on the ground. A few paces away, just inside the tent entrance, sat Mehmet, a gun balanced on his thigh, eyes fixed on Khalifa's face.

'I loved him too once, you know. More than anyone in the world. Anyone.'

The boy was silent.

'I was like you. I would have died for him. Happily. But now . . .' He dropped his head. 'Now there's nothing but pain. I hope you never have to feel that. Because to love someone and then hate them is a terrible thing.'

They sat motionless, Khalifa staring at his hands, the boy staring at Khalifa. A faint thudding came drifting into the tent, growing gradually more insistent. The boy stood and, keeping his gun trained on his prisoner, pushed back the flap.

'Looks like you'll be leaving soon,' said Khalifa.

Outside men were hurrying past. The thud of rotors grew louder, the air vibrating with the sound until eventually it was all around. The boy leaned out and looked up, smiling, enjoying the warmth of the sun and the buffeting of the wind. His prisoner was right. Soon they would be leaving. He and Sayf al-Tha'r. And soon, too, all bad things in the world were going to end. That was why they'd come out here. To make paradise on earth. To do God's bidding. He felt a surge of hope and happiness.

'I'll never hate him,' he said, turning back towards Khalifa, knowing he wasn't supposed to talk but unable to stop himself.

'Never. Whatever you say. He's a good man. No-one ever cared for me except him.' His smile widened. 'I do love him. I will always be at his side. I will never fail him.'

He stared down, eyes bright with love and innocence, and then, suddenly, there was a deafening roar and something ripped through the canvas above. It slammed the boy onto his knees, slicing the side of his head away, spilling blood and brain across his shoulder. For a second he remained like that, teetering, the smile still fixed on his bloodied mouth, and then he pitched face forward on top of Khalifa, knocking him backwards onto the floor. More bullets spat down from above, slamming into the boy's limbs and torso, causing his body to jerk like a marionette, before the helicopters trained their weapons elsewhere and the body was still, fingers bent into claws as though clinging to the edge of a precipice.

For a moment Khalifa was too shocked to move. Then slowly, gingerly, he rolled the corpse away and stood. The roof of the tent was a tangle of shredded canvas, the sandy floor pitted with craters. If the boy hadn't fallen on top of him he'd have been killed, no doubt about it. He bent and felt for a pulse, knowing it was futile, and then ran his fingertips over the boy's eyes, closing the eyelids.

'He didn't deserve you,' he whispered.

Flames had started licking up the back of the tent, filling the interior with smoke. Coughing, Khalifa heaved off his blood-sodden robes and snatched up the boy's gun. He took a final look down at the punctured corpse and then threw back the flap and ducked outside.

The camp had become an inferno. Everywhere there were flames and smoke. Shadowy figures loomed through the haze, some running, others sprawled lifeless on the ground. High above three helicopters hovered, raking the ground with gunfire. An oil drum erupted. The noise was deafening.

He took in the scene at a glance and then began running. He'd gone only thirty metres when a seam of bullets came chewing across the sand from his right, forcing him to dive behind a crate. He started to get up, then ducked again as two khaki-clad figures stepped from the smoke directly ahead, both wearing gas masks. For a moment he thought they'd seen him. Then one signalled to the other and they disappeared back into the maelstrom. Khalifa counted to three, got up and began running again.

He skirted a pile of burning drums, leaped over a smouldering corpse, then glanced up to check the position of the helicopters. One of Sayf al-Tha'r's men staggered out in front of him and collapsed onto the sand, hands clutching his stomach, blood pumping between his fingers. Khalifa dropped to his knees beside him.

'Sayf al-Tha'r,' he cried. 'Where's Sayf al-Tha'r?'

The man stared up at him, bubbles of blood frothing at the corners of his mouth.

'Please,' yelled Khalifa. 'Where's Sayf al-Tha'r?'

The man's mouth was working, but no sound was coming out. One of his hands was clawing at Khalifa's shirt, smearing it with blood. Khalifa took the hand and held it.

'Tell me! Please! Where is he?'

For a moment the man just stared at him, uncomprehending. Then, with a supreme effort, he pulled his hand free and pointed behind him, towards the excavation site.

'Rock!' He was choking. 'Rock!'

He slumped backwards, dead.

Khalifa muttered a quick prayer, came to his feet and ran on, oblivious to the turmoil around him. He reached the edge of the excavation crater and threw himself behind a bale of straw, frantically scanning the outcrop away to his left.

'Where are you, brother?' he hissed. 'Where are you?'

Initially he couldn't see him. There was too much activity, too much confusion. Then, just as he was getting desperate, a curtain of smoke momentarily parted and he spotted a small figure hunched at the base of the rock, a thick black cable snaking away from a box at his feet down into the excavation trench below. It was a hundred metres away, but there was no mistaking who it was. Nor what he was doing.

'Got you!' he cried.

He started running. There was a flash of movement to his left and he swung and fired, a black-robed figure flailing backwards into a pile of shields. Another figure half rose from behind a wooden crate and again Khalifa fired, bullets thudding into the man's chest. Seconds, that was all he had. Seconds.

He hit a heavy bank of smoke and everything went dark. He tripped over, stumbled, somehow managed to keep his footing and staggered on, fighting for breath, uncertain if he was even going in the right direction still. The smoke seemed to go on and on, and he was beginning to wonder if he'd ever get out of it again when, as suddenly as it had come, it cleared. There, just a few metres away, the rock face rearing massively above him, was Sayf al-Tha'r, finger poised above the detonator button, ready to destroy the remains of Cambyses' army. Khalifa powered forward and leaped, slamming into his brother and knocking him back against the rock.

For a moment Sayf al-Tha'r lay still, winded, his body limp, a trickle of blood leaking down his temple from where it had hit the jagged stone. Then, with a painful rasping, the breath rushed back into his lungs and he launched himself at Khalifa, tearing at his face and hair, mouth twisted into a foaming knot of fury.

'I'll kill you,' he roared. 'I'll kill you!'

He got his hands around Khalifa's head and slammed it against the rock, once, twice, three times.

'You betrayed me, Yusuf! My brother! My own brother!'

He yanked him onto his knees and punched him in the mouth.

'You can't fight me! I'm too strong. I've always been too strong. God is with me.'

He punched him again and again, and then threw Khalifa

426

sideways onto the sand, struggling upright and turning back towards the detonator. Desperately, Khalifa lashed out with his foot, catching Sayf al-Tha'r just behind the knee, buckling his legs, knocking him down. He scrambled on top of him and pinned his arms to the ground.

'I loved you!' he cried, tears filling his eyes. 'My brother. My blood. Why did you have to become like this?'

Beneath him Sayf al-Tha'r bucked and writhed.

'Because they're evil!' he spat. 'All of them. Evil.'

'They're women and children! They've done nothing to you.'

'They have! They have! They killed our father!' He got one hand free and clawed at Khalifa's eyes. 'Don't you see that? They killed our father. They ruined our lives!'

'It was an accident, Ali! It wasn't their fault!'

'It was their fault! They destroyed our family! They're evil. All of them! Devils!' With ferocious strength he threw Khalifa off and, leaping to his feet, kicked him in the ribs. 'I'll butcher them! Do you hear me? I'll butcher them! Every last one!'

He kicked again and again, shunting Khalifa downwards to the very edge of the excavation crater. Desperate, the detective looked around for something to use as a weapon. There was an ancient dagger lying on the sand nearby, its iron blade green and notched, and he grabbed it, slashing at the figure above, trying to keep him away. Immediately Sayf al-Tha'r was on him, grabbing his wrist and, knees pressing down on his chest, slowly twisting the knife so the point was aiming at Khalifa's throat.

'They think they can treat us like animals!' he screamed. 'They think they are above the law. But they're not above God's law. God sees their wickedness. And God demands vengeance!'

He began to push the dagger downwards. Khalifa tried to hold it away, arms trembling with the strain, wrists twitching, but his brother was too strong. Inch by inch the tip edged closer to his throat until eventually it was pressing right up against his Adam's apple, breaking the skin. He held it for a moment longer, and then slowly eased his grip. He gazed up into his brother's eyes. Suddenly the noise of battle receded and it was just the two of them.

'Do it,' whispered Khalifa.

Although he alone was holding the dagger, Sayf al-Tha'r's hands were trembling violently, as though he was struggling with an unseen force.

'Do it,' Khalifa repeated. 'It's time. I want to be free of you. Be with my brother again. My beautiful brother. Do it. Do it!'

He closed his eyes and braced himself. The knife pushed a hair's breadth further into his throat, a trickle of blood running down his neck. Then it stopped. There was a pause and, slowly, the blade was withdrawn. Something thudded onto the sand beside Khalifa's head and the weight was lifted from his chest. He opened his eyes again.

His brother was standing over him. They gazed at each other for a brief second, each looking deep inside the other, searching for something they could understand, something they could hold onto, and then Sayf al-Tha'r turned back towards the detonator. He took one pace, two, and then a crack of gunfire blasted him sideways against the rock and down onto the ground. For a moment he sat slumped against the stone, a ribbon of blood spilling from his mouth, hand clawing limply at the sand. Then another flurry of bullets punched into his chest and he toppled away and down, rolling over and over into the crater, where a tangle of desiccated arms and legs closed around him, as if the army was claiming him as one of its own.

Khalifa looked up, horrified. Ten metres away Daniel was standing, gun in hand. He came slowly forward and, bending, ripped the cable from the detonator. Khalifa slumped back and looked up at the sky, eyes blinded with tears.

'Oh God,' he whispered. 'Oh Ali.'

428

Dravic heaved Tara away from the ridge, the mayhem below disappearing from view behind a slope of sand. She punched and clawed at him, but he was far too strong, manhandling her as though she was no more than a rag doll. She didn't waste her breath screaming, knowing the sound would make no impression on the cacophony of gunfire and explosions that filled the air.

'I'm going to teach you a lesson you'll never forget,' he snarled. 'You've fucking ruined everything and now you're going to pay.'

He kept pulling her until they were well below the summit of the dune, then forced her down onto her face, digging his right foot into the slope and jamming his left knee into the small of her back. She tried to punch up into his crotch, but he was too tall and her fist flailed harmlessly against his thigh. He grabbed a hank of her hair and yanked her head back, exposing the pale arc of her neck. The stench of his sweat filled her nostrils like ammonia.

'By the time I've finished with you you'll wish you'd only been raped!'

'You're a brave man, Dravic.' She was choking. 'Killing women and children. A real fucking hero.'

He laughed and yanked her head back further, her vertebrae cracking in protest.

'Oh I'm not going to kill you,' he said. 'That would be far too kind. I'm just going to scar you a bit.'

He fumbled in his pocket and pulled out his trowel, holding it up in front of her eyes, showing off the well-honed edge.

'I like to think that after today you'll never look in a mirror without remembering our time together. Although you'll have to beg me to leave you an eye to look in the mirror with.'

He ran the flat edge of the trowel across her cheek and down onto her breast, slapping the tip of it against her nipple. The areola hardened slightly.

'Well, well.' He chuckled, easing back the material of her shirt to expose her chest. 'You are a dirty girl, aren't you? Seems you like it rough after all.'

'Fuck you, Dravic.'

She tried to spit at him but there was no saliva in her mouth. He leaned right down so his face was almost against hers, his lips wet and quivering.

'What shall we start with, then, eh? An ear? An eye? A nipple?'

He lifted the trowel to his mouth, licked it and then lowered it again to her breast, leaning back slightly to avoid her hand, which was vainly trying to claw at his eyes. She could feel the trowel against her skin, knew he was about to cut her and, in a final desperate effort to free herself, she clasped a handful of sand and flung it backwards into his face.

'You bitch!' he bellowed, letting go of her hair and raising his hands to his eyes. 'You fucking bitch!'

She squirmed out from under him and rolled onto her back. He was half standing, half kneeling, legs to either side of her, eyes weeping from the sand. With every ounce of strength she possessed she drew her right foot back and drove it into his crotch, pulping his testicles. He screamed – a hysterical, high-pitched woman's scream – and doubled over, coughing violently.

'I'll cut your face off.' He was slobbering. 'I'll fucking slash you.'

He stabbed at her with the trowel, but she dodged the blow and began scrambling away along the side of the dune. Dravic swarmed after her. He lunged, missed, lunged again, grabbed the corner of her shirt, and suddenly they were both rolling, tumbling madly down the slope, over and over each other, lost in a blur of sand and sky and flailing limbs.

At the bottom Tara somersaulted away from the dune and slammed onto the sand. For a moment she lay still, dizzy and disorientated, then staggered to her feet. Dravic had tumbled away from her on the lower part of the slope, and was now ten metres away. He too was coming to his feet, the sharpened trowel still clenched in his hand. Blood was dripping from his nose.

'You bitch.' He coughed. 'You fucking bitch.'

He started towards her, his feet sinking deep into the sand. Surprisingly deep, given that they were now back on level ground. Tara backed away, ready to turn and run. The giant heaved his leg out and took another step, but went in even deeper, above the knees. Suddenly he wasn't looking at her any more. He leaned back and tugged at the leg, but something seemed to be holding it from below and it wouldn't come.

'Oh no!' There was fear in his voice. 'Oh no, not that!' He looked up at Tara, face suddenly weak with terror. 'Please, not that!'

For a moment he was still, something almost childlike in his pleading eyes, and then he began to fight, face contorted in a rictus of strain and horror. He bucked up and down, trying to yank his legs free, but all he did was drive himself deeper into the quicksand, sinking to the level of his thighs, then his groin and then his waist. He leaned back, placed a hand to either side of him and pushed, but his arms just sank in too. He dragged them out, still clutching his trowel, and tried again, but with the same result. The sand was now lapping against his ribs. He began to weep.

'Help me!' he screamed at Tara. 'For God's sake, help me!' He was holding a hand out towards her, desperate. 'Please! Oh please! Help me!'

Tears were streaming down his face, his arms windmilling. He started screaming, a high bestial wail of despair, his fists beating on the sand, his upper body heaving and writhing as though he was being electrocuted. But the desert refused to ease its grip, slowly pulling him down, taking him up to the level of his armpits, then his shoulders and then all that was left of him was his huge head and the upper part of one arm, the trowel still clasped in his hand. Unable to watch any more, Tara turned away.

'Oh no!' he screamed at her back. 'No! Don't leave me alone! Please don't leave me alone! Help me! Get me out!'

She began to walk back up the dune.

'Please!' he wailed. 'I'm sorry for what I did! I'm sorry! Please don't leave me like this! Not on my own! Come back! Come back, you bloody whore! I'll kill you! I'll fucking kill you! Oh God, help me! Help me!'

His screams continued until she was about halfway up the dune, then ceased abruptly. Near the top she turned and looked back down. She could just make out the topmost part of his head still protruding above the sand and, beside it, his trowel. She shuddered and carried on to the summit.

The battle was all but over by the time Tara reached the dune-top. Fires were raging everywhere and the air was heavy with smoke and fumes, but the gunfire had dropped off and the three hovering helicopters had landed. Khaki-clad figures, obviously soldiers, were picking their way methodically through the wreckage, stopping every now and then to pump bursts of bullets into the black-robed bodies lying strewn across the ground. Camels wandered aimlessly to and fro. She couldn't see any of Sayf al-Tha'r's men still standing.

She surveyed the scene for a while, then noticed two small figures set apart from the rest, close to the base of the great black rock. They were some distance away, but one was wearing a white shirt and she was sure it was Daniel. She started down the side of the dune. At the bottom she pulled her shirt over her face against the fumes and began moving through the carnage. Soldiers were everywhere. She tried to stop one to ask what was going on, but he simply walked right past her as though she didn't exist. She tried again, with the same result, so she just continued onwards towards the pyramid rock, skirting the edge of the excavation trench and eventually coming to the two figures she'd seen from above. Daniel was nearer, sitting on the sand gazing down into the trench, a machine-gun slung across his shoulder. Khalifa was beyond him, leaning against the outcrop, a cigarette in his mouth, face swollen and bruised, shirt stained with blood. They looked up as she approached, but neither said anything.

She went to Daniel, squatted beside him and took his hand, squeezing. He squeezed back, but still said nothing. Khalifa inclined his head towards her.

'You are OK?' he asked.

'Yes. Thank you. You?'

He nodded and drew deeply on his cigarette. She wanted to ask what was going on, who the soldiers were, what it all meant, but sensed he didn't want to talk and so said nothing.

Nearby a camel was chewing at a bale of straw, the crate on its back peppered with bullet holes. The sun was up and the air was growing hotter.

Five minutes passed, ten, and then they heard the distant pulse of an approaching helicopter. It grew louder and louder and then swung in over the top of the dune opposite, hovering above the valley for a moment before coming down fifty metres from where they were sitting. Sand sprayed towards them and they turned their heads. The camel loped away along the side of the crater.

As soon as it was on the ground the pilot killed the engine and the rotors slowed. Several soldiers hurried towards it and there was the clatter of a door being slid back on its far side. They heard an indistinct babble of voices, and then four figures appeared from around the front of the helicopter. Three of them Tara recognized – Squires, Jemal and Crispin Oates. The fourth, a fat balding man dabbing at his head with a handkerchief, was a stranger. They trudged across the sand, incongruous in their suits and ties, and stopped a few metres away.

Tara and Daniel came to their feet.

'Good morning to you all,' cried Squires jovially. 'Well, this has been an adventure, hasn't it!'

42

THE WESTERN DESERT

For several seconds no-one said anything. Then the fat man spoke.

'I'll leave this to you, Squires. I've got other stuff to deal with.'

'At least introduce yourself, old boy.'

'For Christ's sake, this isn't a goddam picnic.'

He spat and, turning, waddled away, wiping at his neck with his handkerchief. Squires watched him go.

'You must forgive our American friend. A sterling fellow in his own way, but somewhat underschooled in the arts of common politeness.'

He smiled apologetically and, reaching into his pocket, produced a boiled sweet which he proceeded to unwrap, his long white fingers tugging at the cellophane like the legs of a large spider. There was an extended silence, broken eventually by Khalifa.

'It was a set-up, wasn't it?' he said quietly, flicking his cigarette down into the trench. 'The tomb, the text, all this . . .' He waved his arm around him. 'All a set-up. To lure Sayf al-Tha'r back to Egypt. Back to where you could get him.'

Squires raised his eyebrows slightly but said nothing, just finished unwrapping his sweet and popped it in his mouth.

Despite the heat Tara felt something cold creeping across her skin. 'You mean . . .' She couldn't get her thoughts clear.

'The tomb was fake,' said Khalifa. 'Not the objects. They were genuine. But the wall decoration, the text: all modern. Bait to attract Sayf al-Tha'r. Brilliant, when you think about it.'

Tara stared at Squires, a look of mingled shock and incomprehension on her face. Daniel's face was pale, his body tense, as though he was waiting for someone to hit him.

'So who exactly are you?' asked Khalifa. 'Military? Secret service?'

Squires sucked thoughtfully on his sweet. 'Elements of both really. Best not to get too specific. Suffice it to say each of us represents our respective governments in what might loosely be termed an intelligence capacity.' He brushed some fluff from his sleeve. 'So what gave it away?' he asked Khalifa.

'That the tomb wasn't real?' The detective shrugged. 'The *shabti*s from Iqbar's shop initially. They were genuine, certainly, but of a later date than the tomb they'd been taken from. Everything else was First Persian Period. They were Second. If they'd been earlier I could have understood. It would simply have meant they'd been stolen from an older tomb and reused. Later, however, just didn't make sense. How could an object from the fourth century BC end up in a tomb that had been sealed a hundred and fifty years earlier? There were possible explanations, but it got me thinking there was something not right about the whole thing. It was only when I saw the tomb itself that I was certain.'

'You clearly have an acute eye,' said Squires. 'We thought we'd got it just right.'

'You had,' said Khalifa. 'It was perfect. That's what gave it away. Something my old professor told me. No piece of ancient Egyptian art is ever entirely precise. There's always at least one

435

flaw, however tiny. I went over every inch of that tomb and there wasn't a single mistake. No drips of ink, no misaligned hieroglyphs, no correctional marks. It was faultless. Too fault-less. The Egyptians were never that exact. It had to be a fake.'

Daniel's hand slipped out of Tara's and he moved a couple of paces away from her, shaking his head, a barely perceptible smile pulling at his mouth. She wanted to go over to him, hold him, tell him he couldn't have known, but she sensed he didn't want her near.

'Even then I still wasn't sure what was going on,' continued Khalifa. 'Someone had clearly gone to a lot of trouble faking a tomb. And the purpose of that tomb seemed to be to lead who-ever found it out here into the desert. I guessed one of the security services was involved. It was them who were following me in Luxor. And the British embassy too.' He glanced at Oates. 'I couldn't see how it all fitted together, though. Still couldn't until about half an hour ago, when the helicopters arrived. Then it all fell into place.'

There was a brief burst of gunfire from somewhere on the other side of the camp. A gust of hot wind blew across them.

'Ironic, really,' sighed Khalifa. 'The amount of money you must have spent setting this whole thing up would have been enough to solve most of the problems that create people like Sayf al-Tha'r in the first place. How much did it cost you to bury this lot out here? Millions? Tens of millions? God, you must have emptied every museum storeroom in Egypt.'

Squires said nothing, sucking meditatively on his sweet. Then, suddenly, he began to chuckle.

'Oh dear, oh dear, Inspector, you do seem to have got the wrong end of the stick. The tomb was indeed a fake, as you so cleverly deduced. And, as you also realized, its purpose was to lead whoever found it out here into the desert. We didn't have to bury anything, however. It was already here.'

He noted the look on Khalifa's face and his laughter redoubled.

'Oh yes, this is the lost army of Cambyses. The real thing. Just as it was buried two and a half thousand years ago. All we did was to frame a plan around it.'

'But I thought . . .'

'That we'd planted it out here ourselves? I fear you've rather overestimated our capabilities. Even with the combined resources of the Egyptian, American and British governments we'd have struggled to fabricate something on this scale.'

Khalifa was staring out across the crater, disbelieving. The tangled remains of the ancient army stretched away as far as the eye could see – arms and legs and heads and torsos, a jumble of ossified flesh and sinew, with here and there an upturned face, eyes wide, mouth open, bobbing helplessly on a tide of shattered humanity.

'When was it found?' he whispered.

'A little over twelve months ago.' Squires smiled. 'By a young American chap. John Cadey. Spent an entire year working out here all on his own. People said he was mad, but he was convinced it was here and so it was. One of the greatest finds in the history of archaeology. Perhaps the greatest find. Just a shame he didn't live long enough to enjoy his triumph.'

Jemal had begun clicking his worry beads, the noise magnified and sharpened by the silence of the desert so that it seemed to fill the air.

'How are we doing for time, Crispin?' asked Squires.

Oates looked at his watch. 'About twenty minutes.'

'Then I think the least we can do is to offer our friends an explanation of how all this came about, don't you?'

He thrust his hands into his pockets and wandered down to the edge of the excavation crater. Beneath him Sayf al-Tha'r's body lay tangled in a filigree of arms and legs.

'It all began, I suppose, with a young man named Ali Khalifa.' He stared at the body for a moment, then turned. 'Oh yes, Inspector, we know all about your relationship. I sympathize, I really do. It can't have been easy, a decent law-abiding citizen like you being the brother of Egypt's most wanted terrorist. Not easy at all.'

Khalifa said nothing, just stared at Squires. Somewhere on the far side of the camp there was a loud whump as an oil drum exploded.

'He first came to our attention in the mid-Eighties. Prior to that he'd belonged to a variety of minor fundamentalist groups, nothing to concern us particularly. In 1987, however, he broke away and, styling himself Sayf al-Tha'r, formed his own organization. Began murdering foreign nationals. What had initially been a domestic matter suddenly became an international one. I became involved on behalf of Her Majesty's government; Massey, who you just met, acted for the Americans.'

Teams of soldiers had started collecting dead bodies and laying them out in rows alongside the excavation trench. Tara watched them, Squires's voice seeming to come from far away. Out of the corner of her eye she could see Daniel staring out across the remains of the army, expressionless, the machine-gun still clutched in his hand.

'We did everything we could to catch him,' said Squires, 'but he was clever. Always managed to stay one step ahead. We very nearly got him in '96, in an ambush down at Asyut, but he gave us the slip again and hopped across the border into the Sudan. After that it was impossible. We got plenty of his followers, but it meant nothing if the man himself was still at large. And so long as he stayed out of Egypt there was no way we were going to catch him.'

'And so you set a trap to lure him back,' said Khalifa.

'Well,' said Squires, smiling, 'it was really more a case of the trap setting itself. We merely added certain details.'

He pulled out a handkerchief and began polishing the lenses of his glasses. Jemal's worry beads were clacking faster.

'The crisis came just over a year ago when he damn nearly assassinated the American ambassador. That really caused a storm. We were put under extraordinary pressure to deliver him. All sorts of wild schemes were flying around. There was even talk of a limited nuclear strike against northern Sudan. Then, however, Dr Cadey made his amazing discovery and we started thinking along altogether different lines.'

Somewhere far off there was a scream, followed by a brief thud of gunfire.

'We'd been monitoring Cadey for some time,' explained Jemal. 'He was working close to the Libyan border and we wanted to ensure he was doing nothing to compromise national security. One day we intercepted a package he'd sent, from Siwa. It contained photographs: a corpse, weapons, clothing. There was a covering note. Just one sentence: "The lost army is no longer lost." '

'Initially we didn't appreciate the potential of the find,' said Squires. 'It was Crispin who alerted us to the possibilities. What was it you said, old boy?'

'That it was a good thing Sayf al-Tha'r hadn't discovered it or he'd be rich enough to equip an army of his own.' Oates smiled, pleased with himself.

'That was the spark. We started thinking: what if Sayf al-Tha'r *had* found it? Something that big would be too good an opportunity to miss. Complete financial independence. All his funding problems over. A godsend. And he'd almost certainly want to see it himself. It was inconceivable a man as obsessed with history as he was would stay sitting down in the Sudan while his men were uncovering a find of that magnitude. Oh no, he'd come back. And when he did . . .'

He raised his spectacles to his mouth, breathed on each lens in turn, and slowly circled his handkerchief around the glass. More and more dead bodies were being laid out alongside the excavation, like rows of big black dominoes.

'We approached Cadey and asked for his co-operation,' continued Squires, 'but he wasn't at all accommodating, and in the end we were left with no choice but to . . . remove him from the equation. Unpleasant, but the stakes were too high to let one man stand in our way.'

Tara stared at him, shaking her head, a look of mingled horror and disbelief on her face. The Englishman seemed not to notice her expression. He merely held up his glasses again, examined them and resumed polishing.

'The problem then became how to lead Sayf al-Tha'r to the army without him actually suspecting he was being led. That was the key: he had to believe it was he himself who was making the discovery. If it occurred to him for one instant the find was in any way compromised he wouldn't touch it with a barge-pole.'

'But why go to all the trouble of inventing a tomb?' asked Khalifa. 'Why not just plant someone in his organization who claimed to know where the army was?'

'Because he would never have believed it,' replied Squires. 'This isn't the Theban Hills, where people are stumbling over new finds all the time. This is the middle of nowhere. It's inconceivable someone would just happen to find the army.'

'Cadey did.'

'But Cadey was a professional archaeologist. Sayf al-Tha'r's people are *fellahin*, peasants. They'd have no business out here. It just wouldn't have rung true.'

'Whereas the tomb of someone who'd survived the army would?'

'In a bizarre way, yes. It was somehow so outlandish it could only be real. Sayf al-Tha'r would have been suspicious, of course. Who wouldn't be? But not as suspicious as he would have been about someone claiming to have found the army itself.'

He gave his glasses a final buff and returned his handkerchief to his pocket. Khalifa pulled out his cigarettes and removed one from the pack. There was a smouldering crate nearby and, crossing to it, he held the cigarette tip against the glowing wood.

'I really can't bear to see you having to light your cigarettes like that, old boy,' said Squires.

Khalifa shrugged. 'Dravic took my lighter.'

'How very thoughtless of him.' Squires turned to Jemal. 'Be a good fellow and lend the inspector some matches, would you?'

The Egyptian pulled a box from his pocket and threw it across.

'Has anyone seen our friend Dravic, by the way?' asked Squires. 'He seems to be keeping a remarkably low profile.'

Tara continued staring at the row of black-robed bodies. 'He's dead,' she said, her voice dull, beyond caring. 'On the other side of the dune. Quicksand.'

There was a brief pause, and then Squires smiled. 'Well, that's one less problem for us to deal with.' He pulled another sweet from his pocket and began tweaking at the wrapper. 'Where was I?'

'The tomb,' said Khalifa.

'Ah yes, the tomb. Well, there was no way we could have dug one from scratch. That would have been wholly impractical. Fortunately there was an existing one that fitted the bill perfectly. Right period and design. Empty. Undecorated. And, most importantly, unknown to anyone aside from a handful of Theban necropolis specialists. Sayf al-Tha'r's people certainly wouldn't have heard of it, which was, as I'm sure you'll appreciate, crucial if the whole thing was to work.'

Part of the sweet was stuck to the wrapper and he stopped for a moment to pick away the cellophane.

'Even with a readymade tomb it still took us almost a year to complete the job.' He sighed. 'Painstaking doesn't get even close to describing it. The decoration had to be created from scratch and then chemically aged to make it appear two and a half thousand years old. And, of course, it all had to be done under conditions of absolute secrecy. Believe me, it was a huge operation. There were times when we thought it would never be finished.'

He finally managed to free the sweet and slipped it into his mouth, rolling the wrapper into a ball and putting it in his pocket.

'Still, we got there in the end. The decoration was completed and the tomb stocked with a selection of funerary items from the storerooms of Luxor and Cairo museums, with a few bits from the army itself. All that remained was to tip off one of Sayf al-Tha'r's informants and wait for his men to decipher the inscription.'

'Except that someone got there first,' said Khalifa.

'The one thing we hadn't expected,' said Squires, shaking his head. 'A million to one chance. Ten million to one. Even then it needn't have been a complete disaster. They might have just taken a few objects and left the decoration intact. As it was, they hacked out the one bit of text that really mattered so that when Sayf al-Tha'r's people did get there the tomb was, from our point of view at least, completely useless. Devastating, really.'

'Although not as devastating as it was for Nayar and Iqbar,' said Khalifa quietly.

'No,' conceded Squires. 'Their deaths were most regrettable. As was that of your father, Miss Mullray.'

Tara looked up, eyes bright with hatred. 'You used us,' she spat. 'You let them kill my father and you didn't think twice about risking our lives too. You're as bad as Sayf al-Tha'r.'

Squires smiled benignly. 'A slight exaggeration, I think, although given the circumstances a perfectly understandable one. Your father's death was, sadly, beyond our control, but yes, we did use you. As with Dr Cadey, we concluded the well-being of the individual must be subordinated to the wider interests of society. Distasteful, but necessary.'

He was silent for a while, sucking on his sweet.

'Initially we had no idea what had gone wrong with the plan. We knew that Dravic had discovered the tomb, but for some reason he didn't seem to be taking the bait. When we found out about the piece of missing text we were faced with an extraordinary dilemma. It was too late to abort the whole thing, but neither could we do anything overt to help Sayf al-Tha'r. We had no choice but to let events take their course.'

Another gust of wind blew over them, stronger than before, making the dune behind hiss and whisper. The noise of Jemal's worry beads slowed and then petered out altogether. Daniel was biting his lip.

'Your arrival at once both complicated the situation and offered a potential way out of it,' said Squires to Tara. 'You were obviously suspicious about your father's death and there was a danger you might start kicking up a fuss. At the same time there was the possibility that, if properly handled, you might be able to help us locate the missing piece and, subsequently, restore it to Sayf al-Tha'r without him ever becoming aware of our own involvement. And that's exactly how it worked out. You played your part perfectly.'

Tara's eyes were burning with resentment. She felt violated, abused. Daniel glanced briefly back at her, then turned away again.

'Admittedly it was touch and go for a while. Had you just let them take the piece at Saqqara everything would have been a lot easier. As it was, you insisted on running away with it, which forced us into a very delicate game. If you'd gone to the authorities or come to us at the embassy, Sayf al-Tha'r would have backed off immediately. We therefore had to persuade you to go it alone. Hence our little charade about an antiquities smuggling ring.'

'Samali,' she groaned.

'One of our operatives, yes. And a very fine performance he gave too.'

'Jesus Christ.'

Her shoulders slumped. Khalifa wanted to go to her, comfort her, but sensed the moment wasn't right and stayed where he was.

'Even then our fortunes were balanced on a knife edge,' continued Squires. 'The whole thing could still have fallen apart. The inspector caused us more than a few worries and it was by no means easy keeping you under control, Miss Mullray.

Although fortunately we had someone on the inside and that rather helped things along.'

He smiled, but said no more. The soldiers had finished laying out the lines of black-robed bodies and were now standing around aimlessly at the edge of the camp. Everything, suddenly, had gone very quiet and very still. There was something expectant in the air, a tension. Squires's final words seemed to repeat over and over in Tara's head. Someone on the inside. Someone on the inside. Slowly her face lifted. Already pale, it had assumed a sort of horrified transparency.

'Oh no,' she whispered. 'Oh, please God, no.' She looked over at Daniel. 'It was you, wasn't it?'

He stared out across the excavation, face blank, eyes roving over the drifts of twisted corpses.

'You knew,' she whispered. 'All along you knew.'

He continued gazing at the army for a moment, then slowly turned to her. There was guilt in his eyes, and regret, but behind them something harder, more brutal. She felt, suddenly, as if she didn't know him.

'I'm sorry, Tara,' he said, his tone expressionless, 'but it was my concession. They were going to give it back, you see. Let me excavate again.'

She stared at him, too shocked to move. She was dimly aware of the others, especially Khalifa, who seemed to have come forward half a step, but even he felt far away. It was as though she was standing in a tunnel with Daniel at the other end and everyone else on the outside. She opened her mouth to try to speak, but no words came out, just a sort of breathless choke. He stared at her for a moment, then turned away again, gazing down at the confusion of fragmented corpses below.

'When?' she managed to whisper.

'When did I get involved?' He shrugged. 'About a year ago. They came to me, told me about the army, how they wanted to use it to lure Sayf al-Tha'r back to Egypt. Said if I helped them I could dig in the valley again. I hadn't excavated for six months by that point. I would have done anything. Anything.'

A momentary spasm flashed across his face, as if there was a part of him that despised what he was saying. It was gone almost immediately and the coldness returned. He stooped and picked up a dagger, the one Khalifa had fought with earlier, turning it over in his hands.

'It was me who came up with the idea of a soldier surviving the disaster. I remembered the Dymmachus graffito in KV9, and created a story around him. I knew of an existing tomb that was perfect, way out in the hills. Did all the work myself. A little bit each day, slowly covering the walls.' He smiled.

'I was happy, in a funny sort of way. Being down there on my own. Painting the walls, creating the text, building up the story. Really happy. And the end result . . . I surprised even myself. I remember the day I finished, just sitting down there and staring at it and thinking, this is a masterpiece. A bloody masterpiece. Although, of course, I can see now it was just a bit too good. And I should have noticed the *shabti*s were the wrong date. Stupid of me. Careless.' He looked at Khalifa, who stared back at him, stony faced.

'There was a dagger?' said the detective.

'Ah, you saw that, did you?' Daniel grinned. 'I couldn't resist it. The leather binding was loose so I pulled it away and scratched Dymmachus son of Menendes on the metal underneath, in Greek letters. It was just a bit of fun, really. An extra piece of authentication.'

Khalifa dragged on his cigarette, shaking his head contemptuously. There was a long pause.

'That was all I was supposed to do,' said Daniel eventually. 'Just create the tomb. But then the piece of text went missing and you came on the scene, and they found out I knew you. They wanted me to contact you, watch you. I wasn't happy about it, but then what could I do? It was my concession. And, to be honest, I wanted to know what had gone wrong as much as they did. The tomb was my creation, you see. I was . . .

completely involved with it. So I left the note at your father's apartment, knowing you'd recognize the writing.'

Tears had started to trickle down Tara's cheeks. She felt as if her clothes had been ripped off and her skin too, leaving her completely naked, allowing everyone to see inside her. She hugged herself.

'If you'd just let them have the piece at Saqqara everything would have been OK,' he said. 'I tried to tell you. But you wouldn't listen. And after that . . .' He raised his hands helplessly.

Tara's tears were coming faster now. There was a broken, disjointed look on her face, as though her features had somehow fragmented and been rearranged in the wrong order.

'You knew about Samali?' Her voice was hoarse.

Daniel nodded. 'As soon as I'd found out what the piece was I called Squires. From the zoo, when I said I was calling my hotel. He told me what to do.'

'And going to Luxor. Walking up into the hills. You knew Dravic would be there? That you were taking us into a trap?'

'What could I do? I had to get the text back to them. It was the only way.'

Suddenly she heard her father's voice echoing out of the past, filling her head: 'You get the impression he'd cut off his own hand if he thought it might further his knowledge of the subject. Or anyone else's hand, for that matter. He's a fanatic.'

'Why didn't you just tell me?' she said, choking.

He dropped to his haunches and laid the dagger back on the ground carefully, not wanting to damage it in any way.

'I tried to,' he said. 'When we were standing on top of El Qurn. Do you remember? But when it came to it I couldn't. I was in too deep.'

He looked up at her and for a brief moment there was something approaching genuine sorrow in his eyes.

'I never meant you to get hurt, Tara,' he said, the vaguest hint of gentleness creeping into his voice. 'When we saw Dravic up on the hills . . . even at that late stage I had second thoughts. I knew they'd have someone watching the tomb, that if we went down there we'd be caught. That's why I tried to go on my own, to leave you out of it. But you wouldn't let me. You insisted on coming.'

'All those things you said . . .' She was trembling uncontrollably. 'All that shit about still caring for me . . .'

'It wasn't shit, Tara. I meant it. It's just that . . .'

He stared at her for a moment and then came to his feet. Suddenly, as if a light had been switched off, the warmth in his eyes was gone and there was nothing, just an icy blankness.

'What?' she whispered. 'It's just that what, Daniel?'

He shrugged. 'My concession is more important.'

For a moment she stared at him, silent, crushed. Then, with a guttural cry of pain and betrayal, she flew at him, clawing at his face, scratching the skin.

'What sort of person are you?' she screamed, hysterical. 'What sort of monster that you could do something like that? I could have been raped, you bastard! Killed! And for what? For the sake of a few dead bodies! For the sake of your fucking concession! For that you'd stand by and watch me die! You're sick! You're not human! You're . . . disgusting! You disgust me! Disgust me!'

He grabbed her wrists and held her away from him, struggling with her. She fought for a moment longer, and then, suddenly, her anger drained away and she staggered back against the rock, gasping for breath, face wet with tears.

'You bastard,' she gasped. 'You filthy, lying bastard. I could have been killed.'

Khalifa went over and laid his hand gently on her shoulder, but she shrugged it off. Oates and Squires exchanged a brief glance, and Jemal's worry beads began clacking again. Daniel raised his hand to his face, glaring at her.

For a long moment no-one spoke or moved. Then there was the crunch of approaching footsteps and Massey came up.

'Did I miss something?' he asked, looking at each of them in turn.

447

'Dr Lacage and Miss Mullray have just been . . . discussing the events of the past week,' said Squires. The American noted the welts on Daniel's face and burst out laughing.

'Jesus, looks like she gave him a right pussy-whipping! You should give her a job!'

The wind had started up again, blowing steadily down the valley, flurrying sand around their feet and ankles. Oates looked at his watch.

'We should be going, sir.'

'Righty-ho,' nodded Squires. 'There's just a couple of details to round off. Why don't the three of you wait for me in the Chinook, eh?'

Oates, Jemal and Massey turned and began walking towards the helicopter. Squires smoothed back his hair, which had been blown about by the wind.

'Not a great deal more to tell you, really,' he said. 'Once Dravic had the location of the army Sayf al-Tha'r started flying in men and equipment from Libya. We just let them get on with it; monitored the whole thing by satellite. We got word he'd crossed the border a couple of days ago and initially we planned to move in tomorrow evening. As it was, Inspector Khalifa's little odyssey forced us to pounce a day early. The Egyptian air force intercepted his helicopters as they came over the border. We took their place and . . . well, I think you know the rest. Sayf al-Tha'r is dead, his organization is destroyed, the world is for the moment a safer place.'

Khalifa sighed wearily. 'And you think that's the end? You think that by killing him you solve the problem? There are dozens of Sayf al-Tha'rs out there. Hundreds of them. Maybe it's time you asked yourselves why.' He stared at Squires for a moment and then, shaking his head, took a couple of steps forward, gazing out at the rows of corpses lying beside the crater. 'And what'll happen to them?' he asked.

'The bodies? Oh, we'll bury them somewhere out in the desert. Somewhere they'll never be found.'

'And the army?' Khalifa nodded at the jumbled morass of bodies.

'We'll leave it as it is,' said Squires, waving a hand dismissively. 'Let the desert cover it over again. In a few months it will have disappeared. And then, who knows, maybe one day someone else will come along and make the greatest discovery in the history of archaeology. Or the greatest rediscovery.'

He winked at Daniel, who stared at him impassively. Khalifa's cigarette had gone out and, taking the matches from his pocket, he tried to light one. The wind was blowing too hard, however, and he was unable to produce a flame. He struck one, two, three and then gave up.

'And that, as they say, is well and truly that,' said Squires with a sigh. 'It's been a difficult road, but it all seems to have worked out very nicely in the end. Indeed, in a curious way the saga of the missing piece probably helped us. Sayf al-Tha'r was so desperate to get it back that it never once occurred to him the tomb itself might be a fake. So in many ways we owe you a sincere debt of gratitude.'

He smiled warmly and crunched the remainder of his sweet.

'I'm going back to the helicopter now,' he said, looking over at Daniel again. 'I'll leave the final farewells to you. Wouldn't want to get in the way or anything. Miss Mullray, Inspector Khalifa, it's been a pleasure. Really it has.'

He nodded at the two of them and, raising his hand in farewell, set off across the sand, hair blowing in the wind.

'So what now?' asked Tara.

'Now', said Khalifa, 'I think Dr Lacage is going to kill us.'

43

THE WESTERN DESERT

Daniel swung the gun from his shoulder and pointed it at them.

'There was no way they could let us go,' said Khalifa. 'Not after all they've told us. We know too much. They couldn't risk it getting out.'

'Daniel?' Tara's voice was bewildered, lost.

'Like the inspector says, you know too much.' His voice was hard, his eyes empty. 'I can't let anything get in the way, not after I've come this far.'

He pointed with the muzzle, indicating they should move down to the edge of the trench.

'Perhaps I should have said no when they first asked me to help them,' he said. 'Not got involved. But then it didn't have to end like this, did it? If the piece hadn't gone missing every-thing would have been all right. Who knows, Tara, maybe we would have met again under different circumstances.'

They had reached the trench. He motioned them to turn round so their backs were to him. A sea of broken corpses stretched away in front of them, rising and falling and swelling and churning, as if twisted by some mysterious current. Beside her Tara could hear Khalifa reciting a prayer. Involuntarily her hand came out and clutched his.

'I don't expect you to understand,' said Daniel. 'I don't really understand myself. All I know is that it was unbearable not being allowed to excavate any more. Watching from the sidelines while other people got the concessions to dig the valley. My valley. People who didn't know a fraction of what I know. Feel a fraction of the passion. Stupid people. Ignorant people. And all the while the fear that maybe they'd find something. Discover a new tomb. Beat me to it. It was . . . horrible.'

The wind was tugging angrily at Tara's hair, although she was hardly aware of it.

I'm going to be shot, she thought. I'm going to die.

'I dream of it, you know,' said Daniel, smiling faintly. 'Finding a new tomb. Dravic was right. It is an addiction. Imagine it – breaking through a doorway into a chamber that was sealed five centuries before the birth of Christ. Imagine the intensity of something like that. Nothing could ever come close to it.'

Away to their right there was a roar and a whine as the blades of the Chinook started to rotate, cutting at the wind. Other helicopters were also starting their engines. Soldiers began filing back through the camp and clambering inside them.

'It's funny,' Daniel shouted, raising his voice to be heard above the scream of the motors and the hiss of the wind, 'when we were in the tomb, you and me, Tara, when I was looking at the images on the walls, translating the text, even though I knew it was a fake, that it was me who'd done it all, there was still a part of me that felt it was real. Like I'd discovered something truly unique. Something wonderful. Wonderful things.'

He began laughing.

'That's what Carter said, you know. When he looked into the tomb of Tutankhamun for the first time. Carnarvon said, "What can you see?" and Carter replied, "Wonderful things." That's why I have to keep digging, you see. Because there are so many wonderful things still to find.'

There was a click as he drew back the bolt of the gun. Khalifa's hand tightened around Tara's.

'Try not to be afraid, Miss Mullray,' he said. 'God is with us. He will protect us.'

'You really believe that?'

'I have to believe that. Otherwise what is there? Only despair.'

He turned to her and smiled. 'Trust in him, Miss Mullray. Trust in anything. But never despair.'

The helicopters began lifting off, the wind buffeting them back and forth. Tara and Khalifa stood looking at each other. She didn't feel any fear, just a sort of exhausted resignation. She was going to die. That was it. There was no point in arguing or struggling.

'Goodbye, Inspector,' she said, squeezing his hand, the wind pummelling furiously all around her. 'Thank you for trying to help me.'

A sheet of sand blew up into her face and the sun seemed to dim. She turned her head out of the wind, closed her eyes and waited for the bullets.

The desert possesses many forces with which to subdue those who trespass into its secret wastes. It can throw down a heat so blistering that skin shrivels like paper in a flame, eyeballs boil, bones seem to liquefy. It can deafen with its silence, crush with its emptiness, warp time and space so that those passing through it lose all sense of where or when or even who they are. It will grant visions of heart-leaping beauty – a cascading waterfall, a balmy oasis – only to snatch them away again the moment you reach out towards them, sending you mad with the agony of unrealized desires. It will raise mountainous dunes to block your path, shift itself into labyrinths from which you have no hope of escaping, suck you downwards into the unfathomable depths of its belly. Of all the weapons in its fearful armoury, however, none is more powerful, more absolute in its destruction, than that which they call the Wrath of God: sandstorm.

It struck now, suddenly, uncontrollably, out of nowhere. One moment there was the wind, the next the desert around them seemed to erupt, a million million tons of sand geysering upwards into the sky so that the sun was blocked out and the air became solid. The force of it was unimaginable. Crates bounced along the ground, bales of straw disintegrated, oil drums were sucked up into the air and spun around like leaves. One helicopter was smashed against the side of a dune, two more collided with each other, exploding in a ball of flame that was extinguished almost as soon as it had flared by a choking blanket of sand. Men were thumped to the floor, a camel cartwheeled down the valley, heads were ripped from emaciated corpses and sent bounding along the ground like giant brown marbles. The noise was excruciating.

Tara was swept forward and down into the crater, crashing into a tangled foliage of corpses. Bones crunched and splintered beneath her, desiccated skin ripped like parchment, teeth snapped from jaw sockets. She was rolled over and over, withered arms and legs seeming to kick and jostle her, sunken faces looming on all sides, until eventually she came to a halt, face buried in an ossified stomach cavity, a shrivelled mouth pressed hard against her neck as if kissing her. For a moment she lay still, dazed, horrified, and then struggled to her knees and tried to stand. The wind was too strong and punched her down immediately. She began to crawl, palms crunching through backs and chests, feet scrambling on a tangled ladder of spines and skulls, bones snapping beneath her like twigs. Sand scoured her flesh and jammed its way up her nostrils and into her ears so that it felt as if she was drowning.

Somehow she reached the top of the crater and flopped onto her belly, pulling the material of her shirt across her mouth. Behind her the army was fast disappearing, swamped beneath a rising tide of sand. At the same time, around the rim of the crater, dozens of new bodies were appearing. A leathery hand emerged from the sand right in front of her face, the fingers splayed as if reaching out to grab her. Spears jabbed upwards; a horse seemed to leap from the side of the dune; a head bobbed up but was then immediately buried again. The howling of the wind was like fifty thousand voices screaming in battle.

She tried to look for Daniel and Khalifa, eyes narrowed to thin slits against the storm, but she could see nothing, just a blinding fuzz of sand. There was a muffled roar away to her left and she cranked her head round towards it, neck muscles fighting against the wind's torque. The roar grew louder and suddenly a helicopter loomed directly overhead, impossibly low, spinning madly round and round, out of control. For a split second she caught sight of Squires's face in one of the windows, mouth wide open, screaming, and then it spun away again, pirouetting insanely towards the deeper darkness that was the side of the pyramid rock. There was a momentary flash of light and heat, a rage of agonized metal and then nothing. She came up onto her knees and, head bowed, began to crawl forward.

After a few feet she stopped and tried to shout out, but such was the intensity of the storm she couldn't even hear her own voice. She crawled a bit further and stopped again, and this time caught a vague blur of movement ahead and to her right. She angled towards it.

They were nearer than she had thought and after only a few metres she was on them. Daniel was astride Khalifa, both hands clutching the machine-gun, which he was trying to point at the detective's head. Khalifa had one hand on the muzzle of the gun, holding it away, and the other at Daniel's throat.

Neither of them noticed her approaching and, struggling up to them, she seized a fistful of Daniel's hair and yanked, toppling him to the ground. The three of them grappled together, flattened by the gale, eyes and mouths filled with sand. For a moment Tara and Khalifa managed to pin Daniel down, but a furious claw of wind tore the detective backwards and away.

Daniel grasped for the gun, which had fallen a metre to his left. Tara lunged for it too, but Daniel lashed out at her, knocking her to the floor, her head narrowly missing the point of a sword. Khalifa had battled back up onto his knees and was crawling towards them, but the wind held him back and allowed Daniel to seize the gun, swing it round and slam the butt into the side of Khalifa's head, knocking him sideways on top of Tara.

A billow of sand momentarily blinded them. When they looked up again it was to see that Daniel had squirmed away almost to the edge of sight. As they watched, he fought his way up onto his knees and then, in defiance of the gale, which was blowing directly into his face, onto his feet, staggering as if drunk, wrestling the gun muzzle towards them. Khalifa looked around frantically. There was a skeletal arm lying on the ground beside him, snapped from its shoulder, and, in desperation, he seized it around the wrist, swung it back and launched it at Daniel. It was a weak throw, but with the wind behind it the arm gathered speed, cartwheeling through the air and slamming into Daniel's throat with the force of a sledgehammer. He staggered backwards into the storm, disappearing from sight. Khalifa rolled onto his front and began crawling after him. Tara followed.

At first they couldn't find him. Then, after they had gone about ten metres, Khalifa tugged her arm and pointed. She followed the line of his finger, shielding her eyes with her hands, and there, on the ground in front of them, emerging from the gloom as though from beneath a curtain, were Daniel's jeans-clad legs, one booted foot twitching slightly, everything from the waist up lost in the murk. They paused for a moment, uncertain, and then continued cautiously forward as the rest of the body slowly hove into view.

'Oh Jesus,' mumbled Tara when she could see all of it. 'Oh Christ.'

He was lying flat on his back, arms flapped out to either side of him, a sword thrusting upwards through his sternum where he had tumbled backwards onto it. It was a short sword, its blade inscribed with the image of a serpent, the sinuous body coiling around the blood-smeared metal as though slithering from the rent in Daniel's chest. The serpent's fangs, Tara noticed, opened up around the sword's tip as though adding their own bite to that of the blade.

'Oh Jesus,' she repeated, turning her head away. 'Oh Daniel.'

For a moment she sat slumped on the ground, oblivious to the tumult around her. She felt as though everything in her life had broken and disintegrated. Her father was gone, Daniel was gone – it was as if the shell of her past had been ripped away, leaving her raw and exposed. For so long she had defined herself by her relationships with these two men, father and lover. And now they were no more and she was . . . what? Unformed, somehow. Atomized. She couldn't see how she would ever put herself back together again.

'Miss Mullray!' Khalifa had pressed his mouth right against her ear, shouting to be heard above the raging bellow of the storm. 'We can't stay here, Miss Mullray,' he yelled. 'We'll be buried. We must go up. Up.'

She didn't respond.

'Please, Miss Mullray,' he cried. 'We must go up. It's our only chance.'

He could sense that she had lost the will to go on, was about to give up and, seizing her face in both hands, he turned it towards him.

'Please!' he screamed, his voice shredded by the maelstrom. 'Be strong. You must be strong!'

She stared at him, sand scouring so viciously across her face she thought it would scrub away all her features, and then nodded. He took her hand and, slowly, they began to crawl away. After a few metres she looked back at Daniel's body, his open mouth already filled with sand, and then the chaos seemed to thicken around him and he was gone. She forced her head round again and struggled forward through the madness.

It seemed impossible the storm could grow any more violent. Now, however, just when it appeared to have reached the apex of its fury, it tapped deep into some hidden reserve of energy and unleashed a vortex of sand and wind to which everything so far seemed to have been no more than a gentle prelude. Unimaginable forces raged all around them. Tara felt as if the clothes would be ripped from her body, the flesh from her back, the meat from her bones, and the bones themselves then twisted and broken and pummelled to dust. She had no idea where she was going or why. She had no idea about anything at all. She just kept moving forward automatically, driven by some imperative beyond reason or thought. Up. That was all she knew. Up.

They reached the foot of the dune and began to climb, creeping on their hands and knees, inching slowly out of the valley, every movement a torment of exhausted muscle and sinew. The air was now so thick with sand that to have raised their eyelids even a hair's breadth would have been to have their pupils instantly scoured, and so they went forward with their eyes closed, feeling their way solely by the gradient of the land. Each clasped the other's hand, lifting and lowering their arms in unison, while with their other hand they kept their shirts pulled close across their mouths, breathing in short sharp gasps. Such was the blasting of the wind that even on their knees it was hard to keep their balance.

How she kept going Tara had no idea. Within seconds she was exhausted and every inch exhausted her further. More than anything on God's earth she wanted to drop down onto her face and lie flat and still.

Somehow, however, she kept crawling, forcing herself inexorably upwards, further and further, until eventually, just as her legs and arms began to buckle, the slope beneath her started to ease and flatten. She struggled on for another couple of metres and then slumped face forward onto the summit of the dune. She heard Khalifa's voice coming to her as if from far away.

'Keep your head down, Miss Mullray. And try to . . . how do you say . . . wiggle your body as much as possible. It will stop the sand piling up on top of you.'

She squeezed his hand to show she'd heard and buried her face in the crook of her arm, the storm howling over her, sand lashing in from all sides like a million biting insects.

I must wiggle, she thought to herself. Wiggle, girl, wiggle!

She kicked her legs feebly and raised her hips up and down a couple of times, but she was too exhausted and after a few moments her body sagged and was still. She was overwhelmed with a sudden, delicious sense of peace, as though she was rolled up in a swathe of black velvet. Images drifted through her mind: her parents, Daniel, Jenny, the necklace her father had given her for her fifteenth birthday. She remembered how she had woken to find an envelope on her mantelpiece, how she had followed the treasure trail up into the attic, how she had laughed with delight as she opened the old trunk and found the necklace hidden deep inside it. She laughed now, the sound growing stronger and stronger until it drowned out the storm and filled the entire world. She gave herself up to the laughter, allowing it to wash over her, to smother her, and then suddenly there was a blinding flash of white light and she remembered no more.

44

Epilogue

Inspector Khalifa was asleep beside his wife, cascades of soft black hair falling across his face. It was so warm, that hair, so fragrant, and as he always did when they were in bed together, he burrowed his way into it, taking long, deep breaths as if to draw its perfume way down into his lungs.

Rather than filling him with calmness and delight, it made him choke uncontrollably. He coughed and spluttered, fighting for breath, and eventually rolled away from her and came unsteadily to his feet. Sand showered from his back and shoulders, his wife and bed evaporated. He was standing on top of a dune, in the middle of a desert, with a blazing sun overhead and a mouthful of sand. The storm, it seemed, had blown over.

He spat and coughed for several seconds, clearing his windpipe, and then suddenly remembered Tara. She'd been beside him when they'd reached the summit of the dune, he was sure of that. Now there was no sign of her. He dropped to his knees and began scrabbling in the sand.

Initially he could find nothing. Perhaps she'd been rolled

further along, he thought, or been dragged back down into the valley. He redoubled his efforts, but to no effect, and was beginning to despair when suddenly his hand snagged on something solid. He scraped furiously around it, scooping out armful after armful of sand until he'd revealed a small trainered foot. He seized the ankle and pulled. The body was clamped tight in the mouth of the dune, and he resumed digging, burrowing like a rabbit, revealing first one leg, then another.

'Come on,' he hissed to himself. 'Faster! Dig!'

He seized both ankles and pulled again, but still she wouldn't come. He changed his angle of attack, working down from above rather than the side, gouging out the sand and flinging it away between his legs. He revealed a shoulder, the back of her head and her left arm. Yanking the wrist free, he felt for a pulse. Nothing.

'Please, Allah,' he cried, voice echoing across the desert. 'Please let her live!'

He clawed off the remaining sand and rolled her onto her back. Her eyes were closed, her lips and mouth thick with yellowy grains, like biscuit crumbs. He felt for a pulse again but still got nothing and so he rolled her back onto her front, clasped his arms around her midriff and yanked, doubling her up. He repeated the movement, jerking her with all his strength, willing her to live.

'Come on!' he yelled. 'Breathe! Breathe, dammit!'

He bent his knees and jerked again and this time, suddenly, her body convulsed as though a bolt of electricity had been driven through it. For a moment she was still, hanging from his arms as though across a swing, and then she began to splutter and choke. He yanked one final time and a pat of sandy vomit spurted from her mouth onto the dune top. She coughed and retched, struggled, and drew in a deep gasping breath of air. He laid her down gently.

'Thank you, Allah,' he whispered. 'Thank you. Thank you.'

She lay for a while recovering, coughing and gagging and

breathing, and then, wiping her sleeve across her mouth, rolled into a sitting position and looked over at Khalifa, who was squatting a few feet away. He nodded at her, she nodded at him, they smiled, and then turned their attention to the valley below.

The army was gone. Everything was gone. There were no tents, no helicopters, no crates, no corpses. Nothing. All was buried beneath a smooth duvet of new-laid sand, as though it had never existed. Only the pyramid rock remained, vast and silent, spearing upwards into the pale morning sky, surrounded once more by a pristine expanse of desert. It had, thought Khalifa, a vaguely satisfied air about it, as though it had witnessed a great drama and was content with the conclusion.

They sat in silence for some while, staring out across the desert, struggling to come to terms with all that had happened, and then Khalifa spoke.

'The mobile phone?'

Tara patted her pockets, but they were empty. 'It must have fallen out.'

'The GPS unit?'

'Daniel had that.'

He nodded and leaned back against the slope of the dune. 'Then I fear we might have a problem getting back.'

'How far are we?'

'Not that far. About a hundred and twenty kilometres to the nearest settlement. But we have no idea of the precise direction. Half a degree out and we could end up walking all the way to the Sudan.'

'Dymmachus made it.'

'Only in Dr Lacage's imagination.'

'Of course.' She smiled. 'I forgot.'

He fumbled in his pocket and pulled out his cigarettes, proffering the pack to Tara.

'You haven't got any ice cubes, have you?' she asked.

'Ice cubes?'

'I'm trying to give up smoking, you see, and whenever I get the urge I suck an ice cube instead.'

'Ah, I see. No, I'm afraid I don't have any ice cubes.'

'Then I guess I'll just have to have the cigarette.'

She reached out, pulled one from the pack and put it between her lips. Khalifa leaned forward and lit it for her.

'That's a hundred pounds I owe my best friend,' she said, closing her eyes and drawing deeply on the filter. 'We had a bet I couldn't last a year without smoking. I did eleven months and two weeks.'

'I am impressed,' said Khalifa. 'I have smoked a pack a day since I was fifteen.'

'Jesus, you'll kill yourself!'

They looked at each other and then burst out laughing.

'I guess it doesn't really matter how many cigarettes I smoke from now on,' said Khalifa.

'You don't think we've got any chance then?'

'No, I don't.'

'I thought you said something about never despairing?'

'I did. In this case, however, I see no other option.'

They laughed again, genuine laughter, not forced. Tara took another deep pull on her cigarette. She didn't think she'd ever tasted anything so delicious.

'You know it's funny,' she said, 'but I actually feel happy. I'm going to die of thirst in the middle of a desert and all I want to do is laugh. It's like . . .'

'A weight has been lifted,' said Khalifa.

'Exactly. I feel clean. Free. Like I own my life again.'

'I understand. I am the same. The past has been settled and forgotten. We can look forward.'

'Although not very far.'

'No,' he agreed. 'Not very far. But forward at least.' He took another long draw on his cigarette. 'I shall miss my wife and children.'

They gazed out across the desert, smoking, silent. The sun

heaved itself slowly upwards and the air began to shimmer. All around dunes rippled away to the horizon. It was curious to think that only a while ago the world had been turning itself inside out. Everything now seemed so serene and ordered. It was beautiful, thought Tara, the land's curvaceous symmetry, the shifting colours of the sand. Before she'd looked on the desert as her prison. Now, even though she was going to die out here, she felt curiously at one with it.

She finished her cigarette and flicked it aside. The tobacco had made her head swim, so that as she looked down it seemed as if the sand below was trembling. Or at least a small patch of it was, close to the base of the great rock. She took a couple of deep breaths, closed her eyes and looked again. The tremble was still there, a sort of bulging, as though the desert was gasping for breath. She nudged Khalifa and nodded towards it. He frowned and came to his feet. She did the same.

'What is it?' she asked.

'I don't know. It's strange. Like water boiling.'

'Is it the heat?'

'Doesn't look like it.'

'Sinking sand?'

'I don't think so.'

He gazed for a moment longer and then started cautiously down the side of the dune, Tara following. The bulging was growing more violent now, the sand swirling and throbbing as if a giant foot was being ground into the valley floor. It stopped suddenly, started again, stopped, and then, with a loud, bugle-like bellow, the desert's surface sheered open and a large ungainly figure heaved itself upwards into the daylight, sand showering all around it. Khalifa cried out in amazement and began running down the side of the dune.

'Jamal!' he laughed. 'Praise be to Allah! Jamal! Camel!'

He reached the bottom of the slope and slowed, anxious not to frighten the creature. It seemed unfazed by his presence, and allowed him to come up and take its harness.

'Welcome, my friend,' he said, stroking its velvety muzzle. 'We are happy you could join us.'

He turned towards Tara.

'It seems my pessimism was premature, Miss Mullray. My friend here can smell water five hundred miles away. Whichever is the nearest oasis, he will lead us to it.'

He came up on tiptoe and whispered something into the camel's ear. It sneezed and then slowly lowered itself onto its knees, front legs breaking first, then the rear ones. Khalifa began unstrapping the crates on its back.

'I used to work with camels,' he said over his shoulder, 'when I was young. Some skills you never forget.'

He pulled the crates off and rolled them aside, adjusting various straps and harnesses. The camel nibbled his ear.

'They are wonderful animals. Tireless, loyal and so beautiful. The one drawback is that their breath is not nice. But then we all have our faults, don't we? Aha!'

He held up a small water canteen he'd found beneath a flap of the saddle.

'Not much left by the sound of it, but enough, I think, to stop us dying of thirst. Please.'

He stepped back and held out his arm, indicating that she should mount. She came forward, laughing, and clambered onto the saddle. Khalifa climbed up behind her.

'My friend warned me to stay away from camels,' she said. 'The handlers are all perverts, apparently.'

'I am a married man, Miss Mullray.'

'I was just teasing.'

'Ah, I see.' He chuckled. 'Yes. English humour. It is, how do you say, an acquired taste. Although Benny Hill – he was very funny.'

He raised his hand and slapped it against the camel's rump, letting out a loud shout. The creature levered itself upwards, pitching Tara first forwards and then back. Khalifa took the reins around her waist.

'If we keep going we should make it in two days,' he said, 'three at the outside. The camel might be the ship of the desert, but I'm afraid this isn't going to be a luxury cruise.'

'I can handle it.'

'Yes, Miss Mullray, I have no doubt that you can. You seem a remarkable woman. I should very much like you to meet my wife and children.'

He slapped the camel on the flank again and it started to lope forwards.

'*Yalla besara!*' he cried. '*Yalla nimsheh!* Hurry up! Let's go!'

They came to the pyramid rock, towering dark and monstrous above them, a vast black monolith erupting from the deep places of the desert, impossibly ancient, inestimably powerful, Time's sentinel. It seemed to throb slightly in the heat and to give off a sound, a sort of deep brooding growl, as though telling them they could pass, but warning them never to return. And then they were past and moving away down the valley.

'I am building a fountain, you know,' said Khalifa after a while. 'I want my home to be full of the sound of running water.'

'It sounds wonderful,' said Tara, smiling.

'There will be blue and green tiles, and shells from the seashore, and plants around the edge. And at night there will be lights to make the water sparkle as though it is full of diamonds. It will be very beautiful.'

'Yes,' she said, closing her eyes. 'I think it will.'

Khalifa flicked the reins and they broke into a trot, the pyramid rock slowly dropping away behind them, as if receding in time. All around the desert shimmered and swelled with the morning heat.

'*Besara, besara!*' he cried. '*Yalla nimsheh, yalla nimsheh!*'

AUTHOR'S NOTE

The Lost Army of Cambyses was written and edited well before the appalling events of 11 September 2001. Although the issue of Middle Eastern terrorism is central to the narrative, the book is nonetheless a work of imaginative fiction and should only be read as such. It is in no way intended to reflect real events.

GLOSSARY

Abu el-Haggag Patron sheikh of Luxor (born Damascus *c.* 1150). A *moulid* in his honour is held annually in Luxor, two weeks before Ramadan.

Abu Sir Group of pyramids to the south of Giza, dating to Fifth Dynasty (*c.* 2465–2323 BC).

Afterlife Books Series of ancient Egyptian texts describing the afterlife. Most date from the New Kingdom, although they can ultimately be traced back to the Pyramid Texts of the Old Kingdom. Their names – Book of the Dead, Book of Gates, Book of Caverns etc. – are modern.

Akhenaten Eighteenth Dynasty pharaoh. Ruled *c.* 1353–1335 BC. Father of Tutankhamun.

Akhet One of three seasons into which the ancient Egyptian year was divided (the others were Peret and Shemu). Akhet was the season of the Nile flood, covering roughly June to September.

Akhetaten City built by the pharaoh Akhenaten on the banks of the Nile, roughly midway between modern Cairo and Luxor. Name means 'Horizon of the Aten'.

Al-Ahram Popular Egyptian newspaper. Title means 'The Pyramids'.

Al-Jihad A militant Egyptian fundamentalist group.

Al-Mukhabarat al-'amma Egyptian general intelligence and security service.

Amarna Modern name for the ruins of Akhetaten.

Amenhotep I Early Eighteenth Dynasty pharaoh. Ruled *c.* 1525–1504 BC.

Amenhotep III Eighteenth Dynasty pharaoh. Ruled *c.* 1391–1353 BC. Father of Akhenaten, grandfather of Tutankhamun.

Ammonians Ancient name for the inhabitants of the oasis of Siwa. Name derives from the ancient Egyptian god Amun, who had an oracle at Siwa.

Anubis Ancient Egyptian god, depicted as a jackal or a man with the head of a jackal. God of the necropolis and mummification.

Basbousa Sweet pastry made with semolina, nuts and honey.

Beit House, home.

Belzoni, Giovanni Battista (1778–1823). Explorer. Discovered the tomb of Seti I in the Valley of the Kings.

Bes Dwarf-god. Protector of pregnant women.

Cambyses Son of Persian emperor Cyrus the Great. Born *c.* 560 BC. Succeeded father as King of Persia 529 BC. Conquered Egypt in 525 BC, becoming the first pharaoh of Twenty-seventh Dynasty. Died *c.* 522 BC at Ecbatane, Syria, possibly by assassination or suicide. Portrayed by contemporary chroniclers as a mad despot.

Canopic jars Four jars holding the viscera of a mummified body.

Caria A region of the ancient Near East, in the south-west of modern Turkey, colonized by the Greeks. Famed for its mercenaries.

Carnarvon George Edward Stanhope Molyneux Herbert, fifth Earl of Carnarvon (1866–1923). Collector and amateur Egyptologist. Patron of Howard Carter.

Carter, Howard (1874–1939). Egyptologist. Discovered the tomb of Tutankhamun (1922).

Cartouche An oval with a horizontal line at the bottom in which a pharaoh's name was written in hieroglyphs.

Colossi of Memnon A pair of colossal seated statues on the west bank of the Nile at Luxor. Formerly part of the mortuary temple of Amenhotep III.

Cromer Evelyn Baring, first Earl of Cromer (1841–1917). English Consul-General and de facto ruler of Egypt from 1883 to 1907.

Cuneiform Ancient Mesopotamian wedge-shaped script.

Dahshur Pyramid field south of Saqqara. Site of the famous 'bent' pyramid of Snofru.

Danishaway Village in the Delta region of northern Egypt. Scene of an infamous incident in 1906 in which four innocent Egyptians were executed following an altercation with British soldiers.

Djed pillar An ancient Egyptian symbol of stability depicted as a pillar surmounted by four horizontal branches. Considered to represent the backbone of the god Osiris.

Davies, Nina MacPherson (1881–1965). Artist. Published several volumes on ancient Egyptian tomb paintings.

Djellaba Traditional robe worn by Egyptian men and women.

Eighteenth Dynasty First of the three dynasties of the New Kingdom, *c.* 1550–1307 BC.

Faience A material made of fired quartz, with a glazed outer layer. Used extensively in ancient Egypt for jewellery, small vessels, *shabti*s, etc.

Fellaha (pl. fellahin) Peasant.

Gates of the Dead Ancient Egyptian name for the Valley of the Kings.

Hajj Pilgrimage to Mecca, one of the 'five pillars' of the Moslem faith. The other four are the *shahada* (declaration of faith), *salah* (prayer, recited five times a day), *zakah* (the giving of alms) and the observance of the fast at Ramadan.

Hatshepsut Eighteenth Dynasty queen, wife of Tuthmosis II, who ruled Egypt *c.* 1473–1458 BC as joint pharaoh with her stepson Tuthmosis III. Her mortuary temple on the west bank of the Nile at Luxor is one of Egypt's most spectacular monuments.

Herodotus (*c.* 485–425 BC). Greek historian, known as 'the father of history'. Famous for his *Histories* outlining the causes and events of the wars between the Greeks and the Persians.

Horemheb Last pharaoh of the Eighteenth Dynasty (although for some Egyptologists he is regarded as the first pharaoh of the Nineteenth Dynasty). Formerly commander-in-chief of the Egyptian army under Tutankhamun.

Imam Leader of congregational prayer in the mosque.

Imhotep Ancient Egyptian architect and physician. Designed Egypt's first true pyramid – the Step Pyramid of the Third Dynasty pharaoh Djoser (ruled *c.* 2630–2611 BC). Worshipped as a god after his death. His tomb has never been found.

'Imma Turban.

Isis Ancient Egyptian goddess. Wife of Osiris and mother of Horus. Protector of the dead.

Iteru Ancient Egyptian name for the Nile. Also an ancient unit of measurement, equivalent to approximately 2 km.

John Soane Museum Small museum in central London in the house of architect Sir John Soane (1753–1837). Diverse collection of objects including the coffin of Nineteenth Dynasty pharaoh Seti I.

Ka'ba A cube-shaped shrine in Mecca, the holiest site in the Moslem world. It contains a stone believed to have been given by the angel Gabriel to Abraham. All Moslems turn towards it when praying.

Karkaday An infusion of hibiscus flowers, popular throughout Egypt.

Karnak A vast temple complex just to the north of Luxor, with buildings spanning almost 2000 years of Egyptian history.

Khamsin A strong desert wind.

Khan-al-Khalili A large bazaar in Cairo, selling everything from jewellery to *shisha* pipes.

Khutbar Sermon.

Kufr Name given to those who do not follow Islam. Unbelievers.

KV39 Tomb just outside the Valley of the Kings. Considered by some Egyptologists to be the tomb of early Eighteenth Dynasty pharaoh Amenhotep I (ruled *c.* 1525–1504 BC).

KV55 Mysterious tomb in the Valley of the Kings, discovered in 1907. Considerable controversy over who was actually buried there, with some scholars suggesting Akhenaten, others Smenkhkare.

Late Period Period of ancient Egyptian history lasting from 712 BC to 332 BC, when the country was conquered by Alexander the Great.

Lepsius, Karl Richard (1810–84). German Egyptologist. Director of Berlin Museum. Published a seminal twelve-volume study of the monuments of Egypt.

Linear A As yet undeciphered script used in ancient Crete.

Lydia Ancient Near Eastern kingdom. In modern Turkey.

Machimos Warrior.

Malqata Site of former palace of Amenhotep III on the west bank of the Nile at Luxor.

Mariette, Auguste Ferdinand (1821–81). French Egyptologist. Founder of Egyptian Department of Antiquities and National Museum.

Mastaba Oblong tomb, made of stone or mud bricks. From the Arabic word for bench.

Medinet Habu Village on the west bank of the Nile at Luxor, and site of the mortuary temple of Ramesses III.

Memphis Capital of the Old Kingdom, an important administrative centre throughout ancient Egyptian history.

Midan Tahrir The hub of modern Cairo. The name means 'Liberation Square'.

Mihrab Niche in a mosque indicating the direction of Mecca.

Minoan Ancient Bronze Age culture based on island of Crete.

Mizmar Musical wind instrument, akin to the oboe.

Molochia An Egyptian dish made from stewed mallow leaves. Rather like spinach.

Mortuary temple Temple where prayers were recited and sacrifices offered for the well-being of the deceased, usually a king.

Moulid Popular festival or fair, usually in honour of a local saint or holy person.

Muezzin Mosque official who summons the faithful to prayer five times each day.

Munshid A devotional singer or chanter.

Necropolis Literally 'city of the dead'. A burial ground.

Nefertiti Great Royal Wife of the pharaoh Akhenaten. Some scholars believe that on Akhenaten's death she took the name Smenkhkare and ruled as a pharaoh in her own right. Immortalized in the famous 'Nefertiti Bust' in the Berlin Museum.

Old Kingdom Ancient Egyptian history is divided into three Kingdoms – Old, Middle and New – with Intermediate Periods between them. The Old Kingdom lasted from *c.* 2575 to 2134 BC.

Osiris Ancient Egyptian god of the underworld.

Ostrakon Piece of pottery or limestone bearing an image or text. Effectively the ancient equivalent of the modern-day doodling pad.

Pectoral Jewel, usually pylon-shaped, worn on the chest or breast.

Pendlebury, John Devitt Stringfellow (1904–41). Egyptologist. Excavated at Amarna. Shot by Germans on Crete during the Second World War.

Peret One of three seasons into which the ancient Egyptian year was divided (the others were Akhet and Shemu). Peret was the season of planting and growth, and lasted roughly from October to February.

Persepolis Former capital of ancient Persia. In modern-day Iran.

Petosiris The name of a noble family buried at Tuna el-Gebel. Their tomb is unique in its use of both Egyptian and Greek styles to portray daily life in ancient Egypt.

Petrie, William Matthew Flinders (1853–1942). Archaeologist and Egyptologist. Worked extensively in Egypt and Palestine.

Pylon Massive entrance or gateway standing in front of a temple.

Qurn High, pyramid-shaped peak overlooking the Valley of the Kings. Means 'the horn' in Arabic. Called Dehenet by the ancient Egyptians.

Rais Foreman or overseer of works.

Ramesses I First pharaoh of the Nineteenth Dynasty (although some consider Horemheb to have been the first). Ruled *c.* 1307–1306 BC.

Ramesses II Third pharaoh of the Nineteenth Dynasty. Ruled *c.* 1290–1224 BC. One of ancient Egypt's greatest pharaohs.

Ramesses III Twentieth Dynasty pharaoh. Ruled *c.* 1194–1163 BC. His mortuary temple at Medinet Habu is one of the most beautiful monuments in Egypt.

Ramesses VIII Twentieth Dynasty pharaoh. Ruled *c.* 1136–1131 BC.

Ramesseum Mortuary temple of Ramesses II, on the west bank of the Nile at Luxor.

Ramessid Umbrella title given to the period of the Nineteenth and Twentieth dynasties.

Ra (or Re) Ancient Egyptian sun god.

Re-Harakhty Ancient Egyptian god combining the attributes of Ra and Horus. State god of the New Kingdom. Usually depicted as a man with the head of a falcon.

Rek'ah Prayer cycle.

Rekhmire Vizier of Tuthmosis III (ruled *c.* 1479–1425 BC) and Amenhotep II (ruled *c.* 1427–1401 BC).

Rohlfs, Gerhard (1831–96). German explorer. Travelled extensively in the western desert, making a landmark crossing of the Great Sand Sea in 1874.

Rosellini, Niccolo Francesco Ippolito Baldessare (1800–43). Italian Egyptologist. Founder of Egyptology in Italy.

Saidee Native of Upper Egypt.

Saqqara Necropolis of the ancient Egyptian capital at Memphis. A vast desert burial ground covering almost seven square kilometres, and including the Step Pyramid of Djoser, Egypt's first true pyramid.

Scarab A dung beetle. Considered sacred in ancient Egypt.

Serapeum A series of vast underground galleries at Saqqara where the Apis Bull – a sacred cult animal of the ancient Egyptians – was buried.

Seth Egyptian deity, brother and murderer of Osiris, associated with deserts, war and chaos. Represented by an unidentified animal.

Seti I Nineteenth Dynasty pharaoh, father of Ramesses II. Ruled *c.* 1306–1290 BC.

Shabti Small mummiform figure, usually of wood or faience, placed in a tomb in order to perform tasks for the deceased in the afterlife.

Sharia Islamic law.

Shepseskaf Final pharaoh of the Fourth Dynasty. Ruled *c.* 2472–2467 BC.

Shisha pipe A water pipe. Found in cafés and private homes throughout Egypt.

Siga A board game, also known as Tab-es-Siga. Similar to draughts. Thought to derive from the ancient Egyptian board game Senet.

Smenkhkare Eighteenth Dynasty pharaoh, ruled *c.* 1335–1333 BC. Some scholars have suggested that Smenkhkare was actually Nefertiti, who ruled as a pharaoh in her own right following the death of her husband Akhenaten.

Snofru First king of the Fourth Dynasty. Ruled *c.* 2575–2551 BC.

Stele Upright block of stone or wood carrying images and inscriptions.

Sura A chapter of the Koran, the holy book of Islam. Each of the 114 *sura*s is divided into a number of *ayat*, or sections.

Susa Former capital of the Persian empire. In modern Iran.

Teftish Office.

Termous Type of bean.

Thebes Name given by the Greeks to ancient Waset, modern Luxor.

Thoth Ancient Egyptian god of writing and counting. Usually depicted with a human body and the head of an ibis.

Touria Hoe.

Tuna el-Gebel Ancient site in Middle Egypt, near the town of Mallawi.

Tuthmosis II Eighteenth Dynasty pharaoh. Ruled *c*. 1492–1479 BC.

Ummah The Moslem community.

Waset Ancient Egyptian name for modern Luxor.

Yuya and Tjuyu A noble couple, lived in the fourteenth century BC. Great-grandparents of Tutankhamun. Their tomb in the Valley of the Kings – KV46 – was found in 1905. Until the discovery of Tutankhamun in 1922, it was considered one of the greatest finds in the history of Egyptian archaeology.

Zamalek District of Cairo. Occupies the northern part of Gezira Island.

Zikr A group of devout Moslems, usually belonging to one of the mystic Sufi brotherhoods, who perform a trance-inducing devotional dance.

ACKNOWLEDGEMENTS

Numerous people helped in the writing of this book, which would never have made it out of my head, let alone into the bookshops, without their advice, assistance and support.

Special thanks to my wonderful agent, Laura Susijn, who believed in me when many others didn't, and to my editor, Simon Taylor, a master of the art of painless revision.

Nicholas Reeves, Ian Shaw and Stephen Quirke provided crucial advice on aspects of ancient Egyptian history and language, and I owe them a huge debt of gratitude, as well as an apology for the many liberties I have taken with the information they provided.

Stephen Ulph and James Freeman filled in the numerous gaps in my knowledge of, respectively, modern Arabic and ancient Greek. Thanks to them, and also to Andrew 'Splodge' Rogerson and Tom Blackmore for their invaluable comments on the manuscript.

Of all the many friends who buoyed me up with words of encouragement, four in particular deserve mention: John Bannon, Nigel Topping, Xan Brooks and Bromley Roberts.

Finally, two special acknowledgements. First, to my aunt Joan, who first planted a love of ancient Egypt in my mind, and subsequently nurtured it through many joyous afternoons in the British Museum.

Secondly, and most importantly, to all my many friends in the Arab Republic of Egypt, who have shown me such unfailing warmth, kindness and generosity.